SHADOWS OF LOVE

Liz had sent a clear signal to Jake to keep his distance, to get on with his life, because she had. "You're right, though," she said, willing to give him that much. "It wasn't all bad. I loved you once. In fact, I loved you so much it hurt." The impulse to touch that long-ago love was strong, too strong to resist, despite the risk. She lifted a hand, and her fingertips played over the warm, weathered skin of his cheek. "I've had enough hurt for two lifetimes, Jake. I don't want to go through that again. I don't want to relive it. I won't. Not even for you."

Hardheaded Jake didn't seem to be listening. There was something strangely intimate about the dim shadows of the stable. Liz could feel it, and she knew that he felt it, too.

"You're more beautiful than ever. I never get tired of looking at you . . . the way your mouth tightens when you're pissed off at me . . . the way you look in the mornings, all drowsy and heavy-lidded." He caught her braid, sliding his hand along its length as his gaze drank her in. Then, slowly, with exquisite care, he leaned in . . .

BOOK YOUR PLACE ON OUR WEBSITE AND MAKE THE READING CONNECTION!

We've created a customized website just for our very special readers, where you can get the inside scoop on everything that's going on with Zebra, Pinnacle and Kensington books.

When you come online, you'll have the exciting opportunity to:

- View covers of upcoming books

- Read sample chapters

- Learn about our future publishing schedule (listed by publication month *and author*)

- Find out when your favorite authors will be visiting a city near you

- Search for and order backlist books from our online catalog

- Check out author bios and background information

- Send e-mail to your favorite authors

- Meet the Kensington staff online

- Join us in weekly chats with authors, readers and other guests

- Get writing guidelines

- AND MUCH MORE!

**Visit our website at
http://www.kensingtonbooks.com**

BE VERY AFRAID

S.K. McClafferty

ZEBRA BOOKS
KENSINGTON PUBLISHING CORP.
http://www.kensingtonbooks.com

ZEBRA BOOKS are published by

Kensington Publishing Corp.
850 Third Avenue
New York, NY 10022

All Kensington titles, imprints and distributed lines are
available at special quantity discounts for bulk purchases for sales promotion, premiums, fund-raising, ed-
ucational or institutional use.

Special book excerpts or customized printings can also
be created to fit specific needs. For details, write or phone
the office of the Kensington Special Sales Manager: Kensington Publishing Corp., 850 Third Avenue, New York,
NY 10022. Attn. Special Sales Department. Phone: 1-800-
221-2647.

Zebra and the Z logo Reg. U.S. Pat. & TM Off.

First Printing: June 2004
10 9 8 7 6 5 4 3 2 1

Printed in the United States of America

For our second batch of Rugrats:
Miss Selina Lynn
Miss Riley Mae
and Master Braeden Michael . . .

And in loving memory of
Janine George, beloved friend.
Sadly missed.

Prologue

It was late, and the light he worked by was a low-wattage bulb. Bright lights were for other things, not for adding another figurative brush stroke to his growing masterpiece. He liked the softened effect the diffused light gave the project, blurring the harsh edges. Three feet by three . . . one square yard of smiling faces, faces with freckles, and others without, some with wide gaps between their incisors. He was a collector of smiling faces, a connoisseur of people, but not just any people. . . . Each of the faces depicted on the collage was a link in a long chain of humanity that had marched through his life. All of them had given him their trust; some had paid dearly for it, their reward an eternal connection of their lives with his.

He made the decisions. He decided who lived and how long, and whether or not they would be found.

He controlled everything, right down to the smallest detail; he was the master manipulator.

The face he concentrated on now was shaped like a heart. Framed by red hair, it was perfect, the eyes bright, mischievous; nose small and well-shaped; the mouth a perfect cupid's bow in a lovely and vulnerable shade of pink untouched by lipstick. Using a small pair of scissors he'd confiscated from his wife's sewing basket, he carefully trimmed the background away from the subject, humming softly under his breath as he worked, the television news anchor droning in the background about the downward spiral of the country's economy. As he finished cutting and put down the scissors, the pretty blonde on screen, perfectly coiffed and serious of expression, shuffled her scripted notes, a signal to her camera crew that she had finished the segment and was ready to start another.

The camera zoomed in for a tight shot, and he continued to hum beneath his breath, calm and unruffled, perfectly content with his work. "The search for Carrie Ann Mallick ended tragically today with the discovery of a shallow grave in northern Ulster County. Carrie Ann, just ten years old, failed to come home from school on Friday. A resident, who asked us not to identify him, discovered the grave site while using his metal detector."

The video clip rolled, and a spare man in a plaid flannel shirt talked to a reporter, his back to the camera. "It's a good area for coins, that field. I'd been there just last week and found me an Indian-head penny almost in that same spot. The ground was solid, and I had to work real hard to get to it. That's how come I noticed the earth had been recently disturbed. When I saw the pipe, I got suspicious and called the police. I heard about all of this burial stuff on the TV."

The clip ended, and Blondie looked straight into the lens. "Police aren't saying much at this point in the investigation, but it is believed that Carrie Ann was a victim of the serial killer, 'the Cemetery Man,' a sadistic murderer who abducts and then buries his victim alive. If you have information about Carrie Ann's whereabouts on Friday, please contact police at . . ."

He finished with the photo, holding it up so that it was in line with the photograph on the television screen, so that the two images of the dead girl were side by side. "Perfect," he said with some satisfaction, then glued the trophy in place.

A heartbeat later, a girl appeared in the doorway to the study. Same height, same age as Carrie Ann, with that same sweet childlike grace that precedes the gawkiness of adolescence. Her mouth, unlike that on the photograph, was compressed into a thin, tense line. "Mom wants to know when you'll be done," she said, her voice barely above a whisper.

He finished what he was doing and then slowly walked to where she stood, reaching down to cup her small, delicate chin in his large, hard hand. She flinched at the warmth of his touch and a grim sort of satisfaction flooded his solar plexus. He kept his tone soft, but it didn't fool her, and she blinked involuntarily, as if in anticipation of a blow. "Didn't we talk about this before? Didn't we agree that you are never to disturb me when I'm in my study?"

A quick, sharp nod. "Yes."

"Yes, what?"

"Yes, sir."

"And what do you have to say for yourself?" He removed the hand, but her gaze remained glued to it. Did seeing it coming make it hurt less? he wondered.

"I didn't want to." Her head drooped, and she spoke to her flat chest. "Mom made me."

"Well, then," he said, reaching down once more,

ruffling her blond hair. "We'll have to have a little talk with your mother, now, won't we?" He motioned her out, killed the power button on the television set, and turned the lock on the door, leaving the collage of faces in darkness.

Chapter One

Jake had to admit a grudging admiration for the woman's ingenuity. Once she set her mind to something, nothing short of hell or the second coming of Christ would deter her from accomplishing what she set out to do, and Liz Moncrief had made up her mind to disappear.

It had taken him two months and a private investigator with a network of New York contacts to track her down. He could only hope that the monster who had terrorized two states for more than three years would have half as much difficulty finding her as he'd had, and a tenth as much aversion for a face-to-face.

It wasn't that he didn't respect Liz's position—*former position*—he corrected mentally, or that he didn't recognize God-given ability when he encountered it. It was that he didn't really like her very much.

Okay, so maybe "not liking" was a mild way of putting it. The truth was that they hated one another.

Working with Liz had nearly given him an ulcer. Everything with her was strictly by the book, from her advanced degree in criminology to her sensible shoes. When he'd known her, she'd been a suit-wearing-FBI-goody-two-shoes, and Jake just couldn't relate. He had something of a reputation for cutting corners, but only when it suited his purposes, and if at times his methods stretched the letter of the law a little, well, it certainly didn't keep him awake nights.

What had kept him sleepless for weeks was the unshakable feeling that the Cemetery Man had found her first. The son of a bitch was fixated on Liz, and being the object of a serial murderer's obsession was a damned dangerous position.

Not that Jake failed to understand the attraction. Liz was a looker, with chestnut hair and eyes the shade of melting chocolate. When she wasn't pissed, which wasn't often, her mouth was full and red, giving her an earthy quality that made a man—*other men*, he corrected mentally—think of sweltering nights and steamy sex— He broke off the thought abruptly as the Buick's engine started to knock.

He'd already made the courtesy phone call to Sheriff Rhys of the local sheriff's department to discuss the situation and warn him that there was a good likelihood trouble with a capital "T" was headed his way. Rhys was at his office awaiting his arrival, and Jake wasn't sure what to expect. The sheriff was operating in a rural area, but that didn't mean the man was stupid. He was going to ask questions, and Jake could only hope that his answers satisfied him.

If Rhys decided to verify Jake's arguments with a call to Quantico, things could get more than a little uncomfortable. He could almost hear Assistant Director Fletcher's gravel-voiced whisper; in fact, it seemed so real that Jake glanced in the rearview mirror to assure himself that he was alone in the car. "Look, English," Fletcher had said, "you're a good man, a valued member of our team, and I don't want to lose you. But the plain truth is you worry me. I see that you were scheduled to see a Bureau psychiatrist last week, and you missed the appointment."

"Something came up." Jake winced at the memory of the unconvincing lie.

"You blew it off," Fletcher corrected.

"Sir, I've kept several appointments. Quite frankly, I didn't see the point. I'm not crazy, and I don't feel the need to 'open up.' "

"That's a matter of opinion—an opinion that's biased, I might add, but we'll set that aside for the moment. Bring me up to speed. What's on your desk at the moment?"

"Sir? I've got a stack of case files—"

"Yes, I know. But what's your primary focus? You can't answer that, can you? Not truthfully, in any case, because if you answer it truthfully you prove my point."

At that moment the floor had seemed to shift under Jake's feet.

"Exactly what do you want from me?" he said.

"I want you to listen. Jake, I realize your connection to Agent Airhardt, and I know that her tragedy touched you deeply, but it's time to move on. We have other matters that, at the moment, are more pressing. We're not closing any doors here—as a murder investigation the case is still open; the Virginia authorities are looking for leads. But the Cemetery Man has been inactive for nearly two years. Let them handle it. If they need our help, they'll call."

Jake tried, but couldn't quite blot out the memory of the first of several major ass-chewings. A few more missed appointments with the Bureau's resident shrink didn't help. Charlie Calendar, Jake's friend and colleague, had done his best to cover for him, but Fletcher had eyes and ears everywhere at Quantico, and Jake's increasingly obsessive behavior hadn't exactly rallied his coworkers to his defense. He put in late hours, and rarely slept. He reviewed the data, the psychological profile, and he came up with nothing.

Unofficially, he was described as "burned-out and more than a little belligerent." It probably hadn't helped that he'd objected to the official verdict, handed down by "Dr. Dread," the in-Bureau shrink six weeks later. Her claim that "Special Agent English is suffering from a form of post-traumatic stress disorder" wasn't well received. She stated that it was her professional opinion that Special Agent English had difficulty dealing with his own emotions, and she worried that he could be a danger to himself or those around him. As if he were hell-bent on proving her right, Jake's temper exploded. His objections had been loud-voiced, and less than flattering to the female psychiatrist, and Charlie had to get in his face to get him to shut up.

Fletcher, livid that his attempts to handle Jake's "problems" in a compassionate and humane manner had been thoroughly unappreciated, had put Jake on immediate enforced leave of absence for a period of six months, with pay, pending further review of his "mental state."

"Mental state, my ass," Jake muttered. "There's nothing wrong with me." That had been weeks ago, and the fact that the Bureau had cut him loose without listening to his concerns still stung.

But that wasn't completely true.

They *had* listened. It wasn't as if they hadn't

seen men like him before, men who couldn't let go of the unsolved cases that were so brutal, so devastating on a personal level that they continued to work them even after retirement. Only they had done it quietly, discreetly. Jake had never been quiet, and he was anything but discreet.

Oh yeah. They'd listened, they'd weighed the facts, and as the case had grown colder and colder, his reasoning had leaked credibility until that well went bone dry. Like the kid who cried wolf, no one heard him—until the Cemetery Man reemerged and the body count once again began climbing, but by that time it was already too late. . . .

"You're still not an official part of this investigation," Jake told himself, "so you flash the credentials, warn the sheriff of what may be coming, and find Liz . . . and with any luck, you'll be out of here before anyone asks to see your badge or looks too close."

There was no time to lose. Once the grim task of meeting with Rhys was taken care of, he'd undertake the even grimmer task of finding and confronting his former colleague. He had no doubt that she would be almost as happy to see him as he was to see her, and he sure as hell hoped she wasn't packing any heat.

While Jake plotted his next move, the engine's knock became steadily more insistent, like a sixteen-pound sledge instead of a ball-peen hammer, impossible to shrug off.

"Shit," Jake said, irritated. "What lousy fucking timing." Then he remembered the neglected notation in his day planner several months back. *Check the oil.*

With the town of Abundance somewhere up ahead, the sheriff checking his watch and wondering where his late date had gotten to, and a serial killer on the move, Jake had no choice but to slow to a crawl. Steam and smoke seeped in pale blue threads from under the hood, smelling of heat and oil. "You can remember every MO and every signature of every case you've ever been involved in, but you can't remember to check the oil. What the hell is wrong with this picture?"

The rest of Jake's vernacular turned the car's interior as thick and as blue as the oily steam rising from under the hood. At the foot of a long grade, the engine stalled, refusing all attempts to choke a few more miles from it. The overhead map light had burned out last year, a week after the first anniversary of the last time he'd had the car serviced. He dug in the side pocket of his leather overnight bag and brought out his cell phone, intending to call Rhys and let him know he'd be late for their appointment, *very late*, but the illuminated screen indicated "no signal."

"Great. Just great." He turned off the key, euthanizing the dying engine.

Shoving the phone back into place, he grabbed the bag, which contained a few essentials—toothbrush, a change of clothing, and his notebook computer—and opened the door. The smell of hot metal and motor oil mingled with the heavy fog, the sickening smell of yet more complications in an already frustratingly difficult, high-pressure situation. Glancing at his watch, Jake unconsciously ground his teeth and began walking in the general direction of the town. The time he was wasting just getting to Abundance was precious. If his theory was correct, and TCM (the Bureau's shorthand for 'the Cemetery Man') had located Liz, then she was in real trouble.

* * *

Not far away from the spot where Jake slogged through the mud, B.B. Bratt crouched in a patch of thick woods, resting his arthritic knee and listening to the ghostly bay of Catskill Belle, his bluetick coonhound. Belle was a Grand Night Champion, with a voice that put chills up B.B.'s spine every time she gave a full-throated cry. A hunter from Alabama had offered him three thousand dollars for his little girl, and B.B. had refused it, but he was beginning to wonder if he'd made a blunder. There was something off about Belle these past two weeks. She'd trail all right, but she wouldn't tree, and he could almost imagine the raccoons doing a little jig down by the creek because that big old scary dog had returned to wiffle and whine around B.B.'s feet.

Her crazy behavior was starting to piss B.B. off. Ten minutes in the woods and Belle quit baying. Another minute or two and, sure enough, she came slinking out of the dark with head down and tail tucked. B.B. was about to scold her good when the brush rattled near at hand and something, or someone, gave a strange-sounding groan. The hound pressed close to his legs, quaking.

A groan and a curse, and someone stumbled out of the brush. B.B.'s miner's lamp hit Samuel T. Turner square in the face—or rather, what was left of it after his failed suicide. B.B. recoiled from him, falling over the hound and knocking down his .22 rifle, which went off with a sharp "crack," the shot spent in the direction of the Skunktown Road.

Turner laughed as B.B. picked himself up off the ground. "Jesus, Mary, and Joseph, Turner! You near made me shit myself! What are you doin' lurkin' around out here in the dark, anyhow?"

The right side of Samuel Turner's face was concave, a section of his jawbone missing, the skin scarred and drawn. The socket where his eye had been shone dark and empty. Perversely, Turner refused to wear an eye patch, and B.B. had garnered from local gossip that Turner was as ugly on the inside as he was on the outside. There was no disputing that the younger man had been in and out of trouble of one kind or another since the age of fifteen.

"Buryin' somethin'," Turner said, taking a threatening step forward, jutting that nightmare mask into the older man's face. Whiskey fumes mixed with the smell of body odor made B.B. gag. Turner glared at him from one dark eye, then, without explanation, he walked away.

B.B. Bratt let go the breath he'd been holding. He was relieved to see Turner go, but the evening's hunt had already been ruined. Bratt had survived two hitches in 'Nam, and he'd seen a good portion of hell, but Samuel Turner still made his skin crawl.

Putting a traumatized Belle in the cab of the pickup, he slammed the Dodge into four-wheel high, spun out of the gas-well road, and headed back to his place. As soon as he cleared the cleft, he picked up his car phone and called his wife, Eunice, asking her to be sure to turn on the porch light. He didn't want any more surprises. B.B. didn't risk a glance back, afraid of who stood watching from the woods, and he remained oblivious to the man lying facedown in the middle of the rutted road with a bullet hole in his back.

Elizabeth Moncrief was on the periphery of what passed for a social scene in Abundance, and she liked it that way. She knew most of the residents not at all, a few well enough to hold brief and impersonal conversations, but Julianne Rhys and Doctor Katherine Fife were the only two residents she'd allowed in. She considered them friends, yet she continued to keep even them at arm's length.

It was easier that way. She didn't like having to explain herself when reliving the past was so painful. She'd had a ton too much pain already.

Failed marriage, lost child, shattered emotions, lack of closure, a raging case of burnout, none of which could be allowed to touch her current day-to-day existence for fear she would enter a tailspin she couldn't pull out of. A low level of isolation and a rigid control were the only things that kept the devils at bay, and kept her from falling apart.

No one in Abundance knew where she had been before she purchased the country house eighteen months ago, or what she had been before she came to Ulster County. Kate Fife hadn't asked, though Liz strongly sensed the dark-haired physician suspected that Liz, like herself, had some personal demons. Julianne Rhys, even more intuitive than Liz, knew more than she let on. But she never asked for more, and for that small courtesy, Liz was grateful.

Julianne came from the rear of the Bell, Book, and Whatnot as Liz stepped over the threshold. Julianne's bookstore had odd hours, due to her law practice. The red-haired Wiccan lawyer took another cup down off a shelf and socked a tea bag into it. "Hey, there. I thought you'd be all fogged in. That's some heavy stuff rising out there. A great night for spooks and hobgoblins."

"Not to mention witches," a very pregnant blonde put in. She was seated in the rocker with Hissy, Julianne's cat, curled in what remained of her lap. "You love this kind of weather, and you know it.

The spookier, the better. Hi, Liz, how's that gorgeous stud of yours?"

"She could ask you the same question," Julianne said with a laugh. "You've caught the literary world's most eligible, and you won't even say 'yes.' "

Liz ignored the conversational thread. She wasn't about to discuss the merits of matrimony with anyone. Her experience with marriage had left her cold, and wary, and more than a little wounded. "He's doing a little better, I think. The vet's out of town, but Kate has been good enough to drop by."

"Kate Fife, M.D.?" Abby said.

"One and the same." Liz shoved her hands into the deep pockets of a cracked wax chore coat. She'd met Abby Youngblood a few times in passing, and she seemed nice, but Liz wasn't anxious to get too close. It wasn't really about Abby, but rather about the way the young woman's expansive waistline brought back memories of Liz's own pregnancy, and along with those memories, a poignant wave of bittersweet emotion. Birthdays and cakes and candles reflected in a bright and shining angel's face flew past in a blinding blur until she felt the numbness stir in the pit of her stomach and creep up to anesthetize her soul, to turn her stiff and remote once more, a shell of a woman with a hollow existence. "I was just on my way to the hardware store and thought I'd stop in," Liz added. Then, to Julianne, "Did the books I ordered arrive yet?"

"They did, actually. They're in the back. I'll get them." Julianne moved past the rocker, pausing to glance back. "Are you sure you don't have time for tea?"

Liz glanced at Julianne, intentionally raising the invisible barrier that kept the world out and special people like Julianne from accessing her thoughts. "Some other time, maybe. I don't want to leave Anglican with the hired man for too long. It's Jersey's poker night, and he'll be impatient to leave." She saw the redhead's puzzled frown and she offered the lawyer a remote smile with her excuse.

"Another time, then, and I intend to hold you to that. Abby's here at least twice a week. We're what passes for girl's night out since J.T.'s out of town and Matt's hunka burnin' love caught up with Abby."

Abby blushed. "Julianne! Will you stop?"

"What?"

Julianne put the books on the counter and rung them up. "Forty-eight dollars even."

Liz dug in her jeans' pocket and paid with cash. Always cash, no checks, no credit cards, no paper trail. She took the change and the stack of books. "Abby, take care. Julianne, I'll see you later."

"You too, and be careful out there. It's more than just creepy with all that fog. It's dangerous."

Outside, the fog was getting thicker. Lampposts and buildings were an indistinct blur. Liz walked a few yards toward her Explorer and sucked in a lungful of relief. She didn't like lying to Julianne. The truth was, Anglican was healing, and her hired man, Jersey Delacour, had already gone home for the night. She'd just wimped out on the tea because of Julianne's friend, Abby. It hadn't been that many months, and the pain was like a sharp stab to the heart. She didn't want to deal with it, didn't want to think about it, didn't want to face the fact that her little girl was gone, that she would never brush her long dark curls again, that she would never hear her voice.

In some ways she was every bit as bad as Richard. He'd found the perfect method to escape the pain, and damn him, there were moments when she envied him that. For her there was no true escape, just avoidance.

While living in Virginia, it hadn't been as easy. There had been too many reminders. It had been far too convenient for friends and colleagues to drop by, and their uneasy sympathetic murmurs and pitying looks had gotten to be more than she could stand—especially since she'd been all too aware of the comments made when she was beyond hearing.

My God, what a pity, losing your kid like that. How does she go on? I'd lose my mind. Her husband did, but Richard never was as strong as Liz . . . or as involved in all of this. If I was her, I'd end it. I couldn't live with the guilt.

Not only was the consensus that poor Richard had been blameless in Fiona's death, but that Liz had been solely responsible. And, God help her, she agreed that, in a way, she had been.

It had been her fault, for getting involved.

For being ambitious.

For being too damned good.

In the end the director had begged her to stay, to finish the job she'd started, but she'd walked away.

"Walked?" Liz said, steadying herself with a hand on a parking meter while she struggled to check her roiling emotions and catch her breath. "At least have the guts not to lie to *yourself.* You didn't walk. You fucking ran." And she didn't even pause until she'd crossed the Pennsylvania border into New York. The rounded green hills that flanked the broad Hudson Valley had proven a godsend, timeless and solid, tamer than the Blue Ridge, somehow even more remote, perhaps because they were far away from Quantico.

When she'd seen the FOR SALE sign at the end of a rutted, tree-lined lane some miles to the northwest, she'd known a painful journey was nearing its end. The centuries-old one-and-a-half-story fieldstone house had a steeply gabled roof and double chimneys, cedar-shake barn, and a stable for horses.

She'd sought out the owner and, amazingly, bought the farm on a handshake and a promise that he'd have half of the asking price within the month. The remainder of the balance would be paid out in an Article of Agreement: monthly installments over the next five years. The former owner had seemed unconcerned. He gave her the mailing address for his fishing camp, signed over the deed, and shook her hand a second time, remarking that she had a face a man could trust.

Liz had nearly welled up at that—irrational tears? Maybe. Yet, she couldn't help thinking, *If only you knew.* She couldn't comprehend how the old gentleman with the silver hair and pleasantly lined face could possibly trust her when she couldn't even trust herself.

She blinked away the memory and opened the driver's door of the Ford, carefully placing her precious bundle of books on the bench seat. Abby Youngblood had been right about one thing. The fog made for dreadful conditions. She kept the headlights on low beam and the sport utility vehicle in second gear, creeping along the Skunktown Road. It wasn't much more than a cow path, and the heavy rains earlier in the day had turned the unpaved surface into a mire. Water rushed along the ditch on both sides of the road on its hurried way to Esopus Creek.

There was something unsettling about a night like this. Maybe it was the concealment the fog offered. Anything, anyone, could find cover in it and watch, unseen, undetected. The thought was enough to raise Liz's hackles. She glanced in the rearview mirror. Had she checked the backseat and cargo bay before getting in?

She hadn't. She'd been too caught up in fighting back the memories of a dead child that the sight of pregnant Abby Youngblood had triggered. She glanced in the rearview mirror again, and when she looked back at the road he loomed up out of nowhere—a half-drowned apparition, covered in mud and barely standing.

Liz stood on the brakes, but the antilock device prevented her from achieving a screeching halt, and she hit him, knocking him back onto the road, where he disappeared into the mist.

For a few seconds Liz sat shaking, too stunned to even cry out. Then she was moving, throwing the gearshift into park and opening the door. "Oh my God. This can't be happening. Are you all right?"

But it was all too real. A long body lay crumpled almost under the front wheels of the SUV. In the misty halo cast by the headlights Liz saw the neat round hole in the back of his shirt, and fumbled in the pocket of her chore coat for her cell phone. She turned it on and dialed 911 before she realized there was no signal. Skunktown Cleft was too deep a valley, the hills surrounding the road too steep, to allow the signal to reach the tower.

She knew that. But she was panicked, and she shouldn't be panicking.

"Calm down, Liz. Just breathe," she said aloud and took a breath, and another. "Well, I can't just leave him here."

She crouched beside him and felt for a pulse in his throat. The first rule of emergency first aid was not to move the victim, yet, as she saw it, she had no other choice. He was alive, but he needed medical attention, and he needed it now. If she left him lying in the road, someone else might come along and finish what she'd started, or he might die of shock right there in the mud. "Just hang on. I'm going to get you to a doctor. But first, we've got to get you on your feet."

Gripping his shoulder, she struggled to turn him over. It took everything she had, and she just hoped to Christ she hadn't made things worse. He was heavy, and it took several false starts, a lot of grunting in the muddy track, but she finally succeeded.

He fell on his back with an audible groan, and at the same time, the beams of the headlights illuminated features that were achingly familiar, a hard, masculine face she had hoped never to see again. "English? Oh, Jesus. This has got to be some sort of sick joke."

He struggled for a deep breath and didn't quite make it, his eyes slitting open, a grimacelike smile flitting over his mouth and then gone. He looked as if he'd just gone ten rounds with boxing's heaviest hitter and lost. "Liz. . . . I take it . . . from that . . . rather forceful . . . hello . . . that you're still . . . steamed." Then he passed out.

Liz's heart stood still. Had she killed him? Shaky and sick at heart, she bent near, her cheek to his mouth, and felt the gentle rush of his breath against her skin. Relief flooded her. "Oh, God, Jake. Don't you do that to me again."

She thought about wrapping him in a blanket and tying his sorry ass to the bumper, but he hadn't done anything quite that bad to her lately, and a good dragging through the mud wouldn't do a damn thing to improve a generally nasty disposition. So she settled for shaking him until the pain brought him around again, then nagged him onto his feet and into the Ford before he lost consciousness again.

Dr. Kate Fife lived in a huge white Victorian on Howell Street. The light was on in the kitchen when Liz pulled into the drive. Reaching out, she lifted one of English's eyelids, receiving a groan in return. "You stay where you are," she warned. "Do you hear me? Any theatrics and I swear, I'll leave you to die where you fall."

A shallow breath. "You're such a heartless bitch. It's what I always . . . loved most about you."

"Stay in the vehicle, Jake. I'll be right back."

As Liz ran up the flagstone walk, the porch light came on and Dr. Kate Fife's slim form appeared in the doorway. "Thank God you're still awake! Can you lend me a hand? I just hit someone out on Skunktown Road."

"Do you have any idea how lucky you are to be alive?"

"Since you've told me at least ten times, I think it's starting to sink in." Jake was flat on his stomach with a view of Kate Fife's slender feet. "What kind of doctor wears tennis shoes, anyway?" he wondered.

"The kind who likes to play tennis."

"Shouldn't you buy something hellishly expensive?"

"Pretentious doesn't go well around here, I fear."

"Don't expect gratitude," a voice warned from a corner of the room he couldn't see. "He's a wimp when it comes to pain."

"Look who's talking," Jake muttered, and Liz went dead silent.

"Small-caliber bullet," the voice above him mused. "Probably fired from a distance, which is why you're still breathing. Do you realize a twenty-two-caliber bullet can carry over flat, open ground for a mile? This one glanced off your shoulder blade. You've got a hairline crack, according to the X ray, so you'll have to keep your right arm immobile for a couple of weeks, and then nothing strenuous for another four."

"No cast," Jake insisted. "I can't afford to lose my mobility." The local anesthetic she'd administered had deadened the pain from the gunshot wound, but the aches and pains from his front-on tackle of Liz's SUV made him feel as if he'd been trampled by a herd of elephants. There was a tugging sensation on his upper right side, and he heard a metallic chink as the slug was dropped into a metal container. "Just like I thought. Twenty-two-caliber. You two know each other?"

They answered simultaneously, Jake in the affirmative, Liz deep in denial. "This is too weird," Kate muttered. "Mr. English—"

"It's Special Agent English, but call me Jake. I hate formality."

"You hate rules," Liz put in, "and discipline, and being told what to do, and anything else that applies to polite society, and human decency, and—"

He let out a low groan, struggling for breath. "Liz," he said in a voice gone suddenly weak, motioning with two fingers on his good left hand to the corner where she stood. "Come closer. There's . . . something . . . you need to hear." She hesitated, but couldn't resist, bending near. "Kiss my ass."

Kate Fife choked on a suppressed laugh. "Well, Special Agent Jake, can you sit up without help?"

Jake rolled to his side and pushed upright, keeping his gaze fixed on the woman who retreated to the corner while Kate bandaged the bullet wound and at his direction brought a clean white shirt from his leather case.

"I'll be filing a report with the local police department—standard procedure with all gunshot wounds," the physician told him. "But I'm sure you already know that. I'll leave the car accident to your discretion since all you sustained were some minor contusions. If you want to file a complaint, you'll have to talk to Sheriff Rhys."

"Oh, shit. That reminds me." He dug in his case and extracted the cellular phone, punched a few numbers, and waited. "Sheriff Rhys."

"This is Sarah from Dispatch, I'm afraid Sheriff Rhys is out on a call. May I ask who's calling?"

"Special Agent Jacob English. We had an appointment." He glanced at his watch. *One a.m.* "Any idea what time he'll be available?"

"I'm sorry, sir. There's been a three-car pileup out on Route two-thirteen. There's just no way to gauge these things."

"So much for immediacy. All right. Tell him I was unavoidably delayed, and that I'll stop by first thing in the morning."

He hung up the phone. Kate Fife was in the adjacent room, writing out a couple of prescriptions, while Liz watched him, a look of acute wariness on her face. Her suspicion aside, she still looked damn good. Two years of self-imposed solitude hadn't changed that. *Two years of self-imposed punishment.* That's what this living the life of the upstate recluse was all about. She'd buried herself as surely as the Cemetery Man had buried her eight-year-old daughter alive two years ago.

She was punishing herself for something she could not have predicted, or controlled, and from Jake's perspective, that was a futile exercise. That didn't mean he couldn't relate. He'd done "futile" a time or two.

"You know of a decent motel close by?" The

question had been directed to Kate Fife, but Liz answered.

"There's a bed-and-breakfast here in town, but I hope your credit card balance can take it. It's pricey and exclusive. As a matter of fact, you might want to keep your mouth shut over there or you'll be lucky if they'll have you."

"Always good with a verbal jab," Jake muttered. "I'm glad to see you haven't lost your touch. I hope your other talents are intact as well, because it looks like you're going to need them." He put away the phone and stepped off the examining table. "Seeing as how you ran me down, giving me a lift over there is the least you can do."

"It's one o'clock in the morning. That's the middle of the night around here. Besides, it's getting close to Labor Day. They'll probably be full up."

"Do you have another suggestion?" Jake asked. She was so full of negatives. It was becoming obvious that had she possessed the power to do so, she would have wished him into nothingness.

"As a matter of fact, I do. Rent a car and go back to Quantico." Pitiless, not to mention oblivious.

"I can't do that. Besides, I just got here."

"You hate New York. You said being in New York was like being in hell."

"Well, at the moment, hell is where the action is, and where I can do the most good." It was said quietly, but it obviously struck a nerve.

Her head snapped up, and the look in her narrowed eyes said it all. She didn't want to hear it. Especially not from him.

"TCM is active, and he's relocated. He's here, Liz, in New York."

"That has nothing to do with me," she said. "I'm out of it now. He won't get a rise out of me. There's no one to impress, no challenge."

"That's not the way this works, and you know it. You don't get to dictate what happens here."

Liz glared at him. He was standing beside the exam table, his long-tailed white shirt hanging open over a pair of dark gray trousers. His skin was tanned, making his sapphire eyes seem even bluer, and his black hair had more than a little gray at the temples.

He was thirty-nine years old, in good physical shape, and he shouldn't be graying. The last time she saw Jake's father, Ranald, he'd been sixty-nine and he'd still had a full head of dark hair. Jake wouldn't admit it, but the pressure cooker of Quantico's Investigative Support Unit was getting to him, and she couldn't help feeling a minuscule pang of remorse for the way she was treating him. "I know how it works, Jake," she said quietly. "Now ask me if I give a damn."

Kate came back into the room with a couple of prescriptions, which she handed to Jake. "You can get these filled tomorrow at Arrow's Pharmacy. Tylenol for the pain, and I'll stop by tomorrow and check your shoulder. I'm scheduled to look in on Anglican tomorrow anyway."

"Anglican?"

"Liz's stud. He came up lame after an injury. You're staying at the farm until you find lodging, right?" She looked from one to the other. "I mean, you are friends—or colleagues, or something, right?"

He was looking at Liz, a level, gauging look, awaiting her rebuff, refusal, reaction. "One night," she said, and she meant it.

They made the drive back to her place in total silence, stopping at his car long enough to tie a white rag to the door handle and grab the garment bag from the backseat. Liz's sanctuary was quaint and old, with a solid, lived-in, comfortable feel. Three huge pines shaded the front of the house, protecting it from the wind that swept down from the Adirondacks and tore through the cleft in the raw months of winter.

The house was dark, and Jake found that odd, but he refrained from asking questions. As a guest in her home, he would try not to irritate her any more than necessary. She got out of the saddle tan Ford, locked it, and took his leather carryall out of his hands. "Kate said you aren't supposed to lift anything."

"I have two hands, Liz. There's nothing wrong with the left one."

She plunged ahead, up the flagstone walk, between rows of perennials, hell-bent on ignoring him. She inserted a key into the lock and pushed the door wide. A pair of dogs boiled out onto the porch, barking and wagging their tails. One was a golden retriever, the other a black lab. Liz didn't make the introductions, but she did fuss over her canine companions. A flick of the light, and they went inside.

The great room had the same aged and weathered look of the house's exterior. It exuded stability, and Jake knew she must have found it comforting after the turmoil of her life in Virginia. A massive stone fireplace occupied a place on the east wall, dominating the room and giving it the rustic air of a mountain cabin. There were bookshelves and a comfortable sofa, overstuffed side chairs, and a roll-top desk, but no stereo, and no television. He stood looking around, taking it all in, puzzling over what had become of the sophisticated high-tech Liz he'd known in Virginia. Few personal items, few luxuries. "You do have indoor plumbing?"

"Down that hallway, first door on the right." She plunked down two pillows and a wool blanket that had seen better days. "I ride early, but I'll do my best not to wake you when I leave."

"You ride?" Jake repeated. "As in horses? I'm not so sure that's a good idea."

It was the wrong thing to say. All traces of the uneasy truce they'd slipped into since she'd offered him a roof to keep the rain off blew up in his face. Her dark eyes seemed lit from within by an anger that wasn't totally directed at him. "Let me make it very clear to you, Jake English. You and I are not friends, and we're not colleagues. You are a guest in my home for one night—one! I don't know what you're doing here in Abundance, and I don't want to know, but I am warning you. You do not tell me what to do, and you stay out of my business. No one knows about Virginia, do you hear me? And I damn sure want to keep it that way. Ruin what I've built here, and I swear to Christ I will make you pay!"

Liz stomped from the room, the dogs tracking at her heels, not stopping until they were safely upstairs. Locking the bedroom door and leaning against it, she tried not to dwell on their earlier cryptic exchange. *TCM is active, and he's relocated. He's here, Liz, in New York.*

That has nothing to do with me. I'm out of it now. He won't get a rise out of me. There's no one to impress, no challenge.

That's not the way this works, and you know it. You don't get to dictate what happens here.

Oh, she knew how it worked, Liz thought darkly. The twisted, sadistic game the Cemetery Man was playing wouldn't end until he was ready to end it, or until one of them was dead.

Chapter Two

The couch was either too damned short or he was too damned tall. He couldn't lie on his back because it hurt like hell, and if he turned onto his stomach, he would stiffen and never be able to move come morning, and for some reason he wasn't at all comfortable with the thought of being unable to get out of Liz's way.

He'd found himself in that very position last night on the deserted road, and she'd done her best to kill him, something for which she had yet to apologize. If he'd been the suspicious type, he might have speculated on whether it was a bona fide accident or something slightly more sinister. Yet, she'd had no clue that he was coming to town, and, in her defense, she hadn't left him lying in the road, hadn't backed up to have at him again, and she'd even taken him to Kate Fife, M.D., which certainly counted in her favor. It was the idea that she'd had time to regret her humane impulse that he found so unnerving. He wasn't exactly her favorite person, and he knew it.

Hell, he wasn't even her favorite ex-husband.

A click of boot heels on the slate tiles, and she came into the great room, but she paused when she saw him sitting stiffly on the edge of the couch. The dogs, Sandy and Fletch, flanked him, one on each side of his knees, watching him intently with large, sympathetic eyes. She'd named the black lab after the assistant director. If it weren't for the fact it would hurt like hell, Jake would have laughed.

Liz's gaze narrowed. "If you're trying to elicit sympathy from any of us, then forget it." Her voice was cold and hard and her words clipped.

Jake wondered if it was some sort of protection mechanism, or if she really felt nothing for him besides a lingering hatred?

"Sympathy? From you? You've got to be kidding. I may have been shot and run down by a truck, but the mind hasn't begun to go quite yet." Fletch put a paw on his knee and Jake gasped. He couldn't remember ever being as stiff and sore as he was this morning. It was a complete mystery, how even his fingernails could ache.

She'd been reaching for a red ball cap on a peg by the door, but at his gasp she turned, regarding him with a critical eye. "What's wrong now?"

"Nothing. Nothing at all. I'm fine, really, and in an hour or two, after my muscles decide to stop seizing up, I might just be able to move." He sucked in a breath, and pain shot through his right shoulder. He'd definitely reached a low point in his life. He'd thought he'd bottomed out the day Doc Dread had pronounced him used up and useless. He'd been wrong. "Oh, hell. Everything hurts, Liz, even my hair follicles. Is it possible to die from bumps, bruises, and a minor flesh wound? Because if it weren't for giving you the immense satisfaction of witnessing my last gasp, I'd very much like to give it up right now."

She stared at him a moment, then took down the ball cap and socked it on her head, pulling her ponytail through the hole in the back. "I don't want you dead, Jake, no matter what you may think. I just want you gone." She took a few steps toward the sofa, then pulled up short. He could almost hear her thought process. *Not too close, Liz. He's dangerous. Be careful not to care, careful not to touch. You have no idea where he's been.*

The dogs whined, glancing back at Jake, as if pleading for Liz to do something. She was mistress here, caretaker of all things, and this poor misbegotten and dreadfully ragged creature was obviously in a very bad way. She looked down at the dogs. "You two aren't exactly great judges of character. You've proven more than once that you have a fondness for skunks."

"Thanks," Jake said. "I needed that. Would you like to kick me now? It should be great fun. I'm utterly defenseless."

She lay a finger alongside her chin. "Would you like to shower?"

He glanced sharply up. "With you?" As appealing as the idea sounded—him, Liz, lots of steam, a little soap—he wasn't sure he was up to the challenge.

An eyebrow went up, an expression that said, *What do you think, stupid?*

"The hot water will help ease your stiffness, and, quite frankly, you're a mess. You've got mud in your hair."

She reached out, pointing to his left temple, and for a brief space he thought for sure she was going to touch him. His breath caught, an automatic response. He hadn't forgotten the warmth of her touch, or what a wildcat she was in bed. *Had been*... he corrected himself. She barely resembled the Liz he'd married in a hasty ceremony more than a decade ago when she was young and he was stupid. They'd burned red hot, but the fire was gone, and there was nothing left but cold gray ash and abject bitterness.

"Oh, God, yes," he said, still thinking of their glory days. He caught himself quickly, stunned that she still had the power to affect him after everything they'd been through, after all the rivalry, the animosity, the cutting sarcasm. "The shower, I meant to say. Hot water is just what I need."

Thirty gallons of wet heat later, Jake emerged from Liz's bathroom a little less stiff and slightly more mobile. Dressed in a pair of faded jeans and a ZZ Top T-shirt, his right arm in a sling, and smelling pleasantly of aftershave, he was every inch the six-foot-two Jacob Harrison English Liz remembered. Volatile, sexy, charismatic, hard to resist, impossible to ignore.

As he walked into the kitchen the sun broke through the windowpanes and hit him full in the face, turning his skin a golden tan, his blue eyes deep and fathomless, the dimple in his chin an intriguing shadow. She'd forgotten how handsome he was. She hadn't forgotten his well-earned reputation as the bad boy of Quantico. She remembered too well the effect he'd always had on her. The Investigative Support Unit worked deep underground at the FBI's training facility at Quantico, Virginia. There were no windows in the sub-basement since no natural light reached sixty feet belowground, yet when Jake walked into a room, Liz had been able to feel the immediate change in the atmosphere. The air around him had crackled. He'd been that vital, that exciting, that potent a presence.

Attractiveness came with a price, however. Jake liked women, and women loved Jake, and there was no reason to think that much had changed.

"Thanks," he said, standing a little awkwardly just inside the doorway. "For the hot water and towels, I mean. It helped."

Liz turned away. "Don't mention it," she said, toying with her ponytail. "It's the least I can do after— Look, Jake, I really didn't mean to hit you." It was as much as she was willing to give, and she gave it grudgingly. "There's coffee if you want some."

"Coffee sounds good. Is it all right if I sit?"

Liz sighed, filling a cup with black coffee and placing it on the table in front of him. Two plates and a platter with scrambled eggs and crisp bacon came next. She slipped into a chair at the opposite end of the table. There was safety in distance, or at least the illusion of it. "I was distracted and made too much. Pork isn't good for the dogs, so you might as well eat."

He snorted as he shook his dark head, a sound that was part derision, part wry humor aimed solely at himself. "You're unique, Liz. One of a kind."

"Funny. You didn't think so when you married me."

"Yeah, I did. I was just too young and too damn foolish to appreciate what I had when I had it."

Liz put up a hand. "Oh, please. You weren't that young."

He gave a grimace. "Maturity comes slower to some of us than to others. I did get beyond being the unmitigated ass. It just took me a while."

"Look, Jake. Let's don't go there, all right? It's over with. In fact, it was over with almost before it got started, and there's no sense in reliving it. Besides, I'm in no mood for a walk down memory lane—especially with you."

"Oh, I don't know," Jake said, a slow smile curving his mouth. "As I recall, it wasn't all bad."

"You weren't living it," she said. "I was." She pushed eggs around her plate, then put down her fork and picked up her coffee mug.

"All right," he said. "All right. Ancient history; how we got together in the first place is a bigger mystery than the pyramids." He polished off his bacon and eggs, wiped his mouth on a napkin, and settled back gingerly to sip his coffee while he watched her.

That kind of attention from Jake had always unnerved her, probably because she'd always been very good at reading his thoughts, and right now his thoughts were focused on his libido.

"I know you don't like me much," he said, "and I can't even say I blame you, but we need to talk. This is serious."

Silence. Maybe he would take the hint and give it up. But from the look in his eyes, she knew the hope was futile. She shook her head, adamant. "I don't want to know."

His tone dropped, his voice barely above a whisper. "You have to know. You have to listen. You don't have a choice, and neither do I."

"No. Do you get that? No! I've built a new life here. I have new friends, and no constant reminders. I don't want to go back. I can't change what happened, and I don't want to be that person anymore."

"Is that why you're using your maiden name?" he asked. "So no one will recognize you? Or did you take it back after your second divorce was finalized?"

They were simple questions, and none of Jake's business. Liz's hackles bristled. It was his way of reminding her that she'd failed to hold a relationship together, not once, but twice. "I happened to *like* my maiden name," she said so sharply that he had to get the point. Her business was just that: her business, a closed subject. At least where he was concerned.

But Jake didn't seem to understand subtlety, and he wouldn't quit. He wasn't finished; she could feel it. The barrage was coming. Like the threat of an electrical storm, it crackled in the air between them. "You know, Liz, you might be able to fool a few of the rubes around this place, but you can't fool this guy. You figure into his fantasies, and he will find you. I could always be wrong, but I don't think Fiona was the finish. I don't think he's through with you yet. We have three victims in New York State so far, all within a twenty-mile radius of this shit-bag little town. Each of those three victims disappeared and was later recovered from a shallow grave and a wooden box. Two of the families received phone calls, tormenting them with false promises about the safe return of their kids. The last call they got provided directions as to where to look for their loved ones. By the time they got the second phone call, the vics were already dead. The last one they found by accident. A guy with a metal detector noticed the grave site and found the airway."

"Go to hell, Jake," Liz whispered, but he wasn't finished, and he refused to let it go.

"He's got up a head of steam, and he'll keep right on killing until he gets what he really wants."

Liz closed her eyes. She hated him for speaking her daughter's name, hated him for being right. He didn't have to say anything, didn't have to speak the words, because she knew what the Cemetery Man wanted. He wanted her. Opening her eyes, she got up so abruptly that she nearly knocked over her half-finished coffee. "Finish your coffee and call a cab. The phone book is next to the phone."

"Damn it, Liz, for once in your life will you listen to me?" he demanded. "I know what I'm talking about!" As she brushed by him, he caught her arm with his uninjured left hand. "For Christ's sake. At least tell me where you're going."

"Go to hell," she said again. "I don't answer to you or to anyone." She stormed from the room, throwing a last warning back over her shoulder as she went out, "Don't be here when I get back!"

The dogs glanced at Jake, then followed. Jake winced at the slamming of the door. What a colossal mess. He went to the phone and dialed headquarters in Virginia, then punched in Charlie Calendar's extension.

"Calendar," came the response.

"Hey, Charlie, it's me."

Jake heard the creak of a chair as Calendar sat straight up. "Jake? Where the hell are you? I must have called your apartment fifty times."

"Out of town," Jake said evasively.

"Could you be any less specific?"

Charlie was a good friend, and Jake hated keeping him in the dark. He did it because he liked the guy, because Charlie had done his best to keep Jake from self-destructing. It just hadn't been terribly effective. "North Dakota."

"What? You're shittin' me! What the hell are you doing there?" A sigh. Calendar had his eyes closed and was rubbing his forehead just above his eyebrows, like he always did when he was stressed. "Oh, Christ. You're not in fucking North Dakota. You tracked her down, didn't you. You found Liz."

"Cut me a break, will you, pal? I didn't call so

you could rip me a new asshole. I had that procedure done a few weeks back."

"And you sure as hell didn't learn anything from it!"

"I did some nosing around. Balldecker's working this case, isn't he?"

"Larry's a good man," Charlie insisted. "Stay the hell out of the way, Jake. If the brass find out you're causing problems, it'll just make things worse."

"Balldecker's a good man . . . and I'm not," Jake said, agitated. He wasn't pissed at Calendar. It was the damned business-as-usual attitude he'd been tripping over for two years. Nobody seemed to get it that the son of a bitch had killed Liz's kid. Oh, they'd sent flowers along with their condolences, but then hiked right back to the same old, same old. TCM went underground, and everyone had breathed a sigh of relief but Jake. He'd known the prick was still out there, still a threat. He'd known that he was waiting. "So they hand me my salary and tell me to find a beach somewhere. It would have been a hell of a lot more humane if they'd taken me out to the shooting range and put an end to it right there." He walked to the window with the portable phone, leaning one upraised arm against the frame. "Jesus. I'm sorry. You sure as hell didn't ask to get dumped on."

"Jake, where are you. I've got some vacation time coming. I'll meet you, wherever you are, and we'll talk."

"Some other time maybe," Jake said. The truth is I've started something here, and I've gotta finish it."

"Jake, we've done all we can with the information we have. The police have the information they need, but it's up to them to do the investigative work. Do you get what I'm saying? It's not your job; you know how this works, Jake. We give them the insight into these wackos, and they bust 'em. The authorities have the stuff on TCM."

Jake quietly put an end to the conversation and settled the phone back on its base. Calendar was one of the good guys, but he didn't understand why Jake needed to be where he was. He hadn't been in Virginia when Liz's kid was abducted, and he hadn't been there to dig up that damned Rosewood box, and then break the news to Liz that her daughter wouldn't be coming home. Charlie didn't avoid sleep to avoid dreams, and he hadn't been put out to pasture because some skirt with a degree had deemed him a liability.

This wasn't another bad decision, Jake assured himself, it was something he had to do . . . for Liz, for her kid, for himself. But it would take time to convince her.

Liz was the key.

But Liz wouldn't listen to anything he had to say, let alone work with him. Liz was the one with the gift, the only one who possessed an intuition finely honed enough to get into the mind of the monster, possibly to predict his next move. The abilities she possessed weren't foolproof, but they were better than waiting for him to strike again and praying that he made a mistake while the body count slowly crept into the double digits.

Without her cooperation, her help, Jake's job was going to be a hell of a lot more difficult—not to mention that it included the impossible task of protecting a woman who loathed him, a woman who was unwilling to face a painful reality. *Face it, Jake. She doesn't want your protection. Hell, maybe she doesn't even need it.*

Maybe he was wrong, about everything. Maybe

he'd miscalculated. Maybe they were right and he was wrong, about all of it. Maybe this creep's obsession with Liz had cooled and he would fixate on something else, someone else. Yet . . . no matter how often he tried to tell himself that maybe Liz didn't need him, his gut told him otherwise.

He wasn't wrong, and he couldn't afford to leave it alone, no matter what former Special Agent Elizabeth Moncrief Airhardt wanted.

Liz was furious—at Jake, at herself. She should never have weakened and offered him a place to stay. Letting him into her world for even one night had been a huge miscalculation, and she would have to be damned careful that it didn't cost her.

Starling, the blood bay gelding she exercised each morning, was waiting for her when she entered the barn. She stopped to check on Anglican, her three-year-old stud, and to fish some sugar cubes from the pocket of her blue jean jacket. Anglican took the treat, nuzzling Liz's empty palm as he searched for more treats.

The morning was cool and green, and a heavy mist still hung over the hollow. The air felt good on her face as she saddled Starling and they struck out through the lower field and into the woods beyond. Instinct insisted that she resist following a pattern.

Patterned, habitual behavior was predictable behavior, and predictability was dangerous from a potential target's perspective. Never take the same course twice, vary the time, the routine as much as possible. She knew all of this by rote, and she intentionally ignored it, even though somewhere deep in her core the rebellion went against the grain.

"Don't fall into that trap, Moncrief. Don't you dare give Jake English any credence. You're out of it now. None of it applies to the here and now." Yet even as she said it, she knew that Jake was no schlepp when it came to knowing his business. He was one of the best-known active authorities on serial offenders. He was called upon to advise and assist law enforcement all over the country; his talent and his astuteness were in high demand, and no matter how much she tried to deny it, she knew that he wouldn't be here in Abundance if the threat wasn't very real.

"Shit," she said, barely hearing the hollow ring of Starling's shoes against the floorboards of the old covered bridge that crossed an unnamed brook and joined her property to that of Catherine Youngblood, matriarch of the Youngblood family and Abby's aunt. "This is his fault. He brought it all back . . . the fear, the speculation. If he'd just stayed the hell out of it."

What? If he'd stayed out of it, her life would have been full of positives? Fiona would be alive today, a vibrant ten-year-old full of life and mischief? Richard wouldn't have ended the marriage, slipping further and further into catatonic oblivion? And she wouldn't have been riddled with guilt, so full of regret that she could barely face her own refection in the mornings without wanting to die?

Jake was a thorn in her side, a grim reminder of everything she'd tried so desperately to forget, but he hadn't caused her problems, and he sure as hell couldn't fix them, despite his blatant Superman complex. She snorted a little at the thought.

How many men could take a bullet in the back, get hit by a truck, and still have the tenacity to nag an ex-wife over an exceptionally tense breakfast. He was fearless, and always had been. It was the one thing that had always driven her crazy, the thing about him that she envied most, if she was truthful with herself.

Jake was everything she admired and all that she detested, and her feelings for him were every bit as conflicted today as they had been when she'd been fool enough to promise that she would love him forever. The marriage had burned hot, and then burned out when he slept with another woman a few weeks after they said "I will."

Closet shrinks would have had a ball with that one, as his actions had screamed fear of commitment despite their vows. She'd been too angry, too devastated to allow reason to seep in, and despite his claims that he'd been dead drunk and didn't even remember his infidelity, she hadn't been able to forgive him. Six weeks into wedded bliss Liz's world had fallen apart for the first time. She'd divorced him as hastily as she'd married him, and because he couldn't persuade her otherwise, he'd signed the papers.

Except for Quantico and an uneasy working relationship, their lives had taken separate paths from that moment on. For several years she worked in the field, away from Virginia. She met Richard, a soft-spoken architect with a calm demeanor and a love of children, and a few months later they were married. By the time she returned to Quantico, Fiona was two years old and life was perfect, a fairy tale, complete with a deep, dark secret. It had been a blessing that Jake had never asked questions about the dark-haired little girl born eight months to the day after she'd filed for divorce.

"Not even fairy tales end happily one hundred percent of the time," she said to the horse beneath her, and Starling blew his agreement. She wasn't sure how far she had ridden into Vanderbloon's Woods, but the mist was burning off when Starling stopped short and refused to go any farther. She nudged his ribs and clucked to him, but he remained reluctant, bringing his hooves off the ground in a rebellious buck. They waged a war of wills for a few minutes and then, weary of it, Liz turned his head and took him back home at a brisk trot. With any luck, Jake would be gone by the time she reached the house.

Deputy Shep Margolis was an uncooperative son of a bitch—not that it was all that surprising. Jake had run into a hundred just like him, small-town, small-time law enforcement who regarded their jurisdiction as their sacrosanct territory, not to be infringed upon by a suit, especially if that suit had a shinier badge, bigger gun, or heftier salary than the deputy's twenty-two grand a year. Deputy SOB threw his shoulders back and looked down his nose at Jake. He obviously relished being behind the wheel of the police cruiser. It gave him a sense of power. "Can't recall as I have ever had to play taxi for a fed. What'd you say your name was again?"

Jake took his time getting into the black and white. Settling back with a slight gritting of teeth, he addressed his own reflection in Margolis's dark glasses, which the man continued to wear despite the fact that the day held a promise of more rain and wasn't all that bright. "English, Jacob, but I answer more readily to Jake. I don't like to stand on formality. It gets in the way of business."

"I can see that. Doesn't your position require a dress code?" Margolis sent a sidelong glance at Jake's jeans and T-shirt. Jake was wearing his shoulder holster, but it was more habit than necessity. He felt naked without it, and being in the vicinity of an ex-wife who would like nothing better than to carve up his balls to serve as an entrée, he couldn't afford to feel even a fragment of vulnerability. Besides, cops like Margolis respected firepower, and, more than anything, Jake hoped to achieve an open dialogue and cooperative relationship with the locals.

It was important.

In fact, it was crucial.

"Dress code? As in uniform? When I'm on Bureau business I dress the part, but I stopped punching the clock a few days ago. I'm on my own time, and this is more of a courtesy call than active duty." It wasn't a lie, just a slight bending of the facts. Days, weeks? It really didn't matter. "Like I said, I don't like formalities. It's better to be able to blend in, and I don't see that many suits around here."

"Oh, you'll blend in all right," Shep said with a smirk. "We get a lot of hotshot profiler types up here in the Catskills. Big demand for it, us havin' so much unsolved crime and all."

Jake's facial muscles tightened as he held back his opinion that the Catskills certainly had its share of assholes. "As a matter of fact, I have information that you had a serial murderer in your jurisdiction just last year. A Mr. William Bentz . . . or maybe my information's incorrect?"

The deputy stiffened. "Bentz was here, all right, but we got him—and we didn't need a glorified shrink to help out, either."

"My degree happens to be in criminology, not psychiatry."

The drive was short, and Jake was grateful. He pulled himself out of the car by grasping the door frame and moving carefully. The heat of the shower had helped relieve the stiffness, but he still felt like he'd been beaten and kicked within an inch of his pride; considering his evening and morning with Liz, maybe he had been. Pride was hard to maintain in the presence of a scornful woman.

He followed Margolis into the police station. "Sheriff Rhys is waitin' for you. His office is the first door on the right."

"So much for professional courtesy," Jake muttered under his breath. Margolis ambled over to the dispatcher-slash-receptionist's desk and propped the cheek of his scrawny ass on the corner of it, casually swinging that leg as he chatted with the young woman manning the phone. The first door on the right had small gold letters on the glass: JOHN RHYS, SHERIFF.

Modest and unassuming. Jake raised his left hand and rapped on the glass. At the hurried invitation to enter, he opened the door and stepped into the office.

Rhys was close to Jake's height, only a little stockier in build. Blond and blue-eyed, he had good features that hinted at his Dutch heritage, a younger, slightly more rugged version of the actor Rutger Hauer. Liz's second husband had been blond. In fact, every man she'd ever dated had been blond with one exception, and that hadn't lasted. Jake hadn't seen any evidence of a man in her life, but someone as fine as Liz wouldn't be alone for long unless she chose to be.

Rhys motioned Jake into the room without missing a beat in his phone conversation. "Miss Ridley. Miss Ridley, just take a breath and calm down." Jake could hear the reply from across the room. The caller was female, and she was agitated. "Yes, ma'am, I do understand how upsetting it is. Yes, ma'am, I agree. Samuel Turner should wear his eye patch in public. I don't like running into him much myself, but, ma'am, I can't arrest the man until he's committed a crime."

Rhys listened, and the tic in his cheek worked. "Unfortunately, scaring folks does not constitute disturbing the peace, and I can't order Samuel to remain indoors. Well, I'm sorry too. Yes, ma'am, locking your doors seems like a sound idea."

Rhys hung up the phone and reached for his Styrofoam coffee cup with one hand while he massaged his temple with the other. "I swear, this place is falling apart," he muttered, then, holding a finger up to stall Jake, he bellowed for Margolis.

Margolis stuck his head in the room so fast that Jake knew he must have been lingering at the watercooler so he could eavesdrop on their nonexistent conversation. "You need somethin', boss?"

"Shep, it seems Samuel is at it again. Miss Ridley ran into him on the street and she had her nine-year-old niece with her. You can pretty much guess the rest. Christ, I hate to do this, but would you mind having a word with him? See if you can convince him to stop frightening the kids?"

"Will do. That all?"

"I sincerely hope so," Rhys said. "Much more and I may change my mind about another term and run for animal control warden, instead." He swallowed some coffee, winced, and sat back to regard Jake with a glance that was open without being overly friendly. "Special Agent English, I was expecting you last night, but that was before all hell broke loose. I got a report this morning from Doc Fife about a gunshot wound?"

"It's Jake, and it's a flesh wound."

"You have any enemies in these parts?"

Only one that he could think of, and she hadn't been in the vicinity at the time. "None that I'm aware of."

"Well," Rhys said, "it was probably just a hunter's shot gone wild, but I still think it would be a good thing to look into it." He shoved his coffee away and sat back in his chair. "Now that we've gotten the preliminaries out of the way, maybe you'd like to tell me what brings you here? It isn't often that someone from the Bureau drops by Ulster County, so I'm assuming it's something big."

"You might say that," Jake replied, shifting slightly to accommodate the nagging ache in his shoulder. "I trust you've been following the killings upstate. Three vics, all female, abducted at or near the vicinity of their residences. One, it seems, was on her way home from her middle school. She lived two blocks away."

"Entombed while alive. The guy the newspapers are calling the Cemetery Man. I don't think there's a parent in the state who isn't a little unnerved by it, including yours truly. I'm not sure what that has to do with the sheriff's department, though I am fairly sure you'll enlighten me."

"I've profiled this case, and I have reason to believe our man's next target will be in this vicinity. I was hoping we could combine our resources and stop this scumbag before he grabs someone else. I don't have to tell you that no one is safe if he's in the area."

Rhys shook his head. "That'd be just great, Jake. Just great. Maybe you'd care to tell me how we're supposed to accomplish that? I've had a little experience with this type of offender, and the problem is, he knows what he has planned; we don't. Unless you've got a crystal ball, there's no way to predict who or where he'll strike next, or even *if* he'll strike."

Jake didn't have a crystal ball, but he had Liz. Her instincts had always been dead on, but getting her to cooperate wouldn't be easy . . . and he felt oddly bound by her insistence that no one be clued into her past. If he shared that confidence with Rhys, she would freeze him out, and his chances of gaining her trust—already slim—would be blown beyond hell. "What about extra man-power? We already have a psychological profile on this guy—"

"Lemme guess," Rhys said, "a white guy, mid-twenties to mid-forties—weighing in on this guy being more mature because he's probably been at it for a while, and he's honed his skills. Intelligent, but an underachiever. Probably works at a menial job. Could have a wife and kids, or maybe not—and he comes from a broken home headed by a domi-neering mother. Of course, you do realize that profile fits about half of the residents of this county? We'd be looking for a needle in a haystack, Jake, and that new cruiser out there has already blown this year's budget. Extra manpower? Shep and I and a part-time deputy who works graveyard on weekends are pretty much it."

"That's it? You're going to sit here and do noth-ing?"

"With all due respect, Jake, I'm doing every-thing I can do at the moment. I've got a belliger-ent asshole who tried to eat a bullet and halfway succeeded scaring the piss out of little old ladies and little kids, but I can't convince him to stay in-doors just because he's disfigured without risking a violation of his civil rights. If you have a better suggestion that doesn't involve making a bad situation worse, then I'm all ears. But, quite frankly, we've already had one serial wacko in residence. What are the odds of it happening again in a town this small?"

"At least call a news conference," Jake suggested. "Get the press in on this and alert the residents so they can keep their kids safe."

"You want me to send a shock wave of fear and hysteria through my peaceful little town because you've got a hunch this guy *might* decide this dot on the map is a good place for him to visit? I really am sorry, Jake, but I need something more concrete than that."

"Like a missing kid, maybe?" Jake suggested. "Would that do it for you, Sheriff?"

Rhys's response shouldn't have surprised him. He knew how law enforcement and the judicial system worked, and Rhys's hands were tied until something actually occurred. Unfortunately, by that time it would be too late, and the sheriff's job would get a whole lot harder. There was nothing worse than having to break the news to a parent whose child had been murdered.

He should know.

He'd been the one to locate Liz's daughter, Fiona. He'd pulled her lifeless little body out of that macabre underground box, and he'd insisted on being the one to break the news. Somehow he'd thought that it might be easier to take if it came from someone familiar. But he'd been wrong about that, too. "I've seen this guy's work firsthand, and for your sake, and for the sake of your town, I sincerely hope it doesn't come to that."

"You'll be leaving, then, I take it?" Did Rhys sound hopeful, or was Jake imagining it?

Jake shrugged, then regretted it as a pain knifed through his shoulder. No fucking way was he telling

Rhys about his enforced leave. "I have some vacation days and could use a little downtime. Maybe I'll stick around. Your town may be a dot on the map, Sheriff, but I kind of like it here." He got out of his chair with a wince, slowly straightening to his full height. "There's a bed-and-breakfast around here, I take it?"

"Shep!" Rhys said, and at that moment Sarah, the dispatcher, appeared in the open doorway.

"John, phone call on line two. It's Rachel. It sounds important."

Shep ambled in as Rhys reached for the phone. "Give Special Agent English a lift to Martha's place on your way to talk to Samuel?"

"Sure thing, boss." Margolis headed out, Jake following a few steps behind. "You're looking kind of peaked, Jake," Margolis said. "Maybe you should see a doctor."

John took the phone call from his ex-wife and spent a full twenty minutes reassuring her that she and the kids were safe in the middle of town. By the time he hung up the phone, he was thoroughly out of patience with peeling hysterics off the ceiling. This whole thing with Turner was getting out of hand. The man either was unaware of the havoc he was creating or he didn't give a damn. Most male residents hereabouts owned at least one rifle, and a few had collections that in less rural areas might have been considered an arsenal. All he needed was for Turner to startle some trigger-happy redneck and he'd have a homicide on his hands. And that would blow the election for him.

The murderous escapades of one William Bentz a year ago were a blight on his service record and that sure as hell didn't help. Bentz, a mild-mannered college professor during the day and serial killer by night, had terrorized Abundance for three long weeks. He'd had John at his wit's end, and if it hadn't been for Matthew Monroe, Bentz would have killed Abby Youngblood.

Monroe had put an end to the professor, but not before Bentz killed three local women. Monroe, a horror novelist, for Christ's sake, had gotten the killer, and gotten the girl, making John look like an inept imbecile.

If he was to be totally honest, Abby's rejection still smarted. He'd been in love with Abby Youngblood off and on for years—since high school. She deserved better than Monroe. A hell of a lot better.

"If you had any sense at all," he told himself, "you'd forget about Abby and move on. It's not like that situation will ever change. She made her choice—who the hell are you to say it was the wrong one?"

That was the problem, John thought. He'd never had a great deal of sense. He followed his heart, which usually ended in a lot of disappointment.

Like Abby. He'd loved her. She just hadn't felt the same way about him, and he really needed to get the hell over it. It was obvious that Abby had.

"Brooding doesn't become you," said a voice from the doorway. "You have to be tall, dark, and handsome to get away with that sort of thing. You're tall, and you're passable looking, but dark? Get real!"

Julianne leaned a shoulder against the doorway. "So, big brother . . . are you going to take your little sister to lunch? Liz Moncrief is meeting me at the café in half an hour. You remember Liz? Dark red hair, brown eyes, mysterious, and available?"

John thought about that, surveyed the stack of paperwork awaiting him, listened to Sarah fielding calls, and made up his mind. "If you don't think she'd mind, I'd love to."

Chapter Three

The local café was small and unpretentious, but the food was good, the service better than adequate, and it did a brisk business on weekdays between six A.M. and eight P.M. Marge Turner, the proprietress, was Abundance born and bred, a sturdy woman of indeterminate age with a smoker's voice. After thirty years of frying burgers and flipping flapjacks, Marge had turned the grill over to Billy Yarrow, her employee, dividing her time between waiting tables and a book of crossword puzzles when business was slow. Business this day was anything but slow, however, so there were at least a dozen witnesses to Samuel Turner's entrance.

Liz opened the door and stepped from the heat of the new afternoon into the semi-cool interior of the café, and at the same time, the argument in the kitchen grew sufficiently in volume to turn heads. Hand still on the doorknob, Liz glanced up in time to see a tall, rawboned man shuffle toward the dining area, pursued by Billy Yarrow, spatula in hand. "Samuel, you can't go in there!" Yarrow growled the warning, then grabbed for Samuel's arm. "Marge! Marge!"

Samuel turned and, cursing, gave Yarrow a shove that sent the smaller man stumbling back. Yarrow's foot caught on a loose tile and he fell, hitting his head on the edge of a utility cabinet.

Samuel Turner laughed, an evil, hollow sound that kept Liz rooted to the spot. She'd glimpsed Samuel from a distance before, but she'd never seen him up close, face to face, until now. Any encounter with Samuel Turner was a sobering experience. At the age of seventeen, Turner had attempted suicide with one of his deceased father's handguns. He'd been emotionally troubled even then, and the business end of a pistol under his chin hadn't helped matters. Instead of putting an end to Samuel's problems, the bullet had compounded them. Thanks to the position and angle of the shot, the bullet had bypassed his brain completely, exiting through the right side of his face and mangling flesh and bone.

Where his right eye had been was an empty socket, withered and hollow and dark, the natural structure of cheek and jaw reduced to a mass of concave scar tissue. Plastic surgeons could have reconstructed the ruination of his face, at least in part, but Samuel had refused. The demons that drove him seemed to feed off the nightmare mask, and he remained a blight on and a terror to the little town.

Liz stared, but with more of a waiting wariness of what his next move might be than actual fright. He caught her stare and held it, his single eye burning with an unfocused hatred of everything and everyone he encountered. He grunted, a thin thread of saliva stringing from the ruined right corner of his mouth as he staggered to the cash register and opened the drawer. He grabbed a fist full of twenties, and Liz instintively moved toward the counter. It was none of her business, but she found it nearly impossible to stand idly by while he robbed the cash drawer. "Put it back," she told him. Her right hand instinctively went for her left ribs, but she'd stopped carrying the Glock months ago, so there was nothing there to grasp—a blessing of sorts. Nothing like a .45-caliber automatic to raise a town's worth of eyebrows.

He muttered something that might have been "Fuck you, bitch," then resumed raiding the register. Liz rounded the counter and took him from his blind side, slamming him into the cash register and wrenching his right arm up behind his back. With her knee pressing into his spine, Turner couldn't move without risking dislocation.

"Let him go! Oh good God, let him go!" Marge Turner tried to push between Liz and her son but failed at the attempt.

Liz frowned at the café's proprietress. "He's robbing you blind. Do you really want that?"

"He's my son!"

Reluctantly, Liz let go, stepping back. But she didn't let him out of her sight.

The older woman reached around her offspring, grabbing some of the cash, shoving it at Samuel. "Take it and go, but next time come and find me. I'll give you what you want, just don't frighten the customers."

Samuel took the wad of bills from his mother's hand, glared at Liz, and pushed through the front door, past John and Julianne Rhys, and into the street. "Marge? Is everything okay? Eb Coleman said Samuel was causing a disturbance. You want me to go after him?"

"That won't be necessary, Sheriff," Marge replied. "He wanted some money, is all. He don't mean no real harm, and I won't press charges." She looked at Liz, and there was a silent apology in her dark eyes that seemed completely at odds with the hardness of her expression. "Find a booth and I'll be with you in a minute. I sent Billy by Doc Fife's. He's gonna need a few stitches."

Marge retied her apron and disappeared into the kitchen.

Julianne took Liz by the arm, propelling her around the counter and toward a booth in back. "My stars! What on earth was that about? Did you really tackle Samuel?"

Liz met her friend's glance, somewhat alarmed. She'd just made a gross misstep. The first rule of living quietly was to not draw attention to oneself. She'd screwed up big-time. "What? No, of course not! He was raiding the register—I just slowed him down a little, that's all. It was no big deal."

John Rhys slipped into the booth opposite Liz, who shared a seat with Julianne. "That's not what we heard on the way in here. Where'd you learn to subdue a man Turner's size, anyway? The Marine Corps?"

It was a joke, but Rhys's curiosity was genuine; it showed in his blue eyes, and it gave Liz a moment of very real discomfort. When Julianne came to her rescue, Liz was grateful. "Anyone can learn self-defense. Besides, it's over with, and you're going to set business aside for an hour if it kills you. Now, pick up that menu and read. There are a few healthy choices there. Just remember: no caffeine, nothing fried." The redhead winked at Liz. "I hear the Summer Salad is yummy."

Liz scanned the menu. She'd been to the café three times, including today. To say that she wasn't a social being was a gross understatement, yet she'd found a friend in the owner of the local bookstore and curiosity shop, The Bell, Book, and Whatnot. It didn't bother Liz that Julianne Rhys subscribed to a rather unorthodox set of beliefs. The woman was bright, intuitive, and she didn't ask a lot of questions. Liz didn't even mind that her lunch date with Julianne had turned into a threesome. She was a little curious, however, as to whether this was a spur-of-the-moment thing or a planned attempt at matchmaking.

She didn't have a problem with the former. She wasn't sure how she felt about the latter. John Rhys hadn't done anything to put her off. In fact, the energy field surrounding him was a clear, bright, lovely shade of blue with waves of brilliant green generating through it. *Sincere, honest, and forthright . . . and he is a man who enjoys a challenge.* But there was just a little haziness around the heart chakra. *So, he's been hurt too, in the not too distant past.*

She wondered if his divorce had been the cause, or if it was unrelated. And she softened just a little. Rhys had a nice face, honest and open, with that good-looking All-American-Boy thing about him that she had always preferred to dark and demonic, like some people she could name—and had nearly killed the night before.

"If you're wondering about John, I badgered him into coming," Julianne offered. "Man cannot subsist on coffee alone. Though he gives it a really good stab."

Rhys smiled, revealing a chipped front tooth, probably from his football days. Julianne had mentioned that he'd been a running back for his high school team. Instead of detracting from his smile, that small chink in his armor gave him character. "Ms. Moncrief, since we were denied a proper greeting, maybe we can start over. It's good to see you again."

"Sheriff." Liz extended her hand, and he took it, his warm, strong fingers enfolding hers for just a moment.

"You seem a little frazzled," she observed. "Is everything okay?"

"Frazzled isn't the word for it. It's been like a madhouse today." He shook his head, biting off whatever comment might have followed. "What'll you ladies have? Lunch is on me."

"You don't have to do that," Liz protested.

"No, I don't have to, but I'd like to. It's been a long while since I've had lunch in such pleasant, not to mention *attractive* company."

"Who are you trying to kid?" Julianne said with typical sibling skepticism. "You eat alone—when you eat. When things get busy, you survive on coffee. You know what Kate said about too much caffeine."

John had his head down as he scanned the menu, and his warning was low-voiced. "Julianne, if you feel the urge to nag someone, then you need to call J.T. I've got enough on my plate, thank you."

"I'm concerned about you."

"Well, don't be. I'm fine." John looked up at Liz, and a slight smile played around the corners of his mouth. "I think I'll have the meat loaf. Ms. Moncrief, do you have family? Brothers and sisters, I mean."

"It's Liz, and, no, I'm afraid I don't."

"That's too bad. Even when she's being a major pain, it's good to have family close by. Someone who cares enough to bust your chops now and then."

She didn't need family for that, Liz thought. She had Jake.

The talk turned to business, and business with Liz meant horses. "I hear good things about your place," Rhys said. "You'd better be careful or you'll get the reputation for having the best stables around."

"I like working with horses. They aren't as pushy

as people, and at times they're much better company. Do you ride, Sheriff?"

"It's John, *Liz*," he said with a smile. "A little,
though I never learned the finer points."

"Stop by some time, and I'll be glad to show you
the ropes."

"I'll do that," he said, that warm smile lingering on
his handsome face. "I surely will—soon. Very soon."

By one-thirty that afternoon, Jake was settled into
a second-floor room at Martha Modine's Colonial
Arms bed-and-breakfast. He'd checked in too late
for the one and only meal included in his stay, and
the bacon and eggs served up with a generous side
of argument he'd partaken of at Liz's early that
morning were nothing more than a memory.

Liz had been right about one thing: Miss Modine's
rates were exorbitant. By the time he paid for a
couple of nights and had his car towed to the local
garage, he was almost out of cash. Dinner would
either have to be cheap, or added to his credit
card. His presence in New York, unsanctioned by
the Bureau, would come out of his own pocket.

Miss Modine pointed out the café as the most
popular local eatery, and gave him directions, but
the two-block stroll might as well have been a five-
mile hike. He was forced to stop twice along the
way, and by the time he arrived, he was winded
and feeling like an invalid, which put him in a foul
mood. A glance through the large plate-glass
window didn't help, either. Liz was laughing at
something one of her companions had said, and
Jake quickly surmised that this suddenly lighthearted
mood of his ex-wife had more to do with John Rhys
than with the voluptuous redhead sharing her side
of the booth.

Jake opened the door, walked past a number of vacant stools, and carefully settled himself into the booth adjacent from the trio. He could feel the weight of Liz's frown and derived a warped and petty satisfaction from the thought that he had just thrown a large, extremely wet blanket over the merry proceedings.

A bottle blonde with a wrinkled face and a two-pack-a-day alto placed napkin and silverware, handed him a menu, and asked if she could bring him liquid refreshment. "Coffee, black, no sugar." She brought his coffee and stood with pencil poised over a pad. "I'll have a burger with catsup, not mayo; hold the onions. And a side of french fries."

"Well, if it isn't Special Agent English," Rhys said from across the narrow aisle. "Jake, are you enjoying your vacation so far?"

"Not particularly," Jake replied, taking a large gulp of steaming black liquid and burning his tongue.

The redhead nudged Rhys in the ribs, then leaned forward and smiled. "Ignore my brother's bad manners. When you spend as much time with Shep Margolis as he does, the social skills are the first thing to go. Julianne Rhys," she continued, introducing herself. "I own the local bookstore and do a bit of lawyering on the side. And this is Elizabeth Moncrief. Liz owns the stable south of town. So, you're with the FBI? How fascinating. What brings you to Abundance?"

Liz was watching Rhys warily, looking for some sign that she'd been unmasked to him by the one man in town who truly knew her.

"I'm here about a murder."

"I thought you said he was on vacation?" the redhead said, and socked her brother again.

"Julianne, do I meddle in your law practice?" Giving her no time to answer, Rhys glanced at his watch. "Ladies, it's been great, but I have to be getting back." He plunked a twenty down on the table between them, smiling at Liz. "Liz, I intend to take you up on that invitation at the first opportunity."

"I'm looking forward to it."

Rhys walked out, his sister preparing to follow suit. "I'm afraid I have to run, too. Liz, drop by the shop, will you? Special Agent English, it's been a pleasure."

Liz picked up her handbag, but she didn't leave immediately. Waiting until the sheriff and his sister had exited, she turned a scornful eye on Jake. "You met with John Rhys?"

"First thing this morning, after you threw me out."

"I didn't throw you out. I asked you to be gone before I got back, and don't you dare play the victim in this. I caught you in bed with another woman three weeks into our so-called marriage. You destroyed my life once, and I will be damned if I will let you do it again."

Jake settled back with his lunch, polishing off the burger in several bites and wiping his mouth with his napkin. It gave him a few moments to observe and to analyze. The dynamics of their relationship weren't difficult to fathom. He had the hots for her—just watching her temper flare did predictable things to his libido. But, then, he'd always wanted her; that much hadn't changed, despite their ill-fated marriage, divorce, and her perfect life with another man who had been far better suited to commitment than him. He liked to think that she felt it, too. Her reactions to him, the way she blew up at the least provocation, indicated that on some level the attraction was still very much alive for her as well. But Liz's head was rock-hard and her will ironclad. She would never admit that they still had chemistry. Not to herself, and certainly not to him.

Not that he wanted to go back there. Oh, no. It hadn't worked the first time. There was no reason to try again. Yet that didn't stop him from thinking about it, or imagining the possibilities.

"Believe it or not, I didn't come here to ruin your life." *I've come here to save it.* A moment of quiet. "This thing with you and Rhys . . . Is it serious?"

She blew out a breath, exasperated. "Even if it were any of your business, I wouldn't tell you. Good-bye, Jake." She slid from the booth and got to her feet, but she didn't leave. "Not that I care, but did you find a rental yet?"

"As a matter of fact, no."

"How did you get here? The bed-and-breakfast is at least two blocks away."

He patted his leg and winced. He felt like one massive bruise. Everything hurt like hell, his reflexes were those of a relatively healthy eighty-five-year-old, and should he step in front of another truck, he was definitely a goner.

"I thought Kate told you to take it easy, at least for a few days."

Jake finished his fries and fished a bill from his jeans' pocket. "Funny thing about that bed-and-breakfast. It doesn't have room service, and this place doesn't deliver, so it was walk or starve. Don't worry about me, though. I'm a little sore, that's all. I'll be just fine."

He gripped the table edge with his uninjured arm and pried himself out of the booth as she watched with a narrow-eyed gaze. "Oh, God. There's blood on the back of your shirt. You must have broken the wound open. Damn it, Jake, why can't you stay put?"

He turned slightly and she almost bumped into him. They were standing almost toe to toe, and because of her much smaller stature, she was forced to look up into his face. "Why? Haven't you figured that out yet? Because I might be all that's standing in the way of you and a shitload of trouble. To hell with everything else, to hell with the hell we put each other through. I like you just enough to not want to stand by and see you get hurt again. Why is that so damned hard for you to understand?"

Her reply was squeezed out, heavily laced with emotion. "You don't want me hurt? Too late for that, English. I had my heart torn out two years ago. Nothing anyone can do to me will ever compare with losing my little girl."

For a few seconds she was open and vulnerable, and Jake had the urge to lower his head and kiss her, to offer whatever comfort he could, to show her he understood, that he cared. She wouldn't welcome it, though, and he had the presence of mind to resist impulse, settling for the brief brush of his knuckles against her smooth cheek. "Yeah, I know," he said softly. "But I have to do this, for my sake. I failed you once. Whether you like it or not, I can't let it happen again."

She lifted her shoulders and took a step back, breaking the intimacy between them. "My Explorer's outside. I'll drop you off on my way home."

The ride was brief and extremely tense, kind of like their marriage. Jake should have been discouraged by that, but he'd had a hell of a lot of experience in dealing with Liz. She'd always been exciting, intriguing, but she'd never been easy. Neither was he, which no doubt had a great deal to do with why they were always at odds.

"Would you like to come up?" he said. "We could catch up, tear each other to pieces. . . . It'll be just like old times."

Like a hopeful fool, he waited for her reply, but

she remained stubbornly silent. "Have it your way, then. You always do." He scribbled a string of numbers on the dust on her dash. "My cellular number. If you change your mind, give me a call—day or night, it doesn't matter. I don't sleep anyway." He got out, slowly, bending down at the open passenger window for one last shot. "Be careful out there, Liz; keep the dogs inside at night and sleep with the Glock under your pillow. I do."

"Get some rest," she suggested. She hesitated, and he thought she might say something else, something he needed to hear, but then, setting her jaw, she jammed the gearshift into reverse and backed out into the street. Jake stood for a few minutes, his left hand balled into a fist at his side. Then he turned and went inside.

"The swelling seems to have subsided slightly, but it would be advisable to keep him isolated and as immobile as possible for at least a few more days. I'll give him another injection of cortisone, and as long as there's no further reinjury, that should hold him until Dr. Gilmore returns from his vacation." As Kate Fife got to her feet, Anglican nudged her shoulder with his velvety nose. Kate spoke to the stallion, stroking his neck. "You be a good boy, and watch out for those rabbit burrows from now on."

"He'll be all right?" Liz couldn't keep the concern she felt out of her voice. Anglican was her favorite, and so close to her that more often than not the stud seemed to know what she was thinking. It was like they were connected on a psychic level, and since the accident, she'd been worried that she might have to put him down. It was probably just paranoia, induced by the abject fear of losing something else she loved. But whatever the root cause, she worried all the same.

"Well, there's no evidence of a fracture, so, yes, I think he'll recover. There's always a chance of reinjury, though. Like a sprain in a human, an injury to an animal can weaken the joint and the tendons, increasing the likelihood of similar problems down the road. Once he's ready to ride again, you'll need to take precautions. Keep him out of fields as much as you can. Use the trails you're familiar with, and avoid uneven ground."

"Thanks, Kate. We're both grateful to you for filling in. He needed immediate attention, and it just couldn't wait."

"No problem," Kate assured her. "Did you ever figure out what spooked him? He's such an even-tempered animal. It's not in his nature to take off like that."

"Not a clue. He must have scented something. It could have been a bear, I guess. There's a black-berry thicket a little distance beyond that." Liz hunched her shoulders in her sleeveless jean jacket. "What do I owe you?"

"A cup of raspberry tea and a little normal conversation that doesn't involve a certain hypochondriac's latest complaint. He insisted on seeing me this morning—in fact, he almost barged in on one of my patients, and she was in the stirrups at the time."

"Mr. Peterson," Liz said. Everyone in Abundance knew about Mr. Peterson's hypochondria. "What was it this time?"

"Anthrax. He swore that he contracted it from the post office during his last visit, because he saw dust gathering in the corners, and he knows how neglectful the cleaning staff is, and it looked like last year's dust, and—I could go on, but I won't." The physician took a deep, cleansing breath, following her friend across the yard, through the rear door and into the kitchen. She took a seat at the antique Windsor table, watching as Liz filled the teakettle with spring water and put it on to boil. "So, talk to me. What's the connection between you and the handsome Mr. English?"

Liz tried for a casual shrug, but it came off as stiff, and, well, tense. "We knew one another, a long time ago."

"An FBI man," Kate said. "I'm impressed. Your circle is obviously a lot wider and more all-encompassing than mine. I know hunters, and farmers, and mechanics."

"It's really not all that uncommon an occupation where I come from."

"Which is?"

"Oh, water's hot," Liz said, making a little too much clatter while arranging cups and saucers. "I suppose I should ask how he is."

"Stiff, sore, and in need of rest. I butterflied the bullet wound together when I saw him this afternoon, and warned him to stay down for a few days, but I don't think he'll listen. Not all of my patients are as cooperative as Anglican." She watched Liz, a little too closely maybe, a look of concern on her face. Kate was thirty-eight, a year older than Liz, and they had a lot in common. They were both what was commonly known in the Catskills as "outsiders," coming from other places, other lives, each finding something they desperately needed in the starkly rugged clefts, rocky outcroppings, and abundant waterfalls of the area. Liz had found a measure of uneasy peace, and precious anonymity. Kate, a sense of community, of belonging. If there was something in her past that put the blue-gray shadows under her green eyes, then she didn't allude to it, and Liz didn't ask. Idle chitchat was one thing; prying was quite another.

"My guess is Jake English likes you—a lot."

"Jake doesn't know what he likes," Liz said with a snort. "He's more than a little fickle, and a genuine pain in my ass. But I'm glad he's okay. I don't want to see him, but I also don't want anything to happen to him."

Kate accepted a cup of tea with two sugars and a little cream. "Well, don't worry on that score. He's a tough one, and I have a feeling he isn't going anywhere, at least for a while. I'm going to see him again tomorrow. Is there any message you'd like to convey? I'd be glad to pass it on."

Liz sipped her tea. "I've said everything to Jake that I intend to say."

The conversation turned to other things, and soon Kate Fife got in her car for the short drive back to town. The young physician was having dinner with Julianne Rhys, since Julianne's significant other was out of town. She'd invited Liz to join them, but Liz had declined. After her confrontation with Jake that afternoon, she wasn't feeling up to being social. His comment that he didn't sleep, and that he kept his handgun under his pillow, refused to leave her. She might have brushed the observation off as black humor except for one thing: she could tell he wasn't joking. Also, there was something different about him, something she sensed every now and then, an uneasiness, a restless quality that hadn't been there before.

Not that Jake's well-being was her concern. He was a big boy and could take care of himself. He didn't need her to worry about him, and she'd wasted far too much time in the past trying to figure him out.

Too antsy to read, or to remain indoors, she returned to the stable to check on Anglican's carpal joint one last time before turning her attention to other matters.

Liz currycombed Faerie King, a palomino gelding that belonged to a dentist from nearby Mantoot, then rubbed him with an old towel and gave him a ration of oats. She made a modest living from the boarding fees, but more than that, she enjoyed the work. At times the grooming, exercise, feeding, and constant care she provided proved exhausting, but it was a satisfying kind of tired. More than anything, the long hours, from daylight to dark, and sometimes into the night, allowed her to keep the past in the past, her focus riveted on the here and now.

Today it was a great deal more difficult to avoid thinking about the past. Jake was a painful reminder of all that had happened, and all that was wrong in her life. She had hoped never to see him again after that last day, the day he came to the house in Virginia with the news that he had found Fiona.

Richard had been growing more and more distant in the tense days following his adopted daughter's abduction, sullen, withdrawn. He had always been a quiet man, sensitive and caring . . . perhaps a little too sensitive. He hadn't been suited to a marriage to someone like her; Liz had been the strong one, and they both knew it—a source of strain even before Fiona's kidnapping.

Jake had been at the house when the final call came through, and he'd listened in while she'd begged for her daughter's life. Whether remorse had goaded the caller into giving the information key to locating her little girl or some motive unguessed at, Liz couldn't speculate, but she remembered watching Jake, her heart in her throat as he left the house. She'd wanted to accompany him, but he wouldn't allow it, and for once she'd taken his counsel.

Jake English had been her last hope, and despite her animosity toward him, she'd kept her faith in his abilities long after Richard had given up the hope that Fiona would be found. She'd been standing at the kitchen sink, staring out the window while waiting for the phone to ring, when the dark sedan pulled into view. But when Jake got out and she saw the grim set of his mouth, her last best hope had been shattered. He rapped softly, and she went outside to hear the news.

You found her, didn't you? Her voice seemed like a distant echo, and she couldn't summon the strength required to block it out.

Maybe we should go inside. Your husband's there, right? You shouldn't be alone—"

I shouldn't be alone at a time like this. That's what you were going to say, isn't it, Jake? You found her—you found my little girl, but you were too late, weren't you? Damn you, English! Answer me!

Liz . . . I'm sorry.

She'd slapped him, a ringing blow that left a scarlet handprint on his lean cheek. She would have hit him again if he hadn't caught her arms and dragged her into a rough embrace and held her while she screamed and railed at him and Charlie watched, grim-faced, angry and embarrassed and unsure what to do with his hands. Richard must have heard, but he didn't even bestir himself from his deepening depression long enough to see what was happening. He hadn't been there to hold Liz up when her knees buckled, Jake had. Richard hadn't searched for her little girl, hadn't combed every inch of the woods outside the small town in Virginia, but Jake English had.

Jake had done everything humanly possible to find Fiona, and it wasn't his fault that it hadn't been enough. Still, she had resented him, blamed him, cursed him for the role he'd played in her devastation and loss, however innocent or well-intentioned.

From that point on, things had turned ugly. She'd coldly insisted he stay away from the memorial service. Needing to lash out at someone or something, she'd told him that he wasn't welcome, nor was he wanted. And for once he had respected her wishes. Much later, she'd heard from mutual friends that he'd hadn't drawn a sober breath in almost three weeks after that. But she hadn't softened. She didn't see him again, and she never came clean about their daughter's paternity.

Leaning on the fence that surrounded the paddock, Liz shook off the memories and forced herself to breathe. The rain had held off, but cumulus clouds towered huge and menacing in the distance, and every now and again a streak of silver jetted downward through a Wedgewood-blue sky in a zigzag path. Liz climbed the fence and one by one led the animals to their stalls and an evening meal of grain and last season's hay.

Whistling for Sandy and Fletch, she went in to supper, but as she closed the door on the deepening twilight, a figure broke from the shadows of the timberline and slowly approached the barn.

It thrilled him, to be so close to her after so long a separation. Two years was a long time by anyone's standards, and by his calculations, it was several lifetimes. She'd made him work for this moment, but he couldn't really say that he resented her for that. Anything worth possessing was worth waiting for, and over the years he'd learned to cultivate a little patience. Timing, after all, was so important, and his search, though anything but easy, had borne fruit.

He'd found her. That knowledge was almost as heady as her obliviousness to his presence was, her unawareness of his scrutiny.

He enjoyed watching her. She was easy to admire, in her close-fitting jeans, her white T-shirt and Levi's jacket with the sleeves torn out. He liked the way her long chestnut-colored braid swung over one shoulder, and how she toyed with it when deep in thought. He would have liked to have touched that braid, too, to feel the cool softness of it sliding through his palm. The urge to approach the house was strong, but he resisted it.

He wasn't quite ready for that. The dogs might bark and alert her, and he didn't want her to know of his presence just yet.

Liz was special, and everything had to be perfect in order to impress her. And he did so want to impress her. He stood in the shadows of the barn for a long time, until the twilight was just a memory in indigo, fingering the hair ribbon that had belonged to her daughter and dreaming of things to come.

A few miles away fourteen-year-old Amanda Redwing huddled in a dim box deep underground. He'd left her with a disposable flashlight that was growing dimmer by the second, but the illumination was almost as terrifying as the total lack of light had been during the first portion of her imprisonment. The chill seeping into the box penetrated her flesh, seeping into her bones. *Cold . . . oh, God, so cold!* Even if the miracle she was praying for happened and someone found her, she feared she'd never be warm again.

How long had she been here? An hour? A day? She didn't know. All she knew was that she was terrified and that someone *had* to find her.

He'd said that it was a game, and if her parents followed the directions he'd left for them, they would lead them right to her. He'd left the pipe in the chamber for ventilation, enough to keep her safe for a long, long time, he'd said. But what if something happened? What if her parents couldn't find her? She was out of food, and there was only a dribble of water remaining in the sport bottle he'd provided.

She got as close to the pipe as she could, put an ear to the hole and listened. She heard a rumble. At first, it sounded like thunder; then she recognized it as a car engine. "Hello?" Her voice sounded odd when projected through the galvanized pipe. "Hello? Is anyone there? I'm in here! Can you hear me? Help me! Oh, please, help me!"

No answer, just the rumble of the engine. She was alone, and she didn't want to be here. She wanted to go home. She wanted to fight with her little brother, and listen to music her mom thought was too loud. She wanted to go to math class, and she didn't want to die.

Tears leaked from under lids so waterlogged they were swollen almost shut. Even after there was no moisture left in her, dry sobs wracked her, leaving her exhausted and weak . . . too weak to do anything but sleep. When at last she awoke, the bulb had burned out, and the box was filling with oily fumes.

"No!" Amanda screamed. "No, please! Don't leave me here! Please, oh, please! Don't let me die!"

Chapter Four

"Sheriff, I'd like to know what you plan to do about this Samuel Turner situation? The man's a menace."

Bradley B. Bratt wasn't the kind of guy who was easily rattled. A highly decorated vet of the Korean conflict, he walked with a noticeable limp, the result of a shrapnel wound in his left leg. A short man, with a barrel chest and a silvered crew cut that stood perfectly at attention, he was fit, agile for his age, and at the moment, highly irritated. John did his best to calm him down. Agitation never did much good in these situations, and he'd already had a bellyful of Samuel.

"Have a seat, B.B. Would you like some coffee?" John took a fresh pen out of the desk drawer and flipped the page on his legal pad. He hated typing. He'd never learned properly, and hunting for the keys was so distracting that it interrupted his train of thought, so he scribbled, and Sarah read his hieroglyphics and transcribed them into the computer. "Now, tell me what happened, and start at the beginning."

"I had Belle in Vanderbloon's Woods. Ms. Young-blood gave me permission to dog the raccoons out there, and it's prime territory for it, too. Well, we'd just struck a trail when Belle went cold and came wifflin' back to me, cowed down, with her tail tucked and everythin'. I was encouraging her to try again when Samuel stumbled out of the brush. I could smell the whiskey on him, and he's a mean drunk. When I asked him what he was doin' out there, he mumbled that he was 'burying some-thin.' "

John's pen stopped moving as he glanced sharply up. "Burying something?"

"That's right," B.B. said, scrubbing at his crew cut with his knuckles. "I tried to forget about it, but Samuel bein' Samuel, I had to wonder if there wasn't something strange goin' on. Hell, I even went by the café on my way over here, just to make sure Marge was still kickin'. It's obvious that boy's a half-bubble off plumb, and there's no tellin' what he might be capable of."

"Did Samuel threaten you in any manner?"

"Well, no, of course not. Why, if he raised a hand to me, I'd knock him right on his keister!"

"I have no doubt you'd do just that." John scribbled a few more lines and sat back. "Is that every-thing?"

B.B.'s face reddened. "What do you mean, is that everything? Isn't it enough?"

"Well, it isn't grounds for an arrest, if that's what you mean. Unless there's something you aren't telling me." John sat back in his chair, and the chair creaked. "Look, just between you and me, I'd like to see Samuel get some help. He needs a few weeks in detox, and he needs several years with a good shrink, but I don't think it's going to happen, and until he commits a crime, there isn't a whole lot I can do about it."

"He was the cause of my rifle discharging prematurely!" B.B. insisted hotly. "Somebody could have been seriously hurt."

"Your rifle discharged prematurely?" John went still. "Where was your location?"

"Vanderbloon's Woods, like I said, by way of Skunktown Road."

"What was your proximity from the road?"

A shrug of B.B.'s broad shoulders. "Four hundred yards, maybe. I hadn't gone far."

"What kind of rifle are we talking about?"

"Twenty-two, with a scope, which I now have to replace, thanks to that half-wit Turner." B.B. got up, shaking his head. "I'm warnin' you, John. Either you do somethin' about Samuel or someone else will. A lot of folks around this town would like to see the last of him, and not everybody has my respect for the law."

"I hear you. I hear you." John circled the notation ".22 rifle, Vanderbloon's Woods," then muttered, "One mystery solved." B.B. Bratt exited, and Shep slid into the chair.

"Lemme guess: the unmasked marauder strikes again."

"This is the fourth complaint in two weeks, and nothing serious enough to warrant an arrest." John pushed a hand into his hair and took a gulp of his coffee. *Stone cold. What else is new?* "You know, Shep, I can't lock a man up because he's hard to look at. I look at Marge, and—"

"And you've got a son, too," Shep said. "I get it. But John Jr. will never get that screwed up, because we won't let him, so take that thought right out of your head." Shep got up, quietly closed the door, and sat back down. When he did, he looked different somehow, a little older, a little more tired. "When I was in the army there was a guy I knew who was a lot like Samuel. His name was Edwards, and I never saw him that he wasn't mad as hell just for bein' born. Well, a bunch of us went out one night, just to blow off steam. Edwards didn't show, so I went lookin' for him." He made a gun with finger and thumb and put the tip of his forefinger under his chin. His voice softened. "Christ, what a mess . . . and the worst part came when I started to dial the medics. Edwards woke up, and he begged me not to. Said he wanted to die, that he had every right to die, and I had no right to play God."

He was silent for a moment before he continued. "His voice was a gurgling whisper, hard to understand, but he said, 'What if it was you? What if it was you'?"

"So what'd you do?" John asked, surprised to see this side of the man who was his brother-in-law and his deputy.

A deep breath, and Shep looked him in the eye. "I sat right there, holding his hand and talking to him until he was gone, because it was what he wanted. He thanked me for it, and I ain't sayin' it was the right thing to do . . . but I know what I'd want if I was ever in that position. The surgeons that saved Turner's life didn't do the man any favors."

John shook his head. "If life is present we have to do everything in our power to preserve it. It sure as hell doesn't solve the problem of Samuel, though, does it?"

Shep stood, adjusting belt and holster. "Well, I can tell you one thing. That boy wants to die, sure as I'm standing here, and if he doesn't end it on his own, someone else will."

"That's what I'm afraid of," John said. "Where are you headed this morning?"

Shep took a gold toothpick from his shirt pocket and popped it between his thin lips. "Unless you need me for somethin' else, I thought I'd set a speed trap out on the highway just this side of Stooley's Roadhouse. Lot of drunks out that way, and I hear our favorite celeb is hittin' the sauce pretty hard these days."

"Monroe?" John frowned. He really didn't need to know, but couldn't help asking. "What's that about?"

"Trouble on the homefront would be my guess. Things are fallin' apart between him and Ms. Youngblood. Maybe she's finally come to her senses. You gonna talk to Turner?"

"I'm gonna talk to him," John affirmed. "Christ alone knows if Samuel will listen. But I need to find out what he was burying on Catherine Youngblood's property."

John gave Sarah the rundown of where she could find him should an emergency arise, then left the office. Summer was his least favorite time of year. The local kids were out of school, and too much time on their hands usually meant a rise in petty vandalism and misdemeanors. It also didn't help that a busload of tourists arrived daily to tour the historic houses and quaint shops. Shep kept an eagle eye out for shoplifters, but that meant John had to handle a double load at headquarters while everyone geared up for the Labor Day celebrations. It was all a major pain in the butt, which had him wondering daily why he didn't just chuck it all and get a nine-to-five job somewhere. Something with a measure of sanity to it, however mundane it happened to be, that he didn't take home with him every night.

With an ex-wife who regularly indulged in hair-tearing hysterics, two kids he saw only on the weekends, and so much tension in the town lately, he was beginning to wonder when the other shoe would drop. There was a sense of impending disaster in the sultry August air, as if something huge was about to happen, and he didn't like it one damn bit. "All I need right now is for English's predictions to have some validity to blow the lid completely off this town." Then he cursed himself for giving voice to his trepidations, and hoped like hell the Fates weren't listening.

Jake needed wheels. After a restless night in what he thought of as the Martha Room—coordinating walls, curtains, and sheets in a rose-strewn pattern that, combined with his present incapacities, had him feeling a little pansy-ish—he spent the morning on the phone in a fierce battle with his insurance company, which refused to pay for a rental. More out-of-pocket expenses. He wondered if his bank account could withstand the strain? Not that it mattered a whole hell of a lot. The Virginia apartment was a place to keep his clothing and the few personal possessions that hadn't lost their meaning, things that could just as easily be stowed away in a storage facility somewhere.

Pinpointing the precise moment when material possessions had ceased to have any significance was something Jake tried not to do, and, gradually, avoidance of such thoughts had become a way of life. Somewhere deep inside he knew that his general apathy for the stuff that mattered to others had a direct connection with Fiona Airhardt's murder. The day he'd located her grave and pulled her out of the ground was the day he'd begun to feel too much, and sensitivity in this business was a real liability. Liz's kid had proved to be the chink in his proverbial armor, the one thing that had penetrated beyond his hard exterior and found the heart of him when he no longer believed that he had one.

He'd tried to get beyond it, but he couldn't seem to get the little girl out of his mind. She haunted him day and night, the image of a child's death mask accompanied by the sick, desperate feeling that he hadn't done enough to save her. Logically, he knew the feeling that he'd failed Liz's daughter was as untrue as it was unrealistic. Oddly, he'd been unable to shake it. It needled him even as he picked up the phone in his room and dialed.

The nearest rental company was in Kingston, and after a great deal of finagling, he got them to agree to bring the car to him, a 1994 Chevy Celebrity. It wasn't exactly what he had in mind, but when an agent was hounded into administrative leave, the good old expense account was always the first thing to go. It was his expenditure, and his credit card balance couldn't afford anything more upscale than that. At least he wouldn't be reduced to getting around on foot.

With his mobility restored, he could concentrate on the matters at hand. The killings had numbered seven in all, including Fiona Airhardt. The first three kidnapping-slash-murders had taken place in a three-county radius in Virginia over a period of twelve months. The victims had ranged in age from eight to eighteen, the eldest, Janey McCann, being small in stature, slight in build, and looking a good deal younger than her actual age.

The common thread lay in gender, height, and weight, which led Jake to two conclusions: either the Unknown Subject's sick fantasies revolved around kids, or he was choosing victims that he could easily overpower. Jake's personal take was that it was the latter instead of the former. But that was a guess, something of which he couldn't be certain. There were only two certainties in this case: that the UNSUB had fixated on Liz, and that he would keep on killing until somebody stopped him.

It was after the second Virginia murder, twenty-eight months ago, that Liz was brought in on the case, and when her special intuitive abilities were leaked to the press there was widespread media coverage. The Bureau had done everything possible to downplay it, but once the press got wind of something, there was no sweeping it under the rug. And the psychic angle was just the thing to turn a sensational story of serial murder into a media circus.

Within six weeks of the Jada Adair murder, victim number two, Liz's face had appeared on the front page of nearly every newspaper in the state, and television news coverage had leaped on the story, too.

Within two days of that first broadcast, the letters started trickling in to various newspapers, each addressed to S.A. Liz Airhardt, FBI. There was no set pattern to the communications, no clues, no latent fingerprints. The killer had been very careful not to leave any trace evidence. The paper used was plain common-stock copier paper, cheap by the ream, sold at discount stores and bought by hundreds of thousands of ordinary consumers—and at least one homicidal maniac. The messages, typed on a manual typewriter, expressed admiration for Special Agent Elizabeth Airhardt. Postmarks varied, as did the times the messages were posted. Only the theme remained consistent.

The creep factor had been high, but not much more could be gleaned from the messages—just that the guy was incredibly organized, carefully planned his every move, and would keep on killing until he was killed or caught. He was likely someone highly adaptable, who went about his daily business without arousing suspicion. He was a regular joe, the guy next door, and he had a broad killing field. First Eastern Virginia, now New York.

Moreover, he knew the areas in which he operated, read the papers, watched local news, and had freedom of movement. He might be employed as some sort of driver. His MO was simple but effective. He gained the trust of his victims, lured them into his vehicle, and they weren't seen alive again. Jake had seen other such cases in which the victims had been brutalized physically and sexually, but the Cemetery Man preferred psychological torture, of a type that was every bit as brutal and dehumanizing.

Out of seven interments, six of the underground chambers had been constructed of cheap-grade plywood and fitted with a flange and a threaded pipe that rose to ground level as an air vent. The containers were strongly constructed, impossible to escape, and they served their grisly purpose without requiring a huge amount of time to construct. If the building material was precut, the coffins could be knocked together in a matter of minutes, and the material was so commonly used that if he were discovered with it, it could easily be explained away.

TCM had deviated from the simplistic design only once. The single exception had been for Fiona Airhardt, whose coffin had been constructed of antique Rosewood. Rosewood was rare and expensive, and the carving on the corners showed a keen attention to detail that revealed a great deal about the murderer's feelings about the child's mother, as well as the extent of the planning that went into her abduction and murder.

Liz was special to him, and therefore the child had been special.

Jake had lived inside this guy's mind for so long that he had no trouble envisioning the diligent preparations that preceded the abductions. He could see this sociopath building his fantasy with great care—lovingly almost—as he imagined and planned for and lusted after his next kill. He could imagine, too, the victims' muffled cries of terror as they awoke in the cramped chamber in time to hear the dirt being shoveled in on top of them.

He made a note on his personal data assistant to call local lumberyards and home-improvement centers to check on recent sales of plywood. Then he'd enlist the help of Rhys and his deputy to weed through the list in the hope that something would pop up. But first he needed to check on Liz.

It was almost twelve-thirty. She should have been back from her morning ride hours ago. The Explorer was parked in the driveway of the farm alongside a Blazer he didn't immediately recognize, and the house was locked, but there was no Liz. He'd had a good look around and was starting to get a little concerned when a pair of riders emerged from the woods on the far side of the lower field. Check that: two people, two horses, but only one rider. Liz was astride; Sheriff Rhys was leading a rather large, spirited gelding, and he was limping.

Now, exactly why did he take satisfaction in that fact? Jake wondered.

Liz laughed at something the sheriff said, and the clear, bright sound rippled over Jake like the cool spray of a forest stream on a blistering hot day. He'd always loved that sound, but it had been a long time since he'd made her laugh. They approached across the field, Liz's horse picking its way carefully through the grass. She had a close hand on the reins so she could keep pace with her guest, and her seat was easy and sure, her expression uncommonly open and relaxed. Then she caught sight of him, and everything changed.

He could almost feel her close off and shut down; it was as if a concrete wall had risen up between them. Jake should have been immune to it by now, but today, for some reason, he found it irritating. Rhys seemed oblivious to the change in Liz, but he didn't look happy to see Jake, either.

"Jake," he said as he closed the distance between them. "What brings you out here?"

Liz took the reins from Rhys's hand and led the horses to the paddock, but she didn't miss shooting a glare in Jake's direction.

"Actually, I was hoping for a short consultation, Sheriff, but it seems a hell of a shame to bother you on your day off."

"No day off, I'm afraid. I'm on my lunch hour, and just about to head back. What's this consult about? Not still waiting for your man to show up here, are you? I'd hate to see you waste a lot of time on something that isn't likely to happen."

Jake shrugged the comment off. "Actually, I was wondering if you'd given any thought to my suggestions?"

"Oh, I've thought about it, but until and unless something happens here, I really don't see the point of upsetting everyone by going public with what amounts to an educated guess."

"You really are taking one hell of a chance with this," Jake insisted. "But, hey. I'm just on vacation. What the hell do I know?"

"Nobody's discounting your expertise, Jake. But I do think you're wrong about this. Why would this guy want to come here?" Then Rhys turned toward Liz, ignoring Jake, and said, "Liz, thanks again for the ride. It was just the tension-breaker I needed."

Jake snorted. The seat of the sheriff's uniform trousers was more than a little dust-covered.

"I had a nice time," Liz said in a soft voice, obviously not meant to carry. "Only next time we try something like this I'll let you take Sheba. She's more suited to beginners—sweet temperament."

"Like her caretaker." As Jake watched, Rhys stepped close and, leaning down, kissed Liz's cheek. "As much as I hate to end this, I really do need to get back." Straightening, he backed away, then with a last wave, got into his Blazer and left in a small dust cloud.

Jake pinned Liz with a glance. "If I didn't know better, I'd think we were all back in high school."

"Save the sarcasm," Liz told him. "I don't have the time for it, and, frankly, I'm not interested."

"But you *are* interested in John Rhys?" She was headed toward the barn, Jake right behind her, his intense gaze fixed on her stiff shoulder blades.

She entered the barn and went straight to the last stall. Jake leaned his good arm against the partition as she bent down to check the animal's leg. "Even if I *were* interested in John, it's no concern of yours. Ex-husbands don't get to tell ex-wives who they can see and who they can't. Any other connection we once had ended a long time ago . . . or have you forgotten?"

She stood so abruptly that she startled the

horse. The animal sidestepped, and Liz reached out to stroke its neck. It quieted immediately, and she left the stall, but made no move to exit the stables. There was a strange air of expectancy between them. Liz was keenly aware that they weren't finished here. And she was keenly aware of Jake, though she didn't want to be.

The soft shadows of the building eased the hardness from his face. He looked as young, as breathtakingly handsome as he had when she'd met him for the first time at Quantico more than a decade ago . . . undeniably sexy.

"Damn it, Liz, why does it always have to be this way? With us at one another's throats? It was good once, before everything got in the way."

"I don't know," she said, "maybe we were just a bad mix from the beginning. Chemistry in reverse." But that wasn't quite true. There had been a time when they'd been good together, very good. But it didn't last, and it left her scarred emotionally, and wary of him, desperate to keep him at a safe distance. It had been this way since the breakup of their marriage.

Breakup, hell. It had disintegrated.

Imploded.

She did her best to block out the emotions from that earlier time, everything she had experienced then: anger, humiliation, fear. She'd been pregnant and alone, and she'd never been that terrified in her life, but Ellen Corbitt, a former college roommate, had been there for her. She and Ellen had always been close, and they'd stayed in touch over the years. Ellen gave her a place to stay until she got on her feet. Through Ellen, she'd met Richard Airhardt, mild-mannered Clark Kent to Jake's Superman. Richard had been everything Jake wasn't: steady, reliable, faithful, patient. Richard had proposed several times, but Liz's wariness had kept her from accepting. In time, she'd said "yes."

Her remarriage had solved more than one problem. It had sent a clear signal to Jake to keep his distance, to get on with his life, because she had. It had alleviated her loneliness, too, and it had kept her away from Virginia for several years. "You're right, though," she said, willing to give him that much. "It wasn't all bad. I loved you once. In fact, I loved you so much it hurt." The impulse to touch that long-ago love was strong, too strong to resist, despite the risk. She lifted a hand, and her fingertips played over the warm, weathered skin of his cheek. "I've had enough hurt for two lifetimes, Jake. I don't want to go through that again. I don't want to relive it. I won't. Not even for you."

Hardheaded Jake didn't seem to be listening. There was something strangely intimate about the dim shadows of the stable. Liz could feel it, and she knew that he felt it, too.

"You're more beautiful than ever. I never get tired of looking at you . . . the way your mouth tightens when you're pissed off at me . . . the way you look in the mornings, all drowsy and heavy-lidded." He caught her braid, sliding his hand along its length as his gaze drank her in. Then, slowly, with exquisite care, he leaned in.

She willed herself not to respond, but by slow degrees her body betrayed her. He wasn't a stranger, he was Jake, old love . . . first true love, lost love . . . and she was hungry. It had been so long since she'd felt the warm strength of a man's touch. Unable to resist, Liz closed her eyes and slowly sank into him.

There was a lingering hint of coffee in his kiss,

overlaid by the fresh taste of spearmint, and he smelled of a light and crisp cologne. His skin was warm and smooth, his muscles taut, but it wasn't just Jake's physical presence that penetrated Liz's awareness and got under her skin. Barriers too long held rigidly in place slipped another notch and her sixth sense kicked in.

Mixed and chaotic emotions washed over her, penetrating her consciousness. She felt Jake's turmoil, his guilt, regret, anger. But anger at whom? There was a sense of underlying frustration, coupled with a longing so deep and so sharp that her first impulse was to reach out and soothe it away. The impulse jolted her back to her senses, and with determination her guard eased back into place.

A moment later, he broke the kiss and stood gazing down at her. "That's been a long time coming," he said.

"So has this," Liz said, slapping him soundly, then stalking from the barn while he gaped.

"Liz? Damn it, Liz, what the hell was that for?"

"That was for cheating! I wanted to do it a long time ago, and I never got the chance!"

"Will you slow down!" he shouted. "We need to discuss this!"

"Don't delude yourself into thinking there was more to it than there is, Jake. We have nothing to discuss."

He caught up with her, though she saw him catch his breath at the stitch in his ribs. "I may not have psychic abilities, but I can still read you pretty well, and you can't tell me you felt nothing just now."

At the paddock fence Liz spun to face him, hands planted stubbornly on her blue-jeaned hips. "I felt something, all right—the same thing any red-blooded woman would feel who hasn't been with a man in years, but like summer itch, it'll pass."

"Yeah? Well, it's been ten years, and it hasn't faded. In fact, if I'm any judge at all, it's stronger than it's ever been."

"You've always been such an unrelenting optimist when it comes to relationships," Liz shot back. "'Ah, hell, Liz, I realize we don't know each other very well, but the sex is great so let's get married! It'll turn out all right. I'll just get a little drunk and sleep with the first slut that comes along. Liz loves me, and she'll forgive me, so it'll be all right—'"

"Oh, for Christ sake! Will you let it go? That was more than ten years ago, and it was a mistake! How long do you intend to punish me for it?" He raked his hand through the hair at his temple. When he spoke again, his voice was tight, but his tone gentler. "It was a stupid mistake, Liz, one I wish I'd never made, and there hasn't been a day go by since that I haven't regretted it."

She didn't reply, and the tension between them didn't lessen This was a no-win situation. If she gave him an ounce of encouragement, he wouldn't quit until he wore her down and forced her to face her feelings for him—feelings that, if she were totally honest, hadn't dimmed completely. She was saved from a lie by the sputter of the ancient John Deere tractor and a shout from her hired man, Jersey Delacour. Jersey was nearing fifty-five and normally unflappable, but now he appeared agitated, and his face, the rich shade of chocolate, looked somehow paler. "Something's wrong," Liz said, pushing away from the fence and walking rapidly to meet the tractor.

"Jersey, are you all right?"

"No, ma'am. You know that little girl from Mantoot that come missin'? Well, I think I found her over there on the back parcel."

"What? What girl?"

"A little white girl," Jersey said, taking off his ball cap and wiping his brow on a red bandana handkerchief. "You ain't seen the news? It's been all over television. The police thought she ran away. I was plowin' back there, gettin' ready to sow the winter wheat, and I run into somethin'—some kind of wooden box. I had it in third gear, and the plow splintered the top. When I got off the tractor to see what it was I run into, I saw her. Curled up like she was sleepin'. Who'd do such a terrible thing to a child? And why in hell would they put her in the ground here?"

"Farmland is softer than woodland," Jake said. "No roots, easy digging. Can you take me to her?"

Jersey glanced at Liz. "You know him?"

Liz nodded. "I know him," she admitted, though there was something in her tone that said she wished otherwise.

"All right, then. That's good enough for me. Hop on."

At Jersey's direction, Jake climbed onto the tractor tongue and held on to the edge of the seat. "Call Rhys and get him out here. Tell him to alert the Mantoot authorities."

Liz stood frozen in place long after the tractor had faded into the woods. It didn't even occur to her to be angry that Jake's prediction had come true. Her thoughts were a chaotic jumble. A young girl was dead, a life ended horribly and prematurely, and her parents, already living a nightmare, were about to know the greatest sorrow of all: losing a child to a monster. She knew how they felt now, at this minute, and she knew everything they would experience. She knew the heartache and the blame, and the hideous, mind-wrenching speculation of what their daughter's last moments had been like.

Had he hurt her?

Was she frightened?

Or did she just go to sleep?

Did she cry out for me?

Did she hate me for not keeping her safe? For not being there when she needed me, for not finding her, bringing her home?

"Oh, dear God," Liz cried out, barely realizing that she was projecting herself into this new tragedy. "I should have been there! I should have been there." As the shout died away, a shame so powerful she could barely withstand it rose up inside her. She fumbled for the cell phone in the pocket of her jean jacket. Jersey had a heart condition, so she always carried it with her. It was more open here, so she had a signal. She flipped it on and dialed. "Sheriff Rhys, please?" Then, "No, of course, he isn't there. This is Liz Moncrief. Yes, I need an officer to come to my farm immediately. It's an emergency. My hired man, Jersey Delacour, was plowing a field this morning, and he unearthed something."

"He unearthed something?" the dispatcher said.

"A burial site," Liz said. "I can't be sure, but it looks like it may be the missing girl from Mantoot."

Chapter Five

The sheriff's department responded immediately. Within fifteen minutes Rhys and his deputy were on-site, asking questions, taking notes. Jersey Delacour relayed how the discovery had taken place, then Rhys took him through it again, step by step, while Liz Moncrief stood off to one side, expression closed, gaze somber.

John hadn't planned on seeing Liz again so soon, and certainly not under these circumstances. He'd already alerted the Mantoot police about the body, and they would be arriving momentarily. It had been a courtesy call, since there was a good likelihood that the victim was from that area. They couldn't be certain until the next of kin provided a positive ID. From what he could see, however, her clothing and hair matched the description that had come in over the Internet. She'd been classified as a potential runaway. The reality of the situation was so much uglier than that.

Once the preliminary investigation was concluded, the body would be released into the coroner's custody, and the girl's next of kin would be brought in to view the remains and provide identification. A positive ID would help bring closure to her parents' nightmare and, hopefully, provide some measure of peace.

Unfortunately, John's nightmares were just beginning.

Shep helped string crime-scene tape and was doubling as crime-scene photographer. "John, do you think that's sufficient, or did you want me to keep going?"

"Do a few rolls of black-and-white," John said. "I want every blade of grass gone over twice, and once it starts to rain, it'll alter everything. The forecast says we've got the day, and part of this evening, but I don't want to take any chances. The weather can change in a snap, and with almost no warning."

Shorthanded as usual, John plied a probe to determine the extent of the grave site. Any earth recently disturbed would be softer than that surrounding it. Next he marked the corners of the grave site with powdered chalk and stood back, dusting off his hands.

Special Agent Jake English didn't wait long to step all over John's jurisdiction. "Sheriff, have you decided how to proceed with the excavation? I checked with the National Weather Service, and there's a possibility of thunderstorms later tonight. I don't have to tell you what heavy downpours can do to trace evidence."

He didn't have to, but the lack of necessity didn't squelch the desire. "I know all about trace evidence, Jake, and sudden changes in weather are a normal occurrence for this area. We could construct overhead protection, but there's a slope just behind us, so it wouldn't prevent runoff."

"What about removing the block of earth and containing it until it can be processed?"

"We could use the impound garage," John said, biting back the assurance that he wasn't a total imbecile. "We won't be ready to move on any of this until late this afternoon at the earliest."

The corners of the grave site were marked with T-handled probes and the area around it searched for every possible avenue of entry. "It looks like Jersey's been in and out of here a number of times this morning," Rhys said. "That's not going to make this any easier."

Jake had already moved on. The access road, paved with inexpensive tar-and-chip and maintained by the township, bordered Liz's land. The road itself gave up nothing, but the access road was soft and sandy from soil erosion and storm runoff. The tractor tires had a one-and-one-quarter-depth herringbone tread that had dug deep through the center of a lighter, less obvious tread. It wasn't much, but it was better than nothing. Jake looked at Rhys. "You have dental stone with you?"

"There's a kit in the trunk of the cruiser," he answered, then called, "Shep! Get the dental stone."

"You mind?" Jake asked when Shep approached with the kit.

Rhys gave the nod and Shep handed him the kit, but it was clear that he objected to an outsider being active in a homegrown murder. Jake added water and mixed the powder into a thin liquid that he poured into the track. Dental stone was a cheap and easy method for preserving evidence.

John Rhys watched from a distance. Jake English was a hotdog, the kind of guy that steamrolled over everything and everyone who got in his way, and he looked good doing it. There was a raffish style about him that rubbed John the wrong way. Didn't matter that the man was right there in the mud with the rest of them—the hairstyle that had come from a stylist, not Chancey's Barber Shop down on Main; the arrogant, self-possessed lift of his chin; and everything else about the man screamed fast-track professional, confident enough to be comfortable in any situation. *Shit,* John thought, *he probably graduated Georgetown U. At the top of his class, too.*

English carefully pulled the cast up once it had hardened and handed it to Margolis for proper cataloging. A forensics team had arrived moments before from the state police crime lab, including a forensic entomologist and a forensic botanist. The former would collect any insect larvae found on the body for study in the hope of establishing a time line as to how long the victim had been deceased; the latter was essential for determining how long she'd been buried by estimating the time when the damage to vegetation occurred. If they could establish how long ago the grave had been dug, they could determine the amount of time between burial and the victim's actual death. Every clue was valuable.

Jake moved aside to give them room, but he didn't go any farther than the spot where Liz Moncrief was standing. John wasn't sure why that bothered him, but it did. He hadn't had time to question Liz, and he wasn't looking forward to that part of the investigation. Maybe it would be better coming from him, though, than from his big-city counterpart, who he suspected would be all too eager to confront her.

There was something about the way Liz reacted to English that raised John's hackles. Not that he had any claim on Liz's time, prior or otherwise, but he liked her, and unless he had interpreted it all wrong, they'd had fun together on their brief ride that afternoon. There was a possibility for something good to develop between them—something positive—if the fed just stayed the hell out of it.

Shep must have been watching the exchange between the two men because he came right on over after finishing the last roll of film. "Hey, Chief," he said. "That fed givin' you trouble?"

"Shep, I've told you a hundred times: don't call me 'Chief,' even as a joke. And, no, he isn't giving me trouble. He made a suggestion—a valid one I think we'd better follow up on. If the weather changes, we run the risk of losing valuable evidence." He lifted his hat and pushed his hair back with one hand, wishing he'd thought of the excavator first. He hated giving English the credit, hated admitting that the other man might have more experience in this kind of investigation—a lot more—and he sure as hell didn't like feeling like some backwater sheriff more suited to figuring out who was soaping windows at Halloween than investigating a gruesome murder. "Get Harold Mackinaw out here with his excavator, and tell him we need a metal container to put that block of earth in for transport. He needs to be here and ready when the team finishes."

"I'm on it," Shep said, getting behind the wheel of the black and white. The car spun on the slick grass, and his exit was less graceful than it might have been. John finally got behind the left rear fender and pushed while Shep applied his lead foot to the accelerator. The cruiser found traction and spun small bits of grass and dirt over John's uniform shirt. Shep stuck his head out the window, "Sorry, boss."

John thrust an arm in the direction of the road. "Now! Go!"

When he turned back, Liz was standing beside him. "Liz, are you all right?" It was a rhetorical question on his part. The horror of the scene was written all over her face. She looked tense, paler than her normal outdoorsy tan. John moved slightly, blocking her view of the grave site and its piteous occupant.

"I'm fine," she said. "Really. Or, at least I will be."

"Well, it's bound to be a bit of a shock. It isn't every day that you get this up close and personal with a murder investigation."

She seemed about to say something, then apparently thought the better of it. "No, not every day. Thank God for that."

"Listen," John said, "Jersey's due to stop by my office and answer a few questions, but I need to talk to you about this, too."

"Routine questions," she said. "I understand. I'd be glad to help in any way I can."

"Have you noticed anybody nosing around the farm recently? Any strange vehicles, anyone giving you or Jersey any trouble? Anything at all out of the ordinary?"

Liz shook her head. "Aside from my run-in with Samuel Turner, no one. I have a new horse at the stable. He's been here a couple of weeks. His owner was here at the time of delivery, and again this morning, and he's due back later this week, but other than that—"

"Somebody new, huh?"

"Bridger, Lyle. He's a dentist, from Mantoot, ex-military man. He takes riding lessons. He has references, rock-solid background. I check out all my clients."

"Anyone else?"

"No one."

John made a few notations on his pocket notepad, looking up as a slight man with dirty blond hair stopped a few yards from Liz and stood, waiting for her to notice him. Seeing that she was preoccupied, he cleared his throat. Liz glanced up. "Kenneth, what is it? Is something wrong?"

Kenneth Simms dragged off his ball cap, lowering his gaze to the ground. "I th-thought you'd w-want to know I f-finished m-mucking out the st-st-st-alls. W-was there anything else for t-to-d-day? If not, I'd l-like to g-get home."

"Nothing that can't wait. I left your check on the desk in the tack room. Give Mary my best, will you? And I'll see you next week?"

"Y-yes'm. I surely w-w-will."

Kenneth ambled off, John watching his progress along the wooded path. "Isn't that Ken Simms? I don't recall seeing him around here before. Is he working for you?"

Liz shrugged. "He does some of the heavier work, so Jersey doesn't have to. He rents a place over by Raccoon Hollow."

"How'd you find him? Did he come to you, looking for work?"

"I gave his wife Mary a lift home one day when their car broke down. It's a pretty rundown place. From what Mary said, Kenneth has trouble keeping a job, so they move around a good bit. She happened to mention he was out of work, and I needed someone, so I offered him the job. He's quiet, for the most part, and hasn't been any problem."

"I'm glad to hear it. Still, I'll need to stop by his place and have a word with him. Could be he's seen something he hasn't mentioned. Given his speech impediment, he might be reluctant to volunteer information for fear of being dragged into some uncomfortable situation."

"Go easy on him, will you? He's reliable, and I don't want to lose him."

"I will," John promised. "And I don't want you to worry. We're gonna do everything humanly possible to get this guy."

She hugged her arms tightly, and John got the impression that she was trying to contain a rising sense of panic. It was a normal reaction to an abnormal situation, as was his impulse to reach out and give her shoulder a reassuring squeeze. "Listen, why don't you go back to the house? There's nothing you can do out here, and this is likely to go on for most of the night."

"I'm not sure that I can. This is my land, John. I feel like I owe her something. I don't know . . . maybe if I'd been more observant . . ."

John shook his head. "Don't go there, Liz. You didn't have any control over this, and neither did I. Only one person could have stopped it, and we're gonna get him. I promise you that."

"Thanks. That helps." She took a tissue from her pocket and wiped at his cheek. "You have a little grass there."

John smiled. "That's the trouble with being a small-town sheriff. Sometimes you gotta get your hands dirty—or your face." A car appeared on the rutted road. A shield on the side proclaimed that it was the Mantoot Police Department. "Duty calls, and I'd better be getting back," he said, and with one last look, he turned and walked away.

"Touching. I remember when you used to do all those little things for me, straightening my tie, smoothing my lapels, reaming me out for coming home late—"

"Or not coming home at all," Liz amended. "What do you want, Jake?"

"In a specific sense, or generally speaking?"

He was maddening as always, and he drove her to distraction, yet in light of what was happening just a few yards away, distraction wasn't such a bad thing. She threw a hot glare his way, and he chuckled. "It always was easy to get a rise out of you. Hot-tempered, hot-blooded Liz," he said, his voice softening as his smile widened.

Liz's heart executed a stuttering beat.

"We were evenly matched in one respect, at least," he said. "I'm glad to see that much hasn't changed."

"We were never evenly matched. We were a match made in hell," Liz insisted. "If you think anything different, you're living in a fantasy world."

"Maybe," Jake said, letting his gaze wander over her. Her cheeks had lost that ashen cast, and her eyes that wary, frightened look. Liz was no coward, but she'd been through hell when she lost her child, and the shock of her hired hand's grisly discovery earlier that afternoon had no doubt brought it all back. "Feeling a little less shaky?"

She hesitated, and he knew that she was grateful to him for being there, even if she refused to admit it. "I need to get back. I have chores to do."

Jake watched her walk to her SUV and get in. Then he watched her drive away until the vehicle was just a dot in the distance. She was damn good at keeping the deep freeze turned up, and he couldn't really say that he blamed her.

If she allowed an open, honest dialogue, she might have to admit that there was trouble on the horizon, the kind of trouble John Rhys might be ill-equipped to deal with on his own.

Jake had come to Abundance to convince her of the seriousness of this threat, but maybe it was wrong of him to try to separate Liz from her denial. Maybe the kindest thing he could do was to go it alone—work with the authorities to catch this asshole, and leave Liz like he found her.

So what if she was hiding from the world? Living a shallow, half-existence? Was he any different? These days, he couldn't even maintain a rich and full fantasy life. Besides, it was her life, her choice, and really none of his business.

"So what if she wants him?" Jake said to himself. "Rhys seems like a nice enough guy." Yet, even as he tried to convince himself that Liz would be happier left to her half-baked choices, he knew that promises were easily made, and even more easily broken. He could tell himself to steer clear of her—but could he do it?

The Mantoot Police Department proved a great deal more receptive to working with Jake than Sheriff John Rhys and his deputy, Shep Margolis, had been. They had told the parents of the missing fourteen-year-old that a body had been found and that they would arrange for them to view the body at the morgue for the purposes of identification as soon as the remains were released to the coroner. An autopsy would be scheduled and performed, all trace evidence collected and cataloged, and the investigation would proceed from there.

The excavator set to work well after dark, removing the top layer of soil with a precision that was amazing. Each scoop of earth that came away was loaded onto a waiting flatbed truck with a large metal container. A block of earth would be extracted that was substantially larger than the actual grave. It was always a second-choice method to on-site grid, and sifting the disturbed earth for fiber evidence, hair, cigarette butts, anything useful. Unfortunately, it had already been a hot, rain-soaked summer, and by the time Mackinaw set to work, thunderheads were beginning to loom on the horizon.

The work was slow and meticulous, and the excavation went on long after the sun went down behind Blue Mountain. The operator's work was painstaking while a growing knot of men in uniform watched. The scene, illuminated by the headlamps of every available vehicle and several powerful portable lights, would have taken on an air of the surreal for the casual observer, but for Jake it was all too familiar.

It was past midnight when the truck and lowboy trailer rumbled away from Liz's farm. Jake stayed until the last man was gone, then he got in his car and made his way back to the farm. The house was dark, the dogs were inside, and Liz no doubt had fallen into an exhausted sleep. Jake thought about knocking anyway, just on the off chance she was sitting alone in the dark. Then he thought the better of it.

Tired and aching from his head to his insteps, he climbed into the car, lit a cigar, and settled back to watch and wait.

The house came alive after dark with creaks and groans, thumps and bangs. Liz had often speculated about whether or not the place was haunted. Not that it mattered greatly. If there were ghosts, then they and Liz had become accustomed to one another and lived together peaceably enough. In fact, there were times when she found the thought of ghostly company oddly comforting.

Tonight was not one of those nights. She sat in the middle of the bed, the covers drawn over the legs of her black silk pajamas, her knees raised and her head resting on them. Arms locked tightly around knees, she rocked quickly, shallowly, to the rapid beat of her heart, starting at every sound. Sandy lay on the foot of the bed, her head on her paws, her brown eyes fixed on her mistress. She looked worried. Fletch, who lay by the door, sighed in his sleep.

Liz had put on the bravest front she could summon in front of John Rhys and especially Jake, but the truth was, she was coming undone. It wasn't fear of what was out there waiting, exactly. She didn't fear death or dying. In fact, there were times when she was so weary of everything that she wondered if it wouldn't be a kind of relief just to feel nothing.

"It's not dying I fear," she whispered to whoever, whatever, was listening. "It's living."

A screech owl called somewhere in the distance. How lonely it sounded. Liz could relate to that. Most days, she drove herself to a point of physical exhaustion, a place where she knew her body was sufficiently tired to allow her the oblivion of sleep. But on nights like this she felt keenly, profoundly alone. That was the problem with living a lie, keeping, guarding secrets. She couldn't afford to allow anyone access to her life.

A whiff of cigar smoke drifted in on the cool night breeze. Liz threw back the covers, and got up, walking to the window. The dreadful rental car sat parked in the shadows near the barn. As she watched, a tiny orange speck, like a firefly in the night, flared and then died.

Liz smiled to herself.

"Jake."

For a long while she stood by the window, unseen, watching as the tension bled from her, then she got back into bed, at last able to sleep.

At the edge of the woods, a lone figure stood, also watching, waiting, observing. He'd gone to the excavation sight, careful to view it from a distance. They'd found the girl and she'd soon be reunited with her parents, just as he'd promised. It was important to keep promises, he thought.

Sheriff Rhys had promised to stop him, but Rhys was ill-equipped to deal with anything this sophisticated. The FBI man, Jacob English, was more his equal, but he still fell one step behind. Without Liz, English's job was pure guesswork. He knew the kind of being he was dealing with, searching for, but every move he made, every counterthrust, was a stab in the dark. Without Liz Moncrief, the game wasn't much of a challenge, and boredom was a heartbeat away.

He'd chosen Liz's land for Amanda for two reasons: because of its isolation, and in the hope of drawing Liz out. It was difficult to tell if the ploy had worked from this distance. He would need to get closer in order to determine his success, and with English playing watchdog at the farm, that might not be so easy.

The smell of freshly brewed coffee roused Jake from an uneasy, dream-filled sleep. He jerked awake, jarring his arm in its sling, which triggered the dull throb in his upper back. He settled back with a groan, squinting at the coffee mug Liz held out. "Did you forget the way back to town, Jake?" she asked sweetly.

"Not exactly," he said, sniffing the mug and trying to remember if arsenic had a distinctive smell.

"I just wasn't ready to go, that's all." Steam was rising off the grass, and water from last night's storm beaded on the car's windshield.

She raised a dark, slanting brow at the half-truth. "I guess you can come in if you want. I made flapjacks—"

"Let me guess: you made too many, and they aren't good for the dogs. Nice to know where I stand with you, even if it is a few notches lower than your flea-bitten pals." He took a sip of hot black coffee, sighed, then handed the cup back. "Do you mind? At the moment, I'm a one-armed man." She accepted the cup without comment, standing back as he swung the door open and pulled himself out with the aid of the steering wheel and a lot of teeth-grinding. "I can see why you like this place," he said as they crossed the front porch and entered the house. "It's quiet out here—peaceful."

"It *was*—until yesterday," she said, crossing the porch and holding the door for him to precede her into the house. "I really should thank you for not gloating. I know how you love being right."

"Not this time," Jake countered softly. He would have given anything to have been wrong about the killer's next move. The first New York burial, occurring months ago, had come as a surprise because it hadn't taken place in Virginia. The Cemetery Man had been inactive for two years, and Jake's take on that was that TCM had either been arrested for some other crime, or killed.

Then an eleven-year-old boy cutting across a field outside Woodstock, New York, on his way home from a friend's house noticed a piece of pipe protruding from the ground beside the same path he always walked on his way to and from his friend Jerry's house. The pipe was wrapped with red ribbon. The boy's father, a police officer who worked in Homicide, went immediately to the scene, and Susie Smith, thirteen and a resident of Woodstock, New York, was unearthed.

Jake spent weeks speculating as to why the sudden change. Had this guy changed his home territory because of his day job? Or because the investigation had gotten too close for comfort? Or was there another reason altogether? Something he wasn't seeing?

The fact that serial killers rarely changed their fixations had been the reason he'd thought of Liz. From there, the pieces had all fallen neatly into place; the hunch that their man had followed her here had been just that, a hunch. "You know that I hate this as much as you do. More, maybe."

"I know that you hate it that monsters like this guy exist," she allowed. "But you get off on the chase—the challenge of pitting your wits against theirs. If you think about it, there's something perverse in that."

"Somebody has to do it, Liz. For the victims. Otherwise—"

She slammed her fist down on the tabletop, making the dishes dance and rattle. "Don't say it. I don't need to hear that. Not now."

Jake sipped his coffee and watched her. There was a subtle change in her this morning. She seemed less fiery, more subdued, despite her little display of temper a second ago. A little fist-banging was nothing where Liz was concerned, and she hadn't even threatened to take his head off. "You bring me coffee. You invite me in. What's up with that, anyway? You didn't exactly put out the welcome mat when you discovered I'd come to Abundance."

She shrugged, and there was an uneasiness in the gesture. "Whatever else you are, you're good at what you do. I need your input, your expertise."

"I'm listening."

She walked to the sink, emptied her coffee cup, and braced both hands on the sink ledge. She spoke without turning to face him, staring at nothing in particular. "What will he do if I pack up and leave? Just disappear?"

Jake was a little amazed that she was thinking of running. But wasn't that exactly what she'd done when she'd cut ties with Virginia and moved here, telling no one where she was heading or what she intended to do once she got there? "I'll answer if you want me to, but I think you already know."

"He'll follow," she said in a hollow-sounding voice. Jake caught the slight tremor in her bare arms. "My God. My God . . ." She turned then, and the look on her face wrenched something deep in his gut. "Where does it end?"

"It ends here, Liz. But only if we work to end it." He wasn't sure what he expected, but it wasn't the low-voiced reply he got.

"I can't help you, Jake. I can't do it, and if you give a damn about me—if I mean anything at all to you—you won't ask."

The expression in her pretty brown eyes was stark, and for a fraction of a second Jake felt the emptiness that engulfed her, an emptiness as cold as the grave.

That's what the sick bastard had done to her, in taking her child. He'd eradicated her spirit. Wiped it away as easily as an eraser rubbing out chalk on a chalkboard. The Liz who sipped her coffee while avoiding eye contact was a mere ghost of her former self. It was one more reason for Jake to hate this guy. One more reason to bury him as surely as he'd buried that kid in Liz's wheat field.

"All right," Jake said with a sigh. "I won't ask that you work with me on this, but I will ask one thing: if you get some insight on this asshole, bring it to me first, before you take it to Rhys." At her questioning look, he tilted the hand near his mug. "Let's just say that while I'm more than willing to work with the sheriff, I'm not at all confident he wants to work with me, and I sure as hell don't like flying blind."

"You're not eating," Liz said, not making any promises, not committing to anything.

"I guess I don't have much of an appetite," he admitted, surprising even himself. "And I really should get moving. I need to stop by Rhys's office, and I have to find a place to stay. The bed-and-breakfast is kind of rich for my taste, and I need something that's a little less like Grand Central Station, something with more privacy."

"Talk to Julianne Rhys. She has an apartment above her shop that's empty."

"I'll do that. Thanks for the tip." Jake pushed his chair back and stood. "Listen, are you okay here? Alone, I mean?"

She smiled, but it was forced, and there was little warmth in it. "I'll be fine." As he headed for the door, she called him back, "Jake?"

Jake turned. "Yeah?"

Awkward. Shy almost. "Thanks. For last night, I mean."

"Hey, sweetheart," he said, doing a really pathetic Bogie impression. "What's an ex-husband for?"

It wasn't until much later that day that Jake realized she hadn't indulged in a smart-mouthed comeback.

* * *

At the police station Margolis was leaning against the patrol car, trying to look important. He glanced at Jake as he got out of the rental and his thin lip curled. "They run out of hot water and towels at Martha's place, English, or are you undercover as a homeless guy?"

"I wouldn't know about the linen situation," Jake admitted, ignoring the deputy's sarcasm. "I haven't been back there."

He managed the steps and was barely winded. That was an improvement. A few more days, and he might be halfway, semi-normal. Rhys was going over some reports when Jake walked in. He showed the sheriff the courtesy of knocking. Rhys looked up from his paperwork, pushing back in his chair. "Jake, I've been expecting you. Come on in. Have a seat." He glanced at the contents of his Styrofoam cup. "You want some coffee? It's lousy, but it's hot."

"Thanks, but I think I'll pass. Did you get an ID on the girl yet?"

"The parents were supposed to go down to the morgue this morning, but the mother collapsed. Her husband's there now, along with a family friend. We should get word shortly." Rhys got up and refilled his cup. "Rough night? You look a little ragged around the edges."

"I've had better," Jake admitted, but he wouldn't give another inch. Like his deputy, Rhys had taken notice that he hadn't showered, shaved, or changed his clothes. The sheriff wasn't slow, and would have guessed by now that he'd spent the night at the farm. Given the man's closeness to Liz, there was no way Jake was going to volunteer that he'd slept in his car. "I see the excavator's truck's in your building. Is there a reason you haven't unloaded and started dismantling the block of earth?"

Rhys sat back, sucking in a slow breath while he struggled to hold on to his temper. "Look, Jake. I know you're probably used to snapping your fingers and having everyone haul ass, but it won't go around here. You're here in an advisory capacity, is that right? Well, I'm not. Abundance is my town, and though I welcome your participation, don't expect to step in and take over."

"Well, shit, I don't want your job, Sheriff," Jake assured him. "I have enough to contend with. What I do want is to stop this guy before he snatches another kid."

"Then we're on the same page. That's good to know. The last thing I need is someone from the big city coming in here and trying to prove he can shoot a hot stream an inch or two farther than me." Rhys shifted slightly, and his tone changed. "The forensic team was called out to a location upstate overnight. Mantoot is lending us a couple of officers with some experience in this sort of thing to help dismantle that block and sift through it for evidence. If there's so much as a hair, we'll find it. They'll be arriving early this afternoon."

"I'd like to lend a hand, if you don't mind," Jake said. It wasn't that he didn't trust the locals to do exemplary work. He was just too involved in this case to leave it alone. Rhys would either grasp that concept, or he wouldn't. Either way, Jake really didn't give a damn.

"Suit yourself," the sheriff said, but what he meant was, *Maybe it'll keep you out of my hair, and off my ass.*

"I'll do that," Jake said. "Speaking of that spirit of cooperation: what do you know about Rufus Vanderhorn?"

"Rufus? Why do you ask?"

"He hasn't started the repair work on my car yet. I was just wondering if he's reliable."

"I'd say so. He's also the only mechanic in town."

"Interesting guy."

"Well, Jake," Rhys said, "Abundance is full of one-of-a-kinds. Take Liz Moncrief, for instance. She shows up one day and buys the Nafter place, a real mystery woman. Beautiful, accomplished, well-educated, able to take care of herself on a lot of levels, and private. You might even say 'guarded.' She doesn't appear to have any connections that I can tell . . . and then you come to town."

Jake's expression was carefully bland. "Exactly what are you driving at, Sheriff?"

"Just that I get the feeling that there's a connection between you two. Something she doesn't want to acknowledge." Rhys frowned. "I guess you could say that I have a personal interest in the lady. And before I get in too deep, I'd like to know what I'm up against."

"A gentleman doesn't kiss and tell, Sheriff. But, then, you already know that. If you want details about Liz's sex life, you need to ask the lady herself, not me. I'll stop back this afternoon to help out with the search for evidence." He didn't glance back as he left the office, but he could feel the sheriff's displeasure with him and knew that Rhys's gaze followed him.

So Rhys had a personal interest in Liz, enough of an interest to ask questions. From the little he'd said, he was sure to get flak from Liz, and he could only wonder exactly what she'd tell her suitor about the connection between them, past and present.

It was almost dark when Liz completed the long drive upstate and pulled into the parking lot at

Woodland Sanitarium. Despite the divorce, she was the closest thing Richard had to family, his only link to the past, the real world. She'd arranged for his transfer shortly after she'd bought the farm. Woodland was the best facility available; as a resident, Richard received the best of care money could provide.

Blood money.

She couldn't help thinking of the insurance settlement she'd received for the loss of her daughter in any other context. One hundred thousand dollars was insufficient exchange for her child. Yet, when combined with the savings they had accumulated during their marriage and put into a trust, it provided the proper care for the man she'd destroyed. It did nothing, however, to alleviate her guilt.

He was sitting by the window in the dayroom when she walked in, looking out the window. Staring mindlessly at nothing. The landscape didn't hold his interest, nor did the deepening indigo of twilight. He stared beyond the outside world, at nothing she could see, and the blank void of his expression tore her heart to bloody shreds.

Liz dropped down to his level, sitting on her heels as she gazed into his blank face. "Richard? How are you today?"

The chatter continued around them as Liz strained to catch a glimmer of reaction from the man with whom she'd shared her life, but she was disappointed.

"You look well. As handsome as ever." It was a kindly lie. He'd aged ten years, and the gauntness combined with his total lack of animation gave him the look of a frail life-sized doll. In no way did he resemble the vital man she had married. Richard was gone away somewhere safe, and the body in the wheelchair was nothing but a shell.

She was feeling a little empty he**rself**, in need of someone to talk to. She took a deep breath, knowing she should hold back, unable to contain the shuddering sigh that escaped her. "Well, it's happened. He's found me. I thought by coming to New York we'd be left alone, and maybe things would get better. But I was wrong—again. It hasn't gotten better. It's gotten worse—so much worse." She clutched the arm of his wheelchair, willing him to look at her. "You don't have to worry, though. None of it will touch you ever again. I promise you that. You're safe here."

There was no sign that any of it penetrated. Richard just sat, his dark blue robe hanging off his scarecrow-thin frame, his eyes blank and staring.

After a moment, Liz rose, fished her car keys from the pocket of her barn jacket, and left the sanitarium. For a long while she sat in the Explorer with the doors locked and her forehead resting on her steering wheel. Then she gathered her strength for the long drive home.

Chapter Six

Julianne Rhys proved a godsend. Not only did the apartment above The Bell, Book, and Whatnot suit Jake's needs, she was willing to rent it by the week, and she had no objection to accepting a check even though he was from out of state. "You're trustworthy," she said. "I have an eye for these things. *And* cute, and it can't hurt having an FBI agent nearby, now can it?"

"Thanks, I think. My stuff is in my car. Do you have any objections to me moving in right away?"

"That'd be great," Julianne said. "Living spaces don't like being empty, and the energy upstairs has been a little melancholy since the last tenant moved out. I trust you'll improve that immediately. You've got a lot of strength, and one weakness—a woman.

Jake laughed. "And you know this how?"

An easy, good-natured shrug. "Some folks read tea leaves; I read people. You've got good vibes, but some vulnerability, too. I like that. I think we'll deal well together."

"I suppose there are worse things than being on

good terms with my landlady," Jake said. "Listen, is there a local watering hole around here? I thought I'd grab a sandwich and a beer. I don't suppose you'd be interested? I could use the company."

"Stooley's Roadhouse, and I'll take a rain check. J.T.'s coming in from Atlanta, and I'm the welcoming committee." She smiled, and Jake was totally charmed.

"J.T., huh? Lucky guy."

"He thinks so."

Jake stowed his gear and locked the door on his way out. Stooley's Roadhouse Bar and Grille was on Route 209, halfway between Hurley and Abundance. Typical of most bars, it was dimly lit, and a haze of cigarette smoke drifted lazily a foot from the rough plank ceiling. Jake slid onto a stool at the end of the bar, ordered a draft, and turned to survey the place while he waited.

He checked the exits first, then the patrons. It was a weeknight, and well past time for the afterwork crowd to drift home. There were only a handful of people there—a couple arguing at a corner table, a guy on the stool next to Jake who was busy eying the chick down the bar while his cigarette ash gained a record length. But it was the table in the corner that caught Jake's eye. The barmaid brought his beer, and he ordered something from the grill, asking her to bring it to the corner table, then he picked up his mug and walked over.

"Christ, this is crap," the table's occupant muttered, downing a shot and chasing it with a brew.

"Mind if I sit?" Jake asked.

The dark-haired southerner glanced up from the pile of paper with which he'd been so preoccupied, and a slow smile replaced his hassled expression. "Jake English? What the hell are you doin' here?"

"Matthew. It's been a long damn time." He shook the writer's outstretched hand. It was good to find a familiar, friendly face in this backwater burg.

"Too long. Jesus," Matt said, shuffling the papers into some sort of haphazard order, then with a sound of low-voiced disgust, he dumped the pile onto a vacant chair beside him. "Ah, hell. Sit down, Jake. Take a load off. Distract me with tales of murder and mayhem, anything to keep me from facing this thing again."

Jake slid into a chair. Matt Monroe was a long-time acquaintance. They'd conferred a few times while Matt was conducting research, and the novelist had spent some time at Quantico. He hadn't run into him in a couple of years, though. "Not going well, I take it?"

"It's probably my mood. It's kinda hard to be objective when your life's in the shitter." He signaled the barmaid. "Rose, set me up again, will you? And bring my friend here a cold one." Rose Redding brought Matt's whiskey, and as she walked back to the bar, he tossed back the double. "A few more of these, and this'll"—gesturing to the manuscript pages—"have bestseller written all over it."

"A few more of those, and you won't be *at* this table—you'll be under it."

Matt settled back with a sigh. "You know what my problem is? Women. That's my problem. I sure as hell don't understand any of 'em."

Jake snorted. "Well, that makes two of us."

"So what brings you here? That kid's murder, or a certain redhead who happens to be livin' south of town?" He put a finger to his lips. "Yeah, I know. She's hidin' out. I ran into her a couple of times. I guess I must be the only person in town who knows, besides you."

"Hell, Matthew, I'm on vacation." He sipped his beer. "As for that certain lady, I have no idea what you're talking about . . . but if you know one who's available, you'll introduce me, right? I've always had a thing for redheads."

Matt just laughed and left it at that. Jake was relieved. The truth was he had no idea where he stood with Liz. She excelled at sending mixed signals, and he couldn't assume anything where she was concerned without risk of falling on his face.

Matt settled back in his chair, pinning Jake with a look. "So, listen. What's your take on this burial thing?"

"Off the record?"

"Is there any other way?"

"The only thing I'm sure of is that this is the same UNSUB we were dealing with two years ago."

"The guy who snatched Liz's kid?" Matt whistled. "Jesus. Does she know this? Well, shit, of course, she does. That's why you're here."

"Actually, I'm here to eat this sandwich and drink this beer, and that's the extent of my plans for this evening. How about you? Don't you have somebody at home, waiting for you?"

The door opened and a very pregnant blonde approached the table. "Hey, sweet thing," Matt said. "Abby, this is Jake English. He's with the FBI. Jake, Abby Youngblood, the undisputed love of my life."

Her brows raised slightly. "You're here about the girl they found south of town?"

"I'm consulting with Sheriff Rhys, yes."

"It's so hard to believe anyone could do something that dreadful."

Matt took Abby's hand and kissed it. "When you gonna say 'yes'?" he questioned softly, earnestly, gazing up into her face. There was something in his voice, a trace of loneliness that Jake recognized and related to. "Jake'll vouch for the fact that I'm a great catch, and I'll make some little girl a wonderful daddy."

"Matthew, don't, please. I don't want to argue. Can't we just go home and spend an enjoyable, quiet evening?"

Monroe grinned, but the expression wasn't completely genuine. It was a mask for his insecurities, his pain. "Yeah, sure. That's what we'll do. We'll go home."

He reached out, grasping Jake's hand. "Jake, you take good care of yourself."

"Count on it."

Abby Youngblood exited with a final wave, Monroe holding the door for her. After they were gone, Jake realized the writer had forgotten his manuscript. Jake picked it up, and placed it on the table, marveling at the power a woman could exert over a man, without even trying. He was damn fortunate to have cut ties long ago, and to have resisted getting involved seriously with anyone again.

His marriage to Liz hadn't failed; he'd sabotaged it. He wasn't proud of his actions. In fact, he considered cheating on Liz the second biggest mistake he'd ever made; getting married at all took first prize.

If he was going to be totally honest with himself, he had a problem with commitment that was directly related to the job. He'd seen too much real-life misery to buy into the happily-ever-after concept. There was something seriously wrong with a world in which monsters like the Cemetery Man could callously end the life of a sweet kid like Kate's Fiona, or that poor child they'd pulled from that damned underground hell at Liz's farm just the day before. Happy endings, Jake was convinced, existed only in fairy tales. They weren't part of the real world, his world, and he'd reconciled himself to that fact a long time ago.

He finished his meal, drained the brown bottle, left a tip on the table and put Matt's latest masterpiece under his arm. The bar was all but empty, and there was nothing for Jake to do but go home.

He wasn't alone. He could sense that, and even though he couldn't see them, he knew they were there. It was dark, blacker than hell's deepest pit, but he could feel the eyes on him . . . watching, willing him to come for them. Screams trembled in the air around him, high-pitched and hoarse from hours of torment. Help me, Jake! Please, help me!

Jake turned in a circle, scanning the inky darkness. His heart hammered against his ribs, and he could feel cold, damp dread soaking his shirt. The fear made him helpless, impotent.

He stepped back and stumbled, falling over something that clutched at him. He glanced down at the severed hand plucking at his ankle, horror welling up inside him. Pale in the darkness, the fingers were torn and bloodstained, its wrist a ragged dark hole. He shot a glance around, but there was no escape. Carnage was everywhere, the smell of blood, thick and metallic and nauseating, rose up around him. Wild to get clear of the killing field, he scrambled back over writhing body parts while the voices pleaded in an endless drone, filling the air, seeping into his pores, "Jake . . . Jake . . . Help me! Please help me!"

He opened his mouth to reply and a hideous, unearthly howl escaped him. It wasn't real. It couldn't be. They were right. He was losing his mind.

I can't help you! Do you hear me? I can't help

you when it's already too late! Jake rolled to escape the disembodied hand—and fell off the sofa onto the carpet. He had a moment of disorientation, not knowing where he was or how he got to be there, his pulse thundering in his ears. Slowly, gradually, he remembered. The apartment above Julianne Rhys's bookshop. He'd gone to Stooley's to toss back a brew and had come home feeling the weight of fatigue. He'd stretched out on the sofa, closing his eyes for just a second, and he must have drifted off.

Someone was knocking, loudly. Shaking off the weirdness of the nightmare, he picked himself up off the floor. As he made his way to the door, he just hoped there was a body attached to the hand making all the racket.

She glanced up as the door swung open.

"Liz."

Jake sounded surprised, but not half as surprised as she was to be standing on his doorstep, begging admittance at two o'clock in the morning. "I'm sorry I woke you. You need your rest, and I'm beginning to see that this was a mistake. I obviously shouldn't have come here."

He didn't argue, just pushed the door wide and stepped back. "Hey, don't do that. You know my door's always open. Do you want to come in?"

Her feet moved her forward into a narrow galley-style kitchen, while her brain screamed for her to turn around before it was too late, before she did something she'd hate herself for, and him. The kitchen was lit by a low-watt bulb over the stove, insufficient to reveal the danger lurking in the shadows. Liz didn't need to see it to know it was there. She felt vulnerable, and that wasn't a feeling she liked.

Dressed in a worn pair of Levi's and a long-tailed white silk shirt open to the last button, his black hair tousled, Jake embodied a wordless sexual invitation. Sleep had etched pillow creases on the left side of his face. Before she could stop herself, Liz reached out, smoothing his warm skin with cool fingertips, as if somehow she could ease the creases away. She heard his swift intake of breath and caught her own as he turned into the touch and pressed a lingering kiss in the heart of her palm. "I don't need explanations. It's enough that you're here."

He reached around her with his good left hand, closing the door, locking it. As he turned back, Liz came into his one-armed embrace. Unshed moisture pricked her eyes. Coming here was crazy, an impulse she couldn't resist, despite the potential for a negative outcome.

By turning to Jake she was opening a door she had sworn would remain locked. The repercussions of this moment had the potential to be huge, impossible to contain or control. She knew all of that, knew she was inviting trouble, and she still couldn't stay away.

Tonight, she needed to be touched.

More than that, she *ached* for it.

Her visit to the sanitarium had left her feeling empty and ineffectual, lonelier than she had ever been, and Jake was the one man she knew she could turn to—despite their troubled past, despite everything. He wouldn't deny her, and he didn't hold a grudge. He was the one man who truly knew her—all of her secrets, her failings and insecurities, her quirks and desires—and he still wanted her. She could see it in his eyes, feel it in the softness of his touch.

There was an intimacy between them that divorce and a decade couldn't wipe away, an ease in the way they came together, pulled apart, fought, that Liz craved. Jake was familiar, but exciting as he had always been, a good man with bad impulses, and a reserve of strength deep enough to sustain them both. He could withstand anything. He was a man who was as invincible, as resilient, as she was fragile.

Jake didn't know what stressor had precipitated her late-night visit, and he wasn't about to pry. She was here, and for the moment, she was his. Gazing down at her, he slipped the clip from her hair, arranging the silken mass around her shoulders. Its softness had always amazed him, and though their time together had been mind-bogglingly brief, he'd never forgotten the sensation of tangling his fingers in it, how it felt to have it fall around his face when they made love and she bent to kiss him. He'd dreamt about it sometimes, when she was living in New England, and after her return to Virginia . . . the wife of another man, the mother of someone else's child.

Liz belonging to someone else had been difficult to bear; working with her, seeing her on a day-to-day basis, had been sheer hell, and he'd had ample time to kick himself for screwing up. It hadn't been easy watching her settle into happiness, especially when his own life revolved around his career and little else. At night he'd gone home to an empty apartment, MSG-laden takeout, and a lonely bed, the grim reminder of everything he'd had, and thrown away like day-old sushi.

"This can't be real," he said. "You're not really here, and in a few minutes I'm gonna wake up, alone and frustrated."

She answered with a kiss, initiating the contact when he'd been reluctant to, her mouth open and searching. Jake groaned, dragging her closer. His

bumps and bruises, three days old and still smart-
ing, seemed to recede into the background, an after-
thought to the passion threading through his veins.
Hungry for her, he deepened the kiss, his good
arm encircling her slim waist, molding her soft
warmth against him. She had to know how she affected him. She had to know that he wanted her,
that he had never stopped wanting her, and unless
this was some sadistic game she was playing, she
wanted him, too. Her dark eyes were alight with
desire, her hands so soft, teasing on his bare skin.

Wordlessly, she fingered the sling supporting
his right arm, and Jake slipped it over his head. It
fell to the floor at his feet, followed by his shirt.
"Are you all right?" she asked. "I mean, can you?"

"I'm great," he said. "In fact, I've never felt
hornier—I mean, better. Listen, Liz. This isn't a
joke, is it? Because if you walk out that door—"

"It's no joke." Leaning in, she nuzzled his throat,
just beneath his ear, then worked her way down to
his shoulder while his heartbeat quickened. He
could feel its sledgelike beat, hammering against
his bruised ribcage, but no pain registered. Just
passion, heavy in his lower abdomen, quicksilver
in his veins. When he caught her hands in his, she
didn't falter, but walked with him to the dark living
room, where together they sank down onto the
sofa.

Gently, she pushed him back onto the pillows.
The need within her to lead the encounter was
strong, and Jake was more than willing to give her
whatever she wanted. He'd never been insecure,
sexually or otherwise, and he could respect a woman
who gave as good as she got. He and Liz had always
been equals, in the workplace, in the bedroom, in
a pitched verbal battle.

Jake lay back, watching as she kissed his shoulder and the bruises on his ribs . . . bruises she'd put there with her SUV, bruises that were a deep purplish green. "I'm sorry I hurt you," she said.

"Not like I didn't have it coming. I shouldn't have been in the road like that." It wasn't what he meant, and they both knew it. Thankfully, she let it pass, or maybe she was too preoccupied, too caught up in the moment and all of the things she was doing to him to have heard. Her hands—small, warm, and experienced—seemed to be everywhere, sliding over his belly, working his zipper down while he slipped off her scant little tank top and unbuttoned her jeans. Her top had spaghetti-straps with a built-in bra, and when he whisked it away, she was bare to his warm scrutiny. "Venus rising," he said appreciatively. "You're beautiful. Liz. That much hasn't changed."

His compliment didn't seem to register, or at least she didn't acknowledge it. Her dark eyes had a hunted look, and he guessed rightly that she hadn't been able to face going home. She wanted sweet forgetfulness, and he was it, and the only question was why had she come to him instead of going to Rhys.

"Jake," she said, running a finger along the cleft in his chin. "Just in case you haven't figured it out, I didn't come here to talk."

Her jeans were easily shed, and so were Jake's. And this time when she pushed him back onto the pillows, the only mystery between them was why she had chosen this night to forgive past indiscretions, and why Jake had suddenly become so damned lucky.

Liz took him in one smooth, sliding motion, fitting herself around him so quickly, so snugly that he couldn't quite bite back an agonized groan. Hot, wet, intoxicating, she straddled his hips, lead-

ing him through a slow dance, so steamy, so sexual
that he forgot to hurt, forgot everything except for
the woman in his arms and how much he loved
her.

When she had wrung every last bit of passion
from him, she collapsed against him, her hair soft
against his damp skin, her face hidden in the
curve of his throat. Jake thanked whatever god was
listening for bringing her back to him as he
stroked her hair and pressed a kiss to her temple.
"You did the right thing, coming here. The smart
thing. It'll make things a hell of a lot easier if
you're with me."

He felt her stiffen, and wondered how in three
sentences, he'd managed to say the wrong thing.
Then she was sitting up, pulling away from him.
"Wait-wait-wait-wait-damn it, Liz! Will you wait a
minute? Where are you going? What the hell did I
say?"

"Home," she said quietly. "I'm going home. It's
late, and I have a client coming in the morning.
She boards her horse at the stable, and she called
earlier to tell me she was terminating our contract.
Seems she got wind of what happened out there,
and she doesn't think its safe to leave her animal
with me. Imagine that."

"All right, then. No problem. We'll go. Just give
me a second to pull myself together." He was already half-dressed, his jeans on and zipped, but his
feet were bare, and he couldn't seem to recall what
he had done with his shoes.

She dressed more quickly than she had un-
dressed and was reaching for her car keys. "That's
just it: Jake, there is no 'we.' " A shuddering sigh,
then she steeled herself and said the words he didn't
want to hear. "I went to the sanitarium tonight,
and I was upset." She smoothed her hair back,

gathering it into a tail with swift, practiced motions, replacing the clip he'd taken from it moments ago.

Had it really been just minutes ago? It already felt like centuries . . . and he thought it was fucking amazing how fast she'd distanced herself from him, throwing up that goddamned wall.

"I needed someone, and you were the most illogical choice. Chalk it up to my not thinking clearly. What else is new?"

"All right," he said. "I get it. You want to ease back into it, and that's okay with me, but baby, please, don't shut me out again."

She had to catch her breath at his soft-voiced plea, and when she replied, her voice was rushed, the words forced out. "It's obvious you're going to read more into this than there is, so let me make it blatantly clear. Clear enough for even you to understand. You and I are past tense, and what we just did doesn't change anything."

"What we did?" Jake snorted. "You want to tell it like it is? Plain talk and no holds barred? We made love just now, and it was good—better than good. In fact, unless you've started faking it, your experience was about an eight on the Richter scale."

She reached out, running a fingertip along the shallow valley between his pecs. "Yeah, it was good. It always was good between us . . . but that's the extent of it. Tonight didn't have anything to do with love." She wouldn't look at him as she spoke the words, and they seemed forced out.

Jake resisted telling himself that she didn't mean it.

She meant it, all right.

His delusions about what had just happened between them, and what would naturally follow, disintegrated as he stared at her. There had been one

time in his life when he'd felt a bigger fool than he
did right now, and that was the first time she'd
walked out on him. "Don't follow me," she said
flatly. "I don't want you sitting in my drive when I
get up in the morning. Having an FBI agent hanging around's bad for business."

She shoved the keys into her pocket and headed
out the door while Jake stood staring after her.
The door closed quietly behind her, her footsteps
fading as she went down the outside stairway.

Perversely, Jake left the door unlocked, just in
case she changed her mind.

Outside, Liz released the breath she'd been
holding. It would have been so easy to give in, to
fall into Jake's world the way she'd fallen into his
arms, but the outcome would have been the same
as before. Disastrous. Like their physical encounter, because it gave him hope, and gave her
someone strong to lean on, even if it was temporary. Surely, he got that. Temporary was definitely
Jake's forte. It was long term he had problems
grasping.

She scanned the area around the Ford, checking the backseat and cargo bay beneath the rela-
tive safety of the streetlamp, then unlocked the
driver's door with a flick of her keypad. As soon as
she shut the door, she locked it again, trying not to
feel sympathy for Jake. She didn't owe him sympathy, and she wasn't responsible for the disappointment she'd seen on his handsome face.

Jake was a big boy. He didn't need her to take
care of him . . . just as she didn't need him.

As Liz's taillights faded, a man emerged from
the shadows of the stairwell and stood glaring after
her. In the bluish light cast by the streetlight over-

head, Samuel Turner's unshaven cheeks looked hollow, his heavy brow shadowing the eye that gazed after Liz long after her passing was just a memory. Then he turned and stumbled into the black tunnel that was the alley beside the Bell, Book, and Whatnot.

Liz was gone, and all thought of sleep had gone with her. Jake showered and dressed and would have made coffee except that there was none. No coffeemaker, either. He'd have to do something about that. He could live without a lot of things, but a coffeemaker was an absolute essential for basic life support, especially in a place like Abundance, which was light-years from the nearest Starbucks.

He did know a place that opened early—or rather, rarely closed—but they didn't serve coffee.

The local morgue was in the basement of Nathaniel Greene Memorial Medical Center in nearby Mantoot. The twenty-minute drive toward the rising sun reminded Jake of just how small Abundance really was. By comparison, Mantoot, boasting a population of just over six thousand, a courthouse, a few shops and restaurants, and three working stoplights, was a cultural mecca. It was a little like leaving Mayberry and cruising into Charleston.

The medical center situated outside of town was well lit, but as Jake pulled into the parking lot, the dusk-to-dawn lights flickered out. A woman dressed in white slacks and a print top with a white background got out of her car, looking half-drowsy as she balanced a handbag, keys, and a Styrofoam cup. She glanced his way, stifling a yawn. The world was waking up, and, thanks to Liz, he hadn't been to bed.

The basement was almost deserted compared to the buzz of activity at ground level and above. Jake found the autopsy assistant munching a doughnut at a desk while reading *People* magazine. He glanced up at Jake's light tap, and quickly swallowed. "The ME isn't due in for another hour and a half. Can I help you with something?"

"Special Agent Jacob English, FBI." He flashed his ID. "I'm here about Amanda Redwing."

"The kid in a box. Jack in a box, kid in a box—Ah, forget it." It was a bad joke, and nobody laughed. "You'll have to sign in." He handed Jake a clipboard with a short list of names. Jake recognized John Rhys's among them. He scrawled his signature on the appropriate line, and his escort showed him into the cold room, pulling open a drawer in a stainless-steel wall full of stainless-steel drawers. "They've already gone over the body for trace evidence. Clean as a whistle. Have a nice visit. I'll be at my desk if you need anything."

Jake said nothing. Cops, MEs, EMTs, and guys in his profession dealt with death on a day-to-day basis. So much so that it often became the subject of tasteless jokes. Black humor was a way of breaking the tension in their high-stress profession. Jake was as guilty as his counterparts in that respect, except when it came to kids.

Kids didn't belong in sliding metal refrigerated drawers like this one. He lifted the sheet and exposed the girl's face. Her skin had a bluish-gray tinge, and a cherry pink lividity showed along the length of hip and thigh that he could see. Carbon monoxide poisoning. Now there was a surprise.

TCM was getting more creative. All of the previous victims had died of asphyxiation due to the sealing off of the airway. So why the change in MO? Had he needed a quick kill? Had he been afraid of discovery? Or was it a mercy kill? A spark of pity for the kid at the last moment? The urge to have it over and done with?

Like all the others, Amanda's fingernails were torn and ragged, some ripped nearly off as she had clawed at the rough wood of a makeshift coffin in a futile effort to escape. The instinct to try to dig her way out of there would have been strong . . . but not as strong as the death trap that held her.

He'd examined the structure at length, and he'd requested and gotten copies of Rhys's crime-scene shots. The hotshot at the desk out there had been right about one thing. It had been constructed like a wooden sardine can, too shallow to allow her to do anything but lie down, or perhaps curl on her side.

Jake had no difficulty imagining what she went through. He'd always had a knack for putting himself in the victim's psyche, as well as the killer's.

For an instant, he was coming to consciousness in that box, realizing that his confinement was all too real while praying it was a nightmare. . . . He felt a surge of confusion, then terror, an adrenaline borne panic so strong it squeezed and compressed his lungs, making breath impossible. A little air came in near his nose and mouth from a small metal pipe. But it wasn't enough, and that only added to the terror. He pushed on the wooden ceiling, as hard as he could, but the space was too small, too cramped, and there was no leverage. He imagined he could feel the weight of the earth pressing down on top of the box, and he panicked, screaming and crying, tearing at it with his hands, trying to rip it apart. His nails tore and his fingers bled, but he kept at it, his cries becoming a horrible howl as he realized he was truly trapped, with no hope of escape. . . .

His breath had quickened so violently that it brought the diener running. "Special Agent English, you're not gonna pass out, are you? Maybe you should sit down?"

Jake snapped out of it, forcing a long, slow breath into his lungs. "Not necessary," he said. "I'm fine, really." He covered the child's hands with the sheet once more, took a last glance at her face . . . a pretty kid with dark hair.

Then he covered her face and gently slid the drawer back into the wall. "I'd like to request a copy of the autopsy report."

"She's on the schedule for later today," he informed Jake. "You'll need to sign a requisition, and I'll have to check with the ME, but since you're law enforcement it shouldn't be a problem."

Jake signed the papers, left a phone number, and said he'd pick them up, rather than trust them to the mail. As he left the cool, sterile atmosphere of the hospital basement behind, walking into the sunlight was like entering another dimension— bright, humid, unquiet.

For a few minutes he just stood in the parking lot, one hand braced on the roof of his rental as he let the warmth of the August sun seep into the skin of his face and tried to shed the cold, stark terror of Amanda Redwing's lonely grave.

Chapter Seven

Cyn Kellog was one of those folks who liked to say she owned horses, but, for her it was more about the actual ownership and all of the trappings that went with it—snakeskin boots, tight jeans, chambray shirt, and a belt with a silver buckle—than any genuine love of horses. Ms. Kellog might have a trim rear, but that didn't make up for her lousy seat, or her iron hand on the reins. As far as Liz could tell, Ms. Kellog was far too impatient to deal with an animal as temperamental as Marmalade.

Especially this morning.

Cyn Kellog wasn't just rattled; she was about as spooked as anyone Liz had ever seen, and the mare picked up on that nervousness and reacted to it. Marmalade was a handful on a good day, even for Liz. The mare had a tender mouth, and fought the bit. Ms. Kellog rode her with great difficulty, so she didn't ride often.

The horse, unaccustomed to her, withheld its trust and tried to turn in a circle when her owner took her out of her stall, wedging the pretty, perfectly coiffed blond against the slats of the adjacent stall. Startled at being pinned, Cyn Kellog let go with a screech that really set the mare off.

Liz threw her a dark look and directed her to wait outside.

"Are you forgetting that I own this animal?" she demanded, unhappy with being told what to do.

"You're going to own an injured animal if you don't get out of here. She not only senses your panic, she reacts to it. If you want to load her in one piece, you'll get out now and let me try to calm her down."

Cyn looked as if she wanted to answer. Her glossy mouth tightened and her blue eyes flashed, but she bit back her reply and stalked out.

It took several minutes, but Liz managed to soothe Marmalade, who stood quivering, ears pricked and the whites of her eyes showing. "Ssssh, baby, it's okay. No one's going to hurt you. Good girl. That's such a good girl." She fished a bite-sized Snickers bar out of her jacket pocket, unwrapped it, and gave it to the mare.

"Liz?"

The mare started a bit at the strange male voice. She took a step back, jostling Liz, who kept a firm stance and a steady hand on the bridle. "Dr. Bridger. I didn't know you were there."

"Can I help in any way?"

Lyle Bridger was five-eight, with a sandy buzz cut and a direct, unflinching gaze. A former career military man, he'd retired a year before and moved to Mantoot with his wife and four children.

"Just step aside and keep still," Liz advised. "She's nervous, so no sudden moves. I'll walk her out."

Bridger accepted her advice without comment, calmly moving aside and waiting while Liz walked the mare to the trailer and urged her up the ramp. It took several false starts and a lot of soft-voiced coaxing, but she loaded the mare without serious incident, closing and latching the gate. "I could have been trampled back there," Cyn Kellog complained.

"Yes, you could have been. Marmalade is a fine animal, but she's high-strung. If you feel you're ill-equipped to handle her, I'd be more than happy to take her off your hands. I can write you a check right now." Better to drain her bank account than to worry about the mare being mistreated.

"Leave my mare here? With you?" Her tone was derisive. "How much do I owe you?"

"Don't worry," Liz said. "You'll get my bill."

Miss Kellog and a female companion drove off in a small cloud of dust. Liz cursed softly, then remembered Lyle Bridger, waiting patiently where she'd left him. "I'm sorry about that," she apologized. "Sometimes the horses are more agreeable and even-tempered than their owners."

"She did seem like an excitable young woman," he observed. His gaze flicked to the truck and trailer disappearing along the lane, then returned to Liz.

She took a deep breath, facing him squarely. She didn't know why she felt compelled to explain. He must know about the body's discovery. She'd woken that morning to a reporter knocking at her door, and she'd been hard-pressed to get rid of him. Her threat to call the sheriff had convinced him to leave, but it wouldn't prevent him from using the sound bite he'd gotten as she brushed past him on her way to the stable. Her irate "No comment" had pleased him on some level. As the owner of the property where the girl had been found, she was part of the morbid story.

Victim or villain, it really didn't matter. She'd been dragged into it, and it would be all over the local news by now.

"In all fairness, Miss Kellog has a valid reason for being upset. Something dreadful happened here a few days ago, and she feared her mare might be in jeopardy because of it. I'm afraid I can't dispute the validity of her fears."

"The girl from Mantoot. I read about it. Newspapers—" He shook his head. "They couldn't wait to interview her poor parents. One can't begin to imagine how they must feel."

"I can," Liz said softly. Then, "You work with children, don't you?"

A disarming smile. "Calming the savage six-year-old long enough to inspect their molars is my specialty. Of course, I have kids of my own."

"Are you ready for your lesson?"

"Not just ready, Liz," he said, "eager, and may I say that I hope things work out?"

Liz spent the morning helping Jersey fix the pasture fence. It was the newest in high-tension fencing, installed just last year, and a section of it had mysteriously been torn to shreds.

"Why don't you take that poor old dog and go on back to the house?" Jersey stopped what he was doing, took off his work glove, and wiped his brow with a damp handkerchief before shoving it back in his hip pocket.

It had been a summer of record temperatures, but so far nothing like the sweltering heat and humidity that had descended on the cleft this morning. It was barely eleven-thirty, and the heat index had reached ninety-four degrees, with seventy-three percent humidity. "This ain't no fit job for a woman, and you know it. Besides, poor old Fletch looks like he's all in from chasing that rabbit. He's liable to come down with a case of old-dog heatstroke. And I know just how that feels, bein' an old dog myself."

"You're not old," Liz argued. "Besides, he's more comfortable than we are." She glanced at the lab, who had found a shady spot under the tailgate of the Explorer to lie in.

Today wasn't about heat, or cool, or comfort. It was about repairing the pasture fence, and she was determined to at least make a sizable dent in the workload. She wouldn't admit to herself that the hard physical work of mending fence was the best way she knew to avoid thinking of things that were best forgotten . . . like her visit to Jake's apartment and the intoxicating feel of him inside her as she made love to him.

In a moment of absolute weakness and vulnerability, she'd fallen into his arms, and under his sexual spell, but it had been a mistake.

She couldn't think rationally when it came to Jake, so she pushed the incident to the back of her mind. That's what it was—*all* it was—she assured herself: an incident. It had been almost two weeks since she'd seen him, and though she had somehow managed to avoid him, he was never far from her thoughts.

Liz sighed. The air was so heavy, it was hard to take a breath. Thirteen days, and in all that time the heat wave hadn't broken. Temperatures in the mid-nineties, combined with high humidity and the brooding quiet among the townspeople after the stunning discovery that there was another killer in their midst, created a level of tension unheard of in this sleepy little Catskill town. Liz felt it too, a sense that something was going to happen, and soon.

But when, and where, and who was next on the killer's agenda?

"Jesus, it's hot," she said. "I don't recall it being this hot last August when we installed this fence."

Jersey chuckled. "That's because it wasn't August. It was October. You seem a mite forgetful these days. You feelin' okay?"

Liz glanced at the ten-foot section of damaged fence. "No, I'm not. I can't afford new fence. What's your take on this? Do you think someone did this deliberately?" She swiped the sweat from her brow with the back of one gloved hand.

"Sure looks that way, don't it? This nylon is tough as nails, but tin shears and a pair of strong arms could still cut through it."

"That's what I was thinking, though I can't say I like the thought of someone deliberately vandalizing my property. Looks like the only question now is who?"

"Can't say. I have been hearin' things, though."

His voice had gone quiet, like he was hesitant to be overheard. Liz glanced up at her hired man. "What sort of things?"

"Big man with a big black heart."

"Samuel Turner."

"That's the one. I heard about what happened at the café. Town's abuzz with how you put him in his place. They're all wonderin' how someone small as you could manhandle Samuel Turner. I expect Samuel's just out to get even."

"I guess the local gossips need something to talk about, but it wasn't that big a deal."

Jersey gave her a long look, one that said he suspected more than he was saying. "Any time David takes on Goliath, it's a big deal. What do you plan on doin' about this? You gonna talk to the sheriff?"

"About a broken fence?" Liz said, looking off into the distance. The mountains looked cool and blue, and she wished she were out there, away from everyone and everything, away from Jake, and Samuel Turner, and the faceless menace who was somewhere out there, waiting, watching. "I can't go to the sheriff. I don't have any proof that Samuel is responsible for this." She glanced at the sky. "It's gonna rain, Jersey. But not till nightfall. And I'm afraid nothing's gonna break this heat. What do you say we call it a day?"

"Sounds good to me. Leone'll have the A.C. cranked up. Think I'll grab me a shower and a nap before supper." He retrieved the tools and put them on the back of his truck. "I'll get Simms out here to help with this bright and early tomorrow. We'll finish it then." He opened the door of the '55 Chevrolet. "You'll call me if you need anything?"

"I'll be fine," Liz assured him. "I've got plenty to keep me busy." She whistled for Fletch, who jumped into the cargo bay of the Ford. Liz closed the tailgate, waved to Jersey, and turned the air up full blast.

The storm she'd predicted didn't materialize until well after dark. The windows were open to catch even a faint breeze, and the rumble of thunder in the distance was like the warning growl of an approaching beast, low and ominous. Storms had never bothered her before, but this evening the tension that had been building for the last few days had reached a peak, and Liz felt restless and edgy. The issues she'd been avoiding thinking about all day with absolute determination seemed unwilling to be sidestepped any longer.

Though she did her best to divert her attention into less self-destructive channels, thoughts of a certain dark-haired FBI agent kept rising up to haunt her. At odd moments, she'd find herself looking away from the article on innovative veterinary practices, seeing instead the look on Jake's face the night she'd pushed him back into the pillows: surprise, wonderment, longing. . . .

He'd wanted her, and she hadn't just given in, she'd thrown herself at him.

Worse than that, she hadn't even thought to use protection. There had been no reason for her to remain on birth control pills after the marriage to Richard dissolved. She'd been living the life of a hermit ever since, and hermits didn't have sex lives. The prospect of dating hadn't crossed her mind in ages.

Not that the sexual encounter with Jake could be considered a date. It had been more like an exercise in blatant stupidity, a fine example of just how out of control she happened to be these days. A moment of weakness and, yes, need.

Surely Jake would understand that. Surely he would realize how deeply she'd been affected by the realization that the Cemetery Man had found her out, by the certain knowledge that the worst was yet to come.

"You have got to be kidding, Liz!" she said, hearing how foolishly optimistic she sounded. "This is Jake you're talking about. The King of 'if it feels good, do it.' You kicked that door wide open, and he'll have a ton of unrealistic expectations about where it will lead."

Liz got up to pace the floor, the magazine she'd been reading falling forgotten to the floor. Head lowered in thought, she groaned. "Oh, God. If I had to fall apart, why couldn't it have happened with John Rhys? He's good, and kind . . . a gentleman, with a sane occupation and a solid reputation, and . . ."

Maybe that was the problem.

Maybe John was too good.

Maybe that was why she'd sought Jake out instead. She'd married a good, solid, dependable man, and where had it gotten her?

Richard had been a good husband, a great father to her child, and she'd destroyed him.

Jake, on the other hand, was tough.

In fact, he was nearly indestructible. He'd survived a grueling career that made young men old fast, without even getting an ulcer. He'd been shot, run down, and unceremoniously dumped by her, yet he still wanted her.

And that night, she'd wanted—*needed*—him.

That was the hardest thing to admit, the one thing she didn't want to face. John Rhys could not have given her what she needed, because John didn't know her like Jake did.

Jake knew her history, and he didn't judge her for it. At least, not where Fiona was concerned . . . or Richard . . . and in an odd way, she was grateful for that. Gratitude, however, didn't explain her lapse, or the fact that she was dreading their next meeting. He was going to gloat, and she just hoped that no one was around to witness it. Kate Fife was already suspicious, picking up on the familiarity-slash-hostility between them, a clear indication to anyone paying attention that something was going on between them.

"Nothing is going on," Liz insisted to herself. "It's over and done with, and out of my system."

It sounded good, but it was a lie, and she knew it. Jake still had the power to affect her physically, to challenge her mentally. He was intense, and sexy, and funny sometimes, and— She cut off the thought abruptly, ruthlessly, as the first flash of cloud-to-ground lightning shot from the sky. It cracked, loudly, followed by a torrential downpour. For a few minutes, the roar of the rain blocked out all sound but Sandy's low, insistent "woof." Liz glanced at the dog, whose shoulders and head came up as if she was hearing something besides the rain. Fletch pricked his ears, then got up and walked to the door, where he stood, hackles bristling.

The dogs were always low-key. They didn't start at every noise, and they got alarmed only when something was really wrong. Liz went to the window, pushing back the curtain to peer out just as the ebony sky went stark blue-white, backlighting the black-clothed figure in the white hockey mask looking in at her, with only the window screen separating them.

She screamed, slamming the window shut, throwing the lock, then stumbling back. She heard him fumble with the window, then try the door. As the knob rattled, Sandy lunged at the door, Fletch joining in, both barking and growling. Her service revolver was in her nightstand, by the bed. As she went up the stairs, she heard scratching at another window screen, and then the rattle of the back doorknob. He would try every window, every entrance, until he found a way in, and she thought it was amazing that he hadn't just smashed the glass and entered that way instead of wasting time trying to gain an easy entrance.

Heart beating so violently in her ears that it blocked out the thunder, Liz fumbled in the drawer, grabbing the Glock. With the reassuring weight of the weapon in her hand, she moved to the stairs and started down. The dogs still paced the downstairs, from the kitchen to the front door, and back again. There was no more rattling of the doorknobs, and he couldn't have gotten in, or Sandy and Fletch would have warned her. She moved to the window where she'd seen the masked figure, sucked in a breath, and pushed back the curtain.

The rectangle of glass was empty. The blue-white flash flickered over the front yard, penetrating even beneath the huge trio of pines, revealing nothing out of the ordinary. Weapon in hand, she unlocked the door and stepped outside as a set of headlights showed further along the drive. A gust of wind-borne moisture spattered the legs of her black silk pajamas, and she shivered despite the cloying warmth of the evening.

The car, a Chevy compact, came to a halt next to her Ford. Jake turned out the lights and got out. He took the steps two at a time, and he didn't even blink at the sight of the weapon in her hand. "Are you all right?"

"As right as I can be with a ghoul looking in my windows."

"I came as soon as I got your call," he said, and Liz went very still.

"Call? Jake, I didn't make any calls. I haven't touched the phone since this afternoon."

"You're joking, right? I heard your voice. You called me by name before the line went dead."

Liz shook her head. "I don't know who it was you heard, but it wasn't me."

He was standing on the top step, getting soaked. Water dripped from his hair and ran in thin rivulets down his face. His expression was stark, and she could almost see his thoughts. They were dark, pessimistic, and his temper was smoldering.

"There's no sense in you getting soaked," Liz said, secretly relieved that he was here. "Come inside."

"In a minute. Listen, do you have a flashlight? I want to have a quick look around."

John Rhys photographed the muddy footprint left on the back porch, then dusted magnetic fingerprint powder over it in preparation for lifting it with a dental-stone cast while Jake surveyed the damage to the window screens. They'd been sliced with a sharp object—a knife or box cutter. The cut was clean, the hole large enough for a man to force his way through.

"I got a good cast of that shoe print. Looks like a size-eight running shoe, but that's just an educated guess. I'll know more once it's been processed. There are some unique characteristics on the inside of the sole, near the arch. I'll notify you when I have something more concrete." Rhys made notes and asked a lot of questions, yet he hadn't added up the facts to draw the same conclusion Jake had.

Jake cradled his coffee mug and tried to keep his opinions to himself for Liz's sake. But it sure as hell wasn't easy.

Rhys was a little too casual about the incident, seeming to treat it with about as much gravity as he might have a Halloween prank. "Now, you said you saw this guy at the window? Did anything about him ring a bell?"

"No, but he took me by surprise. I heard a noise, and the dogs seemed alarmed, so I pushed back the curtain and came face to face with him. He was wearing one of those white hockey masks . . . like in the horror movies."

"Clothing?"

"Black," Liz said. "A hooded thing—a sweat-shirt, I think—and sweat pants. I didn't see more than that." Though she had admitted to Jake that she'd gotten the impression the guy's sweats had been worn many times. She'd mentioned a hole in the right knee, none of which she told Rhys, Jake noted.

Law enforcement officials tended to deal in facts and observations, not perceptions or intu-ition. She was keeping things from Rhys, which meant one of two things: either she didn't trust him, or she didn't want him to look at her like she'd sprouted a second head. Frankly, Jake was hoping for the former while betting on the latter. Not that he didn't want her to cooperate fully with the authorities; he just didn't like the competition Rhys seemed to represent.

Liz, however, was hard to fathom. She always had been, and if he was being totally honest with himself, he had to admit it was a big part of her al-lure . . . along with that shiny, thick mane of hers; the way her ass swayed subtly, seductively, when she walked; and a hundred other things that were en-chantingly, uniquely Liz.

"Stature?" Rhys said.

"Below average," Jake put in abruptly. "You saw that print."

"Thanks for the input, Jake. Now, if you don't mind?" He looked expectantly at Liz.

"He's right," Liz admitted reluctantly. "Below av-erage height, smallish build. Five foot six, maybe."

"Well, it sounds like he wanted to frighten you, more than anything. Otherwise, he would have smashed the window glass, or kicked in the door."

"My, that's comforting," Jake muttered beneath his breath.

Rhys heard, and glanced sharply up, his expression a little bemused and a whole lot irritated. "Since you've obviously got something to say, Jake, how about saying it? Or better yet, why don't you tell me what the hell you're doing out here at this hour?"

Jake took a quick step toward Rhys. "You'd better not be implying that I'm involved in this—"

The sheriff's brows lowered. "Oh, I'm not implying anything, Jake. I'm asking. You do seem to pop up where you obviously aren't wanted, with alarmingly frequent regularity."

Jake set his coffee cup on the table, and at the same time Liz stepped between them. "Jake's here to help. Is there anything else you need?"

Rhys's tone softened. "I guess that's about everything. I'll stop back out tomorrow and have another look around, just in case there's something I missed."

"Thanks, John. For coming out here, I mean."

"My pleasure." An awkward moment passed as Jake frowned at Rhys, and Rhys delayed taking his cue to exit. " 'Night, Jake."

A lingering glance at his rival and Rhys went out.

Liz sent a glare in Jake's direction. "Good night, Jake."

"That's all you have to say to me is 'good night, Jake'?"

"You were expecting?"

Jake shrugged. " 'Thanks for rushing to my rescue. . . . Would you like to stay for breakfast?' "

Liz just shook her head. "You're impossible."

"That makes two of us. That's why we're such a good match." Jake reached out, tracing the tip of his thumb from her hairline to the point of her chin. "When are you going to tell Rhys?"

"Tell him what?"

"That you and I are more than just casual."

"You and I are over," she insisted, but as he stole a kiss, her eyes closed and her lips parted, and her body gave the lie away. She almost melted against him, their tongues touching, caressing, before she jerked back and away.

Jake frowned, brushing the hair back from her cheek. "You say that, yet it doesn't feel like it's over. You know it. I know it. We aren't through with one another. In fact, we're a long way from it." She wasn't ready to admit it, not to herself, not to him. Stubborn. She'd always been stubborn. Muleheaded, his daddy would have said. But then, so was he. His background was pure-D Virginia hardscrabble, and his tenacity went bone deep. He took a deep breath and let go a shuddering sigh. "I've changed, Liz. I'm not the same guy you divorced. Give me half a chance and I'll prove it to you."

"I have an early morning," she said. "And you should go."

"Yeah. I should . . . but I don't want to." Jake did the unthinkable then. He kissed her a second time, a long, slow kiss that she didn't even try to resist. She ran her fingertips over his face as his mouth took hers, as if she couldn't get enough of touching him. "Come on, Liz. Don't throw my ass out into the rain. It's wet out there . . . and dark. I'm new around here. I might get lost, or shot, or run down by a car."

"You're bad for me," she said, tangling her fingers in the damp hair at his nape. "We're bad for each other."

"We've both grown up," he insisted. "We're not the same people. We can make it work. Just give me half a chance, just give us one night." He kissed her temple, then nuzzled her ear, biting the sensitive lobe. "It's one night, Liz. One night when you'll be safe, and I'll be able to sleep instead of lying awake worrying about you."

She sucked in a breath to steady herself, pulling back just enough to stare up into his face. "All right," she said softly. "One night, Jake. Not two, not three. *One.*"

"I hear you."

She was giving herself permission to enjoy him, and everything he could give her. And as she turned the latch on the door and led the way up the stairs to her bedroom, the watcher observing the windows from the heavy cover of the pine tree in front of the house silently dropped to the ground.

He stood in the shadows a long while, looking up at the soft light pouring from the open bedroom window. Liz Moncrief's low laughter bubbled out through the window screen, drifting on the damp night air. That laughter sent a chill through him. Funny how a woman's laughter could do that, could bring back the feel of her hands, rough as they dragged him from his bed and shoved him into the close confines of the box.

He remembered how dark it was inside there. Darker than death, because death was supposed to mean white light and peacefulness. The box had been stuffy and almost airless, except for the holes she'd had punched in it. She called it punishment, the hours he spent in the darkness, breathing the sour smell of his sweat and his piss, and sometimes his shit when he just couldn't hold it any longer. No water, no food, no light. Just the sound of the bitch's laughter, low-voiced and gleeful.

He shook off the thought of her like a dog shedding water, and headed off. It was time to get back.

She would wonder where he'd been. She was bound to ask questions, to whine and to nag until he wanted to wrap his hands around her throat and choke the life from her.

He couldn't do that. He wasn't like his brother. But sometimes he dreamed about it, when he dreamed at all.

When Liz woke, Jake was already gone. The smell of his cologne, light and crisp, lingered on her pillow. Before she was fully awake, and was still in that dreamy place that knew no remorse, she rolled on her side and drank the fragrance in. He certainly had made good use of the one night she'd allowed him, and now she was pleasantly sated, and just a bit tender in all the right places. She stretched and sighed, and Sandy and Fletch thrust wet noses above the mattress edge. " 'Morning, guys."

She showered away all traces of last night's surrender and pulled herself together, then she went downstairs to feed the dogs and make some coffee. She found a note on the table, written in Jake's neat block print.

I'll trace that call to its origin this morning, but we need to talk about last night, and I don't mean the sex. No more avoidance, Liz. I mean that.

Easy for Jake to say, Liz thought with a troubled frown, when she was the one with everything to lose.

She worked in the barn until almost ten, then took a basket with sandwiches and a thermos jug of iced tea to the fence row where Jersey and

Kenneth Simms labored. Simms dragged the hat from his head as Liz got out of the Explorer. Fletch stuck his head out the driver's window and barked at the hired man. His tail was swishing. It wasn't an aggressive bark, just odd. Fletch was better at socialization than his female counterpart, which was why he often accompanied Liz while Sandy kept guard on the home turf.

"Hush," Liz scolded. She opened the tailgate and positioned the basket there. It was hot and humid, and a whitish haze seemed to hang in the air, turning the mountains in the near distance a deep, mysterious shade of blue. Last night's storm hadn't helped to alleviate the oppressive atmosphere one iota. September was fast approaching, but it still felt like mid-July. "I thought you two could use a break. This damned heat's a killer."

Jersey poured two glasses of ice-cold tea, handing one to Simms before he quenched his thirst. "Just what I needed," he said, refilling his glass, but drinking more slowly. "Everything all right at the farm? Mother heard police dispatch got a call from out here."

Jersey's mother was ninety-two, lived in a small cottage on his property, and thanks to her police scanner, knew everything that happened in and near Abundance almost as soon as the authorities did. "There was a bit of a commotion," Liz admitted. "A prowler."

Jersey frowned. "Someone tried to break in? I don't know what this world's comin' to, when a body ain't safe in her own home. Sheriff find anything?"

"A muddy footprint, but that was all. He was gone by the time they got there."

"Sh-sheriff know who done it?" Simms asked. "From the sh-sh-shoe print?"

Simms seemed subdued, as if he was concerned about something. Liz made a mental note to ask after his wife, Mary. The woman was late in her second trimester of her first pregnancy, and the last time Liz had seen her she'd appeared haggard. "Unfortunately, it's not enough to determine who's responsible. The sheriff thinks that it was probably just a prank," she assured them, though her mind screamed otherwise. "And nothing to worry about. Kenneth, how is Mary?"

"N-nervous. And the heat b-b-bothers her."

"First pregnancies are often difficult," Liz said, steeling herself for an avalanche of memories, a torrent of pain and regret. It came, as it always did, washing over her like a tidal wave, so surprising, so forceful, she could do nothing but mumble some half-coherent excuse and make a hasty exit.

"M-Miss M-Moncrief?" Kenneth said, calling her back as she was getting behind the wheel of the SUV.

Liz cleared her throat, but her voice still had a strangled quality to it. "Yes?"

"Got s-s-somethin' for you." He went to his beat-up van and brought back a small object wrapped in brown paper. "F-for you b-bein' so nice to us, an' all."

Liz opened the paper and immediately dropped the small handcrafted rosewood box. The wood over the latch was embellished with a curled-leaf design carved into the wood, just like the design on the coffin Fiona had been buried in. "Where did you get this?" And then when a startled Simms didn't answer, "Where the hell did you get this?"

"A v-vendor at a f-flea market," Simms stammered. "It's a j-jewelry b-b-box. Mary th-thought you m-might like it. It's okay if you d-don't."

Simms seemed to shrink in stature; as always,

when upset, or self-conscious, his stammer worsened. "S-s-s-sorry. D-d-didn't m-mean no h-h-harm."

"Yeah, me too," she said. "Tell Mary I said thank you." She picked up the box and sat it on the seat.

Jersey was staring quizzically at her. "You all right?"

Aside from feeling like a fool, she was fine—just fine, for someone coming apart at the seams. "It's this damned heat. I'm ready for autumn. This summer has gone on forever, and it just won't let go." She got in the SUV, cranked up the air, and headed for Jake's place.

Chapter Eight

It was a short drive, but it gave her enough time to work up a full head of steam. When she arrived and found the door locked and the lights out, she almost panicked. "Jake! Damn it, Jake!" she said, chafing her bare arms with her hands. "I need you to be here! Where the hell are you?"

She was standing by the front fender of her Ford, trying to decide what to do next when a voice came from behind her. "Liz? Is that you?"

Liz spun to face Julianne, who was dressed in a chic teal suit and matching pumps, completely unwilted, despite the heat.

"Oh, my stars! Your energy's as scattered as anything I've ever seen. Come inside, out of this oven, and bring Fletch with you. He'll roast in there, even with the windows open."

A moment later, Liz was being pushed into the same comfortable rocker Abby Youngblood had occupied the last time Liz was in the shop. "Relax and breathe," Julianne commanded. "I'll get you both something to drink." She disappeared into the rear of the shop, returning a moment later with a tray and two ice waters garnished with lemon, and a shallow bowl of water for the dog. Hissy the cat perched on the counter by the cash register glaring at her mistress for allowing a mere canine into her domain. Liz accepted the glass, sipping as she tried to calm down.

"All right. Spill it," Julianne said. "What has you so rattled, and why are you looking for Jake English? Is something wrong at the farm that you need to call out the big guns, or is this personal?"

Julianne had no right to ask, except that they were supposed to be friends, and friends didn't keep secrets from one another, yet there was no way to tell a portion of the truth without telling it all, and she wasn't ready to come clean. "It's complicated," Liz said, "and nothing I can talk about right now."

Julianne raised an auburn brow. "Except with my very handsome, very eligible tenant?" She dragged a chair over and sank onto it. She exuded calm, stability, logic, and for one crazy second Liz considered telling her the truth about everything—Fiona, Richard, Jake, and the maniac who had destroyed her world once and threatened to do so again.

If anyone could understand, Julianne would, but it wasn't fair to involve her in a mess that in no way concerned her. The Wiccan lawyer fixed Liz with a level stare. "Liz, I understand that you like your privacy, but what on earth is going on? And please do not insult my intelligence by trying to brush this off. Your stress level has been off the charts for a couple of weeks. In fact, now that I think about it, you started acting strangely when our handsome Mr. English came to town. Is there something you want to tell me?"

"I lost a section of fence night before last to

something big and nasty. It looks like it was deliberately destroyed."

"Okay. But since when has the FBI investigated damaged property?"

"I didn't want to bother John with it just yet, that's all. He has enough on his plate at the moment."

"So you came looking for the man upstairs." It was obvious that Julianne didn't accept the evasive explanation. Thankfully, she let it go. "Liz . . . you wouldn't keep important information from John, would you?"

"Information?" Alarm bells went off in Liz's brain. "I'm not sure how you mean?"

"Your involvement with another man, for instance?" Liz would have replied, but Julianne stopped her. "I'm not suggesting anything, but let's be realistic. Sometimes things happen, things we don't plan on, and can't always control. Unless I read my brother wrong, John thinks highly of you—in fact, I'd say he's more than mildly interested. And you seemed to like him. . . ."

"We're barely even friends, Julianne. John's a great guy, and I'm hoping you won't read more than there is into that." This time there was no hint of falsehood in the statement. John Rhys was the quintessential good guy, otherwise known as a fine catch. But she wasn't looking for a relationship. All she wanted was to make her problems go away, so that she could get her life back on an even keel.

"He's a great guy who's had his heart broken twice. He would have made one hell of a gambler, because he sure has crap-ass luck when it comes to romance—until recently, anyway. I have a funny feeling that given a little time his luck may change."

Liz shook her head. "I'm not sure I like that gleam in your eye, so let me clarify. Your brother is a very nice man who also happens to be quite attractive, but I have no room in my life for a relationship right now. I'd have to be completely insane to get involved with anyone at this point."

"Crazy Love . . . isn't that a song?" Julianne smiled a secret smile. "I'm afraid the cards say otherwise. As for Jake, I don't know where he is, but I happen to know that John's in his office if you change your mind about those questions. I bet he'd be glad to help out, and you can give him this for me"—she handed a box to Liz—"for the Labor Day celebration." The lid was off, and a candid black-and-white shot of John on the steps of the police station topped the caption, "Reelect Sheriff John Rhys." "His term is up in November, and you can't start a campaign too early. Do you mind?"

"No. I was going by the office anyway. There is something he can help me with."

The reception area was deserted, but John's door was open. The deputy knocked softly, then moved into the room at the signal to "come ahead."

"John, a word with you?"

John had his shirtsleeves rolled up, but he was flushed-faced and sweating. The ceiling fan was turning overhead, but all it did was stir the moisture-laden air and assure that there was not a cool spot in the entire room.

"The air's down again. Pull up a chair." John took a second's pause while he initialed a few papers. "Any new developments concerning Samuel?"

"I've been keepin' a close eye on him. Did you know that he walks to Stooley's? I picked him up last night when he was on his way home, and we had a one-sided conversation about a lot of things."

"You learn anything?"

"Only that he hasn't showered in a week. Jesus, that boy reeks. He ought to have his own emission-control device. How about you?"

John glanced down at the sweat rings under his arms and sighed. "Well, let's not put that to the test, shall we?"

Shep snorted. "That's not what I meant, and you know it. I took a little walk in the woods this morning and had a look around the area where B.B. said he saw Samuel, and as far as I can tell there hasn't been any digging going on out there. What else do you suppose he meant by his comment to Bratt about burying something'?"

"With Samuel, it's damn hard to tell."

"You think Samuel could be involved in what's goin' on at Miss Moncrief's?" Shep wondered.

"I can't rule it out, but I doubt it." John ran a hand through his hair. "I do know he wasn't the one who left that shoe print at Liz Moncrief's. Samuel's a good deal taller. No way could he wear a size-eight shoe."

"So, we've got us a peeper who likes to scare the ladies." Shep sighed his disgust.

"Looks that way, doesn't it? That print won't do much good unless we have a suspect with a pair of shoes to compare it to. And this is just what I needed." John leaned forward, bracing on an elbow, his hand pushed into his hair. "Too damned much paperwork, too little pay, and now I've got a homicide on my hands. This place is goin' to hell, and I can't convince Fred and the town council to increase the budget enough for us to buy new pencils, let alone hire someone full time. I have to be honest, Shep, sometimes I wonder if it's worth it."

"I hear Fred addressed the Committee for the Beautification of Abundance last night. You gonna speak at Muley's Lodge? They're plannin' a pig roast just before the holiday. Might be a good way to get equal time to push the point home that a bigger budget means better law enforcement. You've got your finger on the pulse of this town. Maybe it's time to let everyone know it."

"It's kind of you to say that, but I don't feel like I've got a lot of control at the moment, Shep." John glanced up, about to say more when he saw Liz pause outside.

Shep stood. "Guess I'll go have a look around, let folks see a police presence."

Liz put the box full of posters on his desk. "From Julianne. She's getting a jump on your re-election. Personally, I think your record speaks for itself."

He barely glanced at them.

"That's Shep's take on things, too. Personally, I've got my hands too full to worry about next November. You, on the other hand, are another matter. You worry me plenty—on a lot of levels. Is this business? Or did you just stop by to say hello?"

"Actually, I'm here to apply for a permit to carry a firearm."

He raised his brows and motioned for her to take a chair.

Liz sat down, watching as John fished in a file cabinet and brought out the application. "Fill this out, and be sure to sign it at the bottom."

Liz scanned the sheet. "How long will it take to process it?"

John sat back down, the desk between them, his

smile as warm as the air in the room. "That depends. Generally from three to six months. You know people in the department, however, which works in your favor. I think we might be able to speed things along for you. Of course, you'll have to pass a background check, but I doubt that's going to pose any problems."

Liz filled out the application and signed where indicated, then handed the paper to John, who scanned it. "Handgun: Glock twenty-one, forty-five automatic." He whistled low. "That's some firepower. You didn't mention you were in law enforcement, but given the way you handled Samuel Turner in the café the other day, it certainly makes sense."

"The subject never came up." Liz stood, as aware of John's questions as she was eager to avoid them. "If you can speed things up, I'd appreciate it. My weapon is registered, and I still have a permit to carry in Virginia, but I neglected to apply in New York. Somehow, I didn't think I'd need it."

She'd thought wrong.

"Liz?" As she turned to leave, he called her name. Liz stopped, closing her eyes as he came up behind her, resting his large, strong hands on her shoulders. He was a nice, good-looking, honest, even-tempered man. Turning, she raised her gaze, slowly, hesitantly.

"I came out to your place early this morning to have another look around. Jake's car was parked in the drive, and it didn't appear to have been moved since last night. In fact, the windshield was covered with dew. Is English giving you trouble?"

Only ten years' worth, Liz thought. Yet, in all honesty, she was equally to blame for her ongoing problems with Jake. It wasn't all his fault. At the moment, they were running about sixty-forty in his favor on the blame scale. "No trouble, but in all fairness, there is something you should know."

Reaching up, John tipped up her chin, his blue eyes smiling into hers. "You two know each other," he said softly. Then, at her surprised expression, he laughed. "I may not be big-city sophisticated, but I'm not slow on the uptake, either. Cops are trained to be observant, but I'm guessing you already know that."

"Sophistication isn't everything. . . ." Liz admitted. "A good heart counts for a great deal." She wasn't really surprised when Rhys lowered his head and kissed her. And she couldn't say that some part of her didn't welcome his advances, or long for something normal. It was a nice kiss, an experimental kiss—as though he was testing the waters.

Liz dabbled her toes in that same pool, hoping for a few minutes' reprieve from dwelling on what a mess her life had become . . . until someone cleared his throat from the open doorway. She pulled back, but John didn't let her go completely.

"Look, you don't owe me any explanations," John said softly. "But there is something I would like from you. A real date. Dinner somewhere nice, maybe, and a long walk in the twilight?"

Liz smiled. "That sounds wonderful."

"Good. Then, how about tomorrow night? Seven-thirty? I'll pick you up."

"I look forward to it." Liz drew a breath and turned to face the other man in her life.

Jake's mouth seemed abnormally tight, his lips a thin, hard line in his tan, gorgeous face. "Sheriff, pardon the hell out of me for interrupting your social life, but I need to have a word with Ms. Moncrief."

John stepped back. "She's all yours, Jake—*for now*."

Jake took Liz by the arm, propelling her away from her down-home Catskill Casanova. Halfway across the reception area, she pulled her arm from his grasp. "Damn it, Jake, will you let go?"

Jake saw her question as being a lot more profound than she intended it to be. Letting go was something he obviously was no good at. He'd been trying to let go for a decade, and he hadn't exactly succeeded. Liz was as big a factor in his life at this moment as she'd ever been. Deep down, he feared she always would be, and that didn't bode well for his future. Him loving Liz, Liz hating him . . . the prospect made his stomach clench, and the scene he'd just witnessed in the sheriff's office didn't help matters.

Rhys's mouth all over Liz. He hadn't liked it one damn bit. The sight of Liz enveloped in another man's embrace was hard to take; the sight of Liz enveloped in another man's embrace and obviously enjoying herself made him want to punch something. And that something just happened to wear a khaki uniform. "Damn it, Liz! Tell me you are not going out with Rhys!"

"It's dinner, Jake, between two people who happen to like one another. It's what civilized people do. Not that it's any of your business."

They were outside now, facing off on the steps of the police station, hackles bristling, and terribly aware of one another. Her pupils were dilated in the shade of the awning, and her full lips were slightly parted, and he wanted badly to kiss her and make her forget all about his small-town counterpart. Only the thought that she would be comparing his performance to "homeboy" kept him from it. "You're sleeping with me, but you're letting him buy you dinner? You're not just playing the field, you're plowing it under. Is that why you were looking for me? To rub my nose in it?"

"I came to the apartment because I needed you. As usual, you were nowhere in the vicinity."

"Well, excuse the hell out of me," he shot back. "As it so happens, I've been a little busy, and it had nothing to do with dinner and a nice long walk." He stewed for a few seconds, but he wouldn't keep it from her. "I checked with the phone company, and the call that came in the other night was placed from a phone booth."

Liz frowned. "Mantoot?"

"Main Street, Abundance, across from the apartment. The sick bastard jerked my chain and stood in the shadows to watch me react. It doesn't explain how they recorded your voice, though, or how they got my cell phone number."

Liz rubbed her arms, an auto-response to the fine hairs standing on end. "Your number's written on my dash. You put it there, remember? He was that close."

"They. We've discussed the possibility that there were two of them, and this pretty much clinches it. If our UNSUB was at the farm, then somebody else made the call, and we've got a much bigger problem on our hands."

"I need you to look at something." She walked to her SUV, opening the passenger door. "Kenneth Simms gave it to me this morning—a thank-you gift for my thoughtfulness."

She peeled back the paper to give Jake a look. A polished rosewood box, an exact replica of the coffin in which her daughter had been buried. "Hell of a thank-you," Jake said. "Do you mind?" At her nod, he took it from her, careful not to touch the box itself. "We should give this to Rhys. You know that."

She knew it, but she wasn't ready to give up her secrets, even if it defied logic; and Jake couldn't make that decision for her. For old time's sake, for everything she meant to him, he would keep her secrets.

"Kenneth claims that he bought it at a flea market."

"I'll see what I can do. Where do I find this guy Simms?"

"He's at the farm, mending fence with Jersey, but they were almost finished." He would have climbed in his car, but she grabbed his arm. "Go easy on him, will you? I doubt that he's involved, and Kenneth Simms is fragile. That's part of the reason I didn't tell John about this. It wouldn't solve anything to have him hauled into the police station a second time and grilled about something he didn't do."

Jake looked down at the hand on his shirtsleeve, then up at her, and she let go. He'd go easy on the guy, but only because she'd asked him to.

"You're w-with the F-B-B-I? I d-didn't do n–nuthin' wrong."

Simms stood with his hat in his hands. He was unusually small in stature and had a slight build. Jake judged him at approximately five-four, and it would have hurried him to be one hundred and forty pounds.

They'd pegged the Cemetery Man as being below average size, given the victims' statures. The profile had suggested an UNSUB who was targeting young females who would be easy to subdue and control. It had suggested careful planning as opposed to victims of opportunity, and hinted at a possible infirmity, or other physical disadvantage . . . like a thin build, or very short stature.

In that respect, Simms certainly fit the profile. Yet that didn't mean he'd killed anyone, or that he was stalking Liz.

"No one is accusing you of doing anything, Kenneth." Jake kept his tone intentionally light, as though he were having a pleasant conversation with someone about casual everyday occurrences instead of abduction and murder. "You don't mind if I call you Kenneth, do you?"

"Doesn't m-matter, I guess. W-wish we could've t-talked somewhere else. Mary g-gets real upset. Doc Fife says it ain't g-g-good for the b-baby."

"Mary? Is that your wife's name?"

Simms nodded, and Jake pressed on. He'd wanted to get Simms on his home turf. He needed to see what his home environment was like, and he knew it would throw Simms off his game to have an FBI investigator invade his home territory. Also, there was always the chance that he'd see something Simms didn't want him to see, something that might provide clues as to Simms's duplicity, or provide grounds for a search warrant. "That's a nice name. My grandmother's name was Mary. Are you and Mary from around here? I thought I detected something besides New York in your accent."

"W-West Virginia, from near M-Moundsville. Mary t-too."

"Then we're neighbors, after a fashion. Ever been to Eastern Virginia, Kenneth? That's where I'm from. Pretty country—not as rugged as West Virginia, though. Lot of farms over that way, and horses. You comfortable around horses?"

"They're ok-k-kay, I g-guess. I b-been a lot of p-p-places," Simms said with a frown. "Lookin' for w-work, mostly."

"Kenny?" A young woman appeared in the doorway. She was taller than Simms by half a head, and nearly twice his weight. Her belly was distended with the pregnancy, her voice an annoying high-pitched whine. "The antenna wire must have blown off again. Can you fix it for me?"

Kenneth looked irritated. "I c-can't right n–now."

"But it's almost time for the news. I want to know if they found the man who killed that little girl."

"N-not now," Simms said sharply. "For C-christ's s-sake! C-can't you s-see that I'm b-busy?"

Mary's dumpling face turned in upon itself and she started to wail. With a growl of frustration Simms got up to reason with her, but it was at least ten minutes before she calmed down enough for him to return to the kitchen.

"You gave Ms. Moncrief a wooden jewelry box?" Jake asked.

"She's b-been g-good to me—g-good to Mary."

"I saw it. Nice box. Unique—one of a kind, wouldn't you say?"

"G-guess so."

Jake raised his gaze to the smaller man's and kept it there, a steady pressure. "Can you tell me where you got it?"

"The flea m-market," Simms said. "Near Saugerties. It's a b-big p-p-place. Lots of folks g-go there."

A lot of folks, Jake thought, and one ice-cold killer. "Can you describe the vendor for me? Man? Woman? Short? Tall? Light hair? Dark?"

Simms shrugged. "I d-don't remember."

"You remember buying the gift, don't you? It took a while for you to choose it? Surely you must remember something?"

Simms appeared agitated, and he could barely talk. It was almost painful for Jake to listen. "D-d-don't know. A w-woman I g-g-guess. D-didn't recognize her, b-b-but I d-don't get out much."

"Were you home last night, Kenneth? Around ten P.M.?"

"W-went f-for a d-drive. Mary and I argued. Helps s-sometimes to d-drive. C-clears my head."

"Did you stop anywhere? Anyone see you?"

"No."

"Do you own a pair of running shoes?"

"N—no."

"What do you know about the Redwing girl, the one who was buried on Liz Moncrief's farm?"

"J-just what I heard on the n-news."

"Are you sure about that?" Persistent, a little less friendly.

"Yes, I'm s-sure."

Jake seemed to accept his denial as truth. He got up from the table and walked to the door. "You work with wood, Kenneth?"

"I c-cut f-firewood for f-folks. It's extra c-cash, and we're g-gonna n-need it with the b-baby c-comin'. K-kids c-cost m-money."

Jake went away dissatisfied. Simms claimed that his memory, which had never been much good, had been worsened by the brain injury he'd sustained in an automobile accident several years before. He thought the vendor who sold him the jewelry box was a dark-haired woman, but he couldn't swear to it.

Jake spent an afternoon in Saugerties, talking to the woman who owned the facilities where the flea market was held on weekends during spring, summer, and fall. Ann Rothchild flicked the ashes from her cigarette and squinted at Jake through the thin trail of smoke. They met in her office, a dingy cubicle off the kitchen in what once was a drive-in concession stand. The drive-in parking lot provided ample space for vendors to display their wares, and kept Rothchild's bank balance in the black. It wasn't easy, she informed him, for a widow like herself to make a go of it.

Unfortunately, she didn't bother keeping records, except for the head count and cash flow. She knew the regulars by name, but didn't recall anyone handling jewelry boxes like the one he described.

"Anyone who pays the lot fee can set up to sell for the weekend. I don't keep track of the merchandise they choose to sell. With all the odds and ends, can you imagine what a nightmare that would be?" She coughed, a loose, phlegmy-sounding smoker's rattle, looking him up and down. "You should stop back on the weekend. Could be you'll find what you're looking for."

"I'll do that," Jake promised, feeling like he needed a shower.

On the way back to the apartment, Jake stopped by the hardware store and purchased a coffee-cup warmer and a tube of Superglue. A cardboard box from Julianne's shop made an adequate fuming chamber, and some aluminum foil held a small deposit of glue in contact with the heat source without the risk of fire.

He positioned the rosewood box inside the chamber and waited.

Fuming turned latent prints white. The process works well on smooth, dark surfaces, and just as well on human skin. There were several prints on the jewelry box, and while most were smudged, there was a clean print on the upper left portion of the lid that was in perfect condition. Jake lifted the print with sticky tape and a pair of common tweezers. He photographed the print with a digital camera borrowed from Julianne, then picked up his cell phone.

"Calendar."

"Charlie," Jake said, "I need a favor."

Jake sent the digital image via email to Calendar, who ran it through AFIS, the Automated Fingerprint Identification System. Jake was fresh from the shower when his cellular rang.

"English."

"We got a match," Charlie said. "Simms, Kenneth L. Arrested for breaking and entering five years ago. You know what he stole? A pair of panties! He did eighteen months, with early release for good behavior. Eighteen months for a cheap thrill. Guess he got a tough judge."

"Anything else?"

"Nothing that's on the books, but you know how this goes."

Calendar was referring to the likelihood that Simms had perpetrated a number of unlawful activities prior to his conviction in which he'd never been implicated. "Thanks, Charlie."

"No sweat. I don't suppose you've changed your mind about coming back?"

"I can't. Not yet, anyway. I'm committed."

"You might *be* committed, if you're not careful. Sorry, bad joke." Charlie went silent, and for a moment Jake thought he'd lost him. "Listen, Jake, at least keep the lines of communication open, will you?"

"You'll hear from me." He powered down the phone, ending the call. So Simms had a record for breaking and entering. Jake wondered if he'd told Liz? As his employer, she had every right to know, yet she hadn't mentioned it. Simms denied owning running shoes, and without a search warrant, he couldn't verify or dispute his denial. Rhys could obtain a warrant, but would he, on Jake's request alone?

Jake had no doubt he could convince the sheriff, but that would mean betraying Liz's confidence, and he wasn't quite that desperate yet.

He might not have Liz's knack for sensing what couldn't be seen, but he knew when he didn't like someone, and there was something about Kenneth Simms and his wife Mary that set his teeth on edge.

He put away the notebook computer and sat smoking his cigar and ruminating.

Christ, what a day.

The forensics team of two had looked relieved when he'd offered to help them sift through the small mound of earth in the impound building. It wasn't the first time he'd done something like that, though it didn't qualify as part of his job criteria. He preferred a hands-on approach, and didn't shy away from manual labor if it helped bring them closer to catching the twisted freak who'd killed Fiona and put the Redwing kid in the ground.

The cigar burned down to within an inch of his fingers and he still didn't put it out. The results from the examination of the material used to construct the Redwing kid's makeshift coffin were in, but the report held no surprises, provided no fresh clues.

The box had been built of softwood C-C exterior grade plywood, a type readily available all over the Northern Hemisphere. The wood was unsanded, and generally used for rough construction. All stamps identifying the veneer grade and mill number had been cut away, so that the only means of identifying the material had been by means of a technician's microscope.

None of it surprised Jake. The Cemetery Man was smart, otherwise he wouldn't have been able to avoid capture for so long. Even the rosewood used for the chamber in which Liz's little girl had died had been virtually untraceable. African in origin, the experts had determined that it had been milled before the turn of the twentieth century. They had searched, but no purchases from dealers of rare wood matched it, and eventually, the trail went cold.

Jake wished guys like the Cemetery Man were flukes; unfortunately, for every one they put on death row, a dozen more seemed to take up the torch, inventing new ways to terrify mankind, to prove that human nature could always sink to new lows . . . acts more grisly, more shocking than before.

On nights like this, when the frustration of searching for clues and coming up empty threatened to drown him, Jake wondered if it was worth it. He could always take an early retirement, go home to Virginia, and spend his days and nights trying to forget that such creeps and perverts existed. Yet, just when that thought would gel, Fiona's face would flash in his mind, not the bright, beautiful face of the happy eight-year-old girl, but Fiona as he'd last seen her, her skin a dusky bluish tint in death, her fingernails torn from her fingers.

Jake put the hand with the now spent cigar to his forehead, closing his eyes against the image as he struggled to recover from the emotion sweeping over him. "You know, Jake, she could have been *your* kid," he said aloud. "Hell, not could have, she *should* have been."

A sigh slipped out with him barely realizing it. "Jacob English, major, first-class fuckup." Oh, he had the prestige and respect that came with a top-notch, high-profile career, but when it came to his personal life, he'd scored a big fat zero.

He lived alone; he ate unhealthy, artery-clogging

takeout; and he usually fell asleep on the sofa. If he kept on course, not only would he live the rest of his life alone, he'd die alone, probably in some seedy motel room with an orange and brown color scheme and very little hot water. "Jesus Christ, you're pathetic," he said forcing himself off the sofa. He picked up his car keys on his way to the door. There was one place he knew of that stayed open all night, or most of it, and if he was very lucky, he would be able to drink himself into a stupor without running into Liz or Sheriff John Rhys.

It was a Saturday night and Stooley's was packed. The place had a recent addition, a dining room that doubled as a lounge. It was large enough to accommodate live entertainment, and a local band called Halfway There had just ended their first set and were taking a break and grabbing a quick beer at the bar. Jake spied an empty stool and made for it. The bartender, a big man with a shaved head, asked his pleasure.

"Double bourbon, neat."

The man poured the drink, and seemed to know what was coming as he braced a large hand on the bar. The other hand never quite left the neck of the bottle. Jake downed the liquor and put down his glass. "How did you know?"

The bartender shrugged. "You've got that look, and, believe me, I see it a lot."

He refilled Jake's glass, then left him alone. Some guys turned mean when they drank, and some had a definite improvement in their personalities. Jake got morose. He didn't talk, he brooded; and brooding, in his line of work, and current frame of mind, wasn't exactly a good thing to do.

He had plenty to brood about. Pick a case, pick

a victim, pick a perpetrator. . . . It was all still right there inside his head.

Jake wasn't alone for long, however, because the door opened and Samuel Turner stumbled in. Turner stood out from the crowd without even trying, and he cleared the room of customers. Some patrons grabbed their drinks and headed for the dining room, others made for the exits, and inside two minutes the place was almost empty.

The son of the café's owner slid onto a stool at the end of the bar and in his ruined voice demanded whiskey. The bartender poured him a shot, then asked if Turner had money. Turner glared at the man, who threatened to call the sheriff, until Jake moved to a stool nearby. "Give him what he wants; I'll pay for it," Jake said, sliding a bill onto the bar.

"Mister, in case you're nearsighted, this one's trouble."

Turner didn't thank Jake, and he didn't glance his way. He sucked down the drink, grabbed the bottle the bartender had left, and splashed it into the shot glass. It took a hell of a strong stomach to watch him, but years of investigative work had all but annihilated Jake's gag reflex.

"Maybe you should slow down a little, pal. That's eighty proof and you're suckin' it down like it was lemonade."

"Fuck you," Turner muttered.

Jake didn't react, though he marveled at his companion's ability to charm. "Haven't I seen you around somewhere? No, don't tell me." He pretended to think for a moment. "Yeah. Now, I remember. You're that guy that tried to rob the café and got his balls busted by some short chick. How'd that feel, anyway?"

"What's it to you?" Turner tossed back another

double, and a portion of it ran down over his disfigured chin.

Jake shrugged. "Just curious. A big, mean guy like you—you must have somethin' planned for her, right?"

Turner swung his lowered head around and gave Jake a full-face look at how destructive a man's inner demons could be. "FBI."

Jake smiled. "That's right, and just so you know, that lady from the café, the one who cracked your nuts? She's a real close friend of mine."

Grabbing the bottle, Turner lurched off the stool and headed for the door. He'd gotten what he'd come here for, and he'd find a place where he could drink in peace. Jake could only hope his warning had penetrated deeply enough for Turner to remember it.

Someone clapped Jake heavily on the shoulder. He felt the impact right down to his toes. The bullet wound was healing, but it was still a little tender. He swung around to face Matt Monroe, the closest thing he had to a friend and ally in this town.

Matt was more than a little drunk, but Jake was still glad to see him. "You're startin' to hang out in the same places I do," Matt said with a shake of his head. "Man, that is not a good sign." He crushed his cigarette out and a second later shook another out of the pack. "You here for the whiskey, or the distraction?"

"I'm here because I didn't care for the company at my place," Jake admitted. "What about you?"

"You were alone, huh?"

Jake snorted. He and Matt had always spoken the same language. "You got it."

"That makes two of us," Matt said.

Jake frowned. "Oh, yeah? I thought you and that pretty little blonde were hooked up. What happened?"

" 'Were' just about says it all. I moved out. A man can only take so much. Abby's unreasonable. Doesn't listen to a goddamned word I say." He lit his smoke, and dragged the nicotine into his lungs. "I gave up everything for her—even this." He flicked his ashes into the ashtray and stuck the filter back into his mouth. "What the fuck's the use, anyhow? All women do is turn a man's head around; then, when you can't think straight, they put it to you." He shot a stream of blue smoke to the ceiling. "So, what about you and Liz? Tell me your luck's better'n mine."

Jake sent him a sidelong glance. "Liz is seeing your local law enforcement."

"Rhys?" Matt shook his head. "Well, I sure as hell don't get the attraction, but then Rhys and I never did hit it off."

"That was pretty much my reaction," Jake said. "Nice guy, but I can't relate. So, where you stayin'?"

"In my truck. Hey, Ed!" Matt said. "Set me up again, will you? And give Jake a refill, too. I'm buyin', and we got a lot of catchin' up to do."

The bald bartender leaned over and spoke quietly, his waxed head gleaming in the soft, recessed lighting. "Matt, I'm only sayin' this because I like you, and because you helped out at my sister's charity benefit. Don't you think maybe you should slow it down a little? Shep Margolis is sitting out there in the parking lot, and I think we both know why he's out there. If you insist on gettin' shit-faced, I'll take your keys and have Molly drive you home. She's waitin' on your next book, you know, and she'd kill me if you splattered your talented ass all over some guardrail."

"Molly's a great gal," Matt said. "You're a lucky man, Ed." He dug in his pocket and handed a fifty to a blond waitress who was passing by. "Hey, honey, how about puttin' somethin' else on the jukebox? An' crank it up a little. I can still hear myself think." Matt turned back to Jake. "So, how's business?"

"Off the record: it stinks. Liz had an attempted break-in the other night, but so far we've come up empty-handed as far as suspects are concerned. Rhys would like to call it a prank and dismiss the whole incident. Somehow I think it's a little more serious than that."

"That why you were sweet-talkin' Turner?"

"Just my way of lettin' him know I'm connected to Liz."

"Connected?" Matt laughed. "So you are seein' her."

"Oh, I see her, all right, and we argue, and she tells me off. Same old shit, new day. Listen, from a curiosity standpoint, what do *you* know about Samuel Turner and Kenneth Simms?"

"Simms?" Matt said. "Not a whole lot. Keeps to himself. Kind of quiet and shy. Doesn't seem to bother anybody, but who knows? As for Sam Turner, what you see—" He didn't finish the remark. "Turner's more frightening than anything I've ever created. That's for damn sure."

"Yeah, I got that. You think he's dangerous?"

Matt tossed back a whiskey and chased it with beer. "It's just my opinion, but I think if anyone needs to worry about Samuel, it's Marge. I take it Liz's involvement with Rhys is the reason you're asking me and not him?"

"Something like that," Jake said. "Rhys isn't exactly overtly hostile, but he isn't thrilled about working with me, either."

"Why the interest in Simms?" Matt wondered.

"He may have just provided a piece of the puzzle that'll hang his ass—if it turns out he's involved in it. I can't ask Rhys directly because of a promise I made to Liz. She's tryin' to outrun her past, and she doesn't want anyone clued in about who she was, or what happened to her before she came to this place. Including Rhys."

"So John Rhys doesn't know you two were married?" Matt whistled low. "I'd sure as hell love to be there when he finds out."

"Yeah. Me too."

"Ken Simms works for Liz sometimes," Matt said. "You think there's an earlier connection?"

"I don't know, but I'm sure as hell gonna find out. If there's even a hint that he's behind the Redwing kid's disappearance and murder, I'm gonna bury him so goddamned deep he'll never see daylight again."

Chapter Nine

It seemed strange to see John Rhys out of uniform. Not that Liz couldn't grasp the concept of the sheriff having a life beyond the job. She just hadn't given it, or him, much thought until now. She felt a little guilty about that. He'd been a perfect gentleman thus far.

He'd picked her up in his Blazer, and he'd been punctual. He hadn't complained when she wasn't, and kept him cooling his heels with the dogs for almost twenty minutes while she applied foundation, mascara, and lipstick, then tried to decide between a cool cream linen suit and her favorite jade green silk dress. She hadn't worn either one in ages—not since she'd moved to Abundance. There wasn't much call for fancy threads when her days revolved around horses, hay, and quiet evenings with the dogs. She had no social life to speak of—or at least she hadn't had until John asked her out. When she finally did make an appearance, wearing the silk, he had complimented her and surprised her with reservations at a four-star restaurant in Kingston. Almost since they'd been seated, she'd been thinking about Jake.

She was a female cad . . . and nearly as bad as Jake was.

"I hear the Maine lobster's pretty good, and unless I miss my guess, it won't clash too violently with the chablis."

He smiled, genuine, maybe even a little sexy in a straightforward, clean-cut way. He wouldn't cut corners, and he wasn't the kind to cheat, which brought her thoughts full circle.

Liz looked up from her menu. "I'm impressed."

"Because I know a little about wine? Or because I'm not a total bumpkin?"

"If there's any bumpkin here tonight, it's me," Liz confessed. "It's been a long time. I'm afraid I've forgotten how to do this."

"Funny how that works, isn't it? A few years of being on your own, and a simple dinner between friends becomes a trek to the base camp on Mount Everest." He put down his menu and, reaching out, closed his fingers over hers. His voice turned soft, caressing. "Let's take the pressure off, for both of us. No expectations, Liz. Just a nice dinner—and maybe, if you feel up to it and I don't spill wine on my tie in the meantime, and am adventurous enough—a good-night kiss. I like you, but I don't want to rush things."

Fragments of the night she'd invited Jake into her bed flashed behind her eyes: Jake, his face softened by shadow, rising above her, the feel of his kiss on her breast—and John's only suggestion was a good-night kiss. "You make it sound incredibly easy, relaxed. Do you really think we can pull it off?"

"Sure. Why not?"

Liz smiled. It sounded so good when he said it,

but he didn't know her—not really—and he didn't know about Jake. "You've lived in Abundance a long time, but you don't talk about your family much."

"A bitter and slightly hysterical ex-wife doesn't make for great dinner conversation. The kids are twelve and nine. Alicia and John Jr. I see them as often as I can, but with the unpredictability of my job, it isn't as often as I'd like. Like you say, I'm a hometown boy—born and raised right here, and except for college in Syracuse and the police academy, I haven't strayed. My parents are both deceased, and, of course, there's Julianne."

"Football star in high school, hometown hero," Liz said. "You're this town's linchpin, and you have a lot to be proud of."

"I don't know about the hero part, and the town would do just fine without me." He sipped his wine and looked a little uncomfortable. "Don't put me on a pedestal, Liz. I don't like heights. I'm an average guy with a pretty good grip on reality, but I've done a few things I'm not too proud of. How about you?"

Liz laughed. "Definitely. A lot of things I wish I could change, and there are times when I'm afraid my judgment isn't as sound as it should be."

"Oh, I don't know," John countered. "Not only did you settle in Abundance, you agreed to go out with me. I'd say your batting average is pretty good, even though that wasn't quite what I meant. I was asking about your family."

"Oh." She flushed, wishing herself home, anywhere but here. She wasn't good at this. She was thoroughly out of practice. "My parents live in Virginia. No siblings, but I do have extended family."

"Is that where you met Jake? Virginia?"

Liz gave an inward grimace. She was having a

difficult enough time keeping their evening from becoming a threesome without being reminded of him, and the last thing she needed was to open that particular can of worms with John. Yet she wasn't sure how long she could avoid it, with Jake in town, in her bed, under her skin. Maybe the only way to handle the situation was to be open about it. She took a deep breath, choosing her words carefully.

"Jake's a very hard man to ignore—or to escape." A slight pause, just enough to reveal her hesitance. "The truth is that he and I go way back—back eleven years, to be exact. . . . And, yes, we met at the academy."

"So you're a fed."

"An ex-fed, and you say that like it's a four-letter word instead of three."

"I figured you for a cop, but I hadn't guessed you were with the Department of Justice."

"It isn't something I talk about," she allowed. "As for Jake, we were married very briefly a very long time ago."

"It shows, in the way you look at him."

"The way I—"

John laughed. "Like you want to tear his throat out. Trust me. I've seen that same look often enough from Rachel to recognize it."

His pager gave an alarmed-sounding bleat. John checked the number. "Speak of the devil. I'm really sorry. It wasn't my intention to let my ex intrude."

Why not? Liz thought. *Mine certainly has.* "No problem," she said. But it was awkward.

He dug his flip phone out of the pocket of his sage linen jacket and hit talk. "Rachel?"

Liz could hear a female voice on the other end

of the line, raised angrily, her tone as strident as it was frightened. "You say she didn't come home? Did you call Jen's parents? Then you're sure they're together?" He paused, listening, then sighed. "Try to calm down. I doubt she was kidnapped. You know what kids are like. She probably just got caught up in whatever she and Jen were doing and forgot to call."

Rachel's reaction wasn't calm. In fact, she sounded as if she was treading on the edge of hysteria.

"Damn it. Is Shep there? Put him on." A few seconds passed. "What's your take on this? All right. Yeah, I'll be right there. See if you can't get her to calm down a little."

He hung up the phone, and the gaze he raised to Liz's was apologetic. "I hate to do this, but it looks like I'll have to call it a night, and pray like hell you'll consider giving this another try."

"Your ex-wife sounded worried."

"Frantic is more like it. Rachel tends to over-react. Our daughter hasn't returned from her friend's house, and Rachel thinks she's been kidnapped. I'm sure it's a false alarm, but given the problems we've had around here lately, I can't take any chances."

John was trying to stay calm, but she could see the tension in the muscles around his mouth, and she knew what he was thinking. *Please, God, not Alicia. Not my child.*

She'd had the very same thoughts when Fiona had been taken from their Virginia backyard. She'd been with a baby-sitter that day, an older lady from the neighborhood who stayed at the house when Liz was working. It seemed that during that period in her life, Liz had spent more hours consulting with local authorities as they tried to crack the case than she had with her family.

How many times had she speculated, *Maybe if I'd been home that day, maybe Fiona would have been spared the horror of what followed. Maybe the marriage wouldn't have been shattered beyond repair. . . . Maybe . . .*

That it could be happening again, to this wonderful man's little girl, tore her soul to shreds and left her quivering inside. The fear, the guilt, the rage, were so overwhelming it was hard to find her voice.

"Do you think Rachel would mind if I came along? I don't want to cause any problems, but if I go home I'll just worry, and maybe there's something I can do."

She already knew what to do. The one thing she'd been fighting all along. The thing she was still resisting.

She just hoped it wouldn't be necessary. Maybe when they got there his little girl would be safe with her mother.

Please, God, let it be the case. Please, God, not another child stolen and sacrificed to one man's perversion.

"I've got to be honest, I'd appreciate the moral support," John admitted. He signaled the waiter and paid for their drinks. "You ready?" Then, at her nod, "Let's go."

For once Shep had the sense not to alarm the neighborhood by leaving the strobe lights on the car running. There was something about that red and blue flashing light that seemed to fascinate the deputy, and despite repeated warnings from his superior, he continued to use it at every opportunity. Thankfully, tonight was an exception. Shep nodded when John and Liz got out of the Blazer. Liz hung back, close enough to stay abreast and observe, far enough to give the officers space to do their job—all the more important since both men had a personal stake in this.

John was grateful. Shep Margolis's expression said more about the seriousness of the situation than anything. "Before you say anything, you need to know that Alicia's all right. She just got home."

"There's more to this, isn't there?" John said. He could feel the tension in the air. It emanated from Shep, a wiry man in his early forties. In fact, Shep was so damned tense, he almost hummed. John had seen the deputy like this only one other time in all the years they had known one another. The day Shelley La Blanc's nude and battered body was found in an isolated wooded area not far from Abundance. Shep had been sweet on Shelley, a waitress from the café, and even though his feelings hadn't been reciprocated, her death had hit him hard.

"Alicia was with that little friend of hers, Jennifer Stringer. When Alicia came in the door, Rachel was so relieved that she was there that she called Jennifer's mother, but Jen hasn't made it home. I hate to say it, John, but I got a bad feeling, real bad."

John had to agree, but as sheriff he also had to observe a certain protocol. "We'll put out an APB— twelve-year-old white female, red hair, brown eyes, four-eleven, ninety pounds. Go on and call it in. As soon as we can determine this is an abduction and not something else, I'll contact the state police. They get the final say on whether they put out an Amber Alert."

As Shep used the car radio to put out the APB,

John took out his cell phone and dialed Jennifer's parents. The girl's father picked up on the first ring, his voice tight with tension. "Ed? John Rhys. Did Jennifer come home yet?" At Ed's negative answer, John's stomach lurched. "I don't mean to alarm you, but I've instructed my deputy to put out an APB on her. If there's any news on this end, I'll call. Yeah, I'm sure she'll show up soon, too."

John had turned and headed up the walk when the door opened and Rachel and Alicia stepped out. Alicia was gangly, in the way preteens sometimes are, and had his fair hair and features. John Jr. looked more like his mother. Alicia broke from her mother's side and threw herself at him. As he caught her, John knew an overwhelming sense of relief.

"Dad!"

"Hey, baby," John said, just holding her close for a few seconds. "God, I am so glad you're okay. But we do need to talk. Do you know what happened?"

"Mom's upset. She won't say why. I thought something happened to you, and she didn't want to tell me."

Rachel met John's gaze over their little girl's head, hugging her arms tightly to her chest, glaring at him. "I'm fine, sweetheart," John assured her, "and so is Uncle Shep, but Jen hasn't made it home yet. Tell me about where you were, and what you were doing, and don't leave anything out, okay?"

"We were at Miller's Pond. We rode our bikes there to swim, and we were gonna look for tadpoles. Jimmy was with us."

"Jimmy Moore, Jen's friend?" She nodded her head; John prodded for more information. "And then what?"

"That man showed up, and we got scared, and came home."

"What man?"

"The nightmare man," she said, almost apologetically. "I know it's not nice to call him names, but he's scary."

"Samuel? Is that who you saw?"

Alicia nodded. "And you came straight home?" John prompted.

She nodded again. "I took the shortcut, through the alley." She bit her lip, looking worried. "You don't think he took Jen, do you, Dad?"

"No, baby. I don't think he took her. Listen, can you say hi to my friend? Her name is Liz, and she has horses."

"Real ones? That is *so* cool!" Shooting a look at her father, she sobered. "I mean, it's nice to meet you." She put out her hand, and Liz took it, and just for a second, her fingers brushed something Alicia was holding.

A feeling of cold dread shot through Liz, settling dead center in her chest. Cold dread, deep sorrow, and absolute panic. In that flash instant, there was such confusion. Where was she? Why was he doing this to her? She'd trusted him.

"Is she okay?" The girl's concern jolted Liz back to reality.

"Liz?"

"Yes, I'm fine! Just fine. I must have zoned out for a second. What's that you have?"

She opened her hand to reveal a small audio device about one inch square. It was clear plastic, and had a short metal clip attached. "Jen's HitClip. I forgot to give it back. It's Britney. Wanna hear it?"

"Not right now," John suggested. "Liz has to get home, and your mom's waiting. I'll stop back a little later, but Uncle Shep's gonna hang around for awhile." The girl seemed unimpressed by that, but the little boy who came barreling out the walk picked up on it.

"Hey, Uncle Shep, can I sit in the squad car?"

"A monkey like you?" Shep said. "In my cruiser? Well, why not?"

John Jr. hung out the window. "Hey, Dad! Look at me!" He flipped the switch for the lights, and the strobe kicked on, throwing red and blue across the front of the simply constructed white frame house, until Shep reached in through the open window and turned it off.

John ruffled the boy's hair, kissed his cheek, then came back to where Liz was standing. Alicia's mother hustled her inside. John Jr. remained under the hawklike vigilance of his uncle. "He's got her, John," Liz said, surprised at the tremor in her voice. The realization had been crushing, and it had been all she could do to hold herself together in front of his children. "Don't ask me how I know, I just know."

"Don't ask? After a statement like that? You're kidding, right?"

"Sometimes, I pick up on things," Liz said quietly. "I don't know how it works, but when I took your daughter's hand, my fingertips brushed the audio player that belonged to her friend. He's got her. He's got Alicia's friend, and it's dark, and she's cold, and she's scared to death."

"Do you know how much you sound like my sister?" She watched as he shook it off, the amazement, the irony, and he almost laughed. "I don't know about stuff like extrasensory perception, but I do know that the Stringers had a huge blowup and they're talking divorce. I can tell you from personal experience that affects kids a lot more deeply than adults realize. There's a good chance Jen's hiding out at another friend's house, or on her way to her grandmother's, hoping to throw a scare into her parents and get their attention. She's run away twice so far this year. She'll be back home by morning."

A wave of sadness washed over Liz. He was so naive, and he was about to be disillusioned in a huge way. Murder was not an everyday occurrence in small towns like Abundance, where everyone knew everyone else—and all their secrets, passions, and lies. But John had been very wrong about one thing: there was a monster out there, and he had Alicia Rhys's friend. Shrugging it off wouldn't get her back.

John took her home, walked her to her door, and spent one awkward moment searching for the words to apologize for a disastrous first date. Liz stepped close, kissing him gently on the lips, a sweet kiss. Then she stepped back.

"I wish it had turned out differently," he said, gazing down at her, "but I have to get going. I promised Alicia I'd stop back at the house, and I need to have a little talk with Samuel Turner."

Liz stood on the porch and watched him get back in the Blazer and drive away. John wasn't the only one who wished the evening had turned out differently. The impressions she'd experienced earlier wouldn't leave her, and there was only one thing left for her to do.

Opening the door and whistling for Fletch, she took her keys and left the house. Jake's apartment was dark, and his rental wasn't parked out front. She sat outside for several minutes, then drove to the one other place, the only place she knew of where Jake would be.

Stooley's was out of the way; it was also the only

bar within ten miles. The parking lot was full when
Liz arrived, and Jake's rental was parked front and
center. She found a space two rows back, ordered
Fletch to stay and watch, then entered the bar.

It took her a moment to locate him. He was
leaning on a pool cue while Abundance's most in-
famous resident and Abigail Youngblood's significant other leaned in for a difficult and critical
shot. A row of shot glasses were lined up on that
end of the bar, each one brimming with amber liquid. It was anyone's guess as to who was the winner
or the loser of the contest, but the bartender
looked relieved when he realized she was there to
fetch one, or both, of them.

Jake caught sight of her almost immediately.
She saw his antennae go up before he turned
around. He'd always been tuned into her, and in
the days before their ill-fated marriage, she'd
often thought it a strange coincidence that they
were on the same frequency. Because of it, they'd
worked well together. They just hadn't been able
to work it out on a personal level.

Of course, neither one of them had exactly
stuck with it, or tried to fight for the marriage.
They'd both given in, given up.

"Jake, what are you doing?"

Matt overshot the ball, and it bounced over the
rail and landed an inch from Liz's left shoe. His
bloodshot gaze followed from the ball to her face,
and he grinned. "Liz!" He walked to where she
stood and put his arms around her. "How the hell
are you?"

"I've been better. Matt, don't you have somewhere to be?"

"As a matter of fact, I don't," he said. "And neither does Jake. That's why we're here, together."

"Not anymore, you're not," Liz said, extracting

herself from Matt's hug. "Jake has somewhere to be. Come on, we'll drive you home."

Jake looked suspicious, and she could tell he was hell-bent on being obstinate. "I thought tonight was the big date. What happened? Does Rhys have a nine o'clock bedtime—or did you decide to save the nasty for next time?"

"You and I need to talk," Liz said tightly. "It can't wait, and we can't do it here."

"You? Me? Talk?" He racked up the balls. "Now, there's a first! Have a seat and wait your turn. I'm a little busy right now." He lined up his cue and broke left-handed. "Besides, I'm still a little sore from our last conversation, and trying to gain some perspective. I don't know how anxious I am to go down that road again."

"There's been another kidnapping."

He'd been about to make another shot, but froze at her statement. "When?"

"Tonight," Liz said. "An hour or two ago. The girl's name is Stringer, Jennifer. She's a friend of John Rhys's daughter, Alicia."

"How do you know this?"

"His ex-wife called to say their little girl hadn't come home. When we got there, Alicia had arrived, but the Stringer girl never made it home—"

"So?"

"John's daughter was holding an object that belonged to her friend. One of those audio clips that plays a single. When Alicia said hello, my fingers brushed it. I wasn't looking for anything, but her friend came in loud and clear. He's got her, Jake, and she's terrified."

Jake cursed at that. "Did you tell Rhys?"

"I tried to." Reluctantly. Admitting to this man that John Rhys had dismissed the information she'd provided as a crock of shit rankled. It would only serve to stroke Jake's ego to admit that she needed him as much, maybe more, than he needed her. And his ego was already huge. "Are you going to work with me on this, or not? Because if I have to, I'll go it alone."

Jake came close, close enough for her to smell the bourbon on his breath, feel the weight of his simmering anger. Reaching out, he slid his hand under her hair, barely grazing her flesh as he lifted the silky skein and carefully positioned it so that it fell over one shoulder. He toyed with the wavy mass that had taken an hour to style in order to please his rival, his voice a raspy whisper, brimming with hot emotion, abrading her senses like raw silk. "Oh, I'll work with you, Liz, but for the kid's sake, not because you asked me to."

Jake gave Matt his spare key and left him to sleep it off on the sofa. Then he and Liz drove to the farm. Liz felt more comfortable there, and that was important. The fewer the distractions, the better her focus.

The house was dark when they pulled in. Jake didn't like that.

"You need to leave a light on when you're away. A place this dark is like an invitation for trouble. You need a dusk-to-dawn light, too. Something that illuminates the porch and yard."

"I did leave a light on," she countered. "The bulb must have blown. It seems to happen a lot out here. It's an old house. What's with you, anyhow? You're getting what you came here for. I thought that would make you happy."

She got out, letting Fletch out the tailgate while Jake grabbed his bag. "Nothing about this makes me happy, not the missing kid, not you and Rhys, not even the fact that you and I can't seem to get it right no matter what we do." It was more than he should have been willing to admit. He would have liked to appear invulnerable, but where Liz was concerned, it just wasn't possible. It never had been. "I'd rather be in Virginia, or on the road somewhere. None of this was my idea, you know."

But that wasn't completely true. He'd put together the facts, made an educated guess, and decided to save Liz's soft white behind, whether she wanted him to or not. Coming to Abundance had been his idea. He was supposed to be in Virginia, helping Charlie. Instead he was here, trying to protect a woman who hadn't wanted anything to do with him, or his help . . . until now. As she led the way to the house in silence and unlocked the door, he tried not to read too much into the fact that she had asked for his help.

When she reached for the knob, he stopped her. "I go first."

He already had his pistol palmed. A Glock .45, just like hers. The dogs tracked in ahead of Jake, who flicked on the light. The bulb wasn't burned out, which meant one of two things: either she'd forgotten to turn it on, as she'd said, or someone else had turned it off. To be safe, he checked the rooms one by one, relaxing a little when he saw the dogs settle in on the hearth rug and curl up to nap.

"Okay, so maybe I did forget to turn on the light. I don't recall bourbon ever making you this paranoid," she said. It was a lousy attempt at a joke, a grim reminder of their shared past, and it fell flat.

Jake holstered the pistol. "It's not paranoia, Liz. I've just got a lot to lose."

A little too honest. It was the booze.

She closed up, shied away, got busy making coffee. Liz Moncrief, Queen of Avoidance, proud winner of the blue ribbon in the grudge-holding category. . . . But that didn't stop his gut from wrenching into a tension-driven knot every time he looked at her.

He needed her in his world, his life; he didn't feel quite whole without her, and though he hated to admit it, it had been easier for him all those years at Quantico, even seeing her with another man, than it had been since she quit the program and vacated his life completely.

She lifted his bag, which he'd neglected to close, and one of the straps slipped from her grasp. The bag lurched, and some of the contents fell to the floor: toothbrush, toothpaste, and a folding leather frame that held two five-by-seven black-and-white photos. One of Jake's father, the other of a much younger version of the woman he'd married, then lost to fear and foolish pride. She looked down at her own face, a little stunned that he would have the old photo in his possession after all this time.

"Do you mind?" he said softly, reaching out for the frame. "It's the one thing I didn't have to give up after the divorce."

"You didn't give up anything," Liz countered. "We split everything, fifty-fifty."

"That's where you're wrong," Jake said. "I lost everything that ever mattered to me." He held out his hand, but she didn't give it over immediately. Instead, she took a good long look at the photo of Ranald James English, her expression softening.

"I miss him," she admitted. "He was a truly great man."

"He was a simple man, with simple values, who never missed an opportunity to tell his youngest son where he screwed up. Not that he didn't have ample opportunity. He told me I'd regret losing you, and he was right." Jake took the frame from her and put it away. "The truth is, I miss him, too."

"What happened?" A loaded question. "To the farm, I mean?"

She was taking an interest in things that mattered to him, and Jake tried not to inject more into that fact than was there. It was just small talk, he told himself; she didn't really give a damn, or she wouldn't be going out with someone else. The farm in the foothills of the Blue Ridge was a safe subject. It didn't have anything to do with the tension between them, or the reason for it. It didn't apply to a broken heart, and a broken life.

"I managed to hang on to it. I'm renting it to a carpenter and his wife right now, but I figure when I'm ready to quit the craziness, I'll retire there. There are worse things than getting up every morning and looking out at the mountains, and maybe someday I'll be settled enough to be content raising a few head of cattle, and figuring how best to keep the slugs from eating the cabbages. It was enough for Daddy—"

"You aren't like Ranald, and you'll never be content with anything that sedate."

It wasn't said unkindly. Jake looked up. "You don't need to remind me. I've spent half my life knowin' I don't measure up."

She got very quiet, and a look crossed her face he couldn't begin to comprehend. Maybe it was regret, or grief for all that had passed them by, everything they had lost. "It isn't a matter of not measuring up, Jake. It's about being different. You were born to chase the thrill. You like the exhilaration of the job, the challenge, and you're good at it. There's nothing wrong with getting off on an adrenaline rush, unless someone's waiting at home."

Jake sighed. There was no good defense to combat her criticism, and, oddly, he didn't want to fight. She was within reach, and he so ached to touch her that the emptiness yawning inside him throbbed in his voice. "You hate me; I love you. If that isn't an impasse, I sure as hell don't know what is. And I'm thinking it might be a whole lot easier for both of us if we just concentrate on finding the kid. But first, I'd like to stow my gear. Should I take the sofa?"

"You'll be more comfortable in the guest room. Come on, I'll show you the way." She preceded him up the stairs, the same stairs they had climbed together the night he'd shared her bed. Two days ago, and it felt like a lifetime.

The guest room was next to hers, a neatly fitted room with an old-fashioned double bed, painted iron headboard and footboard, tall chest of drawers, and a hickory rocker. He put his bag on the quilt-covered mattress and the computer case beside it. "No sense in unpacking. I won't be here that long." When he turned around, Liz was leaning against the doorway, her dark eyes soft, full of emotion. That surprised him. She'd seemed so untouchable, so closed off earlier. Even two days ago, when she'd allowed him to touch her body, her heart had remained sealed off, protected. It was a talent she had that he'd never learned, much to his regret.

"Jake?"

"Yeah?"

"I don't hate you. I don't know what I feel, but it isn't hatred. It never was."

Chapter Ten

Jake stared at the empty doorway, and it was a long time before he could breathe normally again. He wasn't sure how to react to that stunning admission, and he wasn't so sure that the confusion he felt was preferable to her hatred. The experts claimed that there was a very thin line between love and hate; at least the two emotional extremes were somewhat related, but uncertainty . . . uncertainty could mean a lot of things, none of them good.

He had to admit, her behavior was suspicious. Make love to him one night, go out on a date with Mr. All-American Law Enforcement the next. Invite him into her home, ostensibly to work, but then admit she didn't know how she felt about him. The whole thing made him extremely uneasy—uncertain where he stood with her. He didn't like that. He preferred dealing in facts, and he didn't like feeling off-balance.

"If this is some carefully devised payback, it's working."

Pulling himself together, he joined her in the kitchen. She had a map of the area spread out on the round oak table, with pins in it, one pin for each victim. "Two states, eight victims. What do they all have in common?"

Jake went to the coffeemaker and poured a cup. "They're all dead."

She set her jaw, and her dark eyes took on a determined light. "Come on, Jake. How does he operate?"

"Liz, we've been over this a hundred times."

"You've been over it a hundred times. I've been away from it for two years. Work with me, refresh my memory." Her voice softened. "How does he operate?"

He sank onto a chair. His shoulder felt as mobile as a rusty gate. He moved, and it alerted him in a bitch of an unsubtle way that it was being overtaxed. It had only been a couple of weeks, even if it felt longer, since the accident. He needed to give it time, yet he wanted to be one hundred percent right now. The booze was wearing off, and he was getting cranky. "If you intend to put me through the wringer, the least you can do is provide some Tylenol."

She raised a cynical brow at that. "You've been drinking, sweet cheeks. You don't get Tylenol. Liver damage."

"I'll risk it. C'mon, Liz. It hurts."

"Who knew that Super Agent was such a wuss?" Liz straightened, abandoning the map, coming around the chair where he sat to stand behind him. She put her hands on his shoulders, and Jake's sigh drifted over her senses, giving her pause to rethink her actions.

It was a small thing, a familiar thing . . . massaging muscles that were stiff and sore and overworked, but it was the small things, the familiar things, that were so dangerous. Like admitting she didn't hate him, that she never had.

Such a small concession.

Such a dangerous first step.

She had expected him to leap upon it, to press her into something for which she wasn't ready and, if she had a lick of sense, never would be. There was no going back from where they'd been, and she didn't just fear for herself. She was more than a little afraid for Jake . . . afraid of what he would do if he ever stumbled onto the truth about their daughter.

She had to admit that he hadn't been the only one with poor judgment, and though he'd dealt the killing blow to their marriage, in some ways her deception later on had been far more cruel.

Squeezing her eyes shut, she worked his shoulders and neck and felt the tension go out of him and through her. She didn't hate him . . . but he would hate her, and he would have every right.

"What happened in my absence?" she asked, redirecting her thoughts. It was too late to correct her impetuous and anger-borne mistake—it had been too late when he penned his signature on the divorce papers. With her temper boiling, and her pride in shreds, there had been only one way out for her. Years later, with their daughter in her grave, there was no point in Jake ever finding out. "There must have been some developments in the case."

He gave her what she wanted. Just like he'd given her the divorce, when he could have fought for the marriage and begged her forgiveness. "After Fiona's death, and your departure from Virginia, everything came to a screeching halt. There were a couple of abductions in the area, but they were custody-related. As near as I could figure, he may have been arrested for something unrelated. It's the only thing that makes sense. God, that feels so good—would you mind? A little to the left . . . oh, yeah. You've got great hands, Liz. Your husband was a lucky man."

"Funny, Richard didn't think so."

"Well, then Richard's an idiot."

She smiled at that. "Thanks. I think." She smoothed the wrinkles from his shirt and started to move away, but Jake grabbed her hand, bringing her around to face him.

"Forget about Virginia for now. I have all the pertinent information. What I don't have is what happened tonight with the Rhys kid and her friend. Walk me through it, step by step."

They went over it again, the interruption at dinner, the scare over John's daughter. Liz pulled her hand from his grasp. She couldn't concentrate with him stroking the heart of her hand with his thumb. When she touched Jake, all she felt was warmth and strength; the impression of reliability was strong. *Permanence*, that was the word that leaped to mind.

Now, that was strange. Jake? Reliable? Permanent?

She almost laughed. Yet as soon as she put a few feet between them, the good feeling faded and she felt hollow, empty. "Alicia reached out, and as I took her hand, my fingertips brushed against the object she was holding. I knew it belonged to her friend, Jennifer Stringer, and when I asked, she confirmed it."

"You picked up on something. What was it?"

"Emotion," Liz said, her voice gone small. "Terror. Panic . . . confusion . . . such sadness. My God, she's so scared—and she's worried—about her family— she's afraid of what they might think. She's afraid she won't see them again."

"Afraid of what they might think? What would they think? The situation is beyond her control."

Liz frowned. "I didn't say I understood it." In her mind, she moved back into the moment when her fingers had brushed the HitClip and emotion had flooded her being; she moved into the emotion. "She's afraid they'll be disappointed."

"What about the pervert who snatched her?" Jake wondered. "Does she know him?"

It was asking a lot from one small encounter, a few seconds, a flash of involuntary sensation. "I can't say for sure, but I think so."

"He's close by, so she may have at least seen him, recognized him," Jake insisted. "It might add an element of trust. And since there was only a struggle in one instance, we know he manages somehow to gain that trust, at least for a few seconds. Long enough for him to get them under control, and then it's too late."

A struggle in only one instance. Liz closed her eyes as her respiration increased. Her daughter had struggled, tried to break away. She'd had scrapes and bruises on her body. Defense wounds.

"So, how does he lure them in?" Liz asked. "The 'I lost my puppy' routine?"

"Maybe," Jake replied. "But not in every instance. At least one of the victims here in New York was severely allergic."

"All right, then he has more than one ploy . . . or he belongs. There's some reason he appears trustworthy."

Jake stood up, leaning his weight on his good left hand, pointing to the four New York burial sites. "Woodstock, Willow, Abundance . . . victims chosen from three towns within a twenty-mile radius. They were all taken at dusk, or just before, and there were no witnesses. At least none that we know of."

"What about the Redwing girl?" Liz asked. "Do you have the stats on her?"

"The forensic botanist reported to Rhys today that the roots had been cut approximately thirty-six hours before she was found."

"So she was buried alive for thirty-six hours," Liz said.

Jake reached out, covering her hand with his, giving it a gentle squeeze. She didn't pull back, something that amazed even her. "Look, Liz, you don't have to do this." He had that look on his face ... the same look he'd worn that day two years before when he'd come to the house and she'd slapped him. He was thinking about Fiona, about her, all she'd lost, everything she'd been through, and he was trying to determine if she was strong enough to take it. "I don't want to make things worse for you."

"Too late for that," Liz said, then immediately regretted it. "Forget I said that. I didn't mean it the way it sounded." She shook her head. "Everything is spinning out of control, and I hate that. I hate that he knows his next move and we don't. I hate that the ball always seems to be in his court, and the truth is that I hate him for doing this to all of us. You, me, Richard, even John. . . . We've all been affected by one man, and I feel so fucking helpless."

She rarely used such language, and her use of it now seemed to amuse Jake. He grinned, and all she could think of was how good he looked. The booze had blurred his hard edges, and he was in need of a shave. The stubble on his cheeks and his chin had a silvery sheen here and there, signs of stress that failed to show in more obvious ways. It all accentuated rather than lessened his appeal. Crazily, Liz wanted to go to him and ease the care lines from that hard face, kiss away the dreadful situation they found themselves in, lose herself in him, just for a little while. She resisted, aware that it was a mad impulse, that it wouldn't solve anything. "It's been a while since I've seen you this pissed," he said.

"I don't like being manipulated."

"Funny you should mention manipulation. The prints on the rosewood box belong to Simms. I had Charlie run them through the database, and he ran across something interesting."

"He has a record."

"You *knew*?"

An uneasy shrug. "He told me."

"And you still hired him?"

The "you idiot" was implied. Liz shouldn't have felt the need to defend her actions. Jake was suspicious of everyone and everything, always looking for hidden motives, for the angle being worked, even when none existed. It was part of what made him such a good agent. "Yes, I hired him. Kenneth's brush with the law happened when he was barely out of his teens. He hasn't had a single incident since. Nothing more serious than a parking ticket. He'd started over, and he's struggling." Another shrug. She hugged her arms. "I know what that's like. I felt sorry for him, and sorry for Mary."

Jake's snort said he didn't buy a word of it. "Peepers don't quit, Liz. They graduate to more serious offenses. You know that. If I were you, I'd put a lock on my underwear drawer."

"Very funny. Kenneth isn't involved in any of this. I'd stake my life on that."

Jake didn't believe it. She could see it in his eyes, that Kenneth Simms was at the top of his short list of suspects. Despite her protestations, he would stay on Simms's case until he either turned up evidence or hit a dead end.

"What about Turner?"

Liz shook her head. "Samuel doesn't drive."

He silently studied her, and she was afraid to ask what he was thinking. She changed the subject as quickly as she could, redirecting the conversation. "What about the locations of the burials? If the Redwing girl was taken from Mantoot and brought here, that's what? Eight, ten miles?"

"Eleven, counting the cow path he used to access your property. I drove that road, and I didn't pass a single vehicle—not one. He knows this area, and he picked it deliberately, because it was secluded, and because it's connected to you. Either he lives around here, or he's spending a lot of time preplanning. This guy is organized. Very organized, and he's definitely no novice. He may have been doing something similar for a long time before Virginia." He pinned her with a look, his dark blue gaze riveting. "I think we need to concentrate on the Stringer girl. That's where you come in."

Liz frowned. "I've already told you everything I know."

"Can't you try to tune in, or something?"

She shook her head. "I can't."

Fletch came to Jake and sat down beside him, close enough to receive any demonstrations of affection this sympathetic human might bestow. Within a few seconds, Sandy appeared, hoping for equal treatment. "You can't? Or you won't?"

"Same thing."

"Is it?"

"I can't just turn it on or off," she insisted, though turning it off after Fiona's death was precisely what she'd done.

Jake didn't seem to hear her. He kept pushing. "You said you felt what the kid was feeling when you touched the thing Rhy's daughter was holding. So why don't we pay a visit to the girl's parents?"

It was a sound idea, but one that Liz resisted.

She didn't like feeling pressured, not by Jake, or anyone. Besides, she'd been where they were now, and she knew how it felt to have a child missing. Anyway, John had expressed confidence that the girl had run away, and even if she believed her impressions to be correct, there was always a chance she was wrong. In fact, she was hoping with everything she had that such was the case. She wanted to be wrong. She wanted the monster who had taken and killed Fiona to disappear into the ether, and for the Stringer girl to be okay.

When she answered Jake, her voice sounded small and far away. "We're getting nowhere with this. I've told you all I know right now." She massaged her temples where a tension headache had blossomed. "I need some fresh air. I think I'll walk out to the stable and check on Anglican. He's doing better, but I still worry."

"I'll come with you," he offered.

"Don't, please. It's just across the drive, and I really need a few minutes alone to clear my head."

Jake didn't argue the point; he just waited a few beats—time enough for her to walk across the lawn—then he opened the door and went out onto the porch, where he lit a cigar. Leaning against a porch post, he watched as the barn lights flicked on and spilled from the open door onto the lawn. The dogs were with her, and he was here, so he knew she'd be okay. He wasn't so sure about his own well-being.

Having Liz in his life again had rekindled all the old hurt, the longings, the conflicting emotions.

He loved her.

In fact, he'd never stopped loving her, and staying at the farm, being close to her, working with her, was the hardest thing he'd done since giving her her freedom. He could protect Liz . . . but there was no one to protect him, no one to pick up a shattered Jake when she broke his heart a second time.

Shep left his sister Rachel's house at precisely eleven thirty-seven P.M. Rachel's doors and windows were locked, and her security lights lit the yard almost as brightly as a football field on game night. Confident that his sister, niece, and nephew were safe for the moment, Shep took the cruiser past the café on Main and turned right at the stop sign onto Pingwing Hollow Road. Pingwing Hollow Road was a shortcut that cut directly through the dark heart of Devil's Cleft, just north of Liz Moncrief's farm. If he took a left when he came to the fork in the road, he would emerge a few miles down the highway from Stooley's Roadhouse.

He motored past several mansions, newly built, sprawling demonstrations of the net worth of the wealthy riffraff invading the Catskills. "This place is almost as bad as Colorado. Next thing you know, Mel Gibson'll be movin' in next door." He hit the siren just for fun, flicking on the strobe and cackling to himself.

"Like they have any right being here," Shep muttered to himself. "Three cars in the drive and one BMW in the carport area. Least they could do is to buy American-made."

As soon as he passed the last house, Shep flicked off the siren and cruised on down the road. The plan was to hang around the highway for a while, trawl for DUIs, then circle back past Rachel's before he returned to the station. There was just the smallest bit of drizzle from an overcast and moonless sky. On nights like this the darkness swallowed up the headlights, and even with high beams, visibility was reduced to a few yards. Shep had reached the age when prescription glasses were a must after the sun went down, and in the rush to get to his sister's place that evening, he'd left them lying on the kitchen table.

He didn't need glasses to see the orange glow above Vanderbloon's Woods, however. He slowed the car and stared, at first unsure what he was seeing. A heartbeat later, he reached for the radio mike. "Car One to Dispatch, I've got a ten-seventy on Pingwing Hollow Road. Location: Devil's Cleft, just north of the Moncrief place. Over?"

"Ten-four, Shep." The radio mike belted out static, then Sarah's voice sounded again. "You want me to relay to the fire department? Over?"

"Affirmative. I'm gonna ride on over and have a look around. Over and out."

Shep hung up the mike and picked up some speed. The closer he got, the brighter the glow was. As he neared the blaze, he saw Samuel Turner. He was standing a few feet away from a brush pile that he had set alight, the firelight playing over his disfigured face and stark naked form. Shep stopped the cruiser and got out. "Boy, what the hell do you think you're doin'?"

Samuel muttered something incomprehensible and hurled his empty whiskey bottle at Shep's head. Shep ducked, but it still hit him a glancing blow on the top of his head, hard enough to force his jaws together and cause him to bite his tongue.

"You just assaulted an officer, you dim-witted jackass!" Grabbing Turner's right wrist, Shep wrenched it up behind his back, clamping handcuffs on him. Turner was taller than Shep, and his inhibitions had been shut down by a gulletful of cheap whiskey. He put up a fight, cracking Shep on the chin with a backhanded swing before the deputy finally wrestled him into the back of the patrol car.

Shep was breathing hard when he keyed the mike. "There goes the uphostery," he said under his breath. "Car One to Dispatch, over?"

"Ten-four, this is Sarah at Dispatch. Shep, where are you? Over?"

"I'm comin' in. The truck's just on scene. It was a brush fire, and I caught the instigator red-handed."

"You made an arrest? Over?"

"Damn straight, I did. But you might want to shield your eyes when we come in. It's Samuel T., and he's naked as a jaybird, not exactly a pretty picture. Over and out."

He was a shadow on the lightless porch by the time Liz had shed some of her frustration and gone back to the house. At first she thought he'd fallen asleep on the porch swing, yet as she approached, she knew that he was wide awake and watching. It was very like Jake, to hang back and watch over her, even when she didn't want him to. "You should be in bed," she said as she went slowly up the steps to the porch. "How are you ever going to heal properly if you take such lousy care of yourself?"

"I'd almost forgotten how the night sky looked in out-of-the-way places like this," he replied, voice quiet and contemplative as he reached out and caught her hand in his. "So many stars."

"City streetlights can blind you to a lot of things. Do you suppose she can see them? Jennifer Stringer? Can she look through that pipe and see the sky overhead? Or is she already dead? How long can she last in that coffin? One hour? Two? Less than?"

"Come on, Liz."

"How long?"

"That depends on how he set it up. If he provides an airway like he did with the others, then it should be enough to sustain her, hopefully, till we find her."

"Hopefully." She shook her head, pacing to the edge of the porch, turning back. "Is that what we're reduced to? A hope and a prayer that everything will turn out okay, and this kid won't run out of air before we find her? So she waits in the darkness, terrified, fighting off panic and the constriction of her lungs—"

He shot off the swing and took her by the shoulders. "For Christ's sake! Will you stop? Don't you see what you're doing? Distance yourself, damn it! It isn't your kid out there, and you're not helping anyone with this self-absorbed bullshit! Not you, not me, and not her."

His fingertips dug painfully into her flesh, a reminder that she lived and breathed while her daughter did not. Her reply felt forced out, laced with taut emotion. "Don't you get it? It *was* my child out there, Jake! Have you forgotten? Because I haven't. I live with that horror every day, I wake with it, I sleep with it. It never leaves me, not for one single moment."

"I haven't forgotten. How the hell could I forget? Don't you think I see her face in my nightmares? Don't you think I realize that if it hadn't been for me screwing up she would have been my kid? My daughter, Liz. How the hell can I forget?" His grip lessened, but he didn't let go. He was frowning down at her, and as she gulped in air, Liz was grateful for the lack of light. "We do the best we can with the knowledge we have, and sometimes it isn't enough. We're human, Liz, and humans are fallible. We trip and we fall, and we make miscalculations, but we do the best we can with what we have at the time."

And we cheat, and we lie, and we tear one another apart, Liz thought bitterly.

A small, vindictive part of her would have doused him with vitriol, but he was being sincere, and she couldn't deny the fact that they were past all that now. Yes, he had cheated . . . and she had kept their child's existence a secret, and now that child was dead.

He would never know her, never hold her, never look into her eyes . . . eyes that had been the same cerulean blue as the ones she now gazed into. They had hurt one another, and he was trying to help. She couldn't fault him for what happened here. None of it had been his doing.

He was a victim, just like Fiona, just like her. . . .

"My God," she said. "I really am out on a ledge, aren't I? Nothing like taking a leap from a five-story building and flattening your ex-husband."

"Don't worry, darlin'," he said, letting his voice slip quite naturally into its native Virginian drawl, "if you stumble or jump, I'll catch you. That's why I'm here."

Sweet, Liz thought. But, then, he could be very sweet, the consummate charmer when he wanted to be. He'd so thoroughly charmed her parents that her mother still sent him a birthday card every year on September tenth, and Jake played league softball with her dad.

She suspected that Jake talked to her parents more often than she herself did. Her mother had never sent Richard a card, but they really hadn't connected with Richard like they had with Jake, despite her marriage to Jake being measured in nanoseconds instead of years. His hair had fallen onto his brow. Reaching up, she brushed it back. "How did we get here, Jake? How did everything get so damned crazy?"

He didn't answer, just drew her into his embrace and held her.

Liz released the breath she'd been holding. It felt so good to be in his arms. She needed his strength, needed someone to hold on to, especially now.

For a long time they stood in the shadows of the porch, oblivious to their surroundings, oblivious to everything but each other. Liz toyed with his collar, then allowed her hands to glide over his shoulders. Jake had a nice build, broad shoulders, deep chest, firm pecs. The rest of him wasn't bad, either. And he hadn't added much to his middle over the years. When her fingertips brushed his abs, she felt them contract. "Where are you goin' with this, Liz?"

"Inside," she said, tilting her face up. He kissed her, needing no further invitation, a long, hard kiss that left no doubt in either one of their minds about where the encounter was leading. When the kiss ended, Liz took his hand and led him into the house.

As she pushed the door closed, shutting out the night, he kissed her again, stroking her cheek with his fingertips. "It'll be all right, baby."

She kissed his cheek, his ear. "I wish I could believe that."

"Believe it. I'm here, and as long as I'm here, you're never alone."

Jake made it all right, at least for a little while. He kissed Liz and touched Liz in places that hadn't been touched by a man in so long, until he'd found her. He nuzzled her neck, worshiped her breasts, and made her ache for him. Then, when he was through toying with her, he pushed her back onto the sofa cushions and rose above her, wringing a passionate cry from the depths of her soul that sounded very much like his name.

Much later, they sat on the swing, Liz wrapped in Jake's arms and a blanket around them both. Darkness was fading, from black to charcoal, to the soft, muted gray of predawn. Liz watched the day break, dreading what lay ahead.

"You're going to town today, aren't you?"

Jake's voice was a low rumble, so sexy and rough-sounding that if they hadn't made love twice already, she would have climbed his frame right there on the swing. The time for avoidance, however, had just about run out.

"Yes."

"And you're going to tell Rhys everything?"

"I have to."

"Are you going to tell him about us?"

Us.

There it was. The expectations. The demands. The line drawn in the proverbial sand, and it was a confrontation she had invited. She couldn't blame him for asking, but she wasn't ready for more just yet. Maybe she never would be. "I need time."

She felt the body behind her tense. He let go a breath. "How much time?"

"I don't know." It was as much as she could give, as honest as she knew how to be at that moment, and it didn't satisfy him.

"If you're talking to Rhys, then I'm coming with you," Jake said. "And Liz? If you don't tell him to back the fuck off, I will."

Chapter Eleven

It was an unscrupulous, underhanded dirty trick, and the only way Liz could think of, spur of the moment, that would keep Jake from interfering. She'd spent most of the long sleepless night thinking about it; it was imperative that she meet with John alone. She had a hell of a lot of explaining to do, and she couldn't rectify the mess she'd made of things with two men she cared for while they were busy indulging in a testosterone-driven springtime strut. She needed time to state her case, to beg John's forgiveness, to convince him that she hadn't lost her mind—and she knew that nothing would be accomplished with Jake gloating because he'd been invited into her bed and John Rhys hadn't. Unfortunately, at the moment there was no reasoning with Jake. She tried, several times, and it always ended in an argument. He wasn't really giving her much choice in the matter.

She waited until he stepped into the shower, then she took his jeans and T-shirt out of the bathroom, ransacked the guest room, taking every item of apparel she could find and stuffing them all into the back of the hallway linen closet. Finally, she grabbed her sunglasses, keys to the SUV, and left.

It was after eight, and John's Blazer was already parked in its usual spot. As she stepped into the reception area, his deputy's voice came clearly from the open doorway. "John, you know he's a threat. Samuel's a ticking time bomb, and he's gonna blow up in our faces unless we do something about it."

"I hear you, Shep. I'm just not sure what you expect me to do. Samuel will be arraigned this morning for being drunk and disorderly, and a half dozen other misdemeanor charges. Magistrate Lawless will set bail, and Marge is gonna walk into his office and cut him a check to bail him out of another scrape. It's standard procedure under the statutes. There isn't a damn thing we can do to stop it."

"He burned his clothes, John. The asshole was reelin' drunk, and when I tried to apprehend him, he clocked me on the chin."

"Resisting arrest and assaulting an officer are two of the charges Samuel has to face. Look, I'm not trying to sweep this mess under the rug, but I can't hold him on the suspicion that he may do something. Samuel's rights are protected under the law, and my hands are tied, no matter how strongly I feel about it, but I am sorry about your jaw. If it bothers you too much, maybe you should call Kate and make an appointment to have an X ray."

"It's my pride that hurts," Margolis muttered. "And I have to explain to Marlene that our local nutcase is gonna be turned loose to do as he pleases. She's been a little spooked with all this weird stuff goin' on, and I told her I'd stay over. Normally, she works the late shift, but the hospital's shorthanded this week. Some kind of blue flu—only white, in this instance. A wage dispute.

She said she'd fill in on day shift until negotiations kick in and this thing's resolved."

"Well, it's a good thing she has you around," John told him.

"That and the .357 I got her for Christmas."

Rhys looked up as Liz paused to knock. "Liz? Is that you? This is a nice surprise." He came out of his chair, grasping her elbow with strong fingers, guiding her into the room.

"I'm sorry to interrupt." She felt suddenly awkward.

Margolis came out of his chair, settling his hat more securely on his head as he nodded to her. "Ms. Moncrief, have a seat. We're through here anyhow. John, I'll check in shortly."

Rhys smiled at Liz. "Come in. Would you like some coffee?"

"No, thanks," she said. "Would you mind if I close the door? I'd like a private word with you."

"Sounds serious."

"It is."

"I have a feeling I'm not going to like this," Rhys said, settling on a corner of his desk. "If it's about last night—"

Liz took a deep breath. No easy way out existed, and she had no choice except to plunge in and present him with the facts. "It's about me, and Jake, and Jennifer Stringer." She dug in her purse for her wallet, extracting her card, handing it to him. She'd gotten rid of all but one, and she wasn't sure why she'd kept it. "I told you that Jake was my ex-husband, and about my former position, but there's so much I didn't tell."

The door to the outer entrance opened and closed in the background, and the receptionist's voice sounded. "Sheriff Rhys is in conference with someone else. Excuse me, sir! You can't just go in there!"

The office door opened, and Jake stormed in. He was dressed in a damp T-shirt and faded black jeans, but it was obvious they weren't the clothes she'd hidden. His hair was wet, his handsome face dark as a thundercloud. "That was really shitty, Liz! In fact, it was worse than shitty. It was shitty and underhanded. I had to call my landlady to ask her to bring me something to wear and a lift here, and I'm not sure I like the look she gave me. Do you know what that's like? To be trapped in a towel and assessed sexually to within an inch of your reputation?"

Liz closed her eyes and sought calm. Could this situation get any worse? "Didn't I say that I wanted to do this alone?" she shot back in a furious whisper. "Alone means that you stay out of it. Will you please go home?"

"You haven't done such a great job of it so far, now have you?" Jake demanded. "Has it ever occurred to you that you might just need some backup?"

John Rhys settled back to watch the fireworks. "Would you two like some privacy, or maybe you'd care to clue me in as to what the hell is going on?"

Liz sighed, the sound of capitulation. "All right. You can stay, but I do this." She turned back to John, who was watching her closely. "The Cemetery Man is here because of me. You know about Quantico, but you don't know the whole truth."

John frowned. "I'm all ears. Why don't you fill me in?"

"My daughter was one of the Cemetery Man's victims," Liz said quietly. "I didn't tell you, or anyone, because I didn't want to be that person anymore. I didn't want the notoriety of being the FBI agent who lost her daughter to a serial murderer. I thought if I just disappeared, started over, that he would leave me in peace, but I was wrong—dreadfully, horribly wrong. I don't know what else to say except that I'm sorry, and offer my help in the Stringer case. I think I may be able to help, if you let me."

"That's all good to know," John said. "Especially the part about Jake, but Jen Stringer showed up at her grandmother's last night. She begged a ride from a neighbor. I anticipate a long talk with her about the dangers of getting into a car with anyone, but I'm glad she's okay."

"Yeah," Liz said, bewildered, relieved. "I'm glad, too."

"Jake, I realize you have a full dance card, but did you by any chance have time to review the coroner's report for the Redwing girl? I see there was a printout sent to you?"

Jake frowned. "Only a few hundred times. I intended to stop by and discuss it with you, but it appears we've both been preoccupied."

"Well, if you two are done here, and you have a minute, maybe we can do it now." When Jake didn't object, he continued. "From what I can see, there are a lot of similarities to previous victims. The weird thing is that Amanda Redwing's cause of death wasn't suffocation. It was carbon monoxide poisoning. What do you make of that?"

"My initial thought was that he's getting more creative, but there are other possibilities. We've suspected that there are two actors at work here, not one. So maybe this was a sympathy kill? Could be that something about the victim triggered remorse in one of our guys, and he decided to end her suffering."

"That makes sense, I suppose. Now, what do we do about it?"

Rhys was being particularly cooperative, almost deferential in a completely official capacity. Jake didn't know what to make of it.

"A press conference at this point might be a good idea. Get word out to the media, and work the sympathy angle. We need to remind these two that the kids had families, humanize them, twist the knife a little. I guarantee, he'll either be there, or he'll be watching. That may just work to our advantage."

"I'll make the arrangements," Rhys said. "You'll sit in?"

"Happy to, but first I have to pick my car up from Stooley's."

"Designated driver, huh? Well, that's a wise thing. We wouldn't want to see your name in the magistrate's docket with a DUI, now would we?" John rose from his chair, glancing out the window. "As a matter of fact, Shep's headed out that way. If you like, I'm sure he'd be glad to give you a lift."

Jake was just angry enough at Liz to jump on it. The kid was out of danger, and she could stew, as far as he was concerned. Besides, the investigation into Amanda Redwing's murder was all too real, and still ongoing. He had business to see to. "I may just do that." A last burning look at Liz, and Jake turned and stalked out.

There was a pause, then Rhys shook his head. "You know, I can't really blame him for being angry."

Liz shrugged. "He was being a shit, and he deserved it."

John sank back in his chair. "So you two are an item?"

Liz wasn't quite sure how to answer. There was no denying that she had feelings for Jake, that the embers of an old love affair still glowed brightly, but exclusivity was something they hadn't discussed. She was as honest with Rhys as she could possibly be. "I don't know what we are."

"Well, since it's a morning for honesty between friends, I'll tell you that I'm a fairly competitive guy. I don't mind some healthy competition, but I'm a little too old-fashioned for a threesome. Somehow, I get the impression that Jake wouldn't go for that, either."

Liz smiled. "I assure you, that was never my intention."

"Then we understand one another," John said. "Do you have plans for Labor Day? It's a big deal around here. Community picnic, fireworks... Guess I'll have to ask my sister, because I still don't have a date. Unless, of course, you're free?"

"Sheriff, you are full of surprises."

"Is that a 'yes'?"

"As it stands, I don't have plans, and I love fireworks."

"I noticed." John smiled. "Monday at noon on the old village green?"

"I'll look forward to it."

As Liz left the office, she heard John Rhys whistling softly to himself. She was relieved that John had been right about Jennifer Stringer, and that the girl was alive and well, but she was confused about the vibrations she'd picked up from the HitClip in his daughter Alicia's hand.

Liz dismissed it, all too glad to have been mistaken. Maybe the worst was over. Maybe the Cemetery Man would be satisfied with the havoc he had wreaked and crawl back into his sick fantasy world, content to relive the past. Yet, even as that thought came, she knew how unlikely it was to be true. Serial murderers killed to fulfill some dark need, and kept on killing until they were caught or killed, or jailed for some other crime and thereby prevented access to potential victims. They didn't just stop.

Jake spent the remainder of his morning in the impound garage working a twelve-inch-by-twelve-inch grid labeled E5. Most of the dirt had already been processed and had turned up no trace evidence. The weather was what the locals referred to as "close," so humid that working up a sweat could be achieved without even moving, and the lab coat and latex gloves he wore didn't help. Plying a dental pick to cautiously remove the soil, then sifting all through a series of screens beneath high-wattage portable Hallogen lights, he felt sweat gather under his arms and creep down his rib cage. Two officers from the crime lab in Albany worked in similar sweat-drenched fashion and utter silence a few feet away.

It was meticulous work that required dogged patience, a sharp eye for the smallest speck that seemed out of place, and allowed no room for error. He was grateful to the lab rats for allowing him to get his hands dirty, and contribute, even if it hadn't gotten them anywhere. At least he was doing something, instead of pacing the apartment and fuming over Liz's seeming inability to make the right choices.

An old, established love over a flash in the pan like Rhys? She might be attracted to the guy, but there was no way it would last. Liz needed a challenge, and John Rhys wasn't it.

Jake felt sure about that, and the thought made him a little more confident and a little less angry as he worked the sifter. The glare of the overhead lights was hard on the eyes, making the steamy atmosphere of the garage even more oppressive. Sweat ran down his face and throat, soaking the front of his T-shirt, but he ignored it and kept working until the last of the dirt had been processed.

Not so much as an eyelash, not a piece of lint. Nothing.

Later that same afternoon, Liz drove to Julianne's shop. Explaining her tangled past to her friend wasn't something Liz looked forward to, and she was almost relieved when she saw the CLOSED sign displayed in the window. She rifled her handbag for a pen and paper, finally settling for a hardware-store receipt. Scrawling a note on the back to inform her friend of her visit, she signed it with her initials and folded the note, slipping it over the brass knocker, just as a shadow fell over her. Liz glanced up into Samuel T. Turner's half-ruined face and nearly screamed.

With his eye patch, Samuel Turner was a dark, hulking man with a disfigured face. Without it, he was the stuff of nightmares. It was all Liz could do to meet his single-eyed gaze. The other socket was shrunken and dark, his cheek and jaw horribly drawn and heavily scarred from being blown half away. "Shop's closed," he said, his voice distorted and hollow-sounding.

He reeked of tobacco, sweat, and alcohol, but the knowledge he'd been drinking despite the early hour wasn't what raised Liz's hackles. There was a darkness about Samuel Turner—not darkness, she amended, blackness—something more sensed than seen and more than a little frightening. She didn't look for his aura; she didn't need to. She could feel the negativity projecting from him, like a black, towering wave, cold as ice. Repelled by it, she stepped back without even realizing it. "What do you want?" Liz demanded, determined not to show her rising fear or anything that might be interpreted as weakness.

Samuel chuckled, an evil sound. "What do you think? You think I forgot?"

"I don't play games, Samuel. Move aside. I have business to take care of." Liz stepped to the side, but Samuel moved to block her. "I said move aside." She sounded stronger, angry.

"Don't like folks orderin' me around—'specially women."

Liz's pulse kicked up a notch. He was at least eight inches taller than she was, and a good deal heavier, and if he wanted to overpower her, he could easily do it. "And I don't like being threatened," Liz warned him, hoping her tone would be sufficient to put an end to this sadistic game he was playing. "Step aside and let me pass or you'll wish the hell you had."

His answering laugh broke off abruptly when Jake grabbed him by the scruff of his neck, slamming him face-first into the clapboard wall of Julianne's shop. "Move, and I'll take you apart." He was covered in sweat, his face darkened with a fine layer of grit, and Liz had never seen such a welcome sight.

Samuel hawked and spat, aiming for Jake's shoe, missing. "Call the cops," he said. "You really think they give a rat's ass? They'll let me go, just like always."

"As much as I hate to agree with him, I'm afraid he's right," Liz said.

"Listen, pal. If you see the lady on the street, you turn and go the other way. You so much as glance in her direction and you're gonna be in a world of shit, courtesy of yours truly. You got that?" Jake gave Turner another push into the wall to get his attention, then released him.

Turner stepped back, gathering his equilibrium, then, sending a chilling glare over his shoulder at Liz, he stumbled off, turned the corner at the end of the building, and disappeared into the alley.

Jake faced Liz. "What the hell was that all about?"

"He came up behind me. He was trying to intimidate me, and I'm afraid he succeeded," she said, pushing trembling fingers through her loose chestnut hair. "I haven't been that shaken in a long time." Liz tried to shed her nervous reaction and regain some calm. It wasn't easy.

"What do you know about him?"

She shrugged. "Just that he's very dark on the inside."

"I pulled his records. He's got a hell of a rap sheet. All misdemeanor charges. His old lady bails him out. She's on a major guilt trip, thanks to pulling him back from the edge. In my opinion, she should have given him a push instead. He's a fucking waste of air."

She couldn't see his eyes behind his dark glasses, and there was no way to tell what he was thinking.

"Do you think Samuel's involved in this?" Liz asked.

"Well, we know he didn't kill the Stringer kid." He glanced at the mouth of the alley where Turner had disappeared. "I don't know, but I don't think there's enough going on upstairs for him to be anything but somebody's patsy. He's too unpredictable, too uncontrolled, and a little too steeped in alcohol to be much of a planner."

Samuel would have been a convenient suspect, but Jake was right. It didn't fit. Eliminating him brought them full circle however, back to having no leads. "I'm relieved Jennifer Stringer's safe," Liz admitted, but she left a lot unsaid. She couldn't forget the brief but frightening episode at Rachel Rhys's place. The flash of empathic insight had come uninvited, and it had been far too strong for her to dismiss it out of hand.

Alicia Rhys had said the miniature audio player belonged to Jennifer. But Jennifer was at her grandmother's, not being held captive in a cramped, dark place as Liz had supposed.

It was the first time her intuitive skills had failed her. She could blame the failure on the stress of Amanda Redwing's body being found on her property, but having a valid reason didn't help her feel any less unnerved by it.

A black Chevy pickup stopped on the street. The driver's window whirred down, and Dr. Bridger's square jaw jutted out. He wore shades the color of charcoal, and he looked fit and tan. "Well, if it isn't my instructor. Lesson's not canceled, is it? You seem a little busy."

"It's not until four P.M.," Liz said.

Bridger smiled, tapping the face of his watch with two fingers. "It's almost sixteen hundred hours."

Liz glanced at her watch. "Oh, God. You're right. I completely lost track of time. I'll be right there," she told Bridger, heading for the Explorer. When she glanced back, Jake was gone. He hadn't even suggested accompanying her, and she guessed quite rightly that he was still angry over her hiding his clothes.

The autopsy report was cut-and-dried, revealing little beyond the basics. Jake had gone over it a hundred times in the past week, and his conclusions were always the same. The official cause of Amanda Redwing's death was asphyxiation due to carbon monoxide poisoning. The toxicology reports revealed no indication that the kid had been drugged. There were no ligature marks, no evidence of sexual assault, and the bruises and scrapes she had sustained were judged to have occurred after burial, as were the splinters found imbedded under her fingernails. Stomach contents had been digested, but an empty snack-sized bag and apple core had been found in the coffin. Time of death was estimated at twenty-four to twenty-eight hours before she was found and her body recovered. Since she had been missing for three days before she was discovered, that left a large chunk of time unaccounted for, and raised a host of questions.

Where had she been during that time? Had she been held somewhere and, if so, how? There weren't any physical signs of restraint, so how had he managed it?

And what about the food? An apple and a bag of chips, the typical male idea of nutrition . . . but why would he feed these kids and provide them with water when he was planning to kill them? It sure as hell was contradictory behavior. "Contradictory, hell. It's downright schizophrenic. Unless there really are two of them."

That had to be it. One who was ruthless, and one who was remorseful. It was the only thing that made sense.

Jake read through the report twice more, then read it again, but nothing jumped out at him the third time, either. The autopsy reports for the Redwing kid mirrored the others, except for the carbon monoxide as the cause of death. No fiber evidence inside the coffin, no DNA under the fingernails. Only Fiona Airhardt had put up a struggle. The rest seemed to have gone along with their killer willingly. He tried to picture that. He imagined being coaxed into a coffinlike structure and lying passive while the lid was nailed down, but it didn't compute.

Kids had a fight-or-flight response that was as strong as their adult counterparts, and though they could be bullied, they should have fought back. All but one of them hadn't. The question was why?

Had the killer somehow managed to subdue that primitive response? And if so, how? The toxicology screens hadn't revealed anything suspicious. So how had he accomplished this feat?

Trust. That had to be it.

But why would Amanda Redwing have trusted this individual? What was it about this guy that put the vics at ease?

It might have to do with his appearance. Maybe he looked like a kindly uncle, or grandfatherly type? Maybe his catch-line was sufficiently convincing . . . *or maybe he wasn't a stranger.*

Jake took a Heineken from the refrigerator and uncapped it, but he didn't drink.

They'd worked that angle before but dismissed it as unlikely. What were the odds that seven victims in seven different towns and two states would all know and trust this guy enough to get into a vehicle with him? All but Liz's daughter.

There was one thing of which he was absolutely

certain. No one would willingly accompany Samuel Turner anywhere. In fact, Turner's ruined face was a hard sight for Jake to take without flinching, and enough to make an adolescent girl run screaming. If Turner was involved—and Jake hadn't ruled him out of the murder of the Redwing kid— he wasn't the primary actor.

He lifted the photos of the dental-stone cast of the tire tracks. There was little more than a thin rim of tread showing that hadn't been obliterated by the John Deere's dirt-digger rear tires, but it had been enough to identify type. "Firestone all-season radials," he said aloud. And the width between the wheel base indicated that they were looking for a van.

"Simms has a van, and he works for Liz. If he were seen out there, he could easily explain it, and who would question him?" Jake still hadn't ruled Simms out as the perpetrator of the attempted break-in. Rhys had spoken with Simms about it and then dismissed him as an unlikely suspect. Jake wasn't as easily satisfied. He didn't like Simms, though he couldn't say why. There was just something about him, something dissatisfied, an underlying meanness that simmered just beneath the surface. He was disgruntled, but was he disgruntled enough to try to terrorize Liz?

And what about TCM? Was there a connection? Kenneth Simms might be able to snatch a victim, but that would have created defense wounds, and possibly even DNA material under the fingernails, which would have then been deposited on the lid of the makeshift coffins—none of which had been found. And then there was his speech impediment. Simms wasn't self-confident enough to talk a victim into a vehicle.

The UNSUB had to know the victims. At this point it's

the only thing that makes sense. Jake took a long swal-
low, but the burning certainty that he'd just hit on
something solid lasted long after the bottle was emptied. He went through everything pertaining to the
victims' backgrounds but found nothing glaring.

There has to be a connection. I'm just not seeing it.
He picked up the phone to call Liz, then put it
down again. Her childish tactic to keep him from
telling John Rhys to back off had been successful,
but he still wasn't happy about it. He had no doubt
that Rhys had made the most of the opportunity
her visit that morning created, and asked her out
yet again, and he could only speculate as to whether
or not Liz had agreed to go.

He didn't know and couldn't guess where this
thing between Liz and the sheriff was going, and
he sure as hell couldn't stop it. But that didn't
mean that he had to roll over and play dead for
Liz, or let her walk all over him.

If he was going to get philosophical about the
whole thing, he would have to chalk up the mixed
signals she was sending to fear. Fear of failure, fear
of commitment, fear of making the same mistake
twice. It didn't matter how often he told her that
her heart was safe with him, she would continue to
judge him by past mistakes until he proved to her
that she could trust him not to become a blither-
ing ass a second time.

"Once burned . . ." He sank onto a chair at the
kitchen table, the top of which was strewn with crime
scene photos. "Patience, Jake. Patience. She'll either come around, or she won't."

It sounded good. Forceful, decisive. It sounded
like he had it all worked out where Liz was concerned, and it was too damn bad he didn't believe
a word of it.

Nursing his beer, he walked to the window and

stood looking out at Main Street. A white van with a luggage rack on the roof and a generous helping of putty and primer pulled into a parking space near the hardware store. As Jake watched, a man got out, put a coin in the parking meter, and walked into the hardware store. A small man, dirty blond hair and a baseball cap. "Well, well, well. Mr. Simms. What perfect timing."

It took Jake all of thirty seconds to set aside his beer and reach the street. Rhys couldn't produce probable cause to obtain a warrant, and Simms, having been interviewed twice, was reluctant to co-operate. The sheriff had to work within the letter of the law. Jake, at the moment, had no such re-strictions. Officially, he was a man on administra-tive leave, enjoying the sights and sounds of down-town Abundance, and he wasn't bound by any-thing but the dictates of his own conscience, which allowed a lot of leeway.

He went directly to the van and found four mis-matched tires. Not a Firestone among them, and they were worn. The tread from the vehicle found by Amanda Redwing's grave was deep, the source tire fairly new.

"Hey!" Jake heard the shout coming from the direction of the hardware, and knew it was Simms without glancing up. "W-what the hell are you d-doin'? G-get aw-way from there!"

Jake straightened to his full height, looking down on the smaller man. "Calm down, Kenneth. I was just having a look at your tires, that's all. It's nothing to get upset about."

"You've g-got n-no right! I d-didn't d-do nothin' wrong!"

"Did I say you did?" Jake asked. "No one's accus-ing you of anything. I was just curious, is all. Did you know you've got four different tires? I think that you've been taken. They're supposed to come in a set."

"I d-didn't buy 'em. I f-found 'em." Kenneth crossed in front of the van and opened the driver's door. With a last glare in Jake's direction, he got in, hit the ignition, and drove off.

"One down," Jake said. "One to go."

The old Congregationalist Church was listed on the registry of historic buildings. Legend had it that a young officer from Washington's army had been wrongly accused of espionage against the American cause and hanged from a tree in the churchyard by a group of vigilantes. As the executioner rode off into the night, a deserting member of his band stayed behind to cut the officer's body down and was rewarded with the fright of his life when the hanged man came back to life. The giant maple was long gone, falling victim to a lightning strike in the 1880s, but a brass plaque marked the spot where it had once stood.

The colonial officer, Draegan Mattais Youngblood, was one of Abby's forefathers. Over the years, the church, which belonged to Catherine Youngblood, matriarch of the Youngblood family, had fallen into disrepair. The upkeep on the family estate had taxed Abby's aunt's dwindling resources so severely that there had been no funds to spare for the upkeep of the old stone church . . . until Matt entered the picture.

His last novel had been at the top of the *New York Times* bestseller list for thirteen weeks, and with another title just arrived in bookstores receiving critical acclaim, his career, for the moment, was looking pretty solid. Matt had wandered around the church property plenty of times. He'd gotten a key from Catherine and assessed the old building. There was something about it that drew him, that invited quiet contemplation, an aura of peace he'd never felt before coming to Abundance. On the day he found out Abby was having his baby, he'd met privately with her aunt and purchased the property with the idea of a complete renovation in mind. He'd kept the purchase a secret from Abby, intending to give it to her as a wedding present, the perfect cottage for the perfect family. It had been a damn good plan, except for one small hitch: he couldn't convince Abby to marry him, and he hadn't been able to face coming to the church in over two weeks.

Matt walked to the edge of the woods and stood staring down at the headstones. Many were leaning, the tall, rounded stones washed bone white by the passing decades. One had fallen down completely. As he approached, the fresh mound on the end was readily apparent. No one had been buried on the property in decades. Catherine wouldn't allow it. "Now, how the hell did that get here?"

He dropped onto his heels for a closer look. A galvanized pipe protruded from the ground at one end. The pipe was capped off—sealed, and it looked new. Matt took out his pocket knife and probed the shallow mound. Six inches of earth and the blade struck a solid object. Scraping a small area away, he uncovered the corner of the wooden box. He made the call from the phone in his truck. "Jake? It's Matt. Get Rhys and meet me at the church on the Youngblood estate. I think I just found somethin'."

Kenneth Simms forked the trampled straw and cold manure from Faerie King's stall, loading it directly onto the manure spreader. Jersey Delacour was working in the tack room mending harness, something the older man hated to do. Arthritis made Jersey's hands stiff and the task harder than it should have been.

Kenneth knew about doing things that went against the grain. He didn't like working near the horses; the sheer size and power of the animals intimidated him, and he didn't like the way they looked at him. He'd heard once that animals could sense things, that they could smell fear, and he wondered if they could smell the blood on his hands?

Kenneth wouldn't have cared, except for them being so much bigger and stronger than he was. Any one of the animals could trample someone his size, or pin him against a stall, and he didn't like feeling wary and helpless. Wariness and helplessness were deeply ingrained in his personality. *She'd* seen to that, and every day of his life his wife Mary reinforced it.

Mary whined continuously. She complained that they didn't have a nicer place to live, she said there wasn't enough money, she wondered why he settled for menial jobs when he could have commanded higher wages, she berated him for his lack of ambition, and she used the baby as an excuse to sit on her fat ass in front of the TV all day while he sought odd jobs, repaired things, and worked for a woman who looked down her pretty little nose at his inability to take proper care of his own.

Oh, she made every attempt to hide it, but he knew what his employer was thinking when she looked at him.

Liz Moncrief lived well. She had a nice house, a lot of land, and she managed to thumb her nose at the rest of the townsfolk. Kenneth resented her for that, resented the low wages she paid him when she could have given him more . . . resented the way he had to greet her, hat in hand, stuttering so badly when she looked at him that he could barely squeeze out a sentence. He could have handled his work and Jersey's too, but Liz Moncrief had decided to keep him in his place, in line, behind a man whose skin wasn't even white.

He put another pitchfork of horseshit onto the spreader, which Jersey would hitch to the tractor and spread on the fields, listening to voices outside. Coming closer, getting louder, each word clearer than the last. She was putting Faerie King in the paddock, talking to Dr. Bridger. Kenneth muttered to himself, a clearly spoken sentence without a single stuttering syllable, something that didn't happen very often. The door opened, and sunlight flooded the center aisle of the stables, hitting him in the face like the beam of light from a police helicopter, just like in the movies. For a moment he stood frozen, unable to move, barely breathing. . . . Then, gradually, he regained control and straightened.

"I have him in the first stall," Liz Moncrief said. "He seems to like that. Anglican is at the rear of the stables. He's needed as much quiet as I can provide, and they don't get along very well."

"You talk as though they have personalities," the dentist replied. "They're horses, animals." Kenneth stole a glance at the man, their gazes meeting briefly, clashing. Kenneth looked pointedly away, breaking the eye contact as he went back to mucking the stalls.

Liz Moncrief shook her head in disbelief at his comment, and Kenneth thought privately that Bridger had made a huge misstep. "I've worked with horses most of my life, and they definitely have personalities. If you want to get into Faerie King's good graces, offer him a candy bar and speak softly when you talk to him. He loves sweets, and he hates anything jarring. You may not know it, but you've chosen a spirited but sensitive animal for your first horse. Military bluff, good-humored or not, won't impress him."

"Candy?" Bridger frowned. "What about good dental hygiene?"

Liz Moncrief laughed. "Spoken like a dentist. His teeth are sound, and a treat now and then won't hurt him."

"Well, I suppose one method of control is as good as another."

"It's not about c-c-control," Kenneth said, drawing their attention. "It's to get him t-to like you. He n-needs to know you're his friend, n-not someone who's g-gonna hurt him."

"Kenneth's right. It isn't about power, it's about persuasion. You just need to win him over. He's still edgy around you, but he'll get over it."

"Just d-don't p-push too hard," Kenneth put in. "With F-faerie K-king, I m-mean."

"So much good advice, and a lot to think about. Kind of like winning over a nervous patient, isn't it? Only he's a lot bigger than the average eight-year-old. Speaking of which, I should get back. The school year starts soon. Time to get organized."

"That's right. You do the annual checkups for the district?"

"Kids love me. They relate to my inquisitive streak. I do have one, you know. And I can be very persuasive when I need to be." He smiled, turning to Kenneth Simms. "Thank you, sir, for the valuable advice. I'll be sure to remember it." He stuck out his hand. Kenneth looked down at it, then reluctantly shook it. When the dentist offered it to

Liz, Kenneth interrupted the handshake before it happened, moving suddenly, bumping into Bridger.

"S-sorry. I'm just in k-kind of a hurry to f-finish. M-my wife, Mary. She's expecting m-m-me."

"No harm done," Bridger said quickly, forcefully. "Kenneth, is it? I haven't said anything to upset you?"

Kenneth shook his head, turning back to his chores. "J-just need to f-finish, th-that's all."

Bridger whistled to himself as he walked to his truck. Liz watched him go. When the black Chevy Silverado drove off, she turned to Kenneth Simms. "Kenneth, is everything okay? Mary isn't having problems with the baby, is she?"

"N-no, ma'am. S-sorry. I j-just d-don't like that guy. He's pushy."

"He can be a little overwhelming sometimes, but he seems an all-right sort—a family man. He has kids. Besides, I need the income. The horse sure acts odd around him, though. It's almost like he doesn't like his scent. Maybe he can pick something up off his clothing—antiseptic, or something." She shrugged and changed the subject. "Do you need a ride home?"

"Jersey'll d-drop me."

Liz left the barn, and Kenneth, who leaned on the handle of the pitchfork, stared after her with a look of pure rage.

Chapter Twelve

It was almost midnight and Jake was once again headed the wrong way down the primrose path. He'd given himself a brief cooling-off period of a couple of days—days of working side by side with Rhys and Company excavating the second grave site and preparing the exhausting search for evidence, but forty-eight hours hadn't helped put things in perspective. He tried to tell himself that the trip to Liz's farm was more than merely masochistic; it was crucial: he needed his notebook computer and his leather overnight bag, both of which he'd left at Liz's house in his heat to get to Rhys's office the morning of their last blow-up. He needed the laptop, yet he also couldn't completely deny that somewhere in the back of his mind he was nursing the vain hope that a miracle would happen and Liz would ask him to stay.

He didn't like to admit it, but he'd been miserable without her. Even the time they spent at one another's throats was preferable to time spent alone with his nightmares, and it seemed that he couldn't close his eyes these days without waking in a cold sweat, heart pulsing so violently it seemed it would explode against his ribs. Maybe there was a correlation between the two: Liz and the night terrors. But, no, actually the time he'd spent in Liz's bed was the only dreamless sleep he'd had in almost two years. Maybe Liz was the ticket to getting a firm grip on reality.

Or maybe he was as crazy as Dr. Dread had indicated.

"I sure as hell didn't ask for any of this," he said to no one in particular. He was the only one in the Buick, to which Rufus Vanderhorn had given a clean bill of health earlier that afternoon. Matt had gone home, so the misery-loves-company thing had fallen flat. Not that he wasn't happy for Monroe. After everything his friend had been through, he deserved a hellishly big break, and maybe he'd finally gotten one.

As soon as the news had reached the Youngblood estate of Matt's gruesome discovery, Abby had sought him out. Jake had witnessed the reunion, noticed how the pregnant blonde looked at Monroe, and envy had eaten a gaping hole right through him. "Matthew, you are one lucky son of a bitch, and if you're smart you'll never do anything to screw it up."

Abby had taken her man home, and Jake had been left to work the case with Rhys and Margolis. The deputy had been quieter than usual as they cataloged and processed the site with the help of the same borrowed three-man team who'd helped excavate Amanda Redwing's grave on Liz's farm. Margolis hadn't indulged in a single caustic remark, and Jake surmised the gravity of the situation weighed as heavily on the deputy as it did on the rest of them.

Another murder, another grave, and no one

could hazard a guess as to what came next. The only sure bet was that TCM would continue to kill until he was caught.

Rhys had performed the preliminaries well enough, though Jake was not about to let him off the hook when it came to Liz. The sheriff continued to be a major thorn in Jake's side on that score. Not only had he picked up on their affair, he hadn't backed off. Instead, he just kept pushing . . . and Liz wasn't helping matters. She refused to tell the sheriff that she and Jake were lovers, and she didn't even attempt to discourage his deepening interest.

Just thinking about it put Jake in a black mood. By the time he reached the farm he was ripe for a confrontation. The house was dark and the Explorer was gone. "How many times do I have to tell her to leave a light on?" He was just about to turn around and go when headlights bounced along the lane a quarter mile away. He got out of the car and leaned against the door to wait, crossing his arms over his chest. If it was Liz, then he had a few choice words for her. If it wasn't, then he'd set himself up as the welcoming committee.

The four-door Ford raised a cloud of dust. The black lab saw him and barked a welcome out the open window, his tail swishing. "Maybe you'd care to tell me where the hell you've been?" he said as she opened the driver's door and stepped out. He hadn't meant for it to sound like the demand of a jealous husband, but in a way, it was. He was an ex-husband, and there was no denying the jealousy that prodded him into acting like a total jackass.

She took a few bags out of the front seat, before turning to face him. "Excuse me, but do I answer to you? Because I was under the impression that you were a guest in my home, not the other way around."

"A guest," Jake repeated, confused. That one had come right out of left field to smack him in the center of the forehead.

"A guest, Jake . . . as in the person who occupies the guest room at the top of the stairs. What is wrong with you? You were easier to get along with after you'd consumed a half-pint of bourbon. Do you have male PMS, or something?"

"I thought that . . ." he began. Then, "Never mind what I thought. You haven't heard, have you? It's all over the local news."

"I've been a little busy, Jake. Besides, I don't have a television, and I don't listen to the radio."

"That's right," Jake said, "I forgot. It makes it a whole lot easier to stick your head in the sand that way. They found another body, a woman."

Her expression changed, and the spark went out of her eyes. Jake hated himself for being the one to kill it. It wasn't supposed to be this way. He was supposed to be the one who made her feel alive, not the one who helped the Cemetery Man break her spirit.

"Oh, God. Where? Where did they find her?"

"At the old churchyard. Matt bought the place and has been restoring it. He was taking care of some things when he noticed the grave."

He saw her brace herself. "Do they know who it is?"

"Yep. Harriet Stringer, the kid's aunt."

"Oh my God. The aunt gave her the device, didn't she? It wasn't Jennifer I was picking up on, it was Jennifer's aunt."

"It looks that way," Jake admitted. "I was helping Rhys and Margolis at the burial site. The coroner took possession of the remains early yesterday. Your friend Rhys and I wrapped things up and I came straight here."

She brushed at the grime on his T-shirt. "You didn't even clean up."

All pretense of coming to pick up his things had fled. "You were a little more important." A shrug, but he couldn't manage nonchalance. "I needed to know you were okay."

Liz didn't feel okay. Another killing, so close to home. She couldn't help feeling responsible. She couldn't help thinking that maybe if she'd opened up to John earlier, this could have been prevented.

The Cemetery Man was close by, and she was the reason that the sleepy Catskill Mountain town had become a killing field. She hugged her packages close and struggled to contain the overwhelming sense of panic. "He's not going to stop like before. He's going to keep on killing."

"It looks that way, yeah."

"This must have hit John hard. His department is understaffed and ill-equipped to handle something of this magnitude."

"All that concern for Rhys, when he's had an on-site expert from the very beginning—an expert who isn't even getting paid, and who hasn't exactly been made to feel welcome. "You'll forgive me if I don't sympathize with Rhys's predicament."

"Jake, you sound jealous. John's problems are very real."

He stiffened slightly. "And mine aren't? I'm as much a part of this investigation as John-Boy, in fact, this asshole has been keeping me awake nights a hell of a lot longer. The sheriff refused to see reality when it was pointed out to him!"

"I'm not dismissing your concerns," Liz insisted. "And this is not a competition."

"It's not? Are you sure about that? Because it sure feels like one from where I'm standing." He reached out to her, his open palm gliding over her warm skin, fingertips brushing her temple, the gentle velvety curve of her cheek, the shadowed hollow beneath. "Throw me a bone, Liz. Give me a little hope that we can get back to where we once were. I'm dyin' here."

Liz put down the bags she was holding and put her arms around him. She could feel the solid, steady beat of his heart, and she could feel the ache of wanting, of loving, and not feeling loved in return, an ache she was forced to own. "We can't go back," she said. "You know that. We can't erase the hurt, or the lies, no matter how much we want to." She wasn't just talking about his infidelity. There was so much more to it than that. So much that he would never know.

She felt the tension drain out of him and realized he'd been holding his breath. Reaching up on her toes, she stroked his face and kissed his lips, a gentle kiss meant to reassure. "Let's just take it slowly, and see where it leads. You're here with me, and I am grateful for that. I couldn't have gotten through this without you."

Jake's arms tightened around her and he buried his face in the silken fall of her hair. Liz kept the embrace for a moment, then stepped back, grasping his hand. "Have you eaten?"

He looked confused for a few seconds, then shook his head. "Late yesterday, but I had coffee—"

"Caffeine overload. That explains your mood." He reached for the bags, but Liz beat him to it. "Come on, Spiderman. I'll fix you a plate while you get cleaned up."

Jake wolfed his food and sat down in Liz's favorite chair by the cold stone hearth. He must have been exhausted, because when Liz came into the great room after tidying up the kitchen, he was asleep. She felt her heart soften as she stared down at him. "I don't deserve you," she whispered, tears filling her eyes as she turned away.

A tepid bath made her feel more human. With her hair piled loosely on the top of her head, she toweled away the moisture and slid into her black silk pajamas. The indicator from the pregnancy test sat on the vanity. She'd been purposely ignoring it for twenty minutes, but she couldn't put it off any longer. There was a lot of reason for concern. Her period was late, and she'd been feeling fatigued. Taking a deep breath, she picked up the wand, then sank back against the sink, unsure whether to laugh or cry.

Burning the midnight oil was becoming a habit with John Rhys. It was twenty minutes past the witching hour when Julianne knocked. John glanced up, relieved it was his favorite witch and only sister, until he noticed the gravity in her expression. He sat back in his chair, hoping the bomb she was about to drop wasn't a big one. "Judging from this late visit and the look on your face, I would assume this isn't just a social call?"

Julianne pulled up a chair and sat down. "Have you talked to Rachel?"

"Not in the last hour, but I think our last conversation pissed her off. If her pattern holds true, she'll rant a little, rave a little, and sulk a lot. After a day of hand-wringing over the latest news, she may have worn herself out sufficiently to fall asleep. I hope so, anyway. I found poor Sarah cringing every time the phone rang. I finally sent her home."

Julianne frowned. "You're too good, do you know that? You do your best to take care of everyone around you, and you really deserve a break."

"Are you going to tell me what's wrong?" John asked. "Or are you feeling the need to be cryptic, because if that's the case, then can we postpone this in favor of a day that has sucked a little less than this one?"

"Rachel called ten minutes ago, so upset I could barely understand her."

John took a sip from the Styrofoam cup positioned precisely six inches from his right hand. The coffee was bitter and cold, just like always. He didn't like it that way, but like his ex's tantrums, he'd come to accept it as a fact of life, at least during work hours. "Yeah, well, that sounds like Rachel. What else is new?"

"She's taking the kids to her mother's in Florida," Julianne said softly. "She didn't tell you because she was afraid you'd try to talk her out of it."

"Goddamn it! She's defying a court order! She can't take those kids across the state line without my consent! Is she trying to lose custody, or is this more payback for me not wanting to stay in the hell she called a marriage?"

Julianne sat quietly as he got it out of his system. It was late, and there was no one to hear him but her anyway. "You have as much right to be hurt and angry as Rachel does to be frightened. You know how I feel about Shep, and on an empathy scale, she ranks lower with me than he does, but this time she happens to be right. I know it, and so do you. It might be better if Alicia and John Jr. are away from here, at least for a while."

"They're my *kids*, Julianne." He grabbed his empty cup and crushed it in an impotent display of anger. "Florida might as well be the moon. What if she gets down there and decides to stay? I can't just pick up and relocate. My place is here, and I don't want my kids to grow up in Sun City. What the hell kind of life is that?"

"John," Julianne said reaching out to take his hand and squeeze it. "Rachel isn't looking for a new life. She just needs to feel safe—"

"And with this place on a roller-coaster ride to hell, she can't feel safe here. I know. Damn it all, I know."

"I heard about Harriet Stringer."

"Everyone has. I can't really talk about this. You know that."

"This whole thing worries me. I'm hearing crazy talk down on Main Street. Women are buying guns."

"I hate to say it, but I don't blame them," John admitted. It was as much as he could relate, and the conversation turned to other things. At ten minutes to one, Julianne kissed his cheek and went home, leaving John to the difficult task of piecing together the last day of Harriet Stringer's life. He had a plaster cast of a shoe print that might or might not be related to the case, but no suspect shoes to provide a match. Harriet's recent past seemed his best bet.

An unmarried thirty-year-old white woman, Harriet had worked as cosmetologist to the deceased at Neely's Funeral Home in Mantoot, she'd had a full and active social life, so tracing her whereabouts and activities prior to her abduction and murder wasn't going to be easy. John had already spoken to Ed and Renée Stringer, but given the upheaval they themselves had been dealing with—marital problems and Jen's decision to run away—the only thing he'd accomplished with the interview was ruling them out as possible suspects, or even likely sources of information.

Ed had admitted that Harriet liked the night-life, spending most of her weekends on the prowl, looking for Mr. Right, and settling for a long line of Mr. Right-Nows. Rhys located two of Harriet's closest friends and compiled a short list of possible male companions, all of whom he would need to track down and interview. The only thing he was certain of at this point was that Harriet had had a dentist appointment that morning.

He'd need to start making calls first thing in the morning. It gave him a migraine just thinking about it.

The outside door opened, and Shep walked in, dressed in jeans and a buttoned-down, short-sleeved Oxford shirt. He slid into the chair Julianne had vacated moments ago. "You're not with Marlene tonight?"

"We're on the outs. Said she 'needed her space.' What the hell's that supposed to mean?"

"You all right?" John asked. His deputy was minus his shades and sporting some heavy-duty dark circles under his eyes.

Shep shrugged. "Can't say she doesn't have a valid point. We have been seein' a lot of each other. How about you? Rachel called, I guess?"

"Actually, she told Julianne, and Julianne told me. I suppose it's better this way. At least we'll know for sure the kids'll be okay, and they haven't seen your mother in a while. She's bound to spoil them rotten."

"She will at that." They were both quiet for a moment. "Heard that fed say that this homicidal prick gets off on media attention and is pissed 'cause we've kept a lid on it. You think there's any truth to it?"

"Hell, Shep. I don't know. But tonight I don't seem to know much of anything." John tented his fingers in front of his face. "English thinks that's why this killing happened hot on the heels of the last one, and took place so close—under our noses. He thinks it was a way of getting our attention."

"You buy what the fed says?"

"Maybe. I don't know. There's something weird going on between English and Liz Moncrief, beyond the obvious. Doesn't it seem a little strange to you that he hasn't been called back?"

"You think he's lying about being FBI?"

"No, I don't think he's lying about that. I'm just not so sure he's telling the whole truth. I was thinking I might just make a few calls, see what turns up."

Shep pushed out of his chair and stood. "Guess I'll just go on home. In the meantime, you might think about getting some sleep yourself. And don't worry about Rachel. She'll bring the kids back just as soon as we catch this guy."

It was good to hear, but it didn't totally alleviate John's doubt, or the feeling that he was treading water with twenty-pound weights tied to his ankles.

There was nothing like a wet nose in the ear to rouse a man from sleep. For a few seconds he wasn't sure where he was or how he got there. It was Liz's great room—he figured that much out after a second or two—but he was on the sofa, not on the chair, with no recollection of getting up and relocating. Fletch nudged him again, and this time Jake sat up. "Okay, I get the message. I'm up. I'm up. And I had the impression that you guys slept eighteen hours a day. Who knew?"

Sandy gave a canine groan and then whined softly. Fletch seemed restless, trotting back to Jake twice as if assuring himself that his targeted human subject was up and moving and not trying to pull a fast one to get back to sleep. Not that Jake didn't think about it. There was a guest room up those stairs with his name on it. A guest room with a bed that was a hell of a lot more comfortable than the sofa. If he shut the door, the dogs couldn't gain access, and maybe he could get a little shut-eye. But as he withdrew the dead bolt and opened the door, the acrid taint of wood smoke struck him and all thought of sleep went straight to hell.

The stable door was ajar, its rectangle outlined by a dull orange glow. The building was on fire, and Liz's horses were inside. "Shit!"

Jake fumbled with his shoes, checking to make sure his Glock was seated firmly in the shoulder holster. Taking the steps at a leap, he ran for the building. The entire back wall was ablaze by the time Jake got inside, the animals in a full-blown panic. Grabbing a blanket, he headed for the stall closest to the blaze, undid the latch, and opened the gate. He didn't have Liz's way with horses, and it took several tries to grab the horse's bridle and calm it enough to throw the blanket over its head. Trying to avoid sucking in a lungful of hot smoke, he hustled it from the stall and down the center aisle.

The gelding balked at the paddock gate.

Jake cursed. He was losing precious seconds, and if he didn't make it back inside, Liz stood to lose so much more. He somehow got the gelding inside the paddock fence and closed the gate. The second animal proved almost as difficult, and by the time Jake entered the building for the third time, oily black smoke swirled several feet deep near the beamed ceiling. As he reached the third stall on the left and Liz's stud, something loomed up in his peripheral vision, something large and disfigured and nightmarish.

Instinct took over. Dropping into a defensive crouch, Jake spun, clawing for his pistol. The instant that his fingers closed over the grip, the business end of a short-handled spade shovel connected with the side of his head. His skull rang like a church bell, subsiding into a low drone as he dropped to his knees and unconsciousness settled in.

The dogs were raising hell. They woke Liz from a restless, dream-filled sleep in which Jake had discovered her pregnancy and had displayed a number of reactions, none of them good. As she threw off the covers and opened the drawer of her nightstand where she kept her handgun, she also attempted to throw off the disturbing effects of the dream. There was no way she was sharing that particular bit of news with Jake. Not now, at any rate. It was too soon. Granted, he'd said that he loved her, that he'd always loved her, but she wasn't quite ready to trust that, or maybe to trust herself . . . and the issue of Fiona's paternity was an obstacle she couldn't seem to maneuver around.

What would he do if she told him the truth? About everything?

She'd been on the verge of doing just that several times, yet her instincts wouldn't allow it. Liz was all too aware that one child could not take the place of another. Fiona would always be cherished by her, and her death had left a void in her life that could not be filled by anyone. Living with that loss every day, she couldn't help thinking that it might be kinder if Jake never knew the truth.

Yet, the decision not to tell him created another

dilemma. She didn't know where this thing between them was headed, and that terrified her. The thought of having Jake in her life was daunting. She wasn't sure she could weather another failed relationship—especially one that involved a child.

Two children, she mentally amended. *One living, one dead.*

"Just let it go," she muttered as she threw on a robe and slippers and headed for the stairs. "You can't tell him, about any of it—not yet—maybe not ever."

It might not even be real. Pregnancy tests weren't foolproof, and it could always turn out to be a false positive. Her period had been late a few times in the past, but there had been no cause for concern then. Not having a sex life eliminated the worry of unplanned pregnancies. All of that had, of course, changed the moment Jake had reentered her life.

Why in hell couldn't Jake English do anything in a small, unobtrusive way? Everything he did, he did with force. At times like this it was downright annoying. He couldn't just lure her back to his bed. He had to get her pregnant.

"For God's sake. Test or no test, you can't know that for sure." Not yet. It was too soon, and she was panicking.

As she came down the stairs, she saw that the door was open and Jake nowhere to be seen. Sandy paced the breadth of the room, reluctant to leave the house without her mistress; Fletch, always more outgoing and adventurous, was raising a ruckus in the yard. The lights in the stables flickered on, then just as quickly blinked out again. In the interim she heard the distress of the horses, smelled the smoke on the night wind. She ran to the phone and dialed. "I need to report a fire at the Moncrief farm. My stable. Yes, please hurry."

Liz hung up the phone and ran from the house, grabbing a light cotton jacket from a peg by the door as she went. Balling the fabric, she pressed it to her face and, low to the ground, entered the building.

Flames shot up the straw bales stacked against the rear wall, licking at the rafters. Two of the horses were in the paddock, but three more were still inside, trapped in their stalls. Consumed by panic, they bumped against the wooden slats. Liz made it to Faerie King's stall and opened the gate, got to her feet, and, grasping his bridle, she led him into the center aisle and gave him a slap on the rump. The gelding, needing no further encouragement, bolted from the burning structure. Starling was next, but when she turned toward Anglican's stall, she nearly fell over something blocking the center aisle . . . something that moved as she stepped on it, and gave a barely audible groan. "Oh God, no," Liz said, dropping to her knees beside him. "Jake?"

She brushed his hair back out of his face and her fingers came away sticky and wet. "Jake?" She shook him. "You have to get up!"

As she tried to rouse him, a shadow fell over both of them. Liz glanced up. Backlit by a haze of red, his disfigured face something out of her worst nightmares, Samuel Turner gave a hollow laugh. "Ain't much good to you now, is he?"

"You're insane," Liz said. Her Glock was still in her hand, half concealed by the wadded cotton jacket. She brought it up, leveling the weapon even as Samuel staggered forward, an empty whiskey bottle held by the neck like a club. "Back off. One more step and I'll send your sorry ass to hell."

"You don't scare me," Samuel said. "Nothin' does."

"I said back off!"

Samuel just laughed, lurching forward in an awkward leap.

Liz pulled the trigger, once, twice. Two shots that tore away a fist-sized portion of his breastbone. He jerked backward, his legs folding beneath him as he toppled. He was dead before he hit the floor.

Numb, her chest aching from the heat and the smoke, Liz locked her arms around Jake and inched him toward the door and the damp night air. Starling was down in his stall, and so was Anglican. Her brain screamed for her to go back in; instinct held her back. Her energy was depleted. If she entered the building a second time, she'd die in the blaze with the horses and Samuel Turner. . . . So she sat on the cool grass and wept her eyes dry.

Chapter Thirteen

Kate Fife lobbied for the emergency room at Mantoot, but Jake wouldn't hear of it, so she did the X rays herself at the clinic and sutured the gash above his ear. "Well, from the looks of things, you don't have a skull fracture, but I expect you to stay flat on your back for twenty-four hours."

"You've got to be kidding," Jake said. He was seated on her exam table, his shirt hanging open and smelling a little like a hot dog that had been smoked over an open fire.

She finished cleaning the scalp wound, then applied surgical glue to close the wound. "Do I look like I'm kidding? You've got a very hard head and a slight concussion, and you need to rest. Twenty-four hours, and I'm being extremely optimistic." Unlocking a supply cabinet, Kate handed him a small white envelope containing a few tablets. "One every six hours for pain," she said. "If there's any blurring of vision, or unusual discomfort, call me. Otherwise, I'll see you tomorrow. And, just so you know, there's an additional fee for uncooperative patients."

Jake snorted.

John Rhys came into the room. "You almost through, Doc? I need a few minutes with Jake."

She glanced up. "He's all yours. Jake? Twenty-four hours."

Jake slid off the exam table, shot a look in Liz's direction, and followed the sheriff outside, leaving Liz alone with Kate.

"It's a mild sedative, to help you rest," Kate said, handing a packet with a half dozen capsules to Liz. "I know how fond you were of Anglican."

"I can't," Liz said.

"You can. I've checked your chart; there's no other medication for this to interact with."

"It isn't that—" Liz broke off, pressing her hand to her face. "I intended to call, in a week or two. I was thinking it might be a good idea to schedule some blood work."

"Uh huh." Kate leaned against the exam table. "Are you feeling ill?"

"Not particularly."

"What was the date of your last period?"

"Thirty-eight days ago."

Kate took a breath, her expression suddenly serious. It was her physician's face. Sober, unruffled, businesslike. "Is there a reason to suspect you might be pregnant?"

Liz pushed her hair behind her ear. "I bought one of the over-the-counter pregnancy tests."

"And?"

"Positive."

"Does Jake know?"

Liz glanced sharply up. "Jake *can't* know—not yet, anyway." She realized how abrupt, how final her reply had sounded, how adamant, and tried again. "There's no sense in involving him at this point. It's all too . . . uncertain."

"You think he might not welcome the news?"

"At this point I can't even hazzard a guess." This was all too new, and she needed a little time to get used to the idea of a baby before she involved anyone, even the baby's father. She knew it was selfish. He had every right to know. She just couldn't bring herself to tell him. Not yet.

"Well, why don't we find out for sure, and take it from there?" Kate handed the order for blood work to Liz. "If you go to the hospital early, we can have the results this afternoon. The sooner you know, the more time you have to make decisions."

"Decisions?"

"Whether or not you wish to terminate the pregnancy, or allow nature to take its course," Kate replied, her tone matter-of-fact. "For a woman in the over-thirty-five age bracket, I always recommend amnio."

Terminate the pregnancy . . . abortion . . . one more thing she hadn't even considered, and she wasn't sure she could consider it now. "I really can't think that far ahead."

"First things first. Let's find out if there *is* a pregnancy before you decide what to do about it." Kate took Liz's hand and gave it a squeeze. "And should you need to talk, I can listen."

Liz sighed. "Jake and I were married once, briefly, and it was a disaster. I didn't intend to become emotionally involved with him again. It just happened. And now, this. God. I've made such a mess of everything."

"You may feel that way now. As your physician and your friend, I would recommend you give yourself some time to adjust to the idea. There are worse things than a new little life, but you know that. And Jake is dynamic, good-looking—"

"And impossible to manage."

Kate smiled. "Show me a man who isn't and I'll show you a woman who's just had a sex change operation. He loves you, Liz. I can see it in his eyes when he looks at you, and I'd be willing to bet he'd love to hear the news you're withholding."

"Nothing's certain at this point." There was a lot Kate didn't know. A lot Jake didn't know, and no way to tell him without risking everything.

Kate winked. "Maybe . . . maybe not. Call me this afternoon. We'll talk then."

Outside, John Rhys and Jake were deep in conversation. "I didn't see him when I entered the stable, but I was a little preoccupied with getting the stock out of the burning building."

"You think he set the blaze?" John said.

"Not a doubt in my mind. It was arson. As for motive? Hell, maybe he had a death wish, I don't know. Whatever his motives, he didn't seem to be in any hurry to leave."

"You had your Glock, but didn't fire?" John asked.

"There was no time. . . . Besides, like I said, the animals were trapped. Look, is there some point to this? Because if you're intent on busting my chops for no specific reason, then I really don't need the added hassle."

"That sounds like a reasonable question," Liz put in, closing the door and leaning against it. "If you don't mind, I'd like to know the answer, too. John, what's going on? You have my statement, which corresponds with Jake's. Why the third degree?"

"No third degree," the sheriff assured her. "But a man did lose his life in your barn, and I need to know what happened. I can't very well ask Samuel, and Jake is my only option."

"Jake didn't kill Samuel Turner, I did. Maybe

you should be questioning me instead of badgering him. He took a nasty blow to the head because he was trying to help me, and Kate says he needs to rest."

John ran a hand over his face, something he did when exasperated that Liz had come to recognize. "So, should I drop him off at his place, or are you taking him back to the farm with you?"

Jake took a step forward, one menacing step that spoke volumes. His face had been darkened by smoke, and the smear of blood at his temple that Kate had missed made him look dangerous. "Look, pal, I've had just about enough of you! Back off!"

Liz slipped between them. Putting her hands on Jake's chest, she looked him in the eye. "This is my business, not yours, and you will let me handle it. The keys are in the Explorer. Wait for me there." He didn't look away, but he didn't do as she'd asked, either, and the tic in his cheek was a solid clue to the depth of his anger. "Jake, don't make this worse. *Please.*"

With a last burning glance in his rival's direction, he walked to the Ford and stood leaning against it, intent on at least observing if he couldn't be involved.

Liz wasn't happy about the situation, but she knew this was as much cooperation from Jake as she was going to get. She'd set the two men up as rivals by her inability, or reluctance, to face her feelings, or her fears, and only she could defuse a coming explosion.

It was decision time; she couldn't avoid it any longer. She had to face facts, face the truth, deal with reality.

Taking a deep breath, she faced John Rhys. "Is that what this is about? My connection to Jake?"

John reached out and touched her. A whisper-soft brush of fingers against her cheek. "What's going on, Liz? I'd really like to know before I make a fool of myself . . . or maybe it's already too late for that. Jake's got the home advantage, doesn't he?"

"John, this isn't a football game," Liz insisted. "It's my life, and Jake's a part of it."

"A big part," he surmised, "and I guess that's not likely to change. Is it?"

She glanced back at Jake; his posture was tense, his face to the wind. He wasn't afraid of anything, and he wasn't cautious. He'd gone into the burning stable to save her horses, and he'd almost gotten himself killed doing it. "No, I guess it isn't, and to tell you the truth, I'm not so sure I want it to."

John Rhys sighed. "Fine. I'll get the hell out of the way, then, but I wouldn't be human if I weren't a little jealous. As for Jake, I hope you don't come to regret this."

Liz's brow clouded. "Regret it? What's that supposed to mean?"

"Only that Mr. Wonderful over there may not have told you everything. How well do you know him, Liz? He lied to you once. Are you sure it hasn't happened again?"

Liz shoved her fists into the pockets of her sleeveless jean jacket. Tension coiled in the pit of her stomach, and she hated that she couldn't turn on her heel and walk away. "It's obvious you have something to say, so do me a favor and just say it."

"A few things have bothered me about Jake since he showed up, things that didn't exactly add up, so I made a couple of phone calls. Did he bother to tell you that he's on an enforced leave of absence? Administrative leave. It seems the Bureau's psychiatrist feels that Agent English is slightly unstable."

"Who told you this?"

"The assistant director." John watched her closely, but Liz couldn't quite match the directness of his gaze. "It was diagnosed as post-traumatic stress. Look, you can think I'm a heel for telling you this, but you have a right to know what you're dealing with. The last thing I want is to see you get hurt."

Liz's gaze had drifted to the silent, angry figure standing alone by her SUV. "Jake would never hurt me. Not like that." It was the one thing of which she was absolutely certain.

"The truth definitely sets you free," John said softly, watching as she walked away, back to Jake. It had been a bear of a week: he had two murder investigations on his hands that so far had gone nowhere, his kids were on their way to Florida, he'd seen to the unpleasant task of breaking the news to Marge Turner—a woman he'd known all his life—that her troubled son had died a violent death, and now he'd lost Liz. Planting his hat on his head, John walked back to his Blazer and got in. "See you 'round, Jake," he told his federal counterpart. Then, to himself as he backed from Kate Fife's driveway, "Some days it just doesn't pay to get out of bed."

After Liz and Jake got into her SUV, she glanced at him. He was stiff with anger. Liz really couldn't blame him. "What the hell was that about? What'd you do, Liz, send me off to stand in the corner while you made a date with the All-American Boy?"

Liz raised her brows at that. "Why are you always so suspicious?"

"It's my job. I've made a career out of being suspicious."

"Well, you need to learn to turn it off when you're at home, because I don't like it."

He scowled at her. "Which means?"

"I don't want to fight, but I would like for us to go home. You need to rest, and I have to assess the damage, call the insurance company, and run some errands. Can you live with that, or not?"

Home, Jake thought. It was a concept he had completely lost touch with, and suddenly it rose up like a vision in the midst of an empty and meaningless existence, a shimmering oasis in a water-starved sea of sand. "As long as John-Boy isn't part of the equation, I can live with it."

Jake's father had bought the diamond sixty years before for Lydia Jennison at an antique store in Fredericksburg, Virginia. The ring, a half-carat diamond in a filigree setting, had wiped out his savings so totally that for the first two years of their marriage, they'd lived in a sharecropper's shack, but Ranald had never regretted it for a single moment. He'd said, quite simply, that his Lydia had been worth every penny of it and more. He would have mortgaged the heavens to make her happy. Their marriage had lasted forty-nine years, until breast cancer ended her life.

Sitting alone on the porch swing, Jake wished for an ounce of his father's certainty that asking Liz to marry him a second time was a wise decision. As he figured it, the odds were sixty-forty against him that she would turn him down. She turned to him in the heat of passion, came to him in crisis, but that didn't mean that she loved him. It meant he was a convenience, and he sure didn't like that thought.

It wasn't that he didn't want to be in her bed, or that he would ever turn her away if she needed him. But he wanted more than that. He wanted her gaze to soften when she looked at him. He wanted to be her first thought when she woke in the morning, and her last thought when she put her head on her pillow at night. He wanted her to want him in her life as badly as he wanted her in his, and he desperately needed her to trust him.

"That's a tall order, my friend," he said to himself. "And I suspect you're about to be disappointed."

"Talking to yourself? Are you feeling all right?"

At the sound of her voice, he closed his hand over the ring, but he didn't put it away completely. "Sure, why wouldn't I be?"

She was silent for a moment, and he could sense her restlessness, her doubt.

"You've never been at a loss for words when you're upset with me," he said, staring off at the blackened beams and charred rubble of the stable. "What the hell did I do now?"

She didn't sit down. Whatever she had on her mind wouldn't allow it. Instead, she crossed her arms in front of her, and leaned her left shoulder against the porch railing. "John called Quantico. I didn't want to believe him, so I talked to Charlie. He told me everything."

Softly. Wearily. Defensively. "Jesus Christ."

"My God, Jake. Why didn't you tell me?"

"Tell you what? That I'm losing it? Defective? Because I'm not."

"That's not what Charlie says."

"Calendar needs to mind his own goddamned business and stay the hell out of mine!" He shot to his feet and stalked into the house, slamming the screen door. Liz followed, unable, or unwilling, to let it go.

"Charlie loves you. He doesn't want anything bad to happen . . . and quite frankly, neither do I."

Jake had been reaching for the coffeepot, but

stopped, his fingers curling in upon one another before they touched the handle of the carafe. She reached out, her fingers sliding over his shoulder, and the tension that gripped him threatened to implode.

"It was Fiona, wasn't it?" she asked, the ache in her voice so keen that it sliced him to the marrow, leaving him open and vulnerable.

Jake couldn't answer. He couldn't get the words past the lump in his throat.

"Jake, please. Please don't shut me out."

It was a long time before he could speak, and he couldn't guess how long they stood in her kitchen, her hand gripping his shoulder while he struggled with his feelings for her, his grinding frustration that he had been unable to save her child or catch her killer. "I wanted to bring her back," he said slowly, his voice a raspy whisper. "But I was too fucking late. She was . . . cold, Liz. I tried to revive her, but she was unresponsive. I was too late."

"And I punished you for it."

"You had every right."

She shook her head, her cheeks damp. "That's not true. I was hurt, and angry, and I couldn't take it out on him . . . so I took it out on you." Putting her arms around him, she stood on tiptoes, pressing her hot cheek to his. "I'm sorry. Oh, God, I am so sorry!"

Tension slowly bled out of him as his arms came around her. "Yeah, me too," he said softly. "For everything." He held her while she cried, just held on and hoped for the strength to get through this. He didn't know if that was possible, couldn't hazard a guess as to whether they could survive hurts inflicted in the past. The only certainty in Jake's mind in that moment was that he would breathe his last before willingly hurting Liz again.

Later, Jake sat on the steps to the front porch, watching evening come down. Dusk deepened and the shadows lengthened. He could hear Liz inside, moving restlessly from room to room. She'd taken the Explorer to town earlier in the day, supposedly to run errands. Privately Jake wondered if she had paid the sheriff a visit, but he didn't ask. Real trust was a mutual endeavor. If she trusted him sufficiently to leave him alone with a kitchen full of knives and two semiautomatics after what she'd learned earlier in the day, he would try to trust her to make the right decisions. As for Rhys, that was another matter altogether.

Whatever she struggled with soon drove her from the house and its shadows. She stopped on the top step, hesitating. "You okay?" Jake asked quietly.

"Me? Yeah, I'm okay." One look at her face and he knew she was lying. She'd been crying; her eyes were puffy and red-rimmed.

"It's okay to fall down once in a while, you know. You don't have to be the proverbial tower of strength all the time."

A tower of strength. Liz would have laughed, but ending on a sob would have been a dead giveaway. Jersey and Kenneth Simms had helped her to bury Anglican. Simms seemed greatly agitated, but she knew it had nothing to do with the stallion's loss. Kenneth Simms didn't like horses. He had never admitted as much, and it hadn't affected his ability to do his job, but she could feel his nervousness around them, sense his fear, just as the animals themselves could. She'd resented his presence at so solemn an occasion. To her, Anglican's death had been devastating.

She avoided the step where Jake sat, needing desperately to stand alone, to be strong. She'd taken a human life, and lost her beloved animal; the stable was a burned-out shell; and her life seemed on the verge of total collapse. "How can one man be so filled with hate?" she wondered, her voice terrible in its softness.

Jake shifted on the swing. "It's not about hate. It's about emptiness."

"Emptiness?" She shook her head.

"Guys like Samuel Turner aren't all there. Oh, they walk and they talk, and they go through the motions, but it's all a scam. Inside, there's nothing. Not a soul, not an ounce of sympathy, or a glimmer of light. They're the walking dead in every sense of the word."

He got up and walked to the edge of the porch where she stood, wrapping her in a warm, secure embrace. Liz sighed, ready at last to capitulate. "Don't feel sorry for him, baby. He got what he asked for. He doesn't deserve your sympathy."

"It all seems like such a waste." She was quiet for a moment as she struggled with the enormity of taking a life, something that in all her years with the FBI had never happened. It wasn't a feeling she liked, or one that she could ever get used to. She wasn't up to playing God—and she knew in that moment that the same principle applied to her personal predicament. She'd made an excuse to be away from the farm long enough to have the blood test, and Kate had called with the results a few minutes ago. HCG hormone levels were present and elevated. The results of the blood test had been positive. She was pregnant.

For a long interval she relaxed in Jake's embrace, soaking up his warmth, taking comfort in the knowledge that he cared.

She didn't have to be alone if she didn't want to be, devoid of a life partner. He was here, he loved and he wanted her, and she loved him. That wasn't easy to admit.

She'd been on the verge of an emotional re-awakening for weeks—and fighting it—since Jake had reentered her life. The insulating cocoon of numbness in which she had lived since Fiona's death had cracked and was threatening to burst wide open.

Lived . . . She almost laughed at her choice of words. That was the ultimate irony. She hadn't lived a single day since Fiona's funeral; she'd merely existed, breathing in, breathing out, going through the motions, feeling nothing, like Jake said of men like Samuel—one of the walking dead. But all of that was changing, and it scared her to death.

"Do you think he was involved? In Amanda Redwing's death, and Harriet Stringer's?"

"If there is a connection, I haven't seen it yet, and Turner just wasn't smart enough to perpetrate a complex crime. He was a loose cannon. I'll have to consult with Rhys. Maybe he's come up with something. Speaking of John-Boy: did you give him a rain check for dinner?"

Liz turned in his arms, looking up into his face. "And if I did?"

"Then I'll redouble my efforts to charm you right out of those jeans you're wearing and do my utmost to make you forget you ever met John Rhys." He kissed her, a long and passionate kiss that left her breathless. Then he kissed her again.

Liz gazed up into those beloved blue eyes and sighed. Was it possible? Could she really let go of her insecurities? Could she fall for Jake again? "John who?"

"Let's go upstairs."

"Kate said twenty-four hours. In fact, you're disobeying her orders just being upright. I believe her words were 'flat on your back.' "

Jake raised a hand, a sign of surrender. "I give up. I'll rest, if you come with me." His arm around her, they walked through the door and up the stairs.

The bedroom was soft in shadow, and a gentle summer breeze rustled the lace curtains. Liz turned so that Jake stood with his back to the bed. Slowly, gently, she unbuttoned his silk shirt and slipped it over his shoulders, her hungry kisses following in its wake.

"She didn't mention avoiding sex," Jake said. "I was there. I would have argued."

"No, she didn't. How's your headache?"

"Headache? What headache?"

She reached for the waistband of his jeans and stopped. "Will you be serious? I don't want to hurt you."

Jake drew a shuddering breath. "I've known all along that you'd hurt me. It's a foregone conclusion." Suddenly, it wasn't physical pain they were talking about, and there was so much more at stake than a mild concussion, or impulsive sex. "It's how karma works, isn't it? I hurt you . . . you hurt me. The ultimate payback."

Liz froze, and for the space of a heartbeat she couldn't seem to breathe. "I don't want revenge, if that's what you mean."

Jake caught her hand, brought it to his mouth, kissing each knuckle without breaking eye contact. "What do you want, Liz? From this thing between us? Are you playing me out of boredom? You gonna decide next week you'd rather see other people? Tell me the truth so I can prepare for it. Are you gonna break my heart again?"

Tears stung Liz's eyes, dampening her lashes.

Somehow, she held them back as she bent, pressing a lingering kiss in the shallow dip between his pecs. "Not intentionally. I don't want to hurt you; I don't want to be hurt. I just want to find a way to work things out. Can we do that, Jake? Can we make it work this time?"

They helped one another out of their clothes and made slow, delicious love amid a tangle of crisp white bed linen. Jake kissed her lips and stroked her silky hair, while whispering naughty nothings in her ear. He nipped her breasts, and Liz noticed their new sensitivity with a secret pang. He squeezed the dip of her waist and ran the tip of his tongue into her navel, making her laugh, then suck in a swift breath as he found the source of her heat.

He'd always been an accomplished lover. It was one of the things that had sparked their first marriage so many years ago, and that much hadn't changed. Yet, with time, he'd grown patient, and now he plied every trick he knew to make her writhe and beg and finally to scream his name.

Much later, with passion just a sweet memory, Liz lay in the circle of Jake's arms, unable to sleep. She'd asked him to stay at the farm, and it seemed to please him. He'd be picking up the rest of his things from the apartment the next morning and bringing them here. He would leave his wet towels on the floor of the bathroom, his socks on the rug by the bed, and she would say nothing. She had so much to make up for. She squeezed her eyes shut, but couldn't quite hold back the tears that leaked from the outer corners of her eyes and ran down her cheeks.

Jake left the farm right after breakfast the next morning and drove to Rhys's office. The sheriff looked restless and unhappy, and Jake could only speculate on whether Rhys's mood was due to the growing pile of paperwork at his elbow or something more personal. " 'Morning, Jake. Coffee? I was just about to warm mine up."

"Thanks, I think I will," Jake said, accepting a Styrofoam cup.

"You might want to save the gratitude until you've tasted it. Shep makes it, and it's the worst coffee in three counties."

"Why let him continue to do something when he does it so badly?"

Rhys sat back. "Because he prides himself on doing it correctly, and it would hurt his feelings if I took that away from him. Besides, he's my brother-in-law, and if making bad coffee is the worst thing he does, I can live with that." He sipped from his cup. "If you add a pint of milk to every pot, it's almost palatable. But you didn't come here to discuss my caffeine addiction." He took a small stack of papers off the top of a pile of paperwork that mimicked the Leaning Tower of Pisa and handed it to Jake. "The latest on Harriet Stringer, including a rap sheet and autopsy report."

"Rap sheet?" Jake said, not bothering to hide his surprise. He took another sip of coffee, so distracted by the reports in his hand that he was actually getting used to the stuff. "What were the charges?"

"Solicitation."

"Prostitution?" Jake pushed his cup to the center of the desk blotter. "Hit me again, will you?"

"Harriet went off to the city when she was eighteen and came home a few years later with a substance abuse problem. To support her habit, she started hanging out in the clubs in Mantoot. Sex for money, sex for drugs. She propositioned an undercover cop, which landed her in jail, which eventually led to rehab. The family swears she's been clean for eighteen months, but that's not what the photos say. Have a look."

Jake picked up the black-and-white photo of a naked white female, barely covered with a sheet. "Pretty." Her hair was blond, and she had a pleasant sort of roundness, full cheeks, shoulders that weren't skin and bone. The next shot showed her hands. She had scrapes and bruises. Her nails had been clipped during the autopsy to be examined for DNA trace evidence. The third photo showed needle marks on the inside of her left elbow. "Heroin?" Jake snorted. "Pills, maybe, but 'H'? This girl doesn't look like a shooter—and that doesn't look like track marks to me."

"My thoughts exactly. Defense wounds on her hands, but no DNA under her nails."

"What was the cause of death? It wasn't asphyxiation."

"Drug overdose." John got up, walked to a locked filing cabinet, and opened it. He took out a plastic evidence bag and laid it on the table. Inside was a syringe. "This was in the box with her. No water, no food, just a loaded syringe. We found Harriet's prints on it, but nothing else."

"So he prepared it for her use?" Jake said. "What was the drug of choice?"

"Pharmaceutical-grade morphine."

"Jesus." Jake shook his head. "Does this make sense to you? Why provide a drug addict the means to kill herself? He allowed seven out of nine victims to suffer for long periods of time before he cut off their air supply, so why change his MO with this vic?"

"You're the profiler," Rhys said. "You tell me."

"Because she was a sympathy kill," Jake said.

"Like the Redwing kid. He knew her. One of these pricks knew her, and knew she'd been addicted. The weaker of the two provided the syringe out of a feeling of remorse. Maybe in his warped mind he sees it as a mercy killing. He was giving her a way out."

John Rhys picked up his cup, then set it down again. "Maybe . . . But where did he get pharmaceutical-grade morphine?"

"Theft," Jake suggested.

"No reported robberies in the area. I checked. It's possible that such a theft could go unnoticed, but unlikely. Commercial pharmacies keep records, as do hospital pharmacies. Everything is locked down and meticulously accounted for."

Jake shrugged. "What about an inside job? Or maybe the SOB got it some other way. Maybe he's employed in the medical field and has access to drugs."

"I'll run down the list of Harriet's friends and neighbors today and see what I come up with." Rhys got up and replaced the evidence in the filing cabinet. "Got a call from the fire marshal, too. Traces of an accelerant, and the burn pattern indicates arson in the fire. Rufus Vanderhorn says he sold a gallon of kerosene to Samuel the afternoon preceding the fire. The question is, how'd he get out there without being seen? He walks everywhere."

"Somebody took him." Jake put the photos back into their manila envelope and got out of his chair. "Sheriff . . . you'll let me know if there are new developments?"

"You'll be the first one I call," Rhys said, and Jake didn't know how much of the assurance was genuine and how much was sarcasm.

"Jake? Before you go, I just wanted you to know that I stepped aside because it's what Liz wanted, but should things change . . ." Rhys smiled, but there was nothing friendly about the expression. "Well, let's just say that if I were you, I'd be damned careful not to screw up. Liz is a vibrant, beautiful woman. I like her—a lot."

Jake planted a palm on the edge of Rhys's desk and leaned down until they were eye to eye. "John, you can like Liz all you want. As long as you do it from a distance." He walked to the door, where he turned for one last parting shot. "By the way. Thanks for interfering. Turns out that by forcing the issue you did me a favor."

Jake cleaned out the apartment—not that there was much left to take—but Julianne wasn't at the shop, so he couldn't thank her for the short stay, or drop off the key. Women at large seemed to be the rule of the day, because Liz wasn't at the farm when he got back, either. He knew where she left the spare key, so he let himself in and took his stuff directly upstairs.

He fully intended to show Liz that he really was a new man, and knew how to do this right. She wouldn't have to stumble over his things or wash smelly socks, unless of course she wanted to. He could be neat, and orderly, and he intended to give her so much love and attention that she would accept the ring when he finally screwed up the courage to offer it to her.

Acceptance was crucial. Hell, it wasn't just crucial, it was everything.

It was also the one thing he'd craved all his life but never felt he'd had. Granted, he'd had the respect of his colleagues at Quantico, but having a few jerks of like mind to hang out with on Friday night at a local club didn't satisfy his need. He kept coming back to Ranald, the father he'd loved but never quite connected with, the one man whose respect he'd wanted so badly, but never quite earned.

Maybe reconciling with Liz would have made the difference, finally making things right. Jake found the leather photo frame and, opening it, carefully placed it on the top of the dresser in Liz's bedroom. He'd brought his stuff in from the bedroom and hung his garment bag in the closet. Then he checked the dresser drawers, finding one that was nearly empty. Liz wasn't the type of woman to get territorial, and she wouldn't begrudge him a place to house his T-shirts, socks, and underwear. It wasn't like he needed a lot of space. He traveled exceptionally light.

In the bottom of the drawer was a leather binder with plastic sleeves to hold important papers, open on one end. Jake lifted it out upside down, and the documents fluttered out. Insurance policies, the marriage certificate for her second marriage, and an official document signed by a judge granting the legal adoption of Fiona English by Richard Airhardt, two months before their return to Virginia.

Jake didn't know how long he stood, staring down at the letter in his hands, barely comprehending what he'd accidentally read.

Adoption . . . Fiona English? He got a queasy feeling in his stomach that had little to do with the effects of Shep Margolis's coffee and everything to do with the papers in his hand.

Adoption? Fiona English . . . not Airhardt.

Liz's little girl had been a toddler when they'd returned to Virginia and Liz returned to Quantico. Jake had always assumed she'd met Richard on the rebound and married again soon after the divorce. He'd never questioned her about it, having given up that right, and Liz had never talked about it.

Picking up the leather binder, Jake dumped its contents on the bed—Liz's history in letters, and legal documents, certificates and awards. He ruthlessly rifled through it all, adding up the details, doing the math, not liking the conclusions he was drawing.

Jake had married Liz in October—he glanced again at the child's birth certificate—and Liz's daughter had been born nine months later, in June.

"Jesus Christ. She was pregnant when she filed for divorce. Fiona wasn't Airhardt's kid. She was mine."

Images flashed behind Jake's eyes: that small blue face, those ravaged hands. . . . He felt again the constriction of his heart and lungs as he tried to revive her. Her lips and skin were cold against his, her flesh hard, like marble. He couldn't shake the image. Dark hair, blue eyes. Eyes like his, but clouded over by death.

Jesus.

Driven by the image of Liz's child—his child— he rifled the documents until he found what he was looking for, a birth certificate. English . . . Fiona Elizabeth English . . . mother: Elizabeth; father: Jacob.

He didn't need to look up. He knew the instant she paused in the doorway. "What the hell are you doing? Those are my personal papers, private documents."

"Really?" Jake said, his voice flat and hard. "The birth certificate—that's yours—like our daughter was yours. Yours, Liz? To keep from me, because I didn't merit knowing I had a child? *Yours*, to give away to another man whenever you felt like it?

Without asking me if I gave a flying fuck? Without ever letting me know she existed? Jesus Christ, how could you do that? *How the hell could you do that?*"

His shout faded to a sickening silence. Liz's sense of dread was so strong, it threatened to choke her.

"It wasn't like that, it—"

"By all means, tell me what it was like! Were you ever going to tell me that Fiona was mine?" He cleared the contents of the bed with a furious sweep of one arm. Then, as if that wasn't enough to satisfy his rage, he overturned the bed, sending it crashing into the wall. His violence spent, he stood quivering with fury, his breath coming in strangled gasps.

"Jake, please. Please, you have to listen to me. I was angry, and hurt, and—"

"You were pissed off at me. So you steal my daughter? In what alternate universe does that make us even?"

Her face had gone stark white, and her eyes brimmed with unshed tears. "Jake, please. Baby, sit down, give me a chance to explain."

"You trusted me to head the team that searched for her when she was abducted, but you couldn't tell me I was searching for my own flesh and blood? My baby girl. And when I found her, you couldn't even let me pay my respects, because I was the hated ex-husband, and I wasn't fucking good enough!" He closed his eyes as the birth certificate fluttered from his fingers to the floor, and his voice grew tight with emotion. "Not good enough to come to my own kid's funeral, not good enough to be anyone's daddy."

"No! Oh, God, no! That isn't true! It had nothing to do with you and everything to do with me. I ran as soon as I found out about the pregnancy. It was selfish and desperate, and I spent years regretting it. My God . . . don't you think I regret it? She's gone, Jake. He took her from both of us, and I can't undo what I did! I'm sorry . . . Oh God, I'm so sorry!"

"Yeah, well, so am I." He threw open the drawer and jammed his clothes back into his bag.

"What are you doing? We need to talk about this!"

"We said everything there is to say." He took the garment bag from the closet and pushed past her into the hallway, down the stairs.

"No! Jake, wait!" Liz followed, reaching the porch in time to see his Buick spin gravel into the grass. "Don't go, please." Sinking onto the step, she covered her eyes with her hands.

Chapter Fourteen

Jake couldn't close his eyes without seeing his little girl's face, and he couldn't let her image rise without the lump in his throat threatening to strangle him.

His child . . . his daughter . . . his baby. Kept from him out of anger, out of hatred, and the worst part about it was that he couldn't find it in his heart to blame Liz entirely.

He wanted to hate her for keeping him away from Fiona, and for preventing Fiona from knowing that he was her father. She deserved his hatred. She'd cheated him out of something vital, something precious. She'd prevented him from being there to catch that slippery wet being when it emerged from her body and into his hands, she'd cheated him out of hearing his child's first angry squall, from helping her take her first step, from hearing her first words, from sharing birthdays and school days, soccer, and Christmas mornings, and his sense of loss was so acute that it made him feel physically sick.

She'd kept him at arm's length, kept him from

knowing his little girl, and so much was lost because of it. He'd never gaze into her wide blue eyes, he'd never explain why the stars came out only at night, and he'd never have the smallest connection to a life he'd helped create.

He wanted to hate Liz for that, but he couldn't, and that left him with no outlet for his anger and grief but the bottle of bourbon sitting in front of him. He was entering the second evening of a two-day binge, and he had no plan to stop anytime soon. He drained the water glass, splashed another three fingers into it, and drained it again, after silently toasting his liver. He didn't give a damn what happened to him; he just wanted to numb the pain.

It was unlike anything he'd ever experienced, a deep, all-consuming ache. It engulfed his heart, made his lungs tight, and filled him with a dark and desperate need to drown it, even if it killed him.

He sat on the sofa, his head in his hands, heeding only the call of the bottle. It sounded curiously like his cell phone, which gave a sick-sounding bleat. Jake ignored it. It was probably Charlie, and if that was the case, he'd call back. There was also a slim chance it was Liz. Maybe she'd sensed that he still had a thread of self-esteem left and had contrived some new way to pummel it out of him, some innovative method of extracting his beating heart from his chest without actually killing him.

"Hell, no, we couldn't have that. Old Jake needs to suffer at great length before we cut off his balls with a dull butter knife and parade them around the neighborhood on that silver platter." The apartment phone rang until his voice mail kicked on. It was the eighth call in an hour and forty-five minutes, and the eighth voice message, and he hadn't listened to any of them. "Yeah, it's gotta be

Charlie, wonderin' where the hell I've been. He's the only one besides Liz who has both numbers."

The apartment was as dark as his mood. He hadn't just neglected to turn the lights on, he'd purposely left them off. His baby girl was in a lightless place, cold, and alone, and he wasn't sure he'd ever get past that. How could he live in the light when she was trapped in eternal darkness?

"Not alone, Jake," he told himself. "Dead. She's dead, and you can't reach her. Can't help her." His nightmares come to life. A shuddering sigh; his shoulders slumped. "Can't ever let her know how much you would have loved her if you'd had half a chance."

A soft knocking sounded. Someone tapping on the locked door. "Jake? Jake, baby, please, I know you're in there. Open the door. Please, I need to see you. I need to know that you're all right." As her voice broke, a single thread of scalding liquid leaked over his lower lid and slipped unchecked down his bristled cheek. "Jake, please. We have to talk about this."

Out of his mind with pain and grief, he sat, silent and still, frozen, Liz's plea as soothing as a sprinkle of salt in a gaping wound. Just the sound of her voice stung his raw emotions almost more than he could bear. He poured bourbon into the glass and tossed it back as the dull ache in his chest grew more acute and another silent tear leaked out. The hand he lifted to his face trembled.

It was a test, all of it. Something or someone had decided to see just how much Jacob English could endure. Unaware perhaps that when he reached the point of total saturation, he would find his own solution to the problem. There was always a way out, and he knew what to do. He wasn't sure just why he delayed.

He took a cigar from the coffee table, shoved it between his lips, and flicked his lighter. As he replaced the disposable on the coffee table, his fingertips brushed the cold blue steel of the Glock. For a fraction of a second, his warm skin played along the trigger guard. All he had to do was reach out, pick it up, put an end to it. It would be so damned easy.

No more nightmares.

No more Liz.

No more pain.

No more Bureau psychiatrist.

He could almost imagine the grim satisfaction on Doctor Dread's pretty face as she heard the news. If he picked up the Glock, he would prove her right . . . and TCM would have claimed his tenth victim. That realization was the one thing, the only thing, that kept him from acting on his self-destructive urges.

He gave off caressing the metal and reached for the bourbon. Oblivion awaited somewhere in its golden depths. He just had to find it.

Outside, Liz waited, ear pressed to the door, listening, hoping for some sound, some sign that Jake was okay. She was worried about him, worried about them. He was hurting, and it was all her fault. She didn't blame him for being angry. He had every right to hate her for keeping him away from their daughter, and she had a million reasons with which to justify her actions—or at least, she'd thought she had until the secret came to light the previous day.

The truth was a great deal more complex.

Liz drew a choked breath. Her chest was tight with unshed tears. Kate Fife would have scolded her for getting emotionally overwrought and advised her to go home and rest, but how could she rest when her life had become an irreparable mess? One child lost, another life newly created growing inside her, so very vulnerable . . . so uncertain. If she told him about the pregnancy, there was a chance he'd stay, but she would never know if he'd given her another chance because he loved her or because of the child.

For several minutes she stood there, hand poised to knock again, her heart in her throat as she struggled with a maelstrom of conflicting emotions. Then, before she could do something even more foolish than coming here to beg his forgiveness, she turned and went down the stairs.

Shep Margolis had wrapped up a ten-hour shift and was on his way home when he spotted the van. It was ancient, a true putty wagon, the original white paint rough-patched and painted with an innocuous shade of gray primer. In Shep's opinion, the damn thing was a violation on wheels, the operator in all probability a doper with a marijuana stash tucked under the seat, but the only thing he could see that constituted probable cause to pull the driver over was a burned-out taillight on the driver's side.

He hadn't had a drug bust in a couple of months, and the only thing Shep hated more than outsiders was the possession and abuse of illegal substances inside his jurisdiction. Pill poppers, junkies, heroin addicts, dealers, purveyors of weed, they were all one and the same to Shep. Dope was behind at least ninety-four percent of the weird shit going down in the county, of that much he was unshakably certain. He'd been to the spot in Vander-

bloon's Woods where two illegals had been growing pot a few years back, and though the field was
rife with common ragweed, not the cash-crop vari-
ety, he suspected there was more out there just
waiting to net some enterprising young yahoo a
nice long stint in the federal pen.

Hoping for something more than a dead taillight, Shep followed the station wagon for several
miles, hitting the strobe in disgust when the operator displayed no erratic driving. The vehicle signaled and came to a stop. Grabbing his flashlight,
Shep opened the door and got out.

He shined the light in the driver's eyes. "Hell of
a shiner you got there. Operator's license?"

"S-somethin' w-w-wrong, offi-c-cer?"

"As a matter of fact, you're drivin' with a
burned-out taillight." The operator was a small
man with a nervous twitch and a pronounced stutter. He dug around in his glove box, and after a bit
of fumbling, produced a license. Shep shined the
flashlight beam on the license, then walked back
to the patrol car while the operator waited.

Shep's knee-jerk reaction wasn't favorable toward Simms. There was something about the man
that set his teeth on edge, like the thought of
chewing on a wad of aluminum foil. He took his
damn good time running a check on him. Replacing
the radio mike, Shep walked back to the car, di-
recting the beam of his flashlight inside the van as
he handed back Simms's licence. "I see you've got
a prior. Bet you're gonna tell me you've aban-
doned a life of crime and you're headed down the
straight and narrow."

"I g-got a record. Th-that was a long t-time ago."

"Model citizen," Shep muttered. "County's lucky
to have you. Haven't I seen you around here before?"

"I l-live outs-s-side of t-town."

"Well, Mr. Simms, you are aware that New York residents need New York driver's licenses? This one's for the District of Columbia. You from the Beltway area?"

"W-worked t-there for a year or s-so. Only b-b-been here a c-couple of months. Haven't had t-t-time to g-get to the DMV, th-that's all."

"I suggest you make time," Shep said coldly. "What's that I see in the back of this vehicle?"

"T-tools, that's all." Simms's fingers tightened over the steering wheel, and a bead of sweat appeared from the edge of his dirty blond hair, streaking its way over his temple before he wiped it away with the back of a work-hard hand.

Shep craned his neck to get a clearer view. "Shovels, a pick, a metal bar. You planning on doing some diggin'?"

"B-been workin' for Ms. M-moncrief. N–new f-f-fence row. I d-dug m-most of the holes."

Shep grunted. "How 'bout that plywood? Looks new to me."

By now, Simms was clearly agitated. "M-man's g-got a right to b-b-buy plywood. Gonna put a p-porch on my p-place."

"You're a regular jack-of-all-trades, Simms. Building fence, woodworking."

"I k-keep b-b-busy. Unless you w-want t-to cite me for that t-taillight, I got to g-go."

"Just a warning, this time. Get it fixed. And if I were you, I'd watch myself. I've got my eye on you." Shep stood on the road, flashlight in hand, as Simms signaled his return to the road and drove away. "That boy's up to somethin'," he muttered to himself. "I can smell it."

A mile down that same road, Simms watched the rearview mirror. He'd come close to shitting his pants when the strobe flashed behind him. He didn't like cops, and he especially didn't like cops who were clearly suspicious like Deputy Margolis. Assuring himself that no one followed, Kenneth made a right turn onto a little used road that snaked past a gas well and seemed to peter out except for two faint tire tracks skirting the edge of a field and disappearing into the trees. At the edge of the woods, Kenneth stopped and got out of the van, removing a carefully constructed screen made of brush and tree limbs, large enough to conceal a pair of vehicles from the casual observer. Kenneth parked the rattletrap van beside the shiny new one, then returned to the natural screen.

"Kenny, where have you been?"

"I fucking t-told you n-not to c-call me that!"

"I'll c-call you w-whatever and w-whenever I p-p-please."

The mocking statement, imitating his stutter, brought the hot blood of embarrassment to Simms's face. His mouth tightened as he thought about the shovels in the back of the van. His fingers itched to take one to his tormentor's head, just like he'd done to *her* so many years ago, just like that crazy prick Turner had done to the FBI man the night of the stable fire. He really wished he could have hung around long enough to see it, but it was risky enough that he'd driven within a few hundred feet of the stable, with the headlights out, waiting to see if Turner had acted on his sly suggestions.

The loss of the stable meant the loss of Liz Moncrief's income. He'd hoped that it might be enough to convince her to disappear again, before it was too late. The ploy hadn't worked, and when Lyle discovered what he'd done, Kenneth had paid for "stepping out of line." He fingered the black eye, still quite tender, and hatred welled up inside him for his older half brother. Lyle was bigger, and stronger, and meaner than Kenneth; there were times when Lyle's capacity for coldness amazed him.

If not for Lyle's obsessions, he wouldn't be here now, up to his ears in this mess.

"They'll p-put you in a b-box, if you're n-not careful! Y-you were g-gonna shake her hand at the f-f-farm. T-they say s-she knows th-things. Y-You're so s-s-stupid s-sometimes!"

Lyle's face darkened, a precursor of things to come. "You mean *you'll* put me in a box, isn't that right, Kenny? It's what you fantasize about, isn't it? You're such a worthless little maggot. I bet you've creamed your pants plenty of times just thinking about it."

"You're s-sick, L-Lyle. Just like sh-she was s-sick. F-fuckin' c-crazy b-b-bitch. Sh-She hated every-b-body."

Lyle aimed a punch at Kenneth's head, then chuckled at the smaller man's involuntary cringe.

"I b-brought the s-stuff, like you s-said. L-let's get it over w-with. W-where is sh-she?"

"Oh, she's not here." Lyle straightened. "Anxious? You will be when you hear what I have in mind." He put his arm around Kenneth's emaciated shoulders, lowering his voice to a seductive croon. "Oh, Kenny, you're gonna have a hard-on for this one. It's the ultimate coup."

"I can't believe you kept this to yourself all this time: your little girl, your marriage, Jake."

Julianne reached across the table to give Liz's hand a squeeze, and a feeling of serenity washed over Liz. Her defenses were down. She was too consumed with worry over Jake to keep her guard up. "I didn't want it all dragged out into the open."

"Well, it looks like that's no longer an option," the redhead said with a shrug. "It's difficult to hide a pregnancy. People will figure it out, and speculate. And, then, there's your ex. You *are* going to tell him?"

Not telling Jake wasn't an option. She loved him, more than she had ever imagined she could love anyone. He had every right to know. He'd had a right to know about Fiona, too, and withholding that information had nearly destroyed them. It was a mistake she would not make again. "Jake and I aren't exactly on speaking terms at the moment. To put it bluntly, he's furious with me, and I can't blame him for that. He has every right to be angry—to hate me. I kept her away from him."

"I haven't run into him, but I doubt it's a matter of hating you. From what I could tell, the man is crazy about you."

Liz smiled, but the expression was tinged with sadness. "You didn't see the look on his face when he uncovered the truth. It sure looked like hatred to me." She took a deep, fortifying breath and changed the subject. "I don't suppose John has mentioned how the investigation into Harriet Stringer's death is going?"

"Not a word, and the reaction on Main Street isn't good. People are nervous—understandably so. I tried to tell him he needs to make a statement, but at this point, he isn't listening to his much wiser younger sister. Instead, he's drinking too much coffee, and avoiding sleep."

Liz frowned. "Did you know Harriet very well?"

"Well enough, I suppose, but we weren't close. She ran with a different crowd, if you get my drift.

She lived in the apartment over her brother's garage and commuted to her job in Mantoot. Why do you ask?"

"Just a thought," Liz said. "Do you think her family would mind if I had a look around her place? I picked up on her before, and I was hoping I might be able to come up with something useful." It cost Liz dearly to ask. She'd closed herself off for so long, not allowing anything to penetrate beyond the mundane, that to open that door was frightening and intimidating. If she had a choice, she would have stayed out of it, but she had to do something.

"Renée's a member of my Circle. I'll give her a call. I'm sure she won't mind."

Renée Stringer didn't mind. In fact, she met Liz at the door that same evening and led her up an outside stairway to the garage apartment. "It needs a really good cleaning, but I didn't want to disturb anything until John finished his investigation. Harriet was a pack rat. She couldn't seem to discard anything, and it got much worse after she started using."

Julianne's friend, Renée Stringer, was a small woman with straight blond hair and brown eyes. She was dressed in jeans and a white T-shirt with a large pentagram on the back. Her nails were long and lacquered firecracker red. Attractive, in a Wiccan kind of way. She would definitely stand out from the crowd. "I tried to pick up something earlier, but when I step in the door all I can sense is chaos. I don't know if it was Harriet coming through or all of this junk." She shook her head and sighed. "Well, listen, good luck, and yell if you need anything. I'll be out back, harvesting my herb garden."

"Thanks," Liz said, realizing belatedly that

Harriet's sister-in-law had made her exit, and she
was alone. Flashes of recall lapped at the shadowy
recesses of her mind. She saw herself clutching the
rag doll Fiona had dropped when her abductor
had grabbed her. She felt the dark, desperate need
to force the images from the doll, to forge a connection to her daughter's abductor, to gain insight
into where her child was so that she could bring
her home. The images wouldn't come.

Her breath quickened, and somewhere deep inside she saw herself coming apart at the seams. . . .
Standing in the middle of the room, she forced
herself to recoil from the image, to regain control.
Then, more deliberately, she started again.

She began by doing a slow walk around the living room and kitchen, just letting the space speak
to her. Impressions flitted through her mind,
lightning fast, glimpses of places and people and
emotions, none of which seemed significant
enough to examine.

Renée was right. Harriet had been a collector—
of things, people, experiences. There was a half-
filled wine bottle on the kitchen counter with
several glasses grouped around it and nearby an
ashtray overflowing with ashes and broken, crumpled butts. Liz glanced at the cigarettes and saw
thick, masculine fingers. Women didn't crush
their smokes out with force; men did. Angry, impatient men. But no one had mentioned a boyfriend.

She glanced inside the fridge, then closed it again
and walked through the living room into the bedroom and finally the bath. A packet of oral contra-
ceptives lay open on the bathroom vanity, a book
of matches beside them. Liz wasn't sure why, but
she picked up the matches, then dropped them
again as darkness swirled around her. For that split
second when she held them, she feared she might

faint. When the booklet fluttered to the tiles, the dizziness faded. Bending down, she steeled herself, picking up the pack while holding her reactions in check.

A black emptiness surged up from the floor with a dull roar. She could feel an icy coldness radiating from its center, fanning her cheeks, and she shivered. Holding the matches in her dominant hand, she reached for the vanity with her left, steadying herself as she reached out psychically. It was like standing at the perimeter of a black hole, a vortex of swirling evil that threatened to suck her in.

Liz pulled back from the destructive force with an audible gasp. She was facing the vanity, her image reflected in the mirrored door of the medicine cabinet. She looked pale, as if she'd seen a ghost.

Not a ghost, Liz corrected, *a killer, and he was close.* . . . So close that for a few seconds she had imagined she felt his hot breath on the back of her neck.

The thought formed, and someone appeared behind her. Liz felt the presence and whirled around, hand fisted in a defensive posture around the pack of matches.

Renée Stringer looked concerned. "Sorry, I didn't mean to startle you. I just came to see if everything was all right."

Liz's breath came back in a rush, but the push of adrenaline hadn't passed, and her heart was pounding. "Yes, I'm fine. Why do you ask?"

"It's just that it's getting late. My husband and I are going to be leaving soon, and we'd like to lock up."

Liz glanced at her watch. It was seven-thirty. She'd been standing in the bathroom holding the matches for over an hour, letting the darkness wash over her. As the effect of the adrenaline faded, exhaustion took its place.

"Did you find anything?"

"I don't know. Maybe." Liz held out the matches.

Renée frowned. "Foxy's Place."

Liz glanced sharply up. "You recognize it?"

"Yeah," Renée said. "Harriet hung out there. She was a weekend regular."

"Do you mind?" Liz asked, moving the matches toward her pocket and then pausing.

"No, of course not."

Liz pocketed the matches and followed Renée from the apartment, but she couldn't shake the eerie sensation of standing at the edge of the abyss, and the warmth of a pink and lavender Catskill sunset couldn't lighten her mood.

"Look, Fred, I'm not asking you to cancel the celebration. All I want is a few extra men in uniform, a show of force. You know how this works. A solid police presence not only reassures the citizens, it may prevent further abductions."

The mayor pushed back in his chair, fingering the gavel on the table in front of him. John would have preferred that the meeting had occurred in his office. Fred and the town council were seated behind a table situated on a raised platform. Their elevated position gave them a psychological advantage. They knew it, and so did he. Standing hat in hand in front of them, he was the supplicant, the petitioner, asking for favors.

"Sheriff, I do know how this works. We all know how this works. We've become a maniac magnet. I don't know what draws these monsters here—maybe it has something to do with the lax attitude of local law enforcement creating a favorable environment for them to operate in. Maybe they've put the word out: if you want to get away with murder, go to Abundance; it's a great place to commit a crime."

Nervous titters. Somebody coughed, embarrassed. Heat crept upward from John's collar. "You need somebody to blame for this, Fred? You blame society, not me. Maybe if government provided a few more social programs to identify troubled personalities before they hit the streets, maybe we wouldn't be creating so many of these violent offenders. They're made, folks, not born, but all we hear is that there's no money allocated in the current budget for improvements. Period. Because you've blown the wad on a fireworks display that'll impress the hell out of the taxpayers. I'm sure it hasn't occurred to you, but your priorities are more than a little fucked up."

At Mrs. Hardwick's gasp, "Sorry, Emma, but I don't think anything milder is going to get your collective attention." He took a deep breath to pace himself, and to try to get a rein on his temper, halfway succeeding, but he was still plenty pissed off. The town council had an iron fist on the budget, and under normal circumstances the low crime rate provided an excellent point of argument against approving any suggested increase. Something as ridiculous as a requisition for extra pencils and legal pads came down to a knock-down-drag-out fight.

"Look, I'm not asking for you to hire a whole squad of full-time employees, but we're gonna have busloads of tourists milling around the town tomorrow until well after dark. Just send out to Mantoot for a couple of rent-a-cops."

They put their heads together, whispered furiously back and forth for a few minutes, then Fred shook his head. "Request denied."

John blew out an impatient breath. His muscles tensed, and it was all he could do to keep his hands relaxed at his sides. Fred was intent on being a bullheaded ass over this, throwing up every obstacle he could pull out of the air in the hope of putting him in his place, and on the defensive. Worse, the tactic was very effective. "Dammit, Fred, our limited manpower has been devoted to solving these murders, as it should be. If you can argue that point, then maybe it's time for you to resign. We can always use the money we save on your salary to obtain the resources we need to maintain a decent police presence."

Fred banged the gavel on its stand, his face a thundercloud. "There will be no further discussion of this matter until the regular meeting in October. This meeting is adjourned!"

"Like hell it is! There's one last thing for you to consider before you stick your head back in the sand." John stalked to the dias, unpinned his badge, and slammed it down in front of the stunned mayor. "Find yourself another stooge—somebody who'll put up with your bullshit. I quit!"

As he headed for the door the commotion his statement caused brought a cold satisfaction. Fred had goaded him into doing what he'd been thinking about doing for almost a year. But he knew his actions weren't without consequences, and he couldn't answer the question that immediately rose in his mind: what the hell would he do now?

Alcohol never solved a man's problems; in Jake's case it didn't even help anesthetize the pain that had driven him to the bottle in the first place, and he was quickly coming to realize that the pain over his daughter's loss wouldn't go away. He'd hoped for the oblivion of passing out, but it seemed that even that would be denied him. He was drunk but appallingly awake when footsteps sounded on the outside stairs. Instantly alert, he listened, hoping to Christ it wasn't Liz.

A heavy-handed knock. Definitely not Liz. "Jake?"

Jake glanced at the clock before he got up and opened the door. It was five minutes of eleven P.M. John Rhys, out of uniform, stood outside.

"You mind if I come in?"

Jake stood back to let him pass, closing the door as he stepped into the kitchen. "If you're here to evict me, the rent's not due till Tuesday. By then I expect to be long gone from this delightful little town of yours and on my way back to civilization."

"You're leaving?" Rhys didn't even attempt to conceal his surprise. "What about Liz?"

Jake raised his gaze without raising his head. If Rhys had been a man who picked up on subtleties, he might have sensed the belligerence in Jake's glance, but it sailed right over the sheriff's blond head. "I'm really not in the mood to discuss Liz with anyone, least of all you. If that's why you're here, you can leave." Jake started to turn away, and Rhys grabbed his arm with just enough force to trigger the pent-up anger inside him. Too much bourbon had annihilated his inhibitions, but it didn't slow his reflexes. He balled his fist and swung, a burning satisfaction exploding in his solar plexus as his fist smashed into Rhys's mouth. The sheriff stumbled back and almost fell, righting himself and regaining his stance as he put a hand to his mouth. It came away bloody.

"What the hell was that for?" Rhys demanded.

"You want a reason?" Jake said. "Because I've got

a few dozen, the first being that you don't lay a hand on me—ever. I'm not your pal, you got that? Far from it."

He saw Rhys's gaze move past him, to the coffee table, the bottle, the Glock. "You finally hit bottom, is that it?"

"That punch must have jarred your wits into working order."

"What the hell happened? Did she dump you?" Rhys laughed. "No, I get it, she didn't dump you. You walked away, again. Christ. When the hell are you gonna wise up, Jake?"

Jake gave him a murderous look. "There's the door, Sheriff. Either arrest me for assaulting an officer, or get the hell out."

"I'm not pressing charges. You didn't strike an officer, you planted one on a civilian. As a matter of fact, I just resigned."

Jake snorted, turning his back on the former sheriff a second time. Amazingly, Rhys's hand closed around his arm again. Jake's temper, hanging by a spider's web–thin thread for two days, imploded. He swung, missed, and took a hard right to the chin. Staggering, he finally sat down hard.

Rhys shook his hand out, grinning through the pain. "Thanks, Jake. I owe you. I've wanted to do that since you got here."

Chapter Fifteen

It was Labor Day morning, and Faerie King was the last of the surviving horses to go. Dr. Bridger had hired a man with a horse trailer to transport the palomino gelding to a farm near Mantoot where the horse would board until Liz rebuilt.

If she rebuilt. At this point, nothing was certain. She hadn't discussed limitations with Kate Fife, but it wasn't her first pregnancy, and she was aware that the first trimester was the time at which the fetus was most vulnerable. Even if she managed to weather the first few months without difficulty, she would not be able to handle the kind of workload she'd held down for the last eighteen months, and she hadn't given much thought to the future.

She seemed to exist in a weird state of limbo, afraid to project that far, too consumed with the changes in her body to make life-altering decisions: to stay, to go, start over, rebuild.

And there *were* changes to contend with. Her appetite was unrelenting; she raided the fridge at odd hours, and she required a lot more sleep than she had just weeks before. As her physician, Kate had already cautioned her to avoid strenuous activities, so she was forced to stand back and watch as the gelding was loaded and driven away.

"Well, that's a sad sight," Bridger allowed. "But I'm sure it's only temporary. We should remember that." He took out his checkbook, scribbled a few lines, added a signature, and tore it out, handing it to Liz. "We're settled up, then? Everything in proper order."

Liz took the check, and in her mind's eye, Bridger's face loomed close, backlit by a glaring light. His voice echoed eerily, as if filtering down through a long tunnel. A chill crept over her, and she shivered, despite the warmth of the day. The vision came in a flash, there and gone, but it was so startling, so threatening, that Liz took an involuntary step backward before she could arrest the impulse.

Bridger's eyes narrowed. "Liz? Are you quite all right? You look pale. Maybe you should sit down."

He reached out, as if to grasp her arm, but Liz waved him off, reluctant for him to touch her. "I'm fine, really," Liz said quickly, confused and a little embarrassed. "It must be the heat. I was hoping it would ease with August behind us, but it's been unrelenting."

"Mmm, it certainly is." Bridger glanced at the sky, then focused on the charred beams and gray ash of the stable. "A pity about the old building, and the animals you lost. The newspaper account mentioned that the fire's been judged an arson. Does Sheriff Rhys have any suspects?"

One, Liz thought, *but he won't be providing any answers.* Samuel Turner had taken his secrets to the grave. "The sheriff hasn't clued me in on the investigation, so I can't really say with any certainty."

"Perhaps it's because he doesn't know. Recent events have me questioning Rhys's competency.

I've kept an eye on the papers. They haven't found the Cemetery Man. Kind of makes you wonder, why the police can't find a killer in an area so small."

"They have no proof that he's here. He could be living in another place, close enough to monitor events—"

"Close enough to kill," he pointed out. "Oh, he's here, in Abundance, or as near as Mantoot."

The conversation gave Liz chills. Anxious to end it, she glanced at her watch. "I'm afraid I have to go. I have an appointment, and I'm already late."

"I'll be in touch," Bridger said. "I'll want to continue those lessons as soon as possible."

Liz smiled in response as he opened the door and got into his pickup but refrained from telling him that it would be months before she would mount a horse again. Her riding days were over, at least for the foreseeable future.

She showered and changed into dark slacks and a cream-colored silk shell, pulled her hair into a low-slung tail and went downstairs. The dogs were waiting by the door. They seemed to know what she was thinking. "Sorry, guys, not this time. It's hot out there, and where I'm headed, there are no dogs allowed." Ignoring their disappointment, Liz locked the door and made her way to the Explorer.

Foxy's was an out-of-the-way place, tucked between a pizzeria and an all-night dry cleaner. Situated on a back alley in the seamier section of Mantoot, its water-stained stucco exterior and buzzing neon COORS LIGHT sign with an unlit "R" didn't make for a good first impression. It was ten minutes of twelve when Liz opened the door and walked in.

The smoked glass of the large front window filtered out the sun's rays and kept the interior cozy and dim. The bartender, ponytailed and in his mid-twenties, glanced up as she slid onto a stool. He wore a neat-fitting white T-shirt, fashionably faded jeans, and one gold hoop earring. A tattoo of a cockatiel covered one forearm from wrist to elbow. "Afternoon, pretty lady. What can I get you?"

Liz ordered a caffeine-free soda and struck up a conversation. It wasn't hard; the man was bored, and there wasn't another customer in the place. "Nice place you've got here."

He laughed. "I take it you don't get out much. Actually, it belongs to a friend of mine. I just work here; the tips are usually pretty good, the patrons are an interesting mix, and it's a great place to meet chicks."

Liz smiled. "Is it?"

"Heck, yeah. You're here, aren't you?" It was said with a grin so totally engaging that it was impossible for Liz to be offended, or to take him seriously. "Tristam." He offered his hand. "I started my masters program last week. What about you? What brings a classy lady like you to a hole in the wall like this? You looking for something in particular, or just a cool dark place to get lost for an hour or two?"

"Actually, I was hoping to ask you a few questions." He raised his brows, and she felt his barriers go up. "Don't worry, I'm not a cop. Just curious. I'm here about Harriet Stringer. Word has it she hung out here. Did you know her, by any chance?"

"Sure, I knew her. Everybody knew Harriet," he said easily. "Shame, what happened. In fact, the place hasn't been the same since we got the news. It's really done a job on the foot traffic. As you can see for yourself, the place is deserted."

"What can you tell me about her? Who'd she hang out with? Girlfriends? Men friends? Hobbies or other interests?"

"Harriet hung out with most of the regulars. Real outgoing, if you get my drift. She was even a member of the softball team a few years back. Played shortstop. They took the championship last year. They beat Stooley's Roadhouse." He pointed to a poster-sized group portrait on the wall behind the bar and a bleached blonde with noticeable roots and a unique-looking medallion around her neck. It was oval-shaped and had a winking, smiling sun in its center.

"Nice necklace," Liz said.

"Yeah. Harriet was really proud of it. She designed it herself. She was into that sort of thing, but it took a backseat to the drugs after she started using. She even pawned it for drug money. She bought it back as soon as she kicked the habit."

"Was there anyone new she talked about recently? Anything you noticed about her that caught your attention or seemed odd to you?"

"Nothing I can think of. She'd been a little more outgoing since she got clean. Junkies tend to go inward, you know; they focus on the drug—whatever their drug of choice happens to be. Getting high is all they think about, making that next score. When she got back from rehab, her focus changed. She started socializing again, picking up the people she'd dumped, making some new contacts. It was all pretty healthy. She even started dating again, though that might not have been a good thing. The guy picked her up here a few times, but he didn't hang around—an older guy. I don't know for sure, but I got the impression he might have been married. Not the kind of guy I would have figured Harriet to fall for—pretty rigid. Ex-military, or something."

Liz frowned. "Did she ever mention this guy's name?"

"Yeah. Maybe. I didn't pay a lot of attention."

Liz sensed a dead end and tried not to be disappointed. Coming here had been a long shot, but she'd felt she had to try. She slid a ten-dollar bill across the bar and stepped off the stool. "Tristam, thanks for the information. Keep the change."

"No problem," he said. "Stop back sometime."

Liz was halfway to the door, keys in hand, when Tristam snapped his fingers. "Kyle! No, not Kyle . . . Lyle. That's it. His name was Lyle."

She turned back, slowly, a chill working its way from her shoulders to her fingertips that had little to do with the air-conditioning. "Lyle? Lyle Bridger?"

"That was it. I'm sure of it. Lyle Bridger."

Jake's place was becoming an unofficial hangout for the heartbroken and the newly unemployed. First Matt Monroe and now the local sheriff. From the angle of the sunlight streaming through the living room windows Jake guessed it to be close to the noon hour. John Rhys's head hung half off the sofa as he did a rousing rendition of the buzz-saw blues. Jesus. He'd never heard such an aggressive snore. No wonder Rhys was divorced.

Gingerly making his way to the kitchen, Jake made a pot of coffee, stealing a cup before it was all brewed. He winced when the hot liquid came in contact with his broken front tooth and a fresh wave of new pain shot through his head. Just what he needed, more discomfort. His head thumped, keeping perfect rhythm with his pulse; his eyes itched; and his tongue felt thick and unwieldy. He hadn't been quite this hungover in longer than he could recall; he'd forgotten how excruciatingly miserable it could be.

Jake finished the first cup and poured a second.

He was going to need it. The light on the answering machine was in mid-spasm. *Blink, blink, blink, blink, blink, shudder, blink.* Biting the proverbial bullet, he did the manly thing and opened his voice mail. There were ten messages, nine of them painful to hear.

"Jake, I know you're angry, and you have every right to be. But we really need to talk. Please. I care about you. I'll be here at the farm." Her voice saddened even more with each unheard call. "I don't know why I'm doing this—except that I need you. Please, we can't let it end like this. . . ." Jake closed his eyes against the sting of tears and a muscle worked in his cheek. He'd be justified in erasing the remaining messages, packing up the Buick, and turning his back to this burg. But something held him there, hand braced on the tabletop, phone to his ear.

The need to hear her voice. A reluctance to walk away when they'd come so damn close to having it all. "Jake . . ." She sighed, and for the space of a heartbeat, he thought he heard tears in her voice. "If you're there, please pick up. Haven't we hurt each other enough? Can't we . . . can't we please try to help one another through this? Jake, please . . . call me back. We need to meet. There's something—" A heavy sigh. "Look, there's something you need to know, but I can't do this over the phone."

Her voice broke, the line went silent, and the next message began. "Jake. It's Calendar. You know how I hate admitting this shit, but I'm a little worried about you. When you get this message, ring me back. You won't get an ass-chewing. I promise to mind my own damn business. I just need to know you haven't checked out on me. Yeah, I know. I'm an asshole, but let me hear you say it, okay?"

There were several more. Jake listened to them all, then he erased them. He would have called Charlie, but it made him uneasy to be reminded of how close to the edge he'd come. He'd been walking a fine line the night before, and if Rhys hadn't shown up when he did . . . Maybe he owed the sheriff something, after all. Then, there was Liz. He thought about dialing her number, but what the hell would he say?

It's fine that you kept my kid from me. It's a minor thing, and I'm over it.

It wasn't a minor thing, and though his feelings for Liz hadn't changed, he didn't know if he could get past it. He didn't know much of anything. He'd gotten through the night, thanks in no small part to his buddy the sheriff, but he was uncomfortably aware that he wasn't firing on all eight pistons, and he couldn't guarantee that it wouldn't happen again. Next time there might not be anyone to punch him in the mouth and jar him out of his self-absorption. Yet, all he could do at the moment was push that thought to the back of his mind and try to get through the day.

Maybe in time he'd see things differently, but right now the pain was new, the wound still as raw and intolerable as the newly broken tooth. He ran his tongue across the broken edge of the incisor. At least the tooth could be repaired. He wasn't so sure about the rest of him.

He had a vague recollection of promising Rhys that he'd help keep an unofficial lid on the Labor Day bash, before they'd both passed out. The sheriff, it seemed, had resigned the position without shedding the mantle of responsibility, and Jake couldn't help thinking that it was a little like his reluctance to cut ties with Liz. When it came right down to it, he had more in common with the sheriff than he liked to admit. They were both world-class suckers. With Rhys still snoring on the sofa, Jake showered and shaved, then headed outside with car keys in hand.

He'd checked the tires on Kenneth Simms's van, but he wasn't quite ready to let go of the notion that Simms might be involved with the local murders. Simms would be working at the farm until noon, helping Jersey Delacour sow the winter wheat. His place was only a few miles out, and Jake could be there and back before Rhys had any inkling that he was gone.

The Simmses's home was a low-rate rental, substandard by any means. The driveway was rutted and the sidewalk broken and uneven. No lights showed in the windows, and Simms's van was absent. Mary Simms answered Jake's knock, wiping her damp hands on a ragged dishtowel. "Can I help you?"

"Mrs. Simms. Jake English. I spoke with your husband, Kenneth, a few days ago."

"Yes, I remember." She ducked her head as if embarrassed, a plain young woman with dark hair and a shy smile. "You were asking questions about the little girl they found at Miz Moncrief's place. I saw that on the TV. Such a dreadful thing. Miz Moncrief, she's a nice lady. Been real good to Kenny and me."

"Is Kenneth here?"

"He's workin', but he'll be home in an hour or two. Is there anything I can help you with?"

Jake hesitated, then pushed ahead. She was eager to help, and at this point he had little to lose. "I think I may have left my pen here the other day. It's silver, with the initials J.H.E. engraved on it. My wife gave it to me, and I hate to lose it."

Mary Simms's eyes brightened. "You're married?"

"Divorced. But it means a lot to me."

"Oh, I'm so sorry to hear that. Would you like to come in and look for it?"

"I don't want to be any trouble."

The phone rang in another room. "I'd better get that." She motioned to Jake to come in, then waddled to the kitchen. Jake took the pen he'd described from his pocket and placed it beside the chair he'd occupied during the interview with Kenneth. Mary's voice came from the kitchen, one half of a conversation she was in no hurry to end. Jake glanced around the living room. A shallow alcove with a flowered fabric curtain served as a closet. Jake swept the curtain aside. Work clothes were piled in one corner, a few pairs of shoes scattered haphazardly beneath and beside the pile of worn denim. Women's shoes, size eight. Jake moved the clothing aside and found a pair of men's work boots, heavily worn, strings broken. The size was compatible with the print found on Liz's porch. But there were no athletic shoes, and it wasn't enough to pin the attempted break-in on Simms.

In the kitchen, Mary hung up the phone. Jake replaced the curtain and walked back to the table and bent to retrieve it just as she reentered the room. "You found it, I see," she said. "I'm glad."

The door slammed, and Kenneth stormed in. His upset at finding Jake talking to Mary was obvious. "W-what the hell is he d-doin' here?"

"Kenny! Don't be rude! Agent English left his pen here the other day—it was a gift, from his wife."

Jake held the pen up, then pocketed it. "I don't know what I was thinking to leave this here. I'm lost without it."

"Y-you need to l-leave. N-now."

"Kenny!" Mary said, clearly embarrassed. "Is there anything else you need?"

"That'll do it," Jake said, turning to go.

As he got in his car, Kenneth Simms's voice drifted out behind him. "D-damn it, M-Mary! H-how many t-times do I have to t-tell you? D-don't let no one in when I'm n-not home. D-do you hear me?"

"I hear you! God, Kenny . . . Why are you so mad? I don't understand you!"

Kenneth slammed from the house in time to watch the FBI agent back his car out onto the dirt road. He'd told Mary he was going to the Quick Mart for a pack of cigarettes, but he only drove to an open field on the top of the next hill and took out a cell phone. It rang four times before Lyle picked up.

"We've got a p-problem," Kenneth said without preamble. "Th-that FBI agent was in the h-h-ouse when I g-got home." Pause. "I d-don't *know* what he w-wanted! He s-said he d-dropped a pen when he was there b-before." After another pause, "I d-don't know. He was l-lyin'! He w-was l-lookin' f-for s-somethin'! He's too c-close, L-Lyle. I d-don't l-like this. Oh, G-god. I d-don't like this."

"Calm down, Kenny." It wasn't a suggestion; it was an order. "Did you do what I told you to do?"

"I p-put the shoes in a D-Dumpster. Nobody s-saw."

"Then there's nothing for him to find. And no reason to be upset. Go home and talk to Mary. Make sure that the homefront is secure. I'll take care of everything. I always do, don't I?"

"I gotta go," Kenneth said, his stomach knotting and clenching. Lyle was right. He always took care of everything. He planned the abductions and carried them out. But he had gotten Kenneth into this mess. Liz Moncrief was Lyle's obsession, and it was Kenneth who now had to worry about how much the police knew, and whether they could link him to the evidence. It was his worry, his risk. No one suspected Lyle. No one would.

Suddenly Kenneth wanted out, and if it hadn't been for the thought of what Lyle might do to him if he crossed him, he would have packed the van and told Mary they were leaving Abundance. He could sell Harriet Stringer's necklace. He was sure he could get a couple of hundred dollars for it. It would be enough to get him away from Abundance, away from New York. If he was lucky, away from Lyle. The thought was tempting.

The idea was to grab a quick lunch and head on over to the festivities to have a look around. Rhys seemed convinced that their man would show up there, perhaps try to disrupt the proceedings, or maybe even target and snatch a youngster. It was their worst-case scenario, and the one thing Rhys hoped they could prevent. As he'd helped himself to Jake's bourbon, Rhys had related the scene at the special meeting of the town council and vented his frustration in a string of profanity to rival anything Jake could have come up with. Who would have guessed that Mr. Clean could be so eloquently profane? Not that Jake could blame the man. Politics was a damn dirty business, and politicians were usually self-serving. If it didn't fit the agenda, it got squashed. Unfortunately, in this particular instance, the sacrificial lamb happened to be public safety.

The café was crowded. Marge Turner hadn't missed a beat, despite the death of her only son,

Samuel. Rumor had it that she'd buried him in the cemetery at the First Baptist Church on High Street, without ceremony, then reopened the café to accommodate the dinner crowd. Marge was a hard woman, and a hard woman to fathom. Whether the callousness came from too many years of dealing with a troubled offspring, or whether it had contributed to Samuel's emotional warp was a matter of endless speculation. Jake heard the whispers of a couple arguing the finer points of environmental causes versus genetics in relation to the Turners when he approached the entrance. They glanced at him and he saw them do a double-take as he kept on walking. When he grasped the door handle, the door swung open and a man exiting nearly ran him down.

Jake stepped back and the man smiled. "Clumsy of me. Guess I wasn't paying attention."

"No problem."

As Jake stepped around him, the guy turned to face him and, putting away his billfold said, "I know you, don't I? Yes, you're a friend of Liz Moncrief's—the FBI."

It didn't take long for Jake to come up to speed. The dentist. Black truck. Customized. New. "Bridger," he said. "Riding lessons."

"You have an excellent memory, and a broken incisor. Mind if I have a look?"

"Not if you have special office hours."

"I'm closed today, but for a friend of Liz's, I think something might be arranged." Bridger tilted Jake's head back and looked down his nose at the broken tooth. "I can repair that, no problem. Would you like to meet me at my office in, say, twenty minutes?" He handed Jake a business card, then got in his van. Van . . . not pickup. *Van,* dark green, tinted windows, curtains in back.

"Hey, Doc," Jake called after him. "You get yourself a new set of wheels?"

Bridger smiled. "Oh, this? It's my wife's."

Bridger's office was located in what used to be a fine old brick home on Main Street in Mantoot. It had a broad, shady porch and a handsomely furnished waiting room. His inner sanctum was no less impressive. From the leather dental chair to the sound system, it was all state-of-the-art and very expensive.

"Impressive," Jake said, taking in the adjustable overhead light. "You do pretty well for yourself."

Bridger chuckled. "I make a comfortable living. My job isn't as exciting as yours, though. I mean, it must be a thrill a minute—the investigative work, the arrests. Come, sit." He patted the dental chair.

Jake wasn't anxious to sit. He kept seeing the dark green van.

Family car?

Or murder wagon?

It could be either. No one had considered Bridger a suspect. Family man, with a pack of kids. Solid background, good reputation, husband, father. But was he also a serial murderer?

It was possible, Jake knew. The man had access to Liz's place. He was obviously an intelligent guy, smart enough to stay one step ahead of the authorities. But what about the facts? The evidence?

"Agent English?" Bridger said. "The tooth?"

"Yeah, in a minute. This is nice. You do this?" He had walked to the adjacent wall, a wall covered by a large handcrafted collage of faces, most smiling . . . a few adults, a pile of kids.

"Yes, as a matter of fact. I like to think I enjoy a

special relationship with my patients. I like them; they trust me implicitly."

"That's funny," Jake said. "Trust and dentists. The two words don't usually go together."

He couldn't seem to turn his back on those smiling faces. Kids, and teens and preteens, and one woman proudly displaying a bright smile. She was thirtyish, a bottle-blonde, kind of plump, small of stature, with a face Jake had seen not so long ago in a set of postmortem photographs in John Rhys's office. In this photo Harriet Stringer had her arm around Bridger, who stared soberly at the camera with a stern expression and lifeless eyes. "These are your patients?"

"All satisfied customers."

"You work with kids a lot?"

"Young people are my specialty. I have four of my own, and a contract with several school districts to do annual exams."

Bridger was opening a drawer. He had his back to Jake, who scanned the huge collage, instinctively searching for other familiar faces. "Harriet Stringer was a patient of yours?"

"Are you nervous, Agent English? Don't be. I'm very good at what I do."

Jake started to turn. Bridger was right behind him, and in his hand was a hypodermic needle. Instincts kicked in, Jake raised his arm to deflect the needle, and took the needle stick in his forearm. The effect was instantaneous. His vision blurred, and the floor seemed to rush up toward him. He threw out an arm to steady himself, grasping Bridger's shoulder.

"You can fight it all you like," Bridger said. His voice was distorted and strange, like an old vinyl single slowed to thirty-three-and-a-third. "But in the end, it will win."

"You," Jake managed. "It was you all along."

Bridger watched his patient fall, then, humming to himself, he took out his cell phone. "Kenny, I need you. Come by the office. Problem solved."

Abundance threw out all the stops for their Labor Day celebration. At one P.M. John Rhys lounged in front of Julianne's shop, a pivotal point on the parade route. Hudson Valley High's marching band led the procession, tubas drowning out the clarinets while somewhere in the distance the scream of a bottle rocket sounded. John kept an eye on the crowd lining both sidewalks. Kenneth Simms was there with his wife, Mary. Mary, just pregnant enough to look miserable in the midday steam bath, fidgeted on a lawn chair. Kenneth scanned the crowd. He seemed nervous, as if he was waiting for someone. But who? John didn't know much about Simms, except that he kept to himself. One might even call him a loner. A loner with a cell phone. John watched as he took it from his belt, listened, ended the call after a few seconds, and replaced the phone.

That was odd. Simms wore threadbare work jeans and a stained T-shirt. His hair was too long and unkempt. He seemed to struggle just to keep body and soul together with the mere basics of life, yet he could afford a cell phone?

Across the street, Shep was busy with crowd control. A fight broke out between two teenage boys over a pretty little thing with blond hair and a large chest. Shep separated the combatants and got in their faces. As soon as he turned his back, they were at it again. John keyed his portable radio mike. "You need help over there?"

"Now, knock it off and get the hell out of here!" Shep's shout came clearly through the speaker.

"Jesus, John. These little assholes are driving me crazy. How's a man supposed to keep everything under control while watching for some lunatic murderer? I sure wish you hadn't resigned. Where the hell's our mayor when we need him? If he can't increase the budget, the least he can do is lend a hand down here with crowd control—unofficially, of course."

"Getting ready to make a speech, as I understand it. Just take it as it comes. You're doin' a great job. If I see anything out of the ordinary I'll let you know. Until then just keep doing what you're doing."

"Sure thing, but I really hate this."

Shep had made his feelings extremely clear when the mayor had contacted him and asked him to assume the position of acting sheriff. He would do it, but he didn't like it. John Rhys was sheriff, Shep his right-hand man, and he wanted to keep it that way. As deputy, he had all the perks without the hassle that came with being top dog, and Shep's ambitions only went so far. Shep had waited until the mayor had completed his official duty, then privately pulled him aside and told Fred that he was "a damned bureaucrat with a head full of air and no sense of the trouble he'd caused for the town by backing John into a corner." John had heard about it firsthand from Fred, who accused John during a heated phone conversation of putting Shep up to it. John had told Fred to kiss his ass, and hung up on him.

Freedom felt fantastic.

"Shep, what do you make of Kenneth Simms?"

"I know I don't like him. He's a major loser. Stopped him the other day for a busted taillight, and ended up warning him to get an updated operator's license."

"He's driving on an expired license?"

"It's current, but it isn't for New York State. It

was issued for the District of Columbia. Fancy that. Why do you ask?"

"No reason in particular. He just strikes me as odd, that's all. I think I may swing by his place later and have an unofficial look around—just to be neighborly."

"If you need backup, just let me know," Shep told him. "Simms is a pimple on the ass of humanity. I'd like nothing better than to see him move on out of here."

A car driven by an elderly woman appeared at the barrier on Elva Avenue. John watched as Shep got her vehicle turned and headed back the way she came, then glanced at his watch.

Quarter of two. Where the hell was Jake? He should have been here by now.

Jake had agreed to lend an unofficial presence, and John had taken him at his word. Of course, by then they'd both been well on their way to total inebriation, and there was always a chance that Special Agent English didn't even remember agreeing to it. . . . Or maybe he'd decided to pay Liz a visit instead.

John tried not to let the thought rankle. Liz was a grown woman, capable of making up her own mind about who she wanted to see, and didn't want to see. Besides, he was getting the feeling there was a hell of a lot going on which he wasn't aware of, and which didn't involve him. *Well, you'll find out soon enough,* he thought.

Bloodshot eyes concealed behind a pair of dark glasses, John watched Fred approach in the company of Mrs. Farley, president of the garden club. Fred looked like he wanted to say something to John, but John turned and walked away before he had the chance. Despite being more than a little hungover, he couldn't help smiling.

Chapter Sixteen

Liz couldn't stop thinking about Harriet Stringer on the drive back from Foxy's in Mantoot. From being in Harriet's apartment, she'd gotten a sense of what the other woman had been like, and the face in the group photo above the bar continued to haunt her. Harriet had been brimming with life and with energy, like a candle flame that burned too high, and someone had snuffed out that flame, coldly, cruelly, kidnapping her and burying her alive.

The question was why? Why her? Had something about her spoken to her killer, even though she had little in common with the previous victims? Did she fit somehow into a sick fantasy? Or had she merely been a victim of opportunity? Something had happened in his life that acted as a stressor at that particular moment he happened upon her. Murderous coincidence? The bad luck of being in the wrong place at the worst time? Or did either even apply? Was there something she wasn't seeing? These were questions she'd asked herself a thousand times in connection with the murders in Virginia, in connection with the murder of her daughter. She had thought they were making some headway with the first killings, and then Fiona was taken, and all of Liz's objectivity was obliterated.

Motive, opportunity, psychological profiles.

Her daughter, Jake's daughter . . . gone . . . missing . . . robbed of life.

The heart had gone out of Liz, and there had been nothing left.

Coming to Abundance hadn't changed any of that; Jake had. He'd made her feel again, against her will, made her feel alive.

It wasn't that she missed their daughter any less. She would always miss Fiona, always love her, and a part of her heart would always be in that tiny grave in Virginia, so that her firstborn baby girl would never be alone. But now there was another life, another child. The thought filled Liz with a strange new warmth, and at the same time filled her with terror. As she had come to terms with the baby's existence, the full implications of her position struck her. She was pregnant, and he was out there, still planning, still killing, still living in his obsessive fantasies.

If someone didn't stop him, it could happen again. Another child, another innocent, lost, taken, and she felt helpless to prevent it, despite her extrasensory abilities. She'd been trained to analyze the facts and draw conclusions. She picked up impressions through touch—objects, people. It was considered a gift, yet what good had it been when Fiona had been abducted and was missing, her life on the line?

Her daughter. Her baby girl. She hadn't been able to find her. Her gifts hadn't been effective.

She hadn't felt like a mystic, a seer, just a woman desperate to rescue her child.

And she'd failed.

Now, there was another child important to her, unborn perhaps, but nonetheless real, precious. Vunerable.

And if someone didn't stop him, her previous thought replayed in her mind, *it could happen again.*

"Think, Liz," she said softly, fervently, "What did you glean from the data when working on these murders at Quantico?" The facts came slowly, pulled out of a time that was shrouded in grief. "This guy is no random actor," she said aloud, "and someone is helping him. The containers are too awkward for one man to handle; he has help, which widens his circle a bit, and it also could work against him." She needed to talk to John, urge him to set up a press conference, something he'd been resisting. There was a chance that if someone hadn't picked up on the killer's odd activities, they may have picked up on those of his partner.

Someone knew something. The trick was to convince that person or persons to come forward, and that meant media coverage, showing the victims' faces on television, getting them into the papers, humanizing them, making it personal.

"What else?" she murmured, worrying a thumbnail with her teeth. Then, "His targets are deliberate, chosen for a reason. He took Fiona to get to me. So why did he snatch Harriet? What was it about her that made her special?"

She kept picturing that smiling face. The bartender had indicated that Harriet was outgoing and well-liked, and except for the time when the drug use took over her life, she had a lot of friends. "Collector of things," Liz said, repeating the impressions she'd picked up while at Harriet's place. "Collector of people."

Harriet had been small in stature, barely five feet tall . . . but her age was out of sync with the other victims, who were all under the age of twenty. Harriet, at thirty-three, was the exception. So why had he deviated from his pattern? Why make an exception?

Liz almost missed a turn in the road. "Jesus. That's it: Harriet *is* the exception. Collector of things, collector of people. The son of a bitch *knew* her! And she knew him."

Serial killers had relationships; sometimes they even married, carrying on double lives. Renée hadn't mentioned a boyfriend, but the bartender had said Harriet was dating Lyle Bridger. Bridger was married, with kids. Not that married men didn't cheat on their wives with pretty young blondes.

She pulled the Explorer off the road and took out her cell phone. She thought about her conversation with the bartender, and her brief exchange with Lyle Bridger that morning. If Tristam was right, then Bridger and Harriet had been intimately involved. Yet Bridger hadn't mentioned the connection when they discussed the killings. That in itself wasn't unusual. He wouldn't want it to become common knowledge. Probably wouldn't want his wife to find out he'd been cheating.

Liz decided she had to ask him about it before going to the police. Lyle Bridger's number was in her directory, along with Cyn Kellog's and the owners of all the horses she had boarded not long ago. Punching the number in, she waited, but Bridger didn't pick up. Instead, his machine kicked on. "This is Doctor Bridger's office. I'm unable to take your call right now. Please leave a message. Your call is important to me."

"Dr. Bridger, it's Liz Moncrief. I'd like to talk to you about an acquaintance of yours, Harriet Stringer. Please return my call at the earliest opportunity." She left her number, then dialed Jake's cell phone, but there was no answer there, either. There was a good chance that he was still brooding, refusing to take any calls. She couldn't get through to a man who wouldn't answer the phone, but she was fairly sure she knew where to find him, and she would stand on his landing and talk through the door until he finally heard her.

He was vaguely aware of his pounding head and an itch somewhere in the vicinity of his eyelids, but when he attempted to raise his hand to scratch it, the restraints kept him from it. His brain, groggy from too much bourbon, was slow to react, and the fight-or-flight response the realization should have triggered was replaced by a vague bemusement.

Too much bourbon . . . He seemed to recall coming out of his stupor and doing a pretty good job of being ambulatory. He'd made it to the café under his own steam and without difficulty. Something about John Rhys tickled his recall, and he let the unformed question sink in for a moment while he drifted in a soft, featherlike haze. The answer floated up like the message in a Magic 8 Ball. Rhys had dropped by the night before—or had it been longer ago than that? He wasn't sure what day it was, or how long he'd slept. Snatches of recall drifted lazily through his brain. He saw Rhys's face, then saw the sheriff stagger and fall.

Instant gratification. He'd pasted the sheriff, and Rhys had retaliated.

Jake's tongue found the broken incisor, and the pieces fell into place. The café, the guy who took riding lessons from Liz . . . ex-military, a lifer, Doctor Something-Or-Other . . . No, *dentist*. He was a dentist, and he'd offered to repair the broken tooth, despite it being a holiday. . . . Jake had followed him to his office in Mantoot, but that didn't explain his hangover, or why his lids felt like they were Superglued together.

Voices sounded far away. Jake forced himself to stay awake and listen as they came closer. Two men. One stutterer. The other was matter-of-fact, his tone commanding. The dentist . . . Bridges . . . no, Bridger . . . and Liz's hired man. Kenneth Simms. Now there was an unlikely combination. Turning his head toward the voices, Jake strained to open his eyes, but they wouldn't budge, and he swore softly.

Footsteps, heavy tread, the soles of shoes slapping concrete. "Ah . . . I see you're awake." There was a pinching sensation at Jake's temple, followed by a few seconds of absolute torture as the duct tape covering his eyes was torn away. Bridger's face loomed in front of Jake, who was wondering if a square inch of skin remained?

"What the hell?" Jake managed. His motor responses were delayed, but his pain receptors were working just fine; he wasn't so sure he wouldn't have preferred it to be the other way around. "Where am I?" It was a shed of some sort, twelve feet by twelve feet, with a warped wooden floor littered with sawdust.

"Just a little place I know—I guess you could call it a workshop. Somewhere we won't be disturbed. Sorry about that incisor. There wasn't time to fix it. Opportunity knocked, and I just couldn't say no. Who knew you'd be so easy?"

"Easy," Jake repeated, frowning. The image of the dentist's chair flashed in his brain, the photo collage. . . "Cemetery Man," he managed, but he felt no sense of victory for putting the puzzle together. Being nabbed by the asshole he'd been stalking wasn't exactly a major coup.

"Some call me that, yes," Bridger admitted, "but I can't take all the credit. If it's accuracy we're hoping to achieve, it should be Cemetery Men."

"Two. Partners. We figured that out."

"I knew you would."

"You're a real giant among men, Lyle. Killing kids. My kid. It takes a lot of balls to confront an eight-year-old."

"Your kid?" Bridger had been busy checking the duct tape that bound Jake's wrists in front of him, assuring himself that it was snug, but now he looked sharply up. "The dark-haired little girl. Liz's daughter? Now, there's a surprise."

Jake struggled against the duct tape, but it was tightly wound and since he had less than ideal leverage, it was too strong for him to break.

"Now, now," Bridger said. "That won't make it any easier. You've been under anesthesia. Give yourself time to recover."

Like he had time, Jake thought. He didn't know what Bridger had planned, but he could make a good stab at guessing, and it didn't bode well for reconciliation with Liz and subsequent growing old together. He was thirty-nine; unless he managed somehow to work a miracle and break the tape, he wouldn't see forty. "Why?" Jake demanded.

"Why you? Or why in general?" Bridger stood back, folding his arms over his chest. "Being an

FBI man, I guess you mean motive? It's not complicated, really. Some people collect stamps, I collect people—little people, actually. She was small, you see. Small, and perfect on the outside, rotten on the inside. Not unlike an apple that rots from the inside out."

"*She* . . . who the hell is *she?*"

"Oh, I can't tell you that. It's not a good idea to tell too much. It was one of her rules: don't tell. She was always very strict. Kenny broke the rules, and there were consequences. She used to lock him in a chest freezer out back of the house. One of her men friends had modified it to provide ventilation through a pipe. He put this gratelike insert where the motor had been. That box was like a coffin. He told me all about it. I would sneak outside after she went to bed and talk to him through the grate."

The grogginess was wearing off. The mental cogs were turning, but Jake still didn't see a way out. "And that's why you do this? Because you had a rough childhood? That's bullshit. You didn't corner the market on being abused, you know, and not every kid who has it rough turns homicidal maniac."

Bridger chuckled. "You don't get it. I used to tell on Kenny just to get him into trouble. The box fascinated me, and he came to depend on me, because he knew I'd look out for him. When he was in the box, I was his world, the only thing standing between him and the hot, sweaty darkness."

"Jesus Christ," Jake muttered, but he wasn't the only listener appalled by the admission.

"Y-you s-son of a b-b-bitch! Y-you d-did it on p-p-purpose, so you could s-sit out there and t-talk to me, smuggle me water through a st-straw? Y-you're the sc-scum of the f-fucking earth, L-lyle!" Kenneth's diatribe ended on a yelp as he planted his palms on Bridger's shoulders and shoved. Being much smaller than his half sibling, his shove had little effect.

Bridger took a step back, his tone placating. "Now, Kenny! I took care of you, didn't I?"

Kenneth gave him another determined shove, causing the larger man to stumble. "I t-told you n—never to c-call me that! Y-you're j-just like her! Y-you took care of me unt-t-till you got t-tired of it, just like n-now!"

"Y-you w-w-went along w-with it," Bridger taunted.

"B-because I th-thought I owed y-you!" Simms made an almost animal sound, a clear indication of his mounting frustration. He'd been carrying a cardboard tray with two Styrofoam cups on it that he had put down upon entering. Now he picked the tray up and threw it across the narrow shack. Hot coffee splattered Bridger's shoes. Simms sniffled. "I hate y-you, L-lyle."

"Kenny, Kenny, Kenny." Bridger put his hands on his brother's shoulders. "You're upset and over-reacting."

"He's f-from the FB-B-B-I, Lyle. You said after M-miss M-moncrief, we'd give it a rest. D-damn it, L-lyle, you p-p-promised!"

"Listen to him, Lyle," Jake said. "Hurt Liz, and the Bureau will hunt you down. Kill us both, and there won't be a stone they'll leave unturned looking for you. The only question is who gets the pleasure of frying your ass: New York or Virginia?"

"Don't listen to him, Kenny," Bridger crooned. "We're smarter than they are. Are you ready to help with Phase Two?"

"I g-guess s-so," Simms said, but he didn't sound enthusiastic.

"Then d-do it." Bridger put an arm around

Kenneth's shoulders, guiding him to the door. "Don't screw this up."

Jake was alone with the warped son of a bitch. Most of the fog had burned off his brain, and he was thinking more clearly. Keeping a clear head was crucial. If he went back to La-La Land, he was done for. He needed to be able to think and to strategize, and he needed the use of his hands. He flexed his fingers—or at least he thought he did. He couldn't feel anything but cold in his hands. His fingertips had gone dead, numb from lack of circulation. "The least you could do is to loosen this tape a little. I'm dying for a cigar."

"Tobacco's so bad for you. It causes cancer, and emphysema." It was said with all seriousness, and punctuated by that too-loud laugh. "I guess in your case long-term effects don't apply, do they?"

"You're a regular laugh riot, Lyle. You get your sense of humor from your mother?"

The change was lightning fast. Something came into Lyle Bridger's eyes, or rather, something drained out of them, and for a few seconds Jake wasn't sure what he was witnessing, or even if Bridger himself was still in the room. "I told you not to mention her name!" he said, a thread of saliva spraying out of his mouth and landing on the breast of his shirt. "Didn't I tell you?" He was in Jake's face, dragging him up by the collar, baring his teeth in a snarl. "Didn't I?"

"Yeah, you told me," Jake said. "I get it. Calm down, Lyle. Just calm down."

Jekyl and Hyde, Jake thought. Two sides of one very twisted man, one friendly and confident, the other an out-of-control monster, filled with black rage. He was beginning to get it, the only question remaining was what the hell he could do about it. How could he use the information he had to work

Lyle? The man was anything but stable. If he pushed him over the edge, he could snap, and there was no doubt that Lyle Bridger was capable of murder. He'd proven it. Four murders in Virginia, five in New York . . .

Fiona, his daughter.

Her face, blue-tinged in death, rose up to haunt him, her bloodied fingernails, and he wanted to wrap his hands around this man's neck and squeeze the life from him. Somehow, he got past the cold fury that churned in his gut. It wasn't a matter of forgiveness; it was about survival. In order to get through this, he not only needed to remember who and what he was dealing with, but how best to work him from a psychological standpoint.

"Listen, Lyle, I'm curious: how'd you and Simms pull this off? You've been offing victims in two states over a period of several years, and you've had authorities baffled. In all this time, they never even came close."

Bridger's mouth twitched. "It's all about details. If you take care of the little things, the big ones fall into place. Take yourself, for instance. You're a minor detail; Liz is the main objective."

"You've been obsessed with her for a long time. It's one thing we have in common."

"I've spent a lot of time getting close to her, observing her from a distance, working my way into her world. I can't wait to see her face when she realizes it was me all along. So close . . . and she never even suspected."

"I bet you've got something big planned for her, is that right?" It was killing Jake to talk to this pissant this way about Liz, to get down to his level. Yet, he'd been truthful when admitting that Liz was their common denominator. Jake loved her, wanted her.

Bridger had robbed her of her little girl and in the process nearly destroyed her. If he succeeded, he would finish the job, and though Jake hated to admit it, he wasn't sure he could keep it from happening. Where the hell was his good buddy John Rhys when he needed him? Now there was an irony: Rhys was guarding his precious townsfolk, neighbors and friends, from Bridger and Simms.

"Yes, I have plans." As Jake watched, Bridger took a hypodermic needle and vial from a small carryall bag. He proceeded to fill the hypodermic.

Jake thought of Harriet Stringer, and his stomach clenched. "What the hell's that for?"

The dentist snapped the cylinder with his forefinger, then shot a thin stream into the air. "Just a little something to take the edge off your nicotine cravings and make you a little more cooperative. I had to use it with Harriet, too, though I have no doubt she enjoyed it a lot more than you will, given her history."

He stuck Jake with the needle, and a strange sensation of euphoria stole slowly over him as his breathing slowed, his sense of urgency slowly faded. Bridger's face loomed in front of him, and he could only hope it wasn't the last thing he'd see.

The parade had passed by and the crowd was beginning to thin when Liz arrived at Jake's apartment. Streams of people headed for the village green with picnic baskets and coolers, or to the café for a quick meal. A new gazebo had been added in the center of the green, a showy piece with a domed roof done in gleaming bronze. Inside the open-air structure a string quartet was setting up. Liz had a clear view of the green from the stairs leading to the apartment above the Bell, Book, and Whatnot; what she didn't see was Jake's Buick parked in its usual spot. Trying not to read anything into the car's absence, she knocked. "Jake? It's Liz. Are you there?"

No answer. No sound of movement, or sense of the place being anything but empty. Being able to sense the presence of living energy was something she took for granted. Dwellings had different vibrations, and a home that was lived in felt different from a house that was empty. Liz could always determine before entering whether a house was occupied or not.

There was a waiting stillness about the apartment that she found unsettling. She tried the knob, and the door opened. Unlocked. That was unusual. Jake was always telling her to leave a light on, and he wasn't likely to leave his apartment unlocked while he was away.

Stepping into the kitchen, Liz allowed the quiet to wash over her before she moved to the living room and then the bedroom beyond. His clothes hung in the closet. The notebook computer case sat close by the nightstand. She lifted the case. Heavy. The computer was inside, the bed unmade. Liz ran her fingertips over the indentation in the pillow and a bittersweet pang shot through her. She felt his pain, his anger, his conflict. He loved her, and she'd hurt him so deeply. . . . For an instant she wavered, unsure how she could ever mend the rift between them.

This wasn't just a lover's quarrel. It went so much deeper than that. Jake's sense of loss was profound, a tear in the fabric of his soul. A wrenching sob escaped Liz's throat before she could stop it, before she realized she was no longer alone.

"Liz, are you all right?"

John. Steady, calm, logical. She turned to face him, hoping her angst didn't show in her expression. "I didn't hear you come in," she said quietly. "If you're looking for Jake, he isn't here." John was out of uniform, which seemed odd. Blue jeans and a white T-shirt, tennis shoes and no socks.

"Actually, I came for this." He held up his billfold. "Must have fallen out of my pocket last night. I found it between the cushions on the couch."

"You were here last night? I didn't think you and Jake were all that friendly?"

"We aren't, but we do have a lot in common, and I guess you could say we struck a truce." He unconsciously rubbed the dark bruise on his chin. "After a fashion."

Liz smiled. "Men. I doubt I'll ever truly understand any of you." She sighed, glancing around. "Have you seen him?"

"He reneged on his promise to help me keep a lid on things at the Labor Day bash. I thought he was with you."

Liz shook her head. "We're not on great terms at the moment. Actually, I was hoping to find him here. I have a lot of making up to do."

"Sounds serious."

"It is."

"I'll take that hint and refrain from asking. It's none of my business, anyway." He reached out and tipped up her chin. "I know I asked this before, but are you sure you're okay?"

Liz choked back irrational tears. She wasn't often given to emotional displays, and had always considered herself beyond all that—except during pregnancy, when all bets were off. "I will be," she said softly. "Just as soon as I find him."

John's brow furrowed in concern. "Is there anything I can do?"

"Yeah, actually, there is. If you see him, tell him I'm looking for him."

Outside, Liz opened the door of the Explorer and got in. She was about to turn the key in the ignition when a voice came through the open window. "Ms. Moncrief?"

Liz snapped out of her trancelike state. "Mary! Good heavens, you startled me!"

"I'm sorry. I didn't mean to do that."

"It's all right, really. I'm just a little preoccupied. How are you?"

Mary Simms's pregnancy was starting to show. It happened that way with some women: they didn't look pregnant until the third trimester. Liz had suffered through months of morning sickness with her first, and had rounded quickly. But other than the irresistible urge to raid the fridge at three A.M., she hadn't noticed many early changes with this baby.

"I'm tired, and my feet hurt," Mary said. It was almost a whine. "Kenneth had some mysterious errand to take care of, so he left me here to watch the parade. I don't know where he's gotten to. He wasn't supposed to be gone this long." She shaded her eyes and peered at the knots of humanity on the village green, but she didn't move away from the SUV.

"Is there anything I can do to help?" Liz asked. She'd always felt concern for Mary Simms, but she was also anxious to get back to the farm. She couldn't help thinking that Jake might have decided it was time to talk this out and had gone there. She couldn't abandon Mary, however. The girl didn't have it easy. Kenneth was unambitious and his work sporadic. If it hadn't been for the partial county assistance they collected, and food stamps, they would have had a very difficult time of it.

"Could you give me a ride home? I know it's out of your way, but I don't want to wait. It's hot, and my feet are swollen. I really need to lie down."

"Of course." Liz got out and helped the girl into the passenger seat. "Be sure and buckle up."

As always, she was a little taken aback by the Simms's living conditions. The four-room house they rented had several broken windows, crudely patched and held together with duct tape. The veneer on the front door was ragged and peeling, and the roof leaked. Kenneth's van was nowhere in sight.

Mary got out and waddled around the Ford, pausing at the driver's side window. One hand braced at the small of her back. The other shaded her eyes. "I'd invite you in, but Kenneth is odd about folks visitin'. Sometimes I don't understand him."

"Men are often hard to fathom, Mary," Liz agreed. "Sometimes I don't get them, either. Don't worry about asking me in. I have some things to take care of anyway."

Mary smiled, and her perfect white teeth made her mass of freckles seem to recede. "You must be a busy lady, runnin' that horse farm and all."

"The horses are gone," Liz said.

"Oh! That's right! The fire," the girl said, brushing her brown hair behind one ear . . . and Liz saw it, an oval-shaped medallion with a winking sunburst in its center. The necklace Harriet Stringer had designed and had been wearing in the softball-team photograph.

Liz's stare moved from the medallion to Mary's quizzical expression. "Ms. Moncrief, are you all right?"

"You'll have to excuse me, Mary. I was just admiring your necklace. It's lovely. Where did you get it?"

"This?" She fingered the chain. "Kenneth got it for me. I found it in his dresser drawer, clean in the back. He doesn't know I found it yet, but I just couldn't resist. I had it on under my clothes, so as not to ruin the surprise. I'll put it back before he comes home. He must have worked real hard to earn the money to buy it for me. My birthday's next week."

"Yes," Liz said. "I imagine he did—work very hard." But she knew Kenneth hadn't worked for it. He'd killed Harriet Stringer and kept the jewelry as a souvenir. In her mind's eye, she saw Harriet's smiling face, and then her daughter Fiona's. . . . So many lives lost. Kenneth Simms overshadowed them all. He'd worked for her. She'd trusted him.

"Mary, I'm sorry. I have to leave now." She shifted into reverse and turned the Explorer, heading back down the rutted lane. She picked up the cell phone, always within reach, and dialed Jake's apartment and then John's office. The dispatcher answered. "Abundance Police Department. Sarah speaking."

"Sheriff Rhys, please. This is Liz Moncrief."

"You haven't heard? John resigned late last night."

"What? No, I had no idea. Is Deputy Margolis in?"

"No, ma'am, but I'm expectin' him back real soon."

Sarah, this is urgent. I have information pertaining to the murder and abduction of Harriet Stringer."

"Harriet Stringer?"

"Yes. Tell him that I just came across evidence that will implicate Kenneth Simms in Harriet's murder. Tell him to call me at home at his earliest opportunity. They need to move on this before he gets away. Did you get that?"

"Oh, yes, ma'am, I got it."

Liz hung up the cell and got out of the Explorer for the short walk to the house, but just as she passed beneath the heavy shade of the huge, towering pines, something—no, *someone*—dropped to the ground in front of her.

Liz screamed once before he clamped a hand over her mouth. With his other hand, he showed her the knife. A Buck knife with a wicked, curving five-inch blade. Lethal enough to kill her, to kill the baby. "You c-come along r-real q-quiet and I won't have t-to hurt you."

Liz nodded slowly.

"Screamin' w-won't do no g-good. Ain't n-nobody t-to hear you, but my n–nerves are jangled en-n-nough, s-so don't p-push me. Y-You got th-that?"

Another nod. If not for his weapon, she might have risked fighting back, or trying to break and run, but the weapon was a very real danger. If he felt threatened, he would lash out, and even a nonlethal stab wound could throw her system into shock, jeopardizing the vulnerable fetus. She couldn't take the chance that she would lose the child.

"We'll t-take your c-car. You d-drive."

Chapter Seventeen

Liz did as Kenneth instructed and got behind the wheel of the SUV. Kenneth sat in the passenger seat, his weapon gripped tightly in his fist. His knuckles were white, and a tic worked in the outer corner of his left eye. She could feel his nervousness, a strange kinetic energy that seemed to swirl around him, unceasing motion, and he hardly seemed to fit the profile of the cold, calm killer known only as the Cemetery Man. "I don't understand, Kenneth," Liz said. "Why are you doing this? I thought we were friends. I trusted you."

"F-friends?" He laughed, a sharp bark of sound. "W-we're n-not f-friends. I sh-shoveled sh-shit from your b-barn. You orderin' me around for low w-wages d-don't make us fr-friends."

There was no mistaking the bitterness in his voice. It was clear that he would not have taken the job had he not needed the position to get close to her, to gain her trust. He had needed access to the farm, and the job had given him that.

"T-take a right at the c-crossroads."

"The sawmill road?" Liz said. "But it's a dead

end. No one uses it anymore." The instant the words were out of her mouth she understood. The sawmill hadn't been operational in years, long before Liz had come to the area. The only traffic on the rutted one-lane dirt road these days was an occasional ATV or young couple seeking privacy.

But the Cemetery Man needed privacy for what he had planned, and he was planning murder.

Her murder.

"You killed Harriet Stringer, Amanda Redwing . . . my dau-daughter."

Her voice nearly broke on the accusation. She knew that voicing it wouldn't help. He had no conscience. He lost no sleep after taking a life. *Lives* . . . she amended. Kenneth Simms was a heartless monster.

"You still d-don't k-know. How s-smart d-does that make you?"

Liz was working on sensory overload. Why did a threat always bring everything into sharper focus? The late summer air felt heavier somehow, she could almost feel the weight of the humidity, as real and as solid as a sopping sponge, every bit as dense. She could smell the dry dust of the dirt road, choking and invasive. It entered through the open windows, clogging her nostrils, constricting her throat. She could feel Kenneth Simms's nervous agitation; he was like a trip wire stretched too tightly. Then there was the fetus, her life force, Jake's, awash in love and so very fragile. At the thought, her pulse quickened. How could she shield it from this awful man?

Simms seemed oblivious to everything but his own concerns, his own bruised ego.

"Big-time FBI . . ." He snorted. "You're j-just like him. You c-can't see what's right under y-your nose."

Liz's antennae went up. "Just like him? What do you mean, 'just like him'?"

"The guy you've been sleepin' with." A smug look settled over his sharp features. "Oh, I seen, all right—watched you take him upstairs the night I slashed the window screens."

"That was you?"

"You s-sound s-s-surprised. You never s-suspected. Sh-sheriff didn't know either. I w-w-was w-watchin' when he looked around the house."

A chill crept up Liz's spine, despite the warmth of the day. It was starting to make sense. He hadn't been trying to gain entry to the house that night. He'd been trying to frighten her, and he'd succeeded. Then, as Jake and John had searched for him, he'd watched from a place of concealment. But how? Where? And then she remembered him dropping to the ground in front of her. The ancient pines at the front of the house. He'd found concealment in the branches. Her stomach clenched at the thought of Simms watching, a voyeur as she and Jake made love. "You mentioned Jake. What do you know about him?"

"M-more than I'd l-l-like to. N-now shut the hell up. W-we're almost th-there."

"Where?" Liz said. "There's nothing here."

"S-stop the c-c-car," Kenneth ordered, and when she didn't move quickly enough to follow his orders, he reached out and turned off the key. "Out, and d-don't do anything st-stupid."

Liz opened the door and stepped out, watching as he put the vehicle in park, then pocketed the keys. Then he grabbed her roughly by the arm, propelling her around a screen of foliage and through the door of a shed. Built of lumber, it had no windows and no electricity. A small gasoline-powered generator sat in one corner, along with a circular saw, hammer, and a few other assorted tools. Sawdust covered the floor.

"This is where you built the coffins," Liz said. "Did you hold your victims hostage here until you were ready to dispose of them?"

"Th-they weren't my victims," Kenneth shot back. His outburst seemed to increase his anger. He grabbed a lantern and kindled a blindingly bright light with the quick turn of a knob. Then, using a small pry bar, he opened a trapdoor in the floor. "Th-there's a battery-p-p-powered flashlight, water, and a little f-food down there. He's t-too out of it t-to know."

He held the lantern closer, and the shaft of light crept across a body. A man lay unconscious in the bottom of the deep pit. But not just any man. Jake.

Liz looked from Jake to Kenneth Simms, who nodded. "G-go on. He'll b-be here s-soon." She hesitated and he raised his fist. "W-walk down, or I'll th-throw you down! The quicker this is over w-with, the b-better."

Liz found the ladder and slowly descended. The walls and floor of the pit had been lined with cement. The concrete, combined with its underground location to make it cooler than the shack. She reached the floor and knelt by Jake, forgetting Kenneth Simms for the moment. He was shivering and sweating, and when she pulled back an eyelid she saw that his pupils were mere pinpricks.

He groaned, slowly surfacing from his stupor. "Liz. What are you doing here?" His voice was slurred.

Liz pushed his hair back from his brow. "I didn't want to come, believe me. I had no choice in the matter. What did Simms give you? Can you remember?"

"Simms?"

His voice trailed away and he seemed ready to nod off again. Liz grasped his shoulders and shook him gently. "Stay with me, Jake, please. It's important. Do you know what he gave you?"

"Some sort of opiate, I think. Skin prickled. Morphine, maybe—I don't know." He groaned. "What are you doing here? You break a tooth, too?"

Liz shook her head. He was too high to make any sense, and she couldn't be sure how much of what she was saying would penetrate his drug-induced haze. "No. I didn't break a tooth. It's much worse than that. Oh, God, Jake. We're in some really deep shit."

"Funny . . . feels like cotton." He laughed at that. "I'm still pissed, you know."

"You have every right to be angry, just don't turn away from me."

He sighed. "I love you, Liz. Even when you make me crazy. Guess I always will."

"I love you, too." She forced the words past the painful lump in her throat, but it was something of an understatement. She didn't just love him. She loved him desperately. "We have a lot to discuss . . . but it'll have to wait until you're a little less stoned."

What was the point in telling him about the baby if it would never have the chance to be born? He'd lost one child. She would not be instrumental in his losing another. "There has to be a way to get out of here."

Kenneth had drawn the ladder up, and closed the opening with a metal grate. The grate provided ventilation, but little light. The lantern light shifted, then disappeared. Simms must have taken it. He was gone, or at least gone from the shed. She doubted he had ventured far.

She felt around the space with her hands. Simms had mentioned food and water and a flashlight. She fumbled in the dark until she found the items. Then she turned on the light. "That helps a little." She checked him over. He seemed okay, except for the drugs and the duct tape that bound his wrists. The latter was one thing she could remedy. For whatever reason, Simms had failed to bind her hands. After a quick examination, she found the edge of the tape and stripped it away.

"If it wasn't for the drugs, that would have hurt. Damn that Lyle . . . he thought of everything."

Liz glanced sharply at him. "What did you say?"

"Thought of everything—"

"Before that. Lyle . . . Lyle Bridger?" Oh, dear God. It all made a sick sort of logic: Simms's derisive remark that she "wasn't so smart, after all." His denial that Harriet Stringer and the others were his victims. Simms wasn't the main actor, he was the point man, working the inside, feeding information to Bridger, an accessory to multiple counts of abduction and murder.

Lyle Bridger provided the cunning, while Simms did the dirty work.

"The dentist. Quite a collection of head shots on his wall . . . including two of the local vics. The Mallick kid and Stringer."

"She went to him for braces," Liz murmured. "She trusted him."

"It cost her."

His replies were progressively less slurred, a little less delayed, more coherent. The morphine head rush was starting to wear off. He shook his hands to restore the circulation, and after a moment or two pushed himself up to a sitting position.

His back braced against the wall, he opened his

arms, and Liz went to him. For a moment, she clung to him, breathing him in, taking comfort in the strength of his embrace, the strong, steady beat of his heart. "Christ, I missed you."

She sniffed, unable to speak, but he seemed to understand and tightened his embrace. "Hey, there's no need for that. We'll get through this. That asshole has taken everything from me that he's likely to get. Everything's gonna be all right."

"You're such an unfailing optimist." She kissed him, briefly, then again, and tried not to think about what lay ahead. "You were right, there are two of them. Kenneth Simms is in this, too. I gave his wife Mary a ride home. She was wearing Harriet Stringer's necklace. When I asked her about it, she said she found it in his dresser drawer. She assumed it was a surprise birthday gift for her."

"Simms is Bridger's patsy. He's also his kin. From what Lyle told me, they're half brothers. From what I could gather before he shot me full of dope, they were whelped by the same bitch. She used to lock Kenny in an old refrigerator behind their house. Lyle admitted that he got his kicks out of the little shop of horrors she cooked up. Simms overheard, and wasn't too happy. I'm thinking he may be the angle I have to work to get us out of here. Bridger can't act alone. It takes two for this particular tango . . . especially since I don't fit the victim profiles."

Liz understood. All of the victims had had one thing in common. They'd been small in stature, which made them more vulnerable, easier to manipulate and overpower, and to transport. Jake was over six feet tall and one hundred eighty pounds. Harriet Stringer's resistance had been nothing compared to what Bridger was about to face. Jake wouldn't be quite so easy a kill. If Bridger was to

succeed, he would need to deviate from his MO.
Given his level of organization, that would require
some careful planning. Unless he panicked, he
wouldn't risk making a mistake.

Outside the shed, Kenneth Simms lit another
cigarette and jerkily sucked the smoke into his
lungs. Where the hell was Lyle? If he had been
here as planned, Kenneth wouldn't have had to
put Liz Moncrief in the cell with her boyfriend. He
had an uneasy feeling that it had been a misstep,
yet at the time he didn't know what else to do. Lyle
had always made the plans, and Kenneth did what
he was told to do. If he'd done wrong, it was Lyle's
fault for not being here when Kenneth arrived.

Not that Lyle would tolerate a misstep. Kenneth
had no trouble imagining Lyle's anger. They were
blood kin, but there were times when Lyle scared
him right down to his marrow. He could be joking
and easygoing one minute, and the next fly into a
towering rage. Lyle's rages had dominated Kenneth's life—he would do anything to avoid them.

For the thousandth time, he thought about getting in his van and driving away. He could disappear, leave it all behind, Mary, the baby, Lyle's
unpredictability—walk away and start over somewhere. California, maybe. Or Washington state. It
was a tantalizing thought, one that he'd nurtured
for years, and Kenneth couldn't say why he'd never
acted on it. Maybe he was just so beaten down, so
cowed from years of being bullied and walked on
that he couldn't think for himself. Mary said so
when they argued, and Mary was always right.

Maybe Lyle had already moved on. Maybe he'd
skipped out, leaving Kenneth holding the bag.
The FBI was going to want blood when all of this

was over, and if they couldn't have Lyle, he was the next best thing.

"S-son of a b-b-bitch," Kenneth muttered. "Lyle, where the hell are you?" He hadn't forgotten Lyle's admission to Mr. FBI. He'd fucking enjoyed Kenneth's misery in the box. The crazy son of a bitch was every bit as bad as she had been. Lyle didn't have Kenneth's loyalty, it hadn't mattered that they were brothers. If he'd wanted to, he could have left Kenneth to languish in the hot darkness of the metal box, without food, without water. Yet what he'd once considered a kindness, in reality had been manipulation. Control. Power. Lyle had decided whether Kenneth ate or drank, lived or died.

Years after, he could feel his panic rising at the memories, and with it his fury. And now he was already in deep water, and Lyle would drag him under. He'd been doing it for years, playing on Kenneth's guilt, and simple gratitude. Through everything, Kenneth had held on to the belief that Lyle had helped him; learning of the betrayal stung.

Lyle had never helped anyone but Lyle, and Lyle's assistance came with a heavy price. Kenneth had always been small, like her. But even a small man was stronger than a woman, something she learned when she tried to bully him into the box one last time. He'd been sixteen, and he'd hated and feared her for so many years that when she entered a room, his thought processes shut down, and he reverted to instincts to guide him, like an animal.

She'd been angry that morning. The welfare check was late in arriving and she was out of cigarettes. Lyle was nowhere to be found, but Kenneth had always been an easy target for her rages. As she shoved him toward the box, his gaze fell on the coal shovel. To this day, he didn't remember picking it up, but it was in his hands when he remembered standing over her, staring down at the bloody mess that had been her face.

Lyle had found them, and after kicking her a few vicious licks to determine if there was any life left in her, he helped Kenneth out of a potentially deadly situation. Lyle helped Kenneth dispose of her body. They wrapped her in an old rug and dragged her out to the woods, where they dug a shallow grave and buried her, piling brush on top of the spot so that it wouldn't be easily found.

Afterward, Lyle would speculate whether or not she had truly been dead, or just unconscious, and countless times he suggested to Kenneth that she'd been buried alive.

Lyle seemed to take a strange satisfaction in that possibility.

Kenneth had felt only relief that she was no longer a factor in their lives—along with moments of fleeting guilt that he had killed his own mother.

He sucked the last drag from the cigarette and crushed it underfoot with more violence than was necessary. He couldn't help thinking about that damned box. He'd never forgotten the terror of being inside it, and to think that Lyle had been heartless enough to take pleasure from his misery was more than he could forgive.

He waited another minute outside. The pink of sunset was showing through the trees. It would be dark soon. It was already dark in that hole where Liz Moncrief and Jake English waited, except for the light the flashlight he'd given them provided. He knew how it felt to be trapped in the darkness. He knew how they all had suffered, and the thought of it made his stomach churn. Lyle didn't know. She'd never locked him in the box. Lyle had no idea . . . he had no heart . . . no soul.

He was just like her.

And he should have been here a half hour ago.

The shed door opened. Jake heard it, and tensed. Liz sat close beside him, as close as she could get, her head resting on his shoulder. Every now and then, he kissed her nose, her brow, her temple. It was small reassurance, but all that he could offer. Their prospects sure as hell didn't look good, but he hadn't given up yet.

She had related her call to John Rhys. Because of his resignation, she'd left a message for the acting sheriff, Shep Margolis, but he'd been called away, and there was no telling how long he'd be gone. Jake didn't know Margolis personally, but the few times he'd had truck with the man didn't inspire much confidence in his abilities. Margolis was one of those guys who believed what he believed, and nothing else. He didn't appear open to possibilities. So how much stock would he put into the call from Liz?

Would he look into it immediately? Or would he delay it until tomorrow?

Jake couldn't guess, but he was pretty sure that tomorrow would be too late. Still, Margolis was a cop, and if Rhys's opinion carried any weight, a damned good one. There was a chance he'd get the call and follow up on it. If he failed to follow through and Jake managed to survive this close encounter with Lyle, he was going to punch Rhys again.

He looked up as Simms's face appeared behind the slats of the grate. "You're awake. You want another hit? Lyle left a syringe."

"How fucking humane of him," Jake said.
"Thanks, but I think I'll pass. Wouldn't want to
sleep through all the fun."

"It ain't no fun," Kenneth said. He glanced behind him, then looked down at them again.

"Well, you'd know. You spent a little time in a
box, didn't you, Kenneth? Time that Lyle helped
to arrange. Nice guy, your brother. Not only did he
get his rocks off by seeing you suffer, he's bought
you a stint on death row when they catch up with
you . . . *and they will.* You can bank on it."

"None of this w-was my idea!" Simms shot back,
his upset obvious. Liz glanced at Jake. He shook
his head, a signal perceptible only to her.

"Shit! Do you really think they'll buy that?" Jake
laughed. "Somebody'll have to pay, and Lyle's a
damn good bet to try and roll over on you. If he
even hangs around. He'll be looking for a way out,
and there you are—just like always."

"Sh-sh-shut up!" Kenneth shouted, crouching
near the grate, wrapping his arms around his head
as he attempted to cover his ears, to shield himself.
He rocked slightly, and Jake could have sworn he
heard him whimper.

"Every victim was found with a sport bottle for
water, and a plastic bag containing bits of food.
We speculated as to why, but no one could ever
come up with an answer that made any sense.
But that was you, wasn't it, Kenneth. You made
sure they had food and water, because you knew
how important it was. Because you felt sorry for
them."

"I d-did what I c-c-could without pissin' him off.
I d-d-don't like it when he g-gets mad. He's j-just
l-like her."

"Like your mother."

"She was no k-kind of mother. She w-was a m-m-monster."

"Any woman that could do that to her own flesh and blood doesn't deserve to draw breath."

Silence. But he didn't disagree, or attempt to defend her. Liz would have spoken up, but Jake pressed a kiss to her ear, whispering, "Let me handle this." Then, to Kenneth, "You don't seem as bad as Lyle, Kenneth. You wouldn't have killed them on your own, would you?"

"N-no."

"So in a way you've been as much a victim as any of the others. I'm thinking out loud, here, but maybe it's not too late for you. Maybe there's a way out—but not if you help him with this. You're a grown man, right? You don't have to do what Lyle says, or go where Lyle goes. Lyle's headed to the death house, but you don't have to go there."

Kenneth didn't reply, because at that moment the door opened, and Lyle joined them. "Kenny, what are you up to? Talking to our guests? What have they been saying to you?"

"N-n-nothin'. J-just keepin' an eye on them, l-like you s-said. He's awake, and sh-she's p-plenty sc-scared."

"Liz? Afraid? This I have to see." Footsteps, and Bridger became more than just a voice. He bent to look through the grate. "She does look rather uncomfortable, doesn't she?"

Liz glared at Bridger, and there was no keeping her quiet. "Goddamn you! I hope you burn in hell for what you did to my daughter!"

Bridger clucked his tongue. "Such anger. Is that good for you?"

Silence.

"Oh, yes, I know about that. I was outside when

you were talking to the sheriff's sister." His gaze shifted to Jake, who stiffened. "Have you told Jake yet? I bet he'd like to hear it. You were going to tell him, weren't you, Liz?"

"Tell me what?"

She looked daggers at Bridger. "I hate you."

"Liz, what the hell's going on?"

Bridger clucked his tongue. "I'm afraid the rabbit died."

"I was going to tell you," Liz said, but you stormed out, and you wouldn't take my calls."

Jake didn't look at Liz. Didn't react. "So, when are you gonna let us out of here, Lyle? I'd like to use the little boy's room. I have to piss like a damned racehorse."

"Preparations are nearly complete," Bridger assured him. "It won't be long. Kenny, can I see you outside?" Bridger disappeared from the grate. Footsteps rang hollow overhead. He had a tread like an elephant.

For the space of a second, Simms looked into the pit. "I h-heard what you s-s-said. I help y-you . . . y-you help me." He slipped something through the grate . . . a leather scabbard. Jake got to his feet and caught it as he dropped it.

"Kenny! What's keeping you?"

"J-just making sure this g-g-grating's t-tight, that's all." Then Simms got to his feet and walked away, and Jake breathed a prayer of thanks for the knife in his hand.

"Shep, what the hell's so all-fired important that you had to drag me over here?" John Rhys, ex-sheriff, stuck his head in the room and frowned. Shep sat behind his desk, looking extremely out of place, not to mention ill at ease. Sarah, the dispatcher-slash-receptionist, stood stiffly beside the desk, her eyes narrowed as they remained fixed on a pregnant Mary Simms, who seemed to cower in her chair under the dual hostile stares. The phone was ringing, but no one moved to answer it.

"Sarah? Why'd you leave your post?"

"Shep asked me to ride along, Chief. I'm sitting in on the interrogation to avoid possible accusations of sexual harassment."

"Sexual—" To laugh outright would have hurt Shep's feelings, so John just nodded. "I see. Well, I'm here now, and Shep is out of danger, so would you mind getting that?" He refrained from chiding her about calling him "Chief." He'd been trying to break her of the habit for three or four years, and he'd been totally unsuccessful. A little thing like his resignation wasn't likely to faze her. 'All right, Shep. Everything's under control. Would you mind telling me why Mary's here?"

Shep was all business. "John, we need to conduct an interrogation to determine her level of involvement. As I see it, we have no time to lose. Her husband may have already skipped town."

"Level of involvement in what?"

"The abduction and murder of Harriet Stringer."

"You're joking, right?" John said, but he knew Shep, and he wasn't the type of guy to joke about police matters. "Humor me, will you? Start at the beginning."

"I went out on a call about an accident, and when I got back to the station, Sarah relayed a message from Liz Moncrief. She said she'd stumbled across evidence that indicated Kenneth Simms in Harriet's murder. So Sarah and I drove out there, and sure enough, she had jewelry on her person that belonged to the victim."

Mary started to weep softly. "I didn't know it belonged to a dead girl. I thought Kenny was goin' to surprise me. I was tryin' it on, that's all."

John picked up the evidence bag that contained the necklace, properly sealed and tagged by Shep. "Well, that's Harriet's, all right. I've seen it before. I'll check with Renée and Ed. They'll know how often she wore it. Did Liz happen to call back?"

"No, and there's no answer at her place. I called the apartment over Julianne's place, and no one's home there, either. This whole situation reeks, John. Whatever's going on here, it isn't good."

"I stopped back over there. Jake left this morning, and he hasn't returned."

"You think he went back to Fedsville?" Shep asked.

John shook his head. "Sure doesn't look that way. All of his stuff is still there. In fact, Liz was looking for him, too."

Sarah put her head and shoulders into the room. "Chief? That was Miss Ridley. She says she was out walking her dogs and she noticed some strange goin's on over on Sawmill Road. A suspicious amount of traffic, in and out. She thinks Caleb Abernathy might be planning a keg party out there, and she reminded me it's private property."

Ann Ridley was a retired schoolteacher, and a real stickler for detail. "She happen to recognize any of the vehicles?"

"Dark green van. Ford Explorer, saddle tan."

"Shit. That's Liz's vehicle." John raked his hand through his short blond hair. "Sarah, would you mind keeping Mary company till we get back? She's not to leave without my knowledge." He caught Sarah's nod, then turned to Shep. "Why don't you and I ride on out there and have a look. This doesn't sound like one of Caleb's shindigs to me."

Chapter Eighteen

The ladder came down slowly, inch by inch. When it grounded on the cement floor of the pit, Simms's face, shining with sweat, appeared at the top. "You g-got to c-come up here now." Then, when Jake moved in front of Liz, "Her fi-fi-first, L-lyle says s-so."

But Jake wouldn't budge. "You go back and tell Lyle to come down here and get her. The only way she leaves me is if he kills me first, and I'm not going to be as easy to take as an eight-year-old girl."

Simms's face worked, and Jake could smell his fear and frustration. His feelings for his brother were as twisted as their relationship. Hatred, fear, resentment, loyalty. Simms had given him the knife, but that didn't mean he wouldn't turn right around and betray them. He'd helped Bridger kill Fiona, and nothing could ever even the score as far as Jake was concerned.

"D-don't make it w-worse. He can g-get real n-mean."

"Lyle might lose his temper, so I should just hand her over to him? You know what, Simms, fuck you!

You're nothing but a goddamned sniveling coward. And while we're handing out insults, fuck
Lyle, too! Liz stays with me."

Liz glanced at Simms. "Kenneth, let me talk to
him, please. Just give us a minute."

"Okay, b-but hurry up." He disappeared.

Liz sucked in a shuddering breath. Jake was
being bullheaded as only Jake could be, and he
wasn't thinking clearly. Their position was anything but advantageous. They needed Kenneth,
and they needed to be out of the place they were
in. Years before, she'd visited her grandfather on
his farm and seen him shoot rats in the grain barrels. The rats ran frantically in circles, even trying
to climb the vertical sides of the barrels, but they
were picked off one by one. It was something
she'd never forgotten. Trapped ten feet belowground, she couldn't help thinking that their situation was similar to that of the doomed rodents.
There was only one way out, and that was to do
what Kenneth suggested. With one of them above-
ground, they had a chance of survival. If they were
trapped in the pit, they had no chance.

Putting her hands on Jake's shoulders, she
caught his gaze and held it. "We're going to do
what he tells us to do."

He shook his head, adamant, and his voice betrayed his tension. "Like hell I will. I let you go
once. I won't lose you again."

She dropped her head forward, resting her
brow on the flat plane of his cheek while she
fought back a rising well-spring of emotion. Her
eyes were closed and the tears came easily. When
she looked at him again, she had regained control.
Her voice was strong and unwavering, and she
even managed a smile. "You'll let me go, because

it's the one chance we have—and because I ask you to."

Her words were penetrating, getting past his anger, and though he didn't like the idea, he saw the logic in it. "Liz, please, don't ask me to do this."

She put her arms around his neck, pressing her body to his as she did when they made love. As seconds passed, she held him close. "I'm not asking, Jake. I'm begging. I know what I'm doing, but I need your help, and that means that you have to trust me. It's our only option."

He didn't say a word, just slowly pulled away. He took her hand, pressing the leather sheath into it, then watched as she concealed it in the waistband of her jeans and pulled her loose cotton shell down over it. "If he lays a hand on you—"

Liz touched his cheek, her fingers caressing his skin. "I love you," she whispered, then turned away to climb the ladder. When she stepped off the last rung, she drew it up. "Just so you don't change your mind." He took a step forward, balling his fists at his side, but he didn't attempt to stop her.

It might have been his high anxiety, but the atmosphere seemed to grow increasingly heavy in the belly of the shed. Jake paced the length of the pit, turned, and came back. He kept his movements in a straight line to avoid walking in circles. Not that it helped relieve the tension, but somehow it gave him a false sense of control.

Walking in circles would indicate being lost, purposeless. He wasn't either. He was waiting . . . waiting to get his hands on Bridger . . . waiting because Liz had asked him to . . . and he wished for the millionth time that he didn't respect her half as much, that he hadn't listened.

But he did respect her, and he loved her, and he knew her protective instincts were strong. She wouldn't jeopardize the baby for any reason. She'd been a good mother to their daughter. He knew that. Christ, he had known that all along. She'd gone to great lengths to protect her, even against him.

Outside the shed, Bridger's van rumbled to life. Jake knew it was Bridger's vehicle by the pitch of the engine. Engines were unique. Each had its own sound, its own voice, and Jake wasn't happy to hear this one, as it could only mean one thing. But as the hot, oily exhaust puffed through the pipe at the bottom of the pit, he realized he couldn't have been more wrong.

Jake sized up the pit again.

There had to be a way out.

By pressing back against the concrete, he could barely see the end of the ladder. He could see it, but he couldn't reach it. "Simms! Where the hell are you?"

Kenneth Simms appeared above the rim.

The raw exhaust burned Jake's throat. "The ladder, Simms. Now!"

Simms shook his head. "C-can't. L-lyle knows I'm up to s-s-somethin'. It's b-better this way—easier."

"I don't give a shit about what Lyle knows! The ladder, Simms!" and Jake fell to a fit of coughing.

"L-lyle'll k-k-kill me!"

Exhaust poured through the pipe at just below knee height. Above his head and out of reach, Simms grasped the ladder, but it was clear he had no intention of lowering it into the pit, and Jake was getting steamed. "Like hell you will," Jake growled, cramming the toe of his right shoe into the pipe and throwing himself upward. He shot just high enough to clear the rim of the pit and to latch on to Simms's right ankle as Simms started to turn away.

Jake's desperate grab caught the smaller man off balance. He swore as he tried to right himself, then toppled into the pit. He landed heavily, too surprised to break his fall, and lay still, his head bent at an odd angle. Jake didn't need to examine him closely to know that Simms was dead.

"Liz," Bridger said. "I was starting to worry. I thought perhaps you'd try to disappoint me and melt into the woods, but that would mean deserting Jake, and I guess you're reluctant to be separated from him. I hadn't originally planned for him to be involved in this, but it's worked out well. A sort of insurance policy to guarantee your cooperation."

"I don't get it," she said. "It's obvious that you've spent a lot of time planning—years, really. Why?"

"Why you?" His glance was level, his eyes the coldest she had ever seen. "Because you are the perfect adversary. It's like a game of chess. It's all about the challenge, a meeting of the minds . . . check and checkmate. I'm about to take your king. He won't last long with carbon monoxide pouring into the holding cell. Don't concern yourself, though. There's only a little discomfort. He'll just fall asleep."

In a panic, Liz spun and made a dash for the van. She clawed at the door handle, but the door was locked. Bridger grabbed her hair, jerking her back a step. Liz stumbled, almost fell. The van was still running, a hose she hadn't noticed before connected to the exhaust leading toward the shed. A few yards away, it disappeared beneath the ground. "Oh, God! Jake!"

"It's probably too late," Bridger said. "His hold on consciousness is slipping."

"Goddamn you," Liz gritted out, her hand closing over the hilt of the Buck knife. Her mind full of Jake and all she had lost to Bridger's insanity, Liz spun, burying the blade to the hilt in her adversary's abdomen, just below the breastbone. She let go, staggering back, her heart in her throat.

A stunned expression on his face, Bridger glanced down at the arterial spurt spattering his clothing, his shoes, the grass, Liz.

"Kenny," he said in quiet amazement, then slowly folded and sank to his knees. A low laugh. "I didn't know he had it in him."

Grabbing a rock, Liz ran to the van, hurling it through the driver's window. Tiny squares of glass rained down; she reached in and tripped the lock, opened the door, turning off the ignition. Then, as she spun toward the cabin, she collided with Jake.

As he closed his arms around her, Liz started to shake. He was warm, and solid, and alive. He smelled of exhaust, and his voice was a mere rasp, but she hadn't lost him. "You all right?" he said.

"I am now," she said, wrapping her arms tightly around his neck, burying her face in the curve of his throat.

The black and white from the Abundance Police Department pulled up behind the van, and John Rhys, former sheriff, stepped out. He walked to where they stood, pausing just long enough to press his fingertips to Bridger's carotid artery. "Shep, call the meat wagon. He's gone."

"There's another one inside," Jake said. "He died from a fall."

John gauged Liz and Jake at a glance. "Jake, you look like hell. Are you gonna make it, or should I call for a second ambulance?"

"I've never been better, Sheriff, but thanks for asking. As for the lady, I want her checked out."

Liz shook her head. "No hospital. I want to go home. Please," she said, pressing close to Jake and knowing she could never get close enough. "Just take me home."

Virginia

He stood observing the workers as they reset the polished marble marker, a tall man in a sharply tailored black suit and open-collared white shirt. The striped tie he'd worn to the private memorial service that morning hung loosely around his neck, the ends of the silk fluttering in the warm spring breeze, their teasing touch just brushing the long-stemmed white roses he held in the crook of one arm.

Jake stood for a long while staring down at the headstone. She knew instinctively that he needed this time alone with their daughter, and though she wanted badly to go to him, she held back. Slowly, he knelt by the graveside, reaching out to touch her name, Fiona Elizabeth, tenderly placing the eight roses, one for each year of her life on this earth, just beneath.

The past eight months had been a period of adjustment for both of them. Lyle Bridger's reign of terror had abruptly ended on a hot September night, yet the investigation into the case had been ongoing. It had taken several months and a great deal of collaboration with various law enforcement people to gather the facts and finally close the file on the Cemetery Man.

During that time Jake had had little chance to dwell on the past. The case had consumed his

days, and life at the farm with a newly pregnant Liz
had filled his evenings. It was a little amazing how,
with the truth out in the open, and no secrets between them, they had slowly, gradually settled into
a comfortably loving relationship. Liz wasn't sure
just how it had happened, and she didn't want to
jinx it by asking unnecessary questions.

It had been enough that they were together, and
that the blue-eyed baby boy for whom she prepared
the nursery was healthy. Autumn had ripened, then
receded, and the wind turned cold. Mary Simms
and her infant daughter returned to her parents in
West Virginia just before Christmas and didn't look
back. Eager to put her dead husband to rest and get
on with her life, Mary had insisted in an interview
that Kenneth Simms had been as much a victim as
the girls he had helped to kill. Perhaps the kindly
deception made it easier for Mary Simms to bear.
The truth was far more twisted, Liz knew.

Close examination of the tires on Bridger's van
after the fact proved conclusively that the Dodge
had delivered Amanda Redwing to her death
chamber and left imprints in Liz's field. Lyle
Bridger had preyed upon selected victims, patients
of his practice. His confident manner and ease
with children and adolescents had instilled trust in
them, a fatal trust. Fiona was the only exception.
Lyle's only connection to their child had been
through Liz. The authorities were still looking into
his background, seeking connections between his
activities and various missing persons cases, but
Jake doubted they would ever know the truth.

Kenneth had been dragged into Lyle's scheme
because of a lifetime of association.

Lyle was Kenneth's link to the past, a link that
Kenneth had either been unwilling or unable to
break. Kenneth had built the coffins and dug the

graves, and because of his feelings of helplessness and guilt for a situation he hated but couldn't seem to escape, he had compensated by providing the victims with water, food, and a flashlight. The authorities would never know the exact reason Kenneth had fed the exhaust into the grave of Amanda Redwing or provided Harriet Stringer with an overdose of morphine stolen from his brother's office. Jake's best guess was that by the time Bridger had located Liz and his two-year lull had ended and he resumed his grisly activities in New York, Kenneth Simms had just about reached his psychological limits. He hadn't been strong enough to break from Lyle, so he had rationalized that giving the last two victims a speedy demise had been somehow justified.

It was all part of Simms's sick cycle: unable to leave the mother who had inflicted such cruel abuse, unable to divorce himself from the half brother who had involved him in a killing spree that had spanned several years and two states. As for Lyle, no one could be certain what drove him, or others of his kind, and Liz was determined not to waste another moment dwelling on the dark side of humankind. She was content to concentrate on the blanket-swaddled infant in her arms, and leave serial offenders to her husband.

"Baby, we need to be at the airport by two," she told him, stepping sufficiently near to lay a hand on his shoulder. His head had been bowed, and before he straightened, he wiped the dampness from his cheek with the heel of one hand.

He put his fingertips to his lips, then to the angel engraved in the upper right-hand corner of the stone, and got to his feet. "Do you have your cellular on you? I need to give Rhys a call. Margolis is supposed to be picking us up at the airport, but

I should verify. Abundance is a busy place, crime-wise, and we may have to call a cab."

It was odd to hear him speak of John Rhys and Shep Margolis without rancor, but when Jake set his mind to accomplish something, nothing could stand in his way, and he'd made up his mind to carve out a place in Liz's world. He played poker once a month with the boys: John Rhys, Shep Margolis, who continued to refer to Jake as "the fed," and Matt Monroe, successful mystery novelist, local celebrity, and adoring daddy to a blonde-haired little girl. Abby had finally conquered her fear of commitment, and married Matt. It was a strange foursome, but only because it was so normal, and Jake seemed to like it that way.

Not even a two-month vacation in Virginia and his partner's unceasing attempts to talk him out of his plans could dull his enthusiasm for the next new phase of his life. He was a new husband, since their marriage in February, and a new daddy to Ranald Jacob, in that order, and his days at Quantico were over. While staying with her folks in Virginia, he'd passed his pschiatric evaluation and applied for and been granted a transfer. As of Monday morning at nine A.M., he would be operating out of the New York field office, and he hadn't even complained.

Jake's friend, Charlie Calendar, waited by the car. He was a good-looking guy in his late thirties who never held back his opinion. "New York," he said with ill-disguised disgust. "You're insane, my friend. You know what they call the New York field office."

"Charlie, my man. It may be hell . . . but hell is where the action is. You ought to try it sometime." Jake leaned over and kissed Liz, tucking the blanket more securely around his son. "You think he's warm enough?"